SIN-BIN

An Enemies to Lovers College Hockey Romance

Sinners on the Ice

Book One

Anastasija White

Edited by Caroline Knecht, https://reedsy.com/caroline-knecht

Cover Design by Rotoscope Design, https://www.instagram.com/rotoscope.design/

This book is intended for an 18+ audience.

For content warnings, please visit https://www.anastasijawhite.com

ISBN 978-609-08-0119-2 (ebook)

ISBN 978-609-08-0118-5 (paperback)

To the ones who have ever felt like giving up on love because of an ex.
Do not settle for someone who makes you feel caged.
The right person will never try to break your wings, they will help you spread them.
They will love you the way you are, the real you.

PLAYLIST

1. "kiss, kiss" - Machine Gun Kelly
2. "hot girl bummer" - blackbear
3. "Pretty Girl" - Maggie Lindemann
4. "We Found Love" - Rihanna, Calvin Harris
5. "IDGAF" - Lil Peep
6. "i hope ur miserable until ur dead" - Nessa Barrett
7. "Dusk Till Down" - ZAYN feat. Sia
8. "Swim" - Chase Atlantic
9. "Breakfast" - Dove Cameron
10. "Midnight Rain" - Taylor Swift
11. "idfc" - blackbear
12. "If You Want Love" - NF
13. "Wrecked" - Imagine Dragons
14. "Late Night Talking" - Harry Styles
15. "hazel inside" - blackbear

Find the rest of **SIN-BIN** playlist here:

Chapter 1

Fucker

AVA

"Oh, Clay, yeah... Do that again... Oh, I'm gonna come... I'm gonna come... Clay, please..."

For the past thirty minutes, that's all I've heard. Moans, dirty talk, spanking, and more moans. Why can't she come already so I can finally get into my room and sleep? I literally hate my roommate.

It's my second week of college. I have dreamt about Great Lake University in Michigan for years. GLU has a unique history, incredible professors, and it's the perfect place for me to focus on my communication and media major. It's not far from my hometown, so it's easy for me to visit my dad whenever I feel like it. I have been looking forward to spending time here, studying and hanging out with my best friend, going to parties. I had it all figured out, and I was going to stick to my plan no matter what.

My roommate proved me wrong within hours. She is a nightmare.

Jordan Patterson is the type of girl who will chew you up and spit you out, and you won't even notice it. She's drop-dead gorgeous, but her personality is the biggest turnoff. As soon as she saw me coming, she scowled and loudly exclaimed that she definitely hadn't hit the roommate jackpot.

I thought the same, but I kept my words to myself.

I would have loved to live with my best friend, Layla Benson, but she's a year older than me, and this is her second year, so it's impossible. I got what I got, and I needed to get used to it, as my adviser said. I would be curious to see her reaction if it were her sitting on the floor outside her room, waiting for her roommate to have an orgasm.

Please, Jordan, come already.

My phone dings with an incoming message, and I pick it up off the floor. I unlock it, see a text from my best friend, and instantly smile. Layla is my person, through and through. We have many similarities, but the one thing we don't have in common is our taste in boys.

Her family's house is across the street from mine, so I have known Layla all my life. We can call each other names, threaten to beat the living shit out of one another if one of us acts unreasonable or stupid. A few times, we've stopped talking altogether...but we are always there for each other, no matter what.

BESTIE:

How about shopping tomorrow?

ME:

All in. But only if I get some sleep.

BESTIE:

Meaning? You went back to your room almost an hour ago...

ME:

My roommate is having sex with someone named Clay.

BESTIE:

Gosh. She works fast.

ME:

Don't remind me. It got quieter, maybe they are done?

BESTIE:

Why don't you go inside? She needs to know it's not okay

ME:

Dunno.

I glance at the closed door. What if I open it and just go in? It's my room too, and I'm tired of waiting.

BESTIE:

Ava Mason, you're a badass. Why do you allow her to treat you like this?

I roll my eyes and rise to my feet. In all honesty, she isn't wrong. I have never let anyone treat me like this. Who does she think she is?

ME:

I'll text you later. I need to put someone in her place.

BESTIE:

That's my girl.

I laugh, shoving my phone into my purse. Then I square my shoulders and put the key into the lock. *It's do or die.*

I open the door and freeze straightaway. *What the hell?*

Jordan is totally naked, down on her knees, and giving head to a guy who is sitting in a chair. But that's not what blows me away. Another dude is on her bed, jerking himself off while watching his friend with my roommate. A nauseating feeling lodges in my throat. This can't be happening.

"You said your roommate left for the weekend." The voice of the guy in the chair is cold and distant, sending chills down my spine.

I don't see his face because the room is mostly dark, illuminated only by dimmed LED ceiling lights. The only detail I notice is his brown hair. He puts his hand on Jordan's head, keeping her in place. She gags on his cock, and uneasiness seeps into my veins.

What have I just dragged myself into?

Voices become louder; someone is coming down the hallway. *Shit.* It would be the worst scenario ever to let someone see my roommate like this. No matter what I think of her, no one deserves that humiliation. I take a step forward and close the door with a thud. I look around without focusing on anything, crossing my arms over my chest and then dropping them to my sides. Still, I stay rooted to the spot.

"Want to join?" the guy from the bed asks me in a mocking voice.

It triggers me, boosting my confidence. I stomp in his direction, stop near the bed, and put my hands on my hips. "Get out."

His smirk fades away as he takes his palm off his dick. He stares into my eyes, but I just hold his gaze and say nothing.

"Girl, we were having fun with your roommate way before you got here. She told us you went home."

"I don't care when you got here. I don't care what she said about me. I want you out of my room. Now."

He frowns, hesitating. The slurping sounds become louder while I refuse to watch. One dick is enough for my colorful imagination for one day, especially one I never planned to see.

"If I knew you would come in and ruin all the fun, I would have never even agreed to fuck this freshman." The guy stands up and heads for his clothes on the floor. He hurriedly puts his T-shirt and his pants on, glancing my direction in silence.

I observe him, trying to remember if I've seen him before. I bite my bottom lip in annoyance because nothing rings a bell. He's good-looking with auburn hair and yellowish-green eyes. His body speaks volumes about all the hard work he's clearly been doing in the gym. Is he from the hockey team? What if he knows my best friend's brother? With how often Layla hangs out with Drake, if this asshole is one of his teammates, I'm screwed.

The guy puts his sneakers on and straightens, looking over my shoulder at his friend. "Dude, are you done?"

"Almost." His voice changes, sounding a bit husky. And sexy. My eyes widen, and I inwardly curse myself. I have no idea what he looks like, and I think his voice is sexy? What's wrong with me?

The auburn-haired guy from the bed hides his hands in his pockets and shifts to look at me. "I'm Clay."

"Uh-huh."

"Not going to tell me your name, beautiful?" He beams, making me chuckle. He just had sex with my roommate. Does he really think I would be interested?

"I don't think you deserve to know my name," I murmur, and his face lights up with a smile. I intrigue him, but ew—I can't even think about something happening between us.

"I'm a resourceful fella, and if you let me—"

"Not going to happen, Clay. Really." I speak softly.

"Shame." He shrugs. "I'll figure out your name with or without you telling me."

"Whatever." I let out a short laugh as I hear the sound of a zipper. Heavy steps follow, stopping right behind my back.

"You kinda ruined the moment," a voice rasps in my ear, its hot breath fanning over my skin.

I spin around and find myself right in front of him. I'm smaller than this guy. My eyes are at his chest, and I involuntarily look up to rake my gaze over him. I can't deny that he's stunning, but the look on his face makes me uncomfortable. So much arrogance and annoyance. A bad boy at his finest. The type I'm attracted to the most but prefer to run away from.

"You kinda ruined it yourself," I retort. "Get out. Both of you."

"No one tells me what to do." His stare darkens, and he frowns.

"Keep telling yourself that." I laugh, happy with my sassy response. I gradually relax, feeling more at ease, but it's short-lived.

He leans into my face. His deep brown eyes burn holes into me. "I hope I never see you around campus."

"Or what?"

His lips stretch into a big, radiant smile. "Or you will regret coming inside this room while I was here."

"It's my room too, and it's not my fault she lied about my whereabouts." I grunt, narrowing my eyes. "Get out."

His pupils dilate, indicating his surprise. He didn't expect that kind of reaction from me. I bet he's used to people running for their lives when he looks at them that way. Not me. I don't care about this guy. I just want him gone. Period.

"Dude, come on. We have places to go. The night is young." Clay calls out to his friend, who keeps gaping at me in silence. It honestly is ridiculous. He's not fucking royalty, yet he expects me to bow down to him. Suddenly, he inches toward my ear, and his lips graze my earlobe.

"I bet I can make you come in one minute. I can make you scream my name while you're riding my dick." He leans away, grinning like a fucking idiot while I feel my cheeks get warm. "But I won't. You're too fucking plain for that. Too simple."

"Fucker," I mutter, sucking in air. How dare he?

Without giving it any thought, I slap him across his face. So hard my palm stings. He fucking deserves it.

I don't even have time to blink before Clay walks around me, shielding me from his friend. "Colton," he says, as I take a few steps back. "Let's go. Okay?"

A second passes, then Colton pushes his friend away and storms to the door. He opens it, turns his head, and locks his gaze onto mine. "You just made a huge mistake."

"I don't see it that way." I put on a brave face, but my palms are sweating. Clay sighs, glances at me, and follows his friend out of the room. Then the door closes and they are both gone.

I take a deep breath and focus my attention on Jordan. She's silent, and it creeps me out. What's wrong with her? I edge closer to her and kneel. "You okay?"

Her mascara is smeared under her eyes, and her cheeks and neck are red. She stares off into the distance, then looks at me. "You ruined everything."

"What?"

"Those two...they are the most popular guys on campus. Girls dream about being with them, and I was lucky they both wanted to get laid tonight." Jordan peels her eyes away from my face. "Clay is good, but not exceptional. While Colton...he's a dreamboat. And when I finally get the chance to lay my hands on him, you decide to step in."

"You sucked him off," I mumble in annoyance. "Not sure he would have wanted to fuck you after his friend."

"I could have convinced him." she snaps, standing up and moving to put her clothes on.

I shake my head in disbelief. I don't know the guy; I just know the type. He would have never fucked her after his friend. A blow job was the only thing he was interested in. She should know better.

"I'm going to take a shower," she sneers through clenched teeth, then trudges to the door. But she stops in her tracks and looks at me over her shoulder. "Colton doesn't tolerate disrespect, Ava. Being his enemy will be extremely bad for your reputation."

"We'll see." I hold my chin up high, watching as she ambles out the door. I exhale loudly as soon as it closes.

I wipe off my makeup, comb my long brown hair, and braid it into a Dutch braid. I feel uneasy, but I try to brush off those thoughts. As soon as I'm in bed, I take out my phone and type a message to Layla.

ME:

I shooed the boys away. Already in bed.
Shopping, here I come.

BESTIE:

Boys?

ME:

Clay and Colton.

BESTIE:

OMFG.

ME:

What the hell does that mean?

BESTIE:

Tell u more tomorrow.

ME:

Not fair.

I whine aloud, hiding under the blanket.

BESTIE:

Meet me at 11 a.m. near your dorm. Night.

I toss my phone on the nightstand and close my eyes. The image of that guy impetuously appears in my head. Memories of his severe glare send shivers down my spine. I shut my eyes tighter, erasing him from my mind. The last thing I want is to have nightmares because of that jerk.

I don't think love at first sight exists, but I believe in annoyed at first sight, and Colton is exactly that. He's obnoxious and self-centered, and I'll gladly keep my distance. He's bad news.

Chapter 2

Badass Bitch

Ava

I flip another page of the book I'm reading on my phone. I love the story, and yet now it fails to hold my attention. Layla is twenty minutes late, and it is driving me insane. I tap my fingers on my thigh, trying hard to concentrate. But I can't, due to my lack of patience. It's never been my best trait.

"Hey, love," my best friend says, and I look up, meeting her gaze. Her chocolate brown eyes are on me, and she grins. I wince and do not return the smile. "Don't sulk."

"Easy for you to say." I stand up, intending to hide my phone in my purse, but Layla snatches it from me.

"*Forbidden Love*? How many times have you read this?"

"Not enough." I grab my phone back and shove it into my purse.

"I thought your favorite was about high school?" Layla teases again, and I crack a smile.

"It still is. Just depends on my mood."

"What's up with your mood?" Her eyes zero in on me, and I can't stop my mind from drifting to the night before. Clay jerking off, naked Jordan, and the asshole. "What happened when you walked into your room?"

"I spoiled their fun, according to the three of them," I huff, my nostrils flaring. "Let's go shopping. I sorta want to forget all that."

"Forget all that?" Layla clasps my hand in hers, dragging me away from the tree and the campus. "After you told me who was in your room? Hell nah."

"Who are they?" I ask, looking at my best friend. Her long blonde hair, which has been collected into two pigtails, bounces with each step. "Jordan said they are the most popular guys on campus."

"They are."

"Have you ever mentioned them to me?" I don't know why I care to ask, but her short reply piques my interest.

"Yes, but only briefly. I don't think I ever called them by name." She shoots me a look. "I'm off-limits for them, just like they are for me. So I don't bother."

God no. Please tell me what I'm thinking is wrong. "Are they in Drake's class?"

"What?" Layla looks at me like I'm crazy. "If they were, I wouldn't care. They are from the team."

Just my luck, I guess. "I kind of thought they were. They're well-built..."

"How much did you see?" Layla quirks her eyebrow, and this time I burst out laughing. "It's not funny."

"Do you like one of them?" I ask between fits of laughter.

"Since I can't have either of them, I actually like both," Layla murmurs, a dreamy expression on her face. "But Thompson is another level."

"Hello," I sing as if I'm Adele. "I have no idea who you're referring to."

"Colton. Colton Thompson. He's a heartthrob."

"He's an asshole, and my hand stung after I slapped him across his stupid face." I'm so proud of myself.

My best friend halts in her tracks, looking at me with her eyes wide open. "You slapped Colton? Like really slapped him?" Her voice is high-pitched, and I frown.

"Like really, *really* slapped him. Not my problem he has no idea how to talk to a girl. He should have watched his mouth instead of verbally harassing me for no reason."

"Wow." She whistles, her eyes sparkling. "Tell me more."

"If I tell you, will you leave me alone?"

"Yes. I promise. No other questions."

"Fine," I mumble, taking a deep breath. She won't leave me alone even if she says she will. I know the bitch like the back of my hand.

I tell her everything on our way to the mall. She gasps, laughs, and swears like a sailor. She knows a lot about the asshole, based on her comments, but I don't ask any questions. I prefer not to know anything more about him.

As we go from one store to the next, I realize my mind isn't on shopping. I wrinkle my nose and pout anytime Layla shows me clothes or shoes. Eventually she starts scowling at me, and I don't blame her. I'm a mood killer.

"Ava, what's wrong with you today?" Layla asks, slumping into a chair in a café we decided to take a break in, a mug of hot cocoa in front of her.

"Just thinking." I set my freshly brewed flat white on the table.

"About what?"

"About things." I nibble on my bottom lip. "Should I be worried? I mean, that asshole threatened me."

"Well, Colton has an awfully bad reputation. He has a temper, and he snaps easily." Layla sips her cocoa, eyeing me from under her long eyelashes.

"Okay. So I probably pissed off the wrong dude."

"You probably did." She lets out a giggle, reaching over the table and covering my palm with hers. "But my brother won't let him do anything to you. As soon as Colton knows you're under Drake's protection, he'll back off. He respects his captain."

"I'm not a little girl in distress," I protest loudly, making my best friend laugh even more.

"You're a badass bitch who can stand up for herself. That's true." She points her finger at me. "Unfortunately, to make Colton back off, you'll need something more than that."

"How can you even like him?"

"Have you seen the guy?" Layla leans back in her chair, looking at me like she doesn't recognize me.

"I did. He's kinda hot, I guess."

"*Kinda*? Girl, what happened to you while I was in college?"

"Nothing." I hesitate. Over time, I have learned that some things are better kept to myself. She won't be happy with me if she finds out. She will probably be furious and won't talk to me for a day or two. Maybe a week. Or a month.

"Ava." She smacks my palm, bringing me back to my senses.

"Sorry. What are our plans for tonight?"

"Don't tell me you forgot." Layla groans, shaking her head in disbelief.

"About what?"

"About the party. Why else would we need to go shopping?"

"Dunno. Maybe you wanted new stuff."

She told me about this party a week ago. It's not that I don't like parties, it just slipped my mind for some reason. Well, maybe I *do* need something new.

"Let me guess," Layla sighs. "Now you need something to wear?"

"Uh-huh."

"I should have reminded you about the party from the beginning. It could have saved me a few hours of shopping." My best friend's eyes roam over my face. "Ready to shake your ass?"

"Ready to drink and maybe hook up with someone," I state, and she raises her eyebrows.

"Your first hookup in college. Hella proud of you, baby." My smile fades away. She's only one year older than me, and she acts as if she is my mom.

"Hold your horses, lady. I'm not going to fuck the first guy I meet."

"Guys from the team will be there. Drake said we can hang out with them." I glance at her as she saunters out of the café. After yesterday, I'm not sure I want to spend time with her brother and his teammates. "These guys are awesome. They are elite. So if you are with them, it means you're cool. Your roomie will be happy to have you as a friend when she sees you at the party."

"I don't need friends like her," I snarl, baring my teeth.

"What's her name again?"

"Jordan Patterson."

"Well, Jordan Patterson made a lasting impression on you." Layla shakes with laughter, draping a hand over my shoulder. I try to push her away, but it's no use. I'm a bit thinner than her, and I'm shorter, even at five foot five. She has no problem holding me in her tight grip, cackling at my attempts to free myself. Suddenly, she pushes me away, and I almost fall flat on my face.

"Layla." I yelp, and she runs into the first shop on her left. I'm so not doing this with her. I trudge further, but a few seconds later, I hear her footsteps. She falls into step with me, glancing at me over and over.

"What?"

"You're in a strange mood, and I can't place my finger on why."

"I'm moody," I bite back. "Is there anything I should know about tonight? What do people wear to these parties? Are there any rules, like on Wednesdays we wear pink, or some shit like that?"

"God, who knew I missed you so much?" Layla snorts, making me scrunch my nose. "It's just a college party. Nothing fancy. You don't need to be prim and proper. You need to be wild, like you always are."

"Fine." I nod and bolt into the shop we've been standing outside of.

After I quickly find something I want to wear and try it on, I amble out of the dressing room and head to the cashier. My phone buzzes, and I dig into my purse, looking for it. I see my dad's face on the screen. "Hey, Dad."

"Hey, sweetie." My dad's voice is deep. He raised me on his own after my mom died when I was six. He's been working his ass off at the fire station to earn more money for us. And even with the extra hours, he is the best father in the world. "How are you?"

"I'm fine...ugh, I'm fine." I struggle trying to take my wallet out of my purse.

"Ava?" my father says. "Is everything alright? What are you doing? Where are you?"

"I'm shopping with Layla."

"Already buying new clothes?" he chuckles.

"More or less. There is an occasion."

"Which is?" Dad asks, and I hear the sounds of a busy street. He's probably out running errands before the baseball game starts tonight.

"My first college party." I speak softly as I pay for my clothes.

"Do you remember what I told you about these parties?" Dad is pretty strict, but he always explains why he needs to say no to some of my whims. He envelops me in his care and love, being my friend and my wise adviser. Always.

"Of course." I take the bag in my hand. A satisfied smile plays on my lips. "No means no. Don't take drinks from people I don't know—"

"Don't drink at all," Dad corrects, and I look up at the ceiling. He's perfectly aware I won't listen. I never do. But I know my limits, and I don't get wasted. Ever.

"Okay."

"I'm serious," Dad barks, making my brows knit together. I walk up to Layla and slap her ass since she's standing with her back to me. She twirls around, glaring, then instantly relaxes as soon as she sees it's me. "Promise me, Ava."

I don't like doing this, but it's my first party. I want to be the one who decides whether I drink or not, so I cross my fingers. "I promise."

Dad exhales sharply. "Did you cross your fingers?"

"Yeah," I reply honestly. If there is one thing I won't do, it's lie to my dad. He hates liars.

"Just promise me you won't get into any shit, okay?"

"I promise." And this time, I don't cross my fingers. I smile. "I love you, Dad."

"Love you too, Ava." His words fill my heart with happiness. "Call me later, before you go to the party, okay?"

"Sure. Talk to you soon."

"Talk to you soon," he says back and hangs up. As soon as I slip my phone into my purse, I turn to my best friend, feeling her gaze on me.

"What did you buy?" Layla tries to peek into my bag, but I hide it from her. "Ava."

"You'll see it tonight." When I stick my tongue out at her, my piercing hits my teeth. "Um...what time?"

"Come to my room at eight? We can get ready together." She winks. "I'll do your makeup. You can do my hair. How about it?"

"Only *your* hair?" I ask innocently, aware that I'll need to help Grace, Layla's roommate, too.

"Grace is lovely." Layla nudges me in my ribs with her elbow.

"I haven't said a bad word about her. I simply want to know what I'm signing up for."

"We'll be going to the party with Grace. She sort of has the hots for Hudson Moore, so she's definitely going."

"Last time you said she had the hots for Drake."

"She did," Layla replies, sounding annoyed. "You know my brother. He's too fussy, and he always chooses wrong when it comes to girls. The good ones who like him, he isn't interested in. He focuses on the girls who aren't right for him, but he's still hoping to find love. I've told him a thousand times already. He looks in the wrong direction."

"Maybe it's for the best? It could have been awkward if something happened between them, right? Like, can you imagine stepping into your room and seeing your brother's ass, or him going down on her?"

"I'm going to vomit." Layla grimaces as she pretends to gag. "I want to scratch my eyes out, Ava. And nothing even happened between them, you stupid cow."

"I love you too, bestie." That's how we always are, laughing, crying, talking, or sitting in silence. It's never a dull moment with her.

We chat more about the party and gossip about our hometown. Now I'm in particularly good spirits, and I don't want to leave Layla's side, but I have to. She has an assignment she needs to finish before we go to the party. So I suck it up and go back to my room.

Opening the door, I stroll inside and notice Jordan on her bed, listening to music. I wanted to help her, but she brushed me off. Now? I have no desire to do anything for her.

I change my clothes, climb in bed with my phone, and open my book. I did my homework yesterday, so I have a few hours to kill by reading one of my favorite stories. But now I'll be hot and bothered after reading about Jax and Paige. Maybe it would be better to read something else? I don't want to jump the bones of just any guy at the party. I'm picky, and I don't like everyone.

Experience is a bitch, and mine was too hard on me.

I stare at the ceiling for a few moments as Jordan's music fills the room. It's Halsey, and I actually love her. Looks like this girl has something in common with me, after all.

I shake my head, dive down to the floor, and take my AirPods from my backpack. I decide to watch *You*. Penn Badgley is too handsome for his own good, and his voice... God, his voice is something else. I have never heard anything sexier—the asshole's voice sounds just like his.

I jolt upright on my bed. Realization washes over me, and I fall back, laughing silently. His voice. I found it sexy because it reminds me of one of my favorite actors. *Phew.* It's safe to say I don't find the asshole attractive. It was just his voice, and I would hate for that to change.

CHAPTER 3

CHAMP
COLTON

I SIT UP IN BED AND LOOK AROUND. WHAT TIME IS IT? I reach over to my bedside table, trying to grab my phone, but I accidentally shove it to the floor. "Just fucking great." I grumble, swinging my arm over the side of my bed and picking it up. It's eleven a.m., and I should probably already be up, but I don't want to get out of bed. I don't want to leave my apartment at all today.

This stupid party has terrible timing.

I launch Instagram, seeing new DMs. With a sigh, I open the first message in Requests, hit the Accept button, and stare at a full pair of boobs. *Right.* I look at the name and frown. *Jordan P.* I don't even know her. Why in hell would she send me her tits? I tap on the girl's profile photo, and realization hits me. It's the one Clay fucked last night.

I roll onto my back, holding my phone in the air while scrolling through her profile. She's attractive, loves sports and music, just something is missing. Sure, she has nice boobs, but I have no desire to fuck her. Especially not after her blow job last night. Not that it was really bad, but I didn't enjoy it that much.

Tossing my phone onto my covers, I slowly stand up and stroll to my closet. I put on a tee and a pair of sweatpants, yawning loudly. I will need a bucket of coffee to wake up. I snatch my phone and head to the kitchen. Good thing I decided to buy some food yesterday; I won't starve before I drag myself out of the apartment.

Before I start making a sandwich, I open Spotify, and MGK's "kiss kiss" fills the room. It's heaven. Literally.

Never in my life could I imagine my asshole father would do something good for me. Well, he did. He rented this apartment, paid for the entire year in advance.

It's my last year in college. My chance to make things right and to work on my grades. If I'm lucky and don't screw up my chances, maybe I'll be signed by the California Thunders. I was their first-round pick when I was nineteen. They have been watching my progress ever since. Who knows if, or when, they will still want to sign me, trade me or pass on me completely once I graduate. With my luck, I don't want to leave anything to chance. I work hard on and off the ice, and my only focus is on my future as a professional hockey player .

I will do absolutely anything for it, and my father knows it.

He gave me a long speech when he brought me to this apartment. He wanted me to focus on my studies and not just on pleasure. And I was almost tempted to say "fuck you" and go back to living on campus. I hate lies, and I know my father couldn't care less about my career. He wants me to work for him, and all this pretense is just about me having my degree, nothing else. In his world, reputation and status are everything.

The thing about me is I'm one of those people who prefers to do the opposite of what they've been told. If someone tells me, *Don't go there; there is trouble waiting for you*, I will say, *How can I stay away? Trouble is waiting for me.* But with this apartment, I quickly changed my mind, and I haven't regretted even once that I took the old man up on his offer. For my own selfish reasons.

Drinking my coffee, I sit down on the couch in the living room. All my muscles are relaxed, and my heartbeat is calm—not how I'm used to feeling on weekends when I don't have any games. Canceling my visit tomorrow feels weird, as going has been my ritual for six months already. Yet I've done it for myself, because the visits have become exhausting.

My phone dings, and I pick it up. This girl doesn't know how to read between the lines, does she? I shake my head as I open her message.

JORDAN P:

Do you like what you see?

ME:

Who are you?

JORDAN P:

Your cock fits my mouth perfectly. Last night proved that better than anything.

I scoff, close Instagram, and dial Clay's number. Stretching across the couch, I grab the TV remote. I need to fill time, so I might as well kill a few hours by watching a show.

"What?" My best friend's voice is groggy and barely audible.

"Hello to you too, moron." I laugh, hearing him groan.

"Thompson, it's not even fucking noon."

"Time to rise and shine, Rodgers." I turn on the TV and browse Netflix in hopes of finding something that will catch my attention.

"When you said you weren't going to go visit your parents, I thought you would be busy railing some chick all night and again this morning." He yawns. "But you went home alone, and now you're calling me before noon...for what?"

"Why did that chick send me pics of her tits? Did she send them to you too?"

"Which girl?"

"From last night. The freshman."

"The one that I fucked? Or the one that fucked you up?" Involuntarily, I grit my teeth and press my palm to my cheek. It freaking stung for an hour last night, and Clay's words reminded me about it. I'm not sure it was just because she slapped me without any remorse. It was more about her defiance. I'm not used to girls behaving like that with me.

"The one that gave me a blow job."

"Nah, she didn't send me anything. She checked me off her list, so now she has her sights set on you. Solely on you," he snickers, clearly not as sleepy as he was a few minutes ago.

"I hate clingy," I mutter under my breath as my eyes land on *You*. I haven't seen the third season, so maybe this is a good opportunity to catch up.

"I know, man. Everyone on campus knows that—except maybe her," Clay explains. "Give her time and she'll back off. Or just find another girl at the party tonight so she knows there is nothing to wait for."

"We'll see." I place my phone between my ear and my shoulder while I set my mug on the table and sit up straight.

"Damn, Colt, really—why did you need to wake me up?"

"Because."

"What are you doing?" Clay yawns.

"Watching Netflix."

"No chill?" he asks teasingly.

"Why is it always about sex with you?"

"Because I'm young, dumb, and broke," he singsongs, trying to sound like Khalid. "Can I come hang with you?"

"Are you suggesting we Netflix and chill together?" I cackle, hearing silence in return.

Then he murmurs, "Sorry, man, you're not my type, like at all. I hope you understand."

"Yeah." I chortle, standing up from the couch and heading back to the kitchen. "Come over whenever you want. I don't have any plans."

"Was your dad angry you decided to stay in town?" I stop in my tracks, suddenly lost in my thoughts. No one knows where I spend almost every Sunday lately. Not even Clay.

"I don't care." I take a few more steps and open the cupboard. M&Ms. My guilty pleasure since I was ten, when Mom bought them for me after a practice.

"Cool. I will grab something to eat and be at your place in an hour or so." Clay doesn't insist on talking about my dad. We've known each other since we started playing hockey together eleven years ago. We have been there for each other through thick and thin, and I appreciate the hell out of him. Even if he can be annoying as fuck.

"Okay. Buy some pizza." I end the call and tuck my phone into my pocket.

The day is not going how I envisioned it, but maybe it's for the best? Sometimes unexpected things are exactly what we need to light up our lives and breathe fresh air into something that's been resting in dust. Plus, I definitely wouldn't say no to having a good laugh with my friend. Weekends haven't been my favorite days of the week for a couple of months now, and it's probably time to start changing that. At least, to start trying to change it.

AT TEN P.M., Clay and I step into a house that's already full of people. Loud music echoes through the walls, finding its way under my skin. Adrenaline rushes through my veins, and I smile. I love this atmosphere, even if I often act like Ebenezer Scrooge. The truth is simple: I was fun, until I realized I was on a path of self-destruction. When Coach said, *Another trick and you're out*, I didn't have much choice but to obey.

Hockey is my life. I carry on with my finance major for it. I breathe for the opportunity to be on the ice again. It's the only thing in the world that makes any sense to me. The only thing that matters. Sometimes it means running myself to death with late-night practices and working to be the best during games. I am a champ, and there is no way in hell I will give up on my dreams.

"Let's get drinks." Clay claps a hand on my back, pulling me out of my thoughts. I simply nod and follow him into the house.

I feel eyes on me, but I don't pay any attention to them. Being on the hockey team taught me how to deal with popularity. There were some bumps and bruises along the way, but I got there. I don't care what people think of me, whether they like me or not. Their opinion isn't worthy of my time or my worries, under any circumstances.

"Where is everyone?" I shout, trying to talk over the music.

"They should be by the pool." Clay looks at me over his shoulder. "Moore sent me a text."

I roll my eyes, and it doesn't go unnoticed by my best friend. He smirks, shaking his head and looking away. What? I'm picky, and I won't be friends with just anybody.

Moore joined the team last year as our left wing, and I had a hard time tolerating his attitude. He's an arrogant, rich prick, and I have no desire to be associated with him. The feeling is not mutual. The dude has wanted to be my friend ever since we met, and I always remind him to back off. On the ice, I try to get along with everyone, for the sake of the game and our team. But outside the rink, I'm different, and not everyone likes the boundaries I set.

"Here." Clay shoves a bottle of beer into my hand. I hold his gaze, contemplating tonight's outcome. I haven't gotten drunk in what seems like an eternity. Maybe I can afford one night of total madness? I chew on the inside of my cheek for a few moments, and then I take a sip.

We move further into the house until I see Drake Benson, our captain. He's a damn mountain of a man. Sometimes, standing near him, I feel small—and I'm fucking six foot three. The way this guy looks speaks volumes, but he's a real softy inside. Guys joke about his behavior a lot, calling him a teddy bear. Truth be told? He doesn't get upset about it at all, and I don't remember him being angry even once. Only during games, but who can blame him? On the ice, our emotions run high. We set our eyes on the win and do everything in our power to succeed, like we're an interconnected whole. One wrong move can rouse the beast in any of us. Not just in someone hotheaded like me.

"Drake, what's up?" Clay calls out to Benson, and he turns his head to look at us. His hat is on backward, and a smile plays on his lips. He's in a good mood, and it's infectious. Being near him, even I act nicer. Maybe that's the reason why I don't like hanging out with him? He's rubbing off on me, and becoming the life of the party is not something I want.

"Hey, Rodgers, Thompson," Drake greets us, and we shake hands. "Nothing. Literally nothing. Playing the role of the babysitter."

"Your sister here?" Clay looks around.

"Yeah, she just went to use the bathroom with her best friend. As soon as they are back, I will be on the lookout again."

"Since when do you look after Layla so closely?" I arch my eyebrow at him, surprised.

He made it clear last year his sister was off-limits. He didn't want any of the guys from the team dating her or fucking her, and I respected that. We all did. Until today, he never tried to forbid her from having fun. Something is off.

"It's not actually about her." He shrugs. "Ava has a tendency to create trouble out of nowhere. I want to make sure everyone knows she's under my protection too, so next time there is a party, I will be free to do whatever I want."

"Ava?" Rodgers furrows his brow. "Isn't Grace her best friend?"

"Grace is her roommate." Drake gestures toward the couch. Layla's roommate is sitting near Moore, flirting with him like there's no tomorrow while he looks bored. I'm not sure she has any chance with him, or anyone from the team. She's a bit much. In everything. "Ava is her best friend."

"Is she new? Because last year, your sister and her roommate hung out with us at all the parties, and I kinda thought they were best friends. Always together. Inseparable."

Benson smiles, shaking his head. "Ava is our neighbor. Layla has been friends with her for an eternity, but she's a year younger than my little sis. *They* are inseparable."

"Is she hot?" My best friend's gaze darkens. That's not what amazes me though. Drake's reaction is interesting, to say the least.

"She is," he rasps, narrowing his eyes. "But she's off-limits."

"That's ridiculous. I totally get it when it's your sister, but her best friend?"

"Her best friend is also off-limits. That's final." Benson's smile fades away, and I blink in total stupefaction. A wild guess crosses my mind, but I keep my mouth shut. It's too early to draw any conclusions. For starters, I need to see the girl and Drake together. Somehow, I'm sure I'm right.

Clay huffs, taking a sip of his drink to hide his irritation. The guy is just like me. He hates when someone tells him he can't do something. He is more than happy to go against anyone, except his teammates. Which means one thing: whoever this girl is, he won't be able to lay his hands on her. He doesn't want to have our captain as an enemy—no one does. Including me. A healthy team atmosphere is the key to future wins. If we are at each other's throats, we won't stand a chance against our rivals.

"What a pleasant surprise." Layla's voice rings in the air, rising above the music. "I thought you decided to skip the party."

I whip my head around to look at Benson's sister, and my eyes land on her. *The freshman.*

Chapter 4

Duck You

COLTON

"Do you see what I see?" Clay's voice is full of amazement. He asks without even looking at me. His gaze is focused on the girl, and a smug smile illuminates his face. He tried to flirt with her last night, asking for her name and promising to figure it out on his own when she refused to tell him.

"Hey, Clay," Layla murmurs, leaning in and giving my best friend a quick hug. Then she whirls to me, beaming. She's a beautiful girl with the whole package: great ass, round hips, big boobs, and a narrow waist. Her eyes shift to my face, lingering on my mouth. Once I helped her to her room because she was totally wasted, and she tried to kiss me. I didn't tell anyone about it. The last thing I need is her brother on my back. "Hey hey, Colton."

"Hey." Her fruity scent envelops me as she hugs me way longer than she did Clay. She pushes boundaries, and I don't like it. I'm friends with her brother, but that doesn't mean I'm friends with her.

"Are you going to introduce us to your friend?" Clay looks between Layla and the freshman.

Benson's sister steps back and wraps her arm around her friend's waist. Does she know what happened yesterday? I hope the freshman kept silent about the slap, for her own sake.

"Looks like you already know everything," she exclaims cheerfully, sneaking a glance at Drake. "My big brother told you about my bestie, didn't he?"

"I did." Drake is pleased with himself, smiling at his sister and her friend. Did I read his previous reaction all wrong? I frown, keeping my eyes on my teammate. Anything is better than looking at that fucking girl.

"Well, a little introduction won't hurt, right?" Layla chimes. "Even if you already met."

"Meaning?" her brother asks, furrowing his brow.

"It's not the first time I've met your sister's best friend." Clay's eyes travel down her body. "This beauty refused to tell me her name. Right, *Ava*?"

"Circumstances, you know?" The girl smirks, and my best friend snorts. He's loving their interaction, how she responds to him, while I feel annoyance spilling into my veins. "I didn't think it was appropriate."

"Why?" Drake asks, locking eyes with her.

At that second, it hits me. I'm so right. It gives me an ace up my sleeve, because I'm one hundred percent sure Layla doesn't have a clue about her brother and her best friend. My body warms up, and I almost grin from satisfaction. *You chose the wrong guy to piss off, girl.*

"Does it matter?" She tilts her head to the side, narrowing her eyes on Benson.

"Nope," he utters, taking a sip of his beer.

"Ahem, so, Clay, Colton, this is Ava. She's my best friend in the whole world." Layla looks at Clay and me then back. "Be nice. She's precious."

"And gorgeous," Clay purrs. I wonder how long it will take Drake to put him in his place. With how his grip on his bottle tightens, I'm not sure he has enough patience. "Say, Ava, can I get you a drink?"

"Rodgers," Drake warns, and I almost feel pity for him. Almost. No matter what I think about her, it's not fair of him to forbid guys on the team from pursuing her...until he stakes his claim, that is. "Wasn't I clear?"

"Oh, come on." Layla whimpers. "Don't tell me you're extending your rules to Ava too."

"What if I am?" Benson stares at his sister, unbothered. She sucks in air, her eyes widening.

"What's going on?" The girl fiddles with her earring, looking between the Benson siblings.

"You're off-limits to the hockey team, love," Clay states. "Drake's rules."

The girl blinks, and her mouth forms a little O. Her reaction makes me curious. She doesn't come across as the disobedient type. She's a good girl who tries hard to make everyone believe she's a rebel. It's obvious.

She takes a deep breath and turns to face her best friend. "I want to dance."

"Um...oh, well, let's go dance then." Layla takes her hand, and a second later they both disappear from view.

"Looks like you're free to do whatever you want." Clay claps Benson on his back. "Your babysitting hours are over."

"You don't know her." Drake shakes his head, then he runs his palm over his face. "I pissed her off."

"And?"

"And I better go and find more beer." Benson sneers and marches away from us.

"I have no idea what the hell is going on there." Rodgers lines up with me, staring at Drake's back, which is moving farther and farther away. "You?"

"We'll see if I'm right."

"Not going to share your thoughts with me? Your best friend?" Clay complains loudly, barely hiding his smile.

"No."

"As always." He looks around. "I honestly thought you would kick her out of the house. You were fuming yesterday, so I was sure you were going to flip and send her packing. It's strange that I was wrong."

"There is still time." I have something more damaging for her than just kicking her out of the party. But only if I'm right, of course.

"Let's find the others. They should be outside," Clay suggests, and I nod in agreement. I am here to have fun. As long as that girl stays out of my sight, I'm good. I think.

We ran out of beer, and I volunteered to go get more. Not because I want to get drunk, but because I'm the soberest among my crew. I'm not even sure Clay saw me leave. For the past thirty minutes, he has been too busy shoving his tongue down some girl's throat. Probably another freshman, since I have never seen her on campus before. Well, we all have bad habits, right? Weaknesses. My best friend has a soft spot for girls, thinking he's too young to settle down and date just one person. He hasn't had a girlfriend since we were freshmen, and he's fine like that. Just like I am.

On my way to the kitchen, I notice Benson. His lips are stretched into a thin line, and his brows are knit together, while his arms are folded across his chest. I walk straight up to him and stop by his side, following his line of sight.

Layla is dancing with some dude. He has his hands plastered to her hips, moving along with her as she grinds her ass over his groin. If I were Benson, I would probably want to kill the guy too. Or just punch him in the face. Either way, I have no idea how he's dealing with his sister's behavior.

"Are you planning his murder?" I ask, and Drake spins to look at me. "I can lend you a hand, if you want it."

"No," he laughs. "Just observing."

"The way I see it, Layla is having fun," I say as his sister gyrates and wraps her arms around the guy's neck.

"Nothing unusual. She hangs out with Trey sometimes." I meet his gaze, and I see a smile playing on his lips. "I know the guy."

"Looking at you, I thought you were planning the best way to kill him," I remark, and Benson only shakes his head.

"Definitely not." He sighs and then adds, "I wasn't even looking at her."

"No?" I frown, watching the crowd with more attentiveness, and a moment later I know what he means. The freshman is dancing near Layla. She's on some kind of pedestal, so it's easy to follow her every move. Her very sexy moves.

I shake my head, trying to clear that stupid thought from my mind. She's not sexy. At all. Yet my body begs to differ. I let my eyes wander all over her, feeling like my veins are ready to blow up from the heat forming in my abdomen. *Shit.*

Looking away, I grit my teeth. This girl is playing on my nerves. I want her gone. "Is the best friend a problem?" My voice sounds husky, and I clear my throat.

"Not really," Drake replies, but it doesn't mean anything. I'm not going to listen to him anymore. I'm kicking her out. Now.

As I barrel through the crowd of people, I keep my eyes on her, and it's a total mistake. The closer I get, the hotter I feel. My freaking dick is getting excited just looking at her; hardness pokes through my jeans. *Yeah, so much for not being a horny stud.* I can't help how I feel. The girl has a perfect body, flawless and feminine with full breasts. She's wearing a crop top, and the sight of her flat stomach draws me in like a magnet. Her round hips look nice in that little skirt.

She's stunning.

Wow, wow, wow. I'm definitely off my game. She's stunning? What the fuck am I thinking? Jesus, with thoughts like that, I might as well ask Coach to kick me off the team so I can go apply for the school's first-string quarterback position. It's absurd.

I frown, stopping right in front of her. Apparently, she's standing on a little coffee table. "Get off the table." I yell, trying to catch her attention through the music. She doesn't seem to hear me or even notice me. She's totally in her element. Her eyes are half-closed as she continues to sway to the music. I grab her palm roughly, and she tenses. Her eyes open, and her pupils dilate. "Get off the table."

The girl snatches her palm away; her face contorts in anger. "No."

"What do you mean, no?" *Is she fucking serious?*

"No means no," she retorts, ready to turn away from me. I take my phone out of my pocket and launch my camera. She quirks an eyebrow at me. "What are you doing?"

"Get off the table. Now." Our exchange has put us on center stage, and I can feel people's eyes on my back. I need to end this fucking charade once and for all.

Just at that moment, the song changes to "hot girl bummer" by blackbear. The girl freezes for a second, but then her full lips stretch into a smile. She bends down a little, looking me in the eyes. I know what she's going to do, and I wish she would change her mind. There are consequences, and she won't like them.

Fuck you, she lip-synchs, showing me two middle fingers.

Some people around us start laughing, and it honestly triggers me. Instead of doing as I say, she puts on a show. *Well, be ready to be humiliated then.*

I hide my phone in my back pocket and wind my hands around her waist. Her eyes become as wide as saucers as I lift her into the air. When I put her down on the ground, her hand lands on my chest as she tries to steady herself. We stare at each other in silence for a good minute. Her skin is smooth and soft under my calloused palms. Her chest rises and falls, the goosebumps visible on her exposed stomach. Up close, her eyes look emerald green, framed by thick black eyelashes. She has a birthmark on her right cheek, and I almost smile staring at it.

What the fuck is wrong with me?

I pick her up and throw her over my shoulder. Wheeling around, I trudge straight to the front door. My palm rests on her ass, keeping her skirt down.

She wiggles; her knuckles hit my back. "Put me down."

I smile, ignoring her miserable attempts to stop me. I am actually enjoying this situation, her frustration. I'm not sure she will want to go to another party anytime soon.

I open the door, take a step outside, and put her down again. She's fuming. Her cheeks are red, and her long brown hair falls over her face. She blows it away, tucking strands behind her ears. My eyes linger on her mouth for a moment longer than they should. Shaking my head, I take a step back.

"You wouldn't dare..." she whispers.

I don't care; you brought this on yourself.

"Bye." With that, I close the door in her stunned face. Then I turn around and head to the kitchen. It's time to get back to the guys, maybe even let loose a little. I deserve it.

"Thompson." Drake growls, stomping in my direction. "What the hell did you do that for?"

"Because." I stare at him defiantly. It's the first time I've gone against my captain since we started playing for the same team.

"You just kicked out my sister's friend. Humiliated her in front of all these people. Didn't I make it clear she was with me? Under my protection?" He raises his voice, his eyes staring daggers at me.

"Sorry, Drake. This time, I'm not going to do what you say. That girl doesn't belong here."

"For fuck's sake." He throws his hands in the air. "She was drinking. It's only her second week here, and she doesn't know her way around. What if someone comes after her? Tries to force themselves on her? Did you think about that before you kicked her out?"

"I..." Those thoughts hadn't even crossed my mind, and I hate to admit he could be right.

"I..." he mimics me, and I glare at him. "You're an ass. A real spoiled ass."

Drake storms past me, bumping into my shoulder on his way to the front door. He opens it and moves to leave. The question burns the tip of my tongue, and I go for it, even if it's shitty of me. I want to test my theory. "Does your sister know you fucked her best friend?"

"Fuck off, Thompson," Benson hisses, slamming the door behind him. I stare at it for a few seconds, thoughts swirling in my head. I was right about them, his answer didn't leave me any doubts. Strangely? I don't feel excited anymore.

I take my phone out of my back pocket and frown. *What the fuck?*

Apparently, she must have grabbed it. I guess I hadn't locked it when I shoved it in my pocket before carrying her out. The girl left a message for me. I stare at the screen for a few seconds. Then I burst out laughing, squeeze it back into my jeans, and make a beeline for the kitchen. It's time to bring the guys the beer I promised.

Her silly text is on my mind. *Duck you.* Autocorrect changed her message, making it completely opposite from what she intended it to be. She's funny though.

I exhale through my nostrils, getting rid of those thoughts. I've wasted enough time on this freshman. I'm not going to let her ruin yet another night for me. I need to find a hookup. My hard-on has me acting irrational and stupid. I need to get laid.

Chapter 5

The Secrets We Keep

AVA

"Asshole. Fucker. Stupid jerk." I mutter under my breath as I walk down the street. "Fucking idiot."

I'm ready to kill anyone right now. My fists are balled, and my pulse is racing. Never in my life did I imagine being kicked out of my first college party. Not by that idiotic guy. I'm going to be a laughingstock on Monday. People will be gossiping about his reasons...which are simple: he's an arrogant prick.

Gritting my teeth, I look around. All I see are campus buildings, and in the dark, they all look the same to me. Where the fuck am I? Did I take a wrong turn? I was sure I needed to go right, but what if I needed to turn left instead? I barely hold myself back from screaming at the top of my lungs. I'm frustrated beyond anything and totally alone.

That thought settles, and I huff loudly. I would love some help, yet I don't want to bother Layla. Especially not when she's with Trey. They were so into each other, I preferred to scoot away and go dance on my own. Away from Trey's friend. Dick, or Dirk—doesn't matter, because he isn't my type at all. He's sleazy, and I don't like sleazy.

As my best friend reminded me, I don't like anyone recently.

Shaking my head, I resume walking. At this point, the only thing I want is to be back in my room. Alone. To just lie on my bed and stare at the ceiling until I fall asleep. I regret going to that party. I should have stayed back at the dorm, watching season three of *You*. That show is epic, and I ditched it for this shit.

I hope that idiot gets what he deserves—a broken nose, for example, or a black eye. Anything.

"Ava!"

I halt in my tracks, spin around, and gawk at Drake. What is he doing here?

Layla's brother stops in front of me, breathing hard. "Why didn't you answer your phone?"

"My phone?" I frown, unzipping my belt bag and taking out my phone. "Well..."

"I called you five times. Five." he snaps, towering over me. "I was worried sick about you."

"You don't need to worry. As you can see, I'm fine." I hide my phone back in my bag.

"This isn't funny, Ava. Something seriously bad could have happened to you."

"Okay." I shift uncomfortably under his gaze. The guy is huge, and I always feel small when he's around. It's not even about my height. It's about my senses.

"Where were you going?" He grins at me, allowing himself to relax.

"To my dorm." I turn, intending to continue my walk, but a palm on my wrist doesn't let me take even one step further. "What?"

"Your dorm is in the opposite direction," he muses, and I let out a loud groan. "My house is this way."

I scoff, remembering Jordan. She was at the party, dancing with some dude, and later I didn't see her at all. What if she went back to our room? Sitting on the floor outside the door doesn't sound appealing. I yank my hand out of Drake's and start walking.

"Where are you going, Ava? Didn't you hear me?"

"I heard you perfectly. We're going to your house." I don't expect him to argue, and he doesn't. He speeds up and catches up with me.

We pass a little park as we stroll close to each other, not saying anything at first. But I know him too well. He has questions, and he's going to ask them now.

"I'm sorry for Thompson's behavior. I have no idea what was wrong with him tonight. Usually, he doesn't have problems listening to me. We have a rule on the team: we always support each other. No matter what we think. If our teammates need help, we're there for them." He hides his hands in his pockets as I glance at him.

"He has a problem with me." Our eyes lock for a few moments. "It's not about him looking for trouble with you; it's me."

"Why?"

"I walked in on Clay and him having sex with my roommate. I ruined their fun, and got into an argument with Thompson." I keep my mouth shut about slapping him. "They cut their night short, and it was all my fault."

"Shit, I'm sorry, Ava. Thompson isn't the best guy to have as your enemy," Drake says quietly, lifting his hand as if he's going to hug me and then reconsidering. "What he did tonight was wrong, and I told him that. I'll talk to him. Again."

"Not sure he will care about any of it." If I'm being honest, I don't want to have anything to do with that idiot. And I don't want him to apologize to me. His shitty words won't mean a thing, and they won't change what people might think about me.

"I'll make sure he cares," he says, and I smile at him involuntarily. It's nice to know someone is worried about me. I look down, and then I remember.

"Thanks, Drake." I take a deep breath before continuing. "But I'm not okay with you making decisions for me. I'm not Layla. I'm just your sister's friend, and you can't forbid me to do what I want."

"Do you want to date someone from the team?" He cocks an eyebrow at me, and I shake my head.

"It's not about dating. Or anything. I want to be free to do whatever I want." I lick my lips nervously. "With whoever I want."

Drake holds my gaze, not saying anything at first. Then he just nods. "Okay. I will make sure to let guys know you are available."

"Hey." I smack him in his shoulder. "Now you're making it sound like I'm a free seat on the bus."

"You took that all wrong." He winks. Layla's brother is impossible, honestly. "We're here."

I look at the red brick building in front of me and feel envious. My dorm is okay, but this one looks better. It's cozier and brighter, as it has big windows and little balconies for each room above the first floor. "Do you have a roommate?"

"Nope."

"Do you have a RA who checks visitors and forbids girls from coming inside?"

"He's at the party right now." Drake laughs heartily. "Besides, he knows I'm not a troublemaker."

"Yeah, you're the nicest one of the Benson's siblings." I nudge him in his ribs with my elbow.

"Should I tell my sister that you called her mean?" He heads into the building, and I trail after him.

"Don't put words into my mouth," I warn, drawing a chuckle out of him. It's always like this with Drake and me. We are easy. We get along. We don't fight, and we have a lot of things in common. I like having him near me. In a friendly way.

"I never put anything into your mouth you don't say or want." Is he going to remind me about that any chance he gets?

"I thought we had a deal."

He stops in front of a door on the third floor and looks at me. "We did. It was just a joke."

"It didn't sound like it." I narrow my eyes, pouting.

"Come on in." Drake lets me in first. I edge into the room and stop near the door. It's dark, and I have no idea what his room looks like. Or where his stuff is. Falling flat on my face doesn't sound appealing.

The door closes, and then lights come on. I squint, looking around. It's a tidy and spacious room of light blue and white. There is a desk near the window and a little bookcase, a double closet with a mirrored door, and a beanbag chair in the corner. A few pictures hang on the wall above his bed. The place is welcoming and comfortable, just like Drake. He's a nice guy, and for the most part, he doesn't even try to hide it. Unless he's on the ice. He's a beast when he plays.

"Like my room?" he asks.

"Yeah, it's nice. It's way better than mine."

"Don't worry, Mason. I lived in your dorm once too." Drake ambles past me and heads to the beanbag chair. He slumps onto it, takes off his sneakers, and shoves them aside. He wiggles, making himself comfortable, and then peers at me.

Why the hell did I think it was a good idea to come here?

"Um...are you going to sleep on the beanbag chair?"

"Do I have another option? There's only one bed."

I blink and then burst out giggling. Drake looks at me in confusion. "It's like the book tropes, you know. Enemies to lovers, when they stay in one room, and there is only one bed, and they need to share it." I thread my fingers through my hair as my laugh dies in my throat. Why did I mention that? "I'm sorry, that was unnecessary."

"Ava, it's not a big deal. Truly. It's just one night." He shrugs, taking off his hat. His short curls fall over his face, covering his eyes. "Besides, I will have the entire day to catch up on my sleep."

"If you say so." I stalk to his bed and slowly take off my belt bag. I toss it on the floor, ready to climb into bed, but then I turn around and go to turn off the lights. "Do you mind if I...?"

"Turn it off." Drake crosses his arms over his chest and closes his eyes. I freeze, looking him over. He's a handsome guy, incredibly popular with girls. Somehow, he always chooses the wrong ones who want him only because he's a hockey player. No matter what, Layla is right: he has very bad taste when it comes to women.

"Ava?"

"S-sorry. Got lost in my thoughts," I hurriedly exclaim. Then I turn off the lights, drowning the room in darkness.

"Go to bed, and you can get lost in your thoughts about whatever you want," he jokes, and I guffaw. "Night, Ava."

"Night, Drake." I plop myself down on his bed and stare at the ceiling.

Seconds turn into minutes, minutes into hours. I just can't sleep. I lie here with my eyes wide open. My mind drifts to the asshole. His brown eyes taunt me, as if he's a demon himself. So alluring, so tempting. His gaze coaxes passion, heat, and I feel lost when he looks at me. *Lost in him.*

I inhale abruptly. What the fuck is wrong with me? I'm thinking about the jerk who treated me like garbage two days in a row. My heartbeat quickens, and anger overwhelms me. I set my jaw hard; my muscles are rigid. I need to calm down. Immediately.

"Drake?" I call out quietly. I have no idea how much time has passed. "Drake, are you asleep?"

"No."

"What time is it?"

Drake reaches to the floor and grabs his phone. "It's three thirty." An hour. I spent an hour thinking about that asshole. I almost growl in frustration.

"I can't sleep."

"Is my bed not comfortable enough for you, princess?" he teases, and this time I don't laugh with him. "Ava?"

"Can you...um... Can you come here?"

"Why?" His voice suddenly drops to a barely audible whisper.

"I don't want to sleep alone."

Drake sighs. "We've been there."

"I know. It was good, wasn't it?"

"We said it would only be once."

I roll onto my back and close my eyes. Disappointment seeps into my veins. "We could have just slept in one bed, but whatever."

I remember that Saturday last April. I went to the store and saw Drake standing near the beer aisle. I was incredibly surprised since Layla hadn't mentioned they would be home. *They* weren't; he came alone. His team lost some stupid game, and he wasn't in the mood to stay on campus. I was going to go to a party with my classmate Thea, but he looked so damn lonely. So I canceled my plans and went to his parents' house to hang out with him. I had known him my whole life and wanted to support my friend. My father didn't see any problem with me staying at the Bensons' place, even if he was perfectly aware that Drake and Layla's parents were out of town.

We were drinking, and it kind of happened on its own. One second, we were sitting on the couch in the basement, watching a movie, and the next—we were all over each other. I was bored. He needed to vent. Win-win. It didn't mean shit, for either of us. Just sex, pure pleasure, and nothing else. There wasn't any awkwardness the next morning. We woke up under a blanket on the couch, agreed not to tell Layla anything, and continued on with our lives as if nothing ever happened. Easy. Just like I'd imagined a friend with benefits would be. I just hadn't imagined it would be Drake.

I'm an idiot.

Suddenly, I feel his presence. I open my eyes and see Drake standing near the bed. He looks down at me, his eyes hooded with lust. He bends down and gently places his hands on my legs, moving them up until he's up under my skirt. He smiles as he tugs on my panties and drags them down. Then he slowly kneels and grabs my hips, moving me closer to him. My skirt goes up to my waist, leaving me exposed to him. I should probably feel ashamed, but I'm not. I feel amazing.

"You asked if it was good..." His hot breath on my thighs sends tingles down my spine. "It was fucking perfect."

The second he touches me, I close my eyes, enjoying his caress. I arch my back, immersing myself in the moment and the man. Coming here with my best friend's brother was the best decision I made all week.

Chapter 6

Never-Felt-Before

COLTON

Clay often says that having a face like mine can make women beg for my attention. Add my reputation and my spot on the hockey team, and the girls are ready to do anything to hop into my bed. The truth is, I'm picky. I don't hook up with just anyone. I choose carefully, because if I go with the flow or join my best friend, I often end up disappointed. And I hate being disappointed after sex. It's like a punch to the gut, a low blow to my confidence.

That's exactly how I feel right now.

I close the door and head to the stairs. It's eight a.m., and I need to get out of this house before anyone sees me. Making a girl cry right after I give her an orgasm? I'm not proud of myself, and I feel like a failure. I just wanted to get laid. To get rid of the stupid idea that crept into my head. To make the image of that freshman disappear from my mind.

There was no other reason for me to go home with my classmate Amy.

The situation I got myself in is another reminder why I don't like having sex with girls I have known for a while. They all think if I finally decide to fuck them, it means I feel something for them, maybe even want a relationship. *Colton Thompson doesn't do relationships because he's too fucked up to be present in one.* No one knows that, obviously. They just think I'm a playboy who hasn't met his other half yet.

My mood is so weird. The thoughts that keep resurfacing in my head are batshit crazy, and I need to do something with them. Canceling my visit was probably an unbelievably bad idea in the long run. I'm bored, and when I'm bored, I start to think—and that's not fucking good for my stability. I need to hurry up; I want to get out of this fucking place as soon as possible.

I stop in my tracks. My eyes are glued to the girl coming down the stairs. The freshman is humming under her breath, swaying her hips as she moves effortlessly. Totally lost in her element, she smiles to herself.

Storming forward, I step into her line of sight. She freezes, meeting my gaze. Narrowing her eyes, she takes a deep breath and starts moving again, until she's four steps above me. "Move."

"Glad to see you're safe and sound," I mock, and her frown deepens.

A second later, it dawns on me. Loud music swims around her—she has her earbuds in, which means she can't hear me.

What is it with me and this girl? She pushes my buttons, and I make a fool of myself each time I see her. I hate it.

I put my hand on the railing, blocking her way. I'm not letting her walk out of here until she...what? I don't understand myself this time for real. Why the fuck can't I let this go? Do I need to have the last word so badly?

"Move," she repeats, louder this time. I grimace, reaching under her hair and snatching an AirPod out of her ear. She gasps, her eyes widening. "What the fuck are you doing?"

"Making sure you hear me." I involuntarily listen to her music—"acting like that" by MGK and YUNGBLUD roars through her earbud. I didn't expect her to like this kind of music. She doesn't seem the type.

She rolls her eyes. "What?"

"I'm glad to see you safe and sound," I say. In all honesty, it bugged me a little that I kicked her out of the party late at night. Drake's words found their way under my skin, making me feel bad about myself. I am a moron, but not a heartless one. At least, I hope not.

"You didn't care about my safety when you threw me out of the party." She extends her palm. "My AirPod. Please."

My eyes roam over her face, which is totally makeup-free. Her hair is a bit disheveled, and she looks...I don't even know how to explain it. She looks satisfied. Even her skin is glowing. Memories of the moans I heard from the floor above Amy's room sound in my ear. Was it her and Drake? He lives upstairs. And he never returned to the party after he left to find her. Putting two and two together, I purse my lips tighter.

"Why are you sneaking away so early?" I ball my fist and hide her earbud in it. "Don't you like morning cuddles?"

She blinks long and hard, but it's not the reaction I expect. She doesn't look embarrassed. Her face doesn't show even the slightest change in emotion; she's totally unbothered. "Cuddles with who?"

"With the guy you spent the night with." I lean on the railing, propping myself on my elbow. I gape at her, ready to see her blush, but it doesn't happen. "With Drake," I add to make it clear that I know her secret.

She shakes her head, a smile curling her lips. "I slept in Drake's room, not with him." She steps down, and her tits are now at eye level. I swallow with difficulty because her breasts are all I want to look at, even if they are hidden under her crop top. "My AirPod, now."

I clear my throat, lick my lips, and tear my gaze away from her chest. "Do you really think I'm stupid?"

"I barely know you," she murmurs, taking another step down, "but something tells me that yes, you're stupid."

It's the third time I've seen her, but she has managed to piss me off like no one ever has. Her disobedience and her wittiness drive me insane. "He ran after you and never came back, and now you're strolling down the stairs from his floor at eight. No one sneaks away that early if they don't have anything to hide."

"What are you hiding then?" She cocks an eyebrow. "Why are you sneaking away this early? Don't *you* like cuddles?"

"That's none of your business," I bark, gritting my teeth. She breaks into laughter. "I have places I need to be."

"Of course." She walks around me, stopping in front of me. I lower my eyes and watch as she tucks her hair behind her ears. "Give me my AirPod and I will be out of your way, just like you want."

I hold her gaze. My breath quickens as I fidget in place. Then the realization hits me: I want her, and that makes me aggravated. I won't touch her. The feeling of her skin still lingers on my palms. I remember how soft it was. I swallow the lump in my throat, confused by my own emotions. It's not right. Any of it.

She extends her palm again, and this time I throw her AirPod into it. I have no idea why I even took it in the first place. She hides it in her belt bag, shakes her head a little, and starts walking down the stairs. I stay behind, watching her in silence. There is something about her—I don't even know how to explain it. I feel different when she's around, and I don't remember ever experiencing anything like it.

I slap my cheeks hard, bringing me back to my senses. What the hell am I doing? Gawking at her? Am I for real? I follow her, walking quickly to catch up with her.

"Does Layla know you slept with her brother?" I ask as she opens the door. It's the same question I asked Drake. Even the circumstances are similar.

She huffs, walks down the steps, and only then turns around to face me. "I haven't slept with Drake."

"That's hard to believe." I hide my hands in my pockets. "A lot of girls dream about being with him."

"I've known the guy since I was a child. He has always been there for me. Always. He cares about me, just like he cares about his sister." She sighs in exasperation. "You're trying to make something out of nothing."

"So you just spent the night with the guy, alone in his room, and nothing happened?"

"I don't even know why I'm having this conversation with you. I don't owe you anything, but I'll say it once more, just for Drake's sake." She steps closer, looking up at me. "If you think that a girl can't spend a night alone with a guy without something happening between them, then that's who *you* are. You measure people against yourself, and not everyone is like you. Remember that. I have known Drake since I was a toddler. I have spent night after night at his place. I have hung out with his sister and him alone more than once. He's family."

She spins around, walking away from me. Her head is high, and her posture is relaxed. I'm sure she lied; I don't have even the slightest doubt. Yet her ability to hide her emotions is impressive. I could learn a thing or two from her, even if I'm the most closed off person on the team. She's on another level.

I stay put; my eyes are trained on her body. She looks so damn fine it hurts. I feel my dick hardening in my pants, and it makes me angry. I don't like what she makes me feel. I'm not used to these emotions, the never-felt-before emotions. They stir me in the wrong way. I need to do something about her.

Turning on my heel, I walk in the opposite direction. My apartment is twenty minutes away on foot, and it's a blessing. I need this time to collect myself, or Monday will be a catastrophe.

When I decided to cancel my appointment, I thought I did myself a favor. Seeing her in the state she is in is pure torture, and I needed a break from it. For my own mental health. For my own future. Now? I'm sure it was a mistake. Next Sunday, I will be there, ready to see her. Ready to talk to her about my days, even if she doesn't remember a thing afterward. I will be there, just for me.

Chapter 7

M&Ms

AVA

"How was Trey?" I ask Layla. She called me two hours ago, suggesting we have dinner together. Since I didn't have any plans, I agreed without hesitation.

"Energetic." My best friend takes a sip of her soda, casting her gaze to the side.

"Energetic?" I repeat, putting my fork on my plate. "It sounds like... I don't even know, like you're talking about an old man who surprisingly had enough energy to fuck you."

She shakes her head. "The sex was good. I just...I'm tired of him. That's all."

I push myself away from the table, leaning my back against the leather bench. "Why?"

"We've been seeing each other for over a year, and our relationship is stuck. Nothing changes at all. I've honestly started to believe I will be better on my own," Layla tells me, wincing a little, as if from sudden pain.

"I'm sorry you feel that way. Do whatever feels right; I'll be here for you."

"Well, I'm not going to break up with him yet. We've had great moments together. So maybe if we talk, things will improve."

"You looked really into each other last night. Maybe it's worth trying." I smile, twirling a strand of hair around my finger.

"Speaking of last night," Layla mutters, "Grace said Thompson kicked you out of the party."

I always forget that people in our social circle talk, just like high school. It reminds me of a beehive. Everyone knows everything, and rumors spread faster than wildfire. That guy made a fool of me last night for everyone to see.

"He did." I tilt my head; my hair falls into my face, and I blow it away. "I was so furious I didn't even think about going back to the party. I just left."

"You didn't deserve to be kicked out. I'm sorry it happened, Ava. I honestly thought that you being friends with my brother would make Colton back off."

Colton. He's just... When I saw him today on my way out of Drake's room, I wanted to disappear. Why him? It could have been anyone. Even Layla. But no, it was him, and he didn't have anything better to do than rile me up. Again. This stupid universe is trying to collide us together any chance it gets.

"Did you find your way back to the dorm okay?" she asks, bringing me back to reality.

I feel my skin warm, and memories of her brother flood my mind. "With Drake's help," I murmur, seeing her jaw drop. "He saw what Thompson did, and he wanted to make sure I was okay...because I wasn't. I got lost, and without him I probably would have wandered around campus all night."

"Aw, poor thing." She pats my palm, smiling at me gently. "I'm so glad Drake found you. You're like a sister to him, so I can only imagine how pissed he was at Colt."

I almost choke on my meatball. That's the same bullshit I told that asshole. *He's family.* Family won't fuck me all night, making me come over and over and over. I clench my thighs together, perfectly aware how wet I am just from the memories. *Fucking Drake and his miraculous tongue.*

"Yeah, you two are like family to me." *I'm so going to hell for my secrets.* "Drake promised to talk to him, but I'm not sure it will change anything."

"Colton is difficult to deal with. Everyone knows that." She glances at the clock on the wall. "But it's my brother we're talking about also. He hates when someone acts up, and he never hesitates to do the right thing."

"Uh-huh." If she continues going on and on about how great her brother is, I'll be tempted to tell her about my time with him.

I don't want a relationship with Drake. The guy is gorgeous, but he's not my type. The sex is amazing though, and no one gets me off like him. So maybe, if I'm honest with her, she would be okay with us being friends with benefits? *Hey, bestie, can I occasionally fuck your brother?* I can't even imagine that conversation. I better find something else to talk about. "Why did you choose this place? It's far away from the dorm."

"Just because," she replies as I dig into my food. "Well, not exactly." Layla looks at the clock again. "I'm waiting for someone."

"Meaning?"

"The hockey team has a tradition. They always come here the day after a party...to talk about stuff. It's a great chance to hear the gossip."

"Why didn't you tell me?"

"Because you would have said no if you'd known." She stares at me, unbothered by my annoyed look.

"You should have asked Grace." I push my plate away.

"I can't ask her." My best friend squints, wrinkling her forehead. "She's in a whiny mood."

"Moore sent her packing, didn't he?" I grab my juice and take a sip. As soon as I saw him and Layla's roommate together, I knew she had zero chances. The dude is arrogant and narcissistic. He enjoys bragging about his daddy's money and how good in bed he is. When his eyes landed on me, I felt like a piece of meat, like an object. I hate guys like him.

"Well, yeah. He found another hookup, a girl from Drake's class." Layla dips her chin, leaning closer. "I'm glad Grace hasn't slept with him. He's an asshole, and she's too good for him."

"I can't argue with that," I add. "Thompson is an asshole too, but their energy is different. Moore is worse; I don't even know why I think that about a guy I haven't talked to at all."

"His dad has money and power, and he loves flashing it in people's faces any chance he gets." Layla licks her lips, looking uncomfortable. "And he has zero respect for girls. He thinks we are good only for sex, nothing more."

"He's even more disgusting than I thought."

"I tried talking to Grace about him, but she was stubborn, like a mule," Layla huffs. "Colton's family is pretty rich too, but you would never guess that."

I open my mouth, ready to answer her, but the door of the diner opens, and a group of guys walk inside. *The hockey team.* I let out a harsh breath, looking away. I should have left before they came. If I leave now, it will look like I'm running away because of the asshole.

"Layla." a voice booms, and I recognize it. It's Clay.

"Hey, Clay." she chimes, waving her hand. I have no idea what my best friend has in mind. "So glad to see you."

"You too." He comes closer and slides into the booth next to Layla. "Hey, best friend."

"Hey." I lock my eyes on his and see humor in them. "How was the party?"

"Pretty good." Clay smiles while all the other guys sit in the farthest corner. They move tables and chairs so they can all fit. No one says a word about their actions. "Woke up with my cock hidden in a very warm mouth."

"Ew." Layla yelps, hitting his forearm. "Talking about your hookups isn't allowed here. Go back to your friends if you want to brag."

"I'm just trying to convince Ava to change her mind."

"Telling me about the girls you fucked definitely won't change my mind." I shake my head and dig into my purse. I take my packet of M&Ms and put it on the table. It's my favorite flavor, with peanuts, but I also love the milk chocolate ones. Nothing beats a classic, in my eyes. I plop one candy into my mouth and meet Clay's amused gaze. "What?"

"Colt." he bellows, and my brows instantly pinch together. "Come over for a sec."

I hear footsteps and brace myself for another round of bickering. Not that I don't like it, but he gets under my skin too easily.

"What?" he asks while I concentrate on Clay. "Hey, Layla."

"Hey, Colt. How are you?"

"I'm fine." His answer is curt, even if he tries to sound nice. "What do you want, Rodgers? Aren't you going to sit with us?"

"Soon." Clay's face lights up with a lopsided grin. "We still need to wait for Benson and Moore. There's no harm in spending a few minutes in pleasant company."

"Questionable," I mutter under my breath, and Layla chortles.

"Aw, sweetie, you break my heart." Clay presses a hand to his chest. He's kind of adorable.

"Rodgers, why am I here?" the asshole demands, irritation rising in his voice.

"Here." Clay reaches over to my M&Ms, snatches the pack, and extends it to his friend. "Aren't these your favorite?"

I cast a glance to the side, watching as Thompson furrows his brow and takes my packet into his palm, staring at it as if it's a precious treasure. He looks like a kid, suddenly so happy and cheerful as he dumps almost all of the candies into his other palm. I open my mouth and close it again, like a damn fish out of water. The audacity.

"Hey. Those are mine." I shriek.

He meets my eyes, a stupid smirk on his lips. "Not anymore." With that, he turns around and goes back to his friends.

What the actual fuck?

"What was that?" Layla's voice is full of amusement as her gaze stays glued to Colton.

"Thompson loves M&Ms," Clay explains, looking between us. "A cabinet in his apartment is packed with them. He's more into the ones with milk chocolate, but he likes the peanut ones too. The classic."

Just like me. I chew on the inside of my bottom lip, uncertain what to make of this.

My best friend tsks. "Why didn't I know that?"

"Because you're not his friend," Clay says just as the door opens. I meet Drake's eyes instantly. He looks surprised for a second, but then he just breaks into a coy grin. Someone is definitely happy to see me. "Oh, your brother is here." Clay stands up, looking down at Layla and me. "See you later, ladies."

He strolls away, and Drake takes his place near our table. Hudson Moore walks past him, but then stops and joins Layla's brother. His eyes travel down from my face to my chest, and a smug smile tugs on his lips. Yet he keeps silent, not saying a word.

"Hey," Drake greets us, his hands hidden in his pockets. I nod and continue to observe him. "What are you two up to?"

"Hey hey," Layla singsongs, looking mischievous. "Just had dinner. You?"

"As if I'm going to believe that." He laughs heartily. "Wanted to hear the fresh gossip?"

"Maybe," she confirms sweetly, shifting her gaze to Moore. She sees him staring at me and frowns. "Um...hey, Hudson."

"Hey, Layla." His voice is low. "Can you introduce me to your friend? I didn't have a chance to meet her last night because your roommate kept me busy—"

"I'm Ava, and I'm not interested," I deadpan.

Fury flickers in his eyes, and he quickly covers it with a pretentious laugh. "You have no idea what you're missing."

I tap a finger on my bottom lip. "Still no."

His face contorts in anger. He reminds me of Draco Malfoy from the Harry Potter movies: platinum blond with blue eyes, but, unlike Tom Felton, he's not attractive at all.

"Moore, if she says no, she means no," Drake exclaims, his gaze heavy. "Go away."

"Whatever." He storms over to the guys from the team.

Thank you, I mouth to Drake, and he smiles at me warmly. "Did you sleep well?"

His eyes go wide, and a blush creeps onto his cheeks. Isn't he the cutest? "Yeah, as soon as you left my bed, I finally got to sleep comfortably."

"What do you mean she left your bed?" Layla is loud, causing everyone to look at us.

Drake and his choice of words. *Dammit.*

"I spent the night in his room. I saw my roommate leaving the house with some guy, and I had no desire to listen to her having sex. So, he let me use his bed, while he slept on his beanbag chair. Your brother is a gentleman." I lend him a hand, because he's obviously going to drown us.

"Oh..." she mumbles, looking between us while I flash her my biggest smile. There is no way in hell I'm going to tell her about my hookup with her brother. "I'm sure it wasn't comfortable." Her gaze softens. "But I'm grateful. You took care of my best friend when she needed it. It means the world to me."

"Don't mention it." He shrugs, licking his lips. Does he have a boner? The bulge in his groin becomes more visible. *Drake, you motherfucker.* "I gotta go. See you later."

"Bye," I say, feeling relief wash over me. He almost exposed us.

"Bye." Layla isn't looking at him anymore. Her eyes are focused on the hockey team. It looks like we're not going to be leaving anytime soon. "Drake?"

"What?" her brother shouts from the table he is already sitting at.

"Any chance you can give us a ride back to the dorms?"

"Sure."

I rap my fingers on my thigh and lean back into the booth. I have no clue what she's planning, but it looks like we are stuck here.

Chapter 8

Mr. Boner in His Jeans

COLTON

I POP ANOTHER CANDY INTO MY MOUTH, LISTENING TO THE guys blabber. I honestly thought about staying home and watching something, but it's a freaking tradition, one that I have no desire to break. After each party, we come here to talk, drink, and eat. Nothing fancy, and I kinda like it. Especially with M&Ms. I smile to myself and glance at the table where Layla and her best friend sit. Benson and Moore just walked in and stopped to have a few words with them.

Suddenly, Moore turns on his heel and stomps over with a wry face. I wonder what happened to make him so angry. He slumps into the chair across from me and mutters under his breath, "Fucking bitch."

"Who?" I tear my gaze away from the table and focus on him. He looks at me and forces a smile.

"That Ava chick. She's hot but a total bitch."

"Ava?" Clay asks, taken aback. Moore looks at him and nods. "Well, she sure has the guts to stand up for herself, but calling her a bitch? Come on."

"Don't ever remember seeing you so smitten." I nudge him in the ribs, but he laughs.

"I'm not smitten." Clay takes a swig of nonalcoholic beer. "I'm just stating the obvious."

"What do you mean she left your bed?" Layla's voice cuts through the atmosphere, and everyone looks at their table. I try to hear what the freshman is saying to her best friend but fail. I just see her smile.

"Do you think Benson fucked her?" Moore narrows his eyes, as if he's planning something.

"Hmm, the thought didn't even cross my mind," Clay mumbles. "You?"

"Me either." Hell no, I'm not letting slip what I know already. I will use it later for my own benefit.

"Maybe he did." Rodgers puts his bottle on the table, watching as Benson turns around and strolls in our direction. "He said she's off-limits for the team."

"I don't care what he says. That chick is a piece of work, but I need to add her to my book," Moore mutters, mostly to himself. His eyes stay trained on the freshman. "She will be on my list, I don't have any doubts."

"Do you want to make a bet?" Clay takes another sip of his beer. Moore peers at him, and a leery smile plays on his lips.

"Yeah, why not?" He extends his hand to my best friend. "By winter break, she will have spent the night in my bed."

"And I say that you won't even get to finger her, let alone fuck her." Rodgers takes his hand, and they turn to me. "Break it."

I blink, putting my M&Ms on the table. "What does the winner get? I want my share too."

"Dunno." Moore shrugs. "I don't care. Make it fun."

"How about..." Clay falls quiet, thinking. Suddenly, he breaks into laughter, shaking uncontrollably. "The last day before winter break, the loser goes to class in a dress and full makeup."

"Are you five?" Moore frowns. "I said make it fun."

"That's fun." I hold his gaze. "Are you backing out?"

He's silent for a second, but then he nods. "Whatever. I know I'll win."

"What about the winner?" I press again, glancing between them.

"The winner..." Moore drums his fingers on the table. "The winner will get five hundred dollars."

"I don't have that kind of cash lying around." Clay furrows his brow. "How about the winner gets a bottle of their choice? Whiskey? Tequila?"

Moore rolls his eyes in annoyance. "Fine. Break it, Thompson."

I break their hands apart, sensing a strange feeling forming in my head. I don't like it.

"Did you just make a bet?" Evans, our left defenseman, shouts, drawing attention to the three of us.

"Maybe." Moore grins, sneaking a glance at the girl's table.

"What is it?" Benson asks.

"Nothing special." Clay shifts in his seat. I have known him for years. He's uncomfortable, and he probably already regrets suggesting the bet. It's a common problem with him. He does things and only *then* thinks about the consequences. "Did you fuck your sister's best friend?"

Clay, you stupid idiot. Subtlety is definitely not his strongest suit.

Benson takes a bite of pizza, chewing on it and saying nothing. Yet his eyes are emitting fire. He's royally pissed, and it doesn't go unnoticed. Everyone is silent, waiting for him to say something.

"Why are you jumping to that conclusion?" His jaw tenses.

"Dunno." Clay lets out a short laugh. "You said she's off-limits, and maybe it's because you want her to yourself."

Benson shakes his head with a smile. "Ava is my sister's best friend, but the truth is she's my friend too. I care about her a lot, and don't want her to get hurt. That's all."

"Yeah, I understand. Sorry about that." Clay becomes serious in an instant as his gaze shifts to Moore. If he succeeds and she knows there was a bet, she will be hurt. No doubt about it. "Just a pity that you—"

"She spent the night in my room after someone kicked her out of the party." Benson stares at me for a moment. "We talked, and she made me realize that I don't have any right to forbid her from doing what she wants. She's not my sister, after all."

"Wait." Clay looks excited. "Does that mean...?"

"Yes." Benson laughs wholeheartedly. "Ava is not off-limits. Just keep in mind that if any of you morons hurt her, you should be ready to get your ass kicked."

Now I feel stupid. If I'm right, and they slept together, how could he be okay with her dating someone from the team? Or even just fucking someone from the team? If she were mine, I would never share her.

"Sorry, guys." Clay stands up and goes to the table where Layla and the girl sit. My eyebrows go up because I have no idea what he is doing. It's unusual, and I don't even know what to say.

"What the hell is he up to?" Moore hisses. "Does he want to win the bet by sweeping the girl off her feet so I won't even have a chance?"

"Fuck if I know," I scoff, snatching my M&Ms from the table and tossing the rest of the candies into my palm.

We stay at the diner for about two hours. I chat with the guys, glancing at Clay from time to time. He's still with Layla and her best friend. The freshman's laugh is melodic. A few times, I catch Benson looking at them too, and I don't know how to explain what I see. But I don't know how to explain my own feelings, so that is no surprise.

I go outside to smoke, the only bad habit I still have. I've had a pack stored in my glove compartment for three months, if not longer. But I don't have even a moment alone, as Benson joins me too. His gaze is severe, not a hint of a smile on his face. I light up my cigarette, looking back at him. If he wants to talk to me, he should be the one to start the conversation.

"What you did yesterday was wrong," he finally says, leaning his back against the wall. "I found Ava totally lost. She had no idea where she was going. She's still learning her way around campus, Thompson."

"I know. I'm sorry." I blow smoke and see him wrinkle his nose.

"You should apologize to her, not me."

I frown. "Not gonna happen."

He runs his palms over his face, threading his fingers through his hair when he reaches it. "What is this all about? She said she ruined your night with her roommate, and you got in an argument. Is that any reason to treat her like she's nothing?"

"She just..." I stop speaking, taking a drag of my cigarette. Does he know about the slap?

"She's just what? As far as I know, Clay was there with you, and he doesn't have any problems with Ava. Only you."

Only me. She doesn't affect Clay the way she affects me.

I lower my gaze to my feet and think. Benson knows how to keep secrets, and he won't make fun of anyone on purpose.

"She slapped me across my face for what I said to her." I look back at Benson and see cheerfulness in his eyes.

He chuckles, shaking his head. "Why am I not surprised?" He pushes off the wall and takes a step closer to me. "Listen, Ava has a temper. She's a freaking tornado, as her father often jokes. And let me tell you, he's not wrong. She slapped you because you offended her, not because she has a problem with you. So don't take it personally, Colton. And please, leave her alone. People love to gossip, and what happened yesterday didn't go unnoticed."

"I just kicked her out," I argue, but he shakes his head.

"It's amusing that you still have no idea how much power you have around here." Benson puts a hand on my shoulder. "People will see her as your enemy. A target of derision and talk. I don't know what Monday will bring for her, but I'm sure it won't be nice. No one wants to be on your bad side, especially girls."

When he puts it that way, he might be right. I swallow the lump in my throat and put out my cigarette. "Okay," I tell him, throwing the butt into the trash can. "She knows I'm sorry. I bumped into her on her way out of your room this morning."

Benson blinks at me, speechless. Then he takes a step back and hides his hands in his pockets. "She didn't want to go back to her dorm when I found her. Besides, my place was closer. It's not like that was the first time we slept in the same room."

I smirk knowingly. "Yeah, you've known each other for years. She's family."

"Exactly." He scratches the back of his neck, looking around. "I probably need to get going. I promised to give Layla and Ava a ride home. So..."

"Sure. And don't worry: I will do my best to behave around her," I reassure him.

"Please do," Drake laughs. Then he walks back to the diner, leaving me alone.

I don't understand anything. I start doubting my own gut. Both Benson and his sister's best friend give me a headache with their actions.

One second, I think they have something going on between them, but the next—they prove the opposite. It doesn't make any sense.

The door opens, and she's the first one to walk out of the diner. My eyes travel up and down her length, and again I'm mesmerized by her. She's wearing tiny denim shorts and a red tee. My stomach twists and turns, and my skin warms up. Our eyes lock on each other's, and I don't want to look away, but this moment can't last forever.

Layla pushes her best friend out of the way. Her eyes land on me, and her face lights up. I give her an awkward grin, stepping out of their way. Yet she strolls right up to me.

"Your best friend asked my best friend on a date."

My brows furrow, and my jaw drops. I don't know what surprises me the most: Clay's invitation, or his fixation on this girl. *Oh, look who's talking, Mr. Boner in His Jeans.* "Cool."

"What if we make it a double date if she agrees? Would you go with me?" Layla puts her hands on her hips with a seductive smile. Is she serious? How on Earth does Clay's date have anything to do with me?

"Sorry, but no." I straighten my back.

"Why not?"

"Because you're not my type," I state, and she scowls. I meet Benson's gaze as he nods, stepping closer and wrapping his arm around Layla's shoulder.

"Come on." He pushes her to start moving. I notice her angry stare, but I don't care. Better to be honest now than sorry later. "Bye, Thompson."

I stay rooted in place, watching them walk to Benson's car. Layla throws her hands in the air every so often. She's pissed, and it annoys her brother. I shift my gaze in the best friend's direction and see her climb into the car in silence. Will she agree to a date with Clay? Does she like him?

I huff, turning around and walking back into the diner. I just want to be home, alone in my apartment. I feel my hard-on in my pants, and it irritates me. What was the point of hooking up with Amy if I'm hornier than I was? *Maybe because you chose the wrong girl, idiot?*

I hate my life and that girl. She's the reason I feel like a fool.

Chapter 9

Breathe In, Breathe Out

AVA

I sit on the floor with my back pressed against the wall. My eyes are closed as I listen to music. The sound of a guitar reverberates through my body, bringing every nerve to life. "I Think I'm OKAY" plays at full volume, but I don't pay any attention to it. I try to silence all the people who surround me in this stupid place. I squeeze my eyes tighter because I don't want to cry anymore. I'm tired of these nonstop tears. I just want my life back. The one where I was a happy freshman, excited about her first year in college, and not this mess it has become.

The first week after the party was strange. People whispered behind my back and pointed in my direction. When I walked into a room, everyone would fall silent. It was like my presence shut down every conversation. A few of my classmates stopped talking to me, and one even refused to be my study partner in one of my classes. I took it all in stride. The silent treatment and the gossip didn't bother me at the time. I was hoping that everyone would soon forget and move on, but I was wrong. The second week was harder than the first one.

No one wants to be friends with me—heck, no one wants to talk to me if it's something they can avoid. I feel as if I don't exist, and it hurts. I've literally been forcing myself to go to my classes. All I want is to stay locked in my room, alone with my books. But that's not an option either. I hate Jordan. She's the worst roommate and human being ever. She makes everything even more difficult, and I have a hard time dealing with it.

It would have been better if Layla was with me, but she barely has time for me these days. She got the flu and went home for a week, and she spent this week catching up on all her assignments and deadlines. Her brother wanted to hang out with me on Monday, but he got a last-minute call and asked to reschedule. I saw him on Wednesday, and my stubborn ass decided to pretend like everything was okay and I was living my best life.

A fool, that's who I was.

Why have I suddenly become invisible? It's all because of Colton Thompson. People think he hates me, and they want to show him where their loyalty lies. In reality? They're just a bunch of stupid idiots. I don't exist for this dude. I haven't seen him even once since the diner. But everyone is ignoring my presence because they believe he wants that. Because I crossed paths with the wrong guy, and no one wants to be in the same boat as I am.

This loneliness is the worst, especially when I was used to being someone people wanted to be friends with. I'm not handling this situation very well.

Someone pats me on my shoulder, and I jerk away on instinct. I open my eyes and meet Hudson Moore's gaze. Another motherfucker I can't stand. What does he want from me? My music stops when I take one of my AirPods out of my ear.

"Hey, Ava."

"Hey."

"I noticed you on my way from class." He smiles, lowering himself beside me. "How are you?"

"I'm fine." I don't want to look at him, so I just stare in front of me.

"You look sad," Moore adds, forcing me to glance at him. I don't talk to anyone about my problems; I keep everything to myself.

"I just don't feel well." I use the answer I give everyone. "Girl stuff."

"You don't have any friends here. People treat you as if you don't exist. Aren't you upset about it?" I want to vomit. Does everyone know already? "I'm just very observant, that's all. Plus, you're kinda on my radar—"

"I don't care," I snap, standing up. Anger rises in my chest; I'm ready to kick someone.

"People think Thompson hates you." Moore joins me in standing, then bends down and takes my backpack into his hands. "No one wants to be friends with his enemy."

"My backpack. Please."

"I can be your friend, or more than a friend." He inches closer.

"Thanks. No, thanks." I grab my backpack from his grip and take a step back. "Bye." I stomp away from him. I have another class in fifteen minutes, so I need to get going.

"Ava, wait." He runs after me. This guy doesn't know how to take a hint, does he? "Will you come to the game next week?"

"Ha." It's so sudden that I even clamp my hand over my mouth. He looks confused with his brows pinched together. "No."

"To the party after the game?"

"No."

"Any chance I can change your mind?" He invades my personal space again, but I back away quickly.

"No." I twirl around and march to class, and this time he doesn't follow me. But he also doesn't fool me—he's not going to give up any time soon.

After my class is over, I walk to the dining hall, lost in my thoughts. Lunch is the only time I can see my best friend. It's rare, so I cherish it, even if I know that I am keeping secrets from her. More and more these days.

Suddenly, someone trips in front of me. Something cold hits my skin, and I yelp. The fuck? I look down, and it's like I'm a character from *Glee*. A fucking slushy.

I examine my tee and then meet Jordan's gaze. She stands in front of me, trying to suppress a smile on her stupid face.

"Are you fucking insane?"

"Oh, I'm so sorry. I'm so clumsy." She barely hides her grin. "If you want to, we can go to our room, so you can change and go back to class. Or you can stay in the dorm. No one will notice your absence anyway."

My chest is suddenly so heavy. I'm starting to suffocate. I open my mouth but don't say anything. Tears burn my eyes. This situation is becoming harder and harder to deal with. It's the first time in my life when people are treating me like I'm nothing, and it's all because some arrogant prick doesn't get along with me.

"Fuck you." I storm past her, heading to the bathroom. Everyone is watching me. Everyone. I see their smirks. I hear their laughs, and I want to disappear. I want to be as far away from this place as possible. I want to be back at home, in my room, knowing I can find comfort in my father's arms. I just want to feel safe again.

I barrel through the crowd and halt in my tracks just a few steps away from the bathroom. He's standing there with his hands hidden in his pockets. His gaze is heavy, and it's focused on me. I feel the urge to slap him in the face, kick him in his groin, or just show him my middle finger again. This desire to take out my anger is strong, but I ignore it. It's the first time we have seen each other in two weeks, and I can honestly admit I would have loved not to see him for even longer.

I resume my walk, yank the doorknob, and open the door wide. It closes behind me with a bang while I edge to the mirror. As soon as my eyes land on my reflection, I want to bawl. My tee is ruined. I suck in air and pull my T-shirt over my head, leaving me in only my bra. I just want to try and save one of my favorite shirts. Maybe it will be possible to fix it before the stain sets?

I turn on the faucet and shove my tee under the flowing water. I wipe it over and over again, rubbing the fabric with only one thought in mind—I want to go home tomorrow. I want to see my dad and be his little girl, nothing else.

The door opens, and I brace myself for jokes. The moment I lock eyes with the person who walked into the bathroom, my fingers start shaking and my mouth becomes dry. What the hell does he want from me? Did he come to rub salt into the wound?

Looking away, I wash slushy off my tee and keep silent. I literally bite my tongue to hold back the words that desperately want to find their way out. I don't want to make my days at college even worse than they already are. Colton is fully capable of making that happen. Experience has shown he doesn't even need to say anything to anyone. His reputation plays directly into his hands.

I feel his gaze all over me. His eyes travel down my form. I was in a hurry to take off my T-shirt, I didn't think about the undergarment I'm wearing. It's a beige pink push-up bra, and it looks good on me, but I'm suddenly very self-conscious. I don't want him to see my lingerie. I already feel vulnerable, and being half-naked doesn't help.

"What happened?" His voice is quieter than I expect. He stops just behind my back, and goosebumps spread across my skin.

"Nothing."

"Why did she throw her drink on you? It didn't look like an accident." He sounds strange. Almost like he cares.

I shake my head vigorously, trying to get rid of the stupid idea. The guy has such a big ego that he still can't forget about the slap. The one that only a few people know about. People who won't say anything to anyone. Or is it about me flipping him off? If so, then he's even more arrogant than I thought.

"Why did she do that?" Thompson takes a step closer, putting both of his hands on the sink and trapping me. My insides flare up, and a blush creeps onto my cheeks. What the hell is he doing?

"She's just a bitch," I mutter, trying to focus on the task at hand. It's hard. His proximity and his scent have started to affect me. He smells nice, very nice, and I want to close my eyes and inhale. I bite my inner cheek to bring myself back to my senses. He's a stupid fucker. I can't be attracted to him. "She knows I have no friends here."

"Meaning?"

"No one wants to talk to me. Or even notice me. People act like I don't exist." I shut my eyes because my voice is trembling. Then I take a deep breath and look at him through the mirror. "That's my life now."

"Why?"

"Because they think you hate me, and no one wants to be on your bad side."

"My bad side?" He blinks, stepping back, and I suddenly feel lonely. I want him back close to me.

"You're a popular guy, and people respect you. A lot of girls want to date you, or just sleep with you," I explain, wondering why I even need to tell him this. He doesn't look like an idiot who doesn't know the power he has over people in this place. Or am I reading him wrong? "After you kicked me out, they all think I offended you or something. They ignore my presence."

"Wait..." he mumbles, frowning. "They are doing this to you because of me?"

I turn off the faucet and examine my T-shirt. Nothing can save it. Its place is in the trash. "Are you seriously that dense?" I ask, turning around and pulling my wet tee back on. Instead of having lunch with Layla, I will have to go back to the dorm and change. "Yes, Thompson, they are doing this to me because of you."

"That's bullshit. I never asked—"

"You sure are an idiot," I snap, anger consuming me. The walls of the room close in on me; my breath becomes ragged. "People at the party saw what you did. They think I wronged you. And for them, that's enough of a reason to have nothing to do with me. You don't even need to ask them."

"Why didn't Benson tell me? I could have fixed it a long time ago."

"Because I haven't told him," I counter, grabbing my backpack from the floor.

The door opens, and a girl rushes inside, stopping in her tracks as soon as her eyes land on Colton and me. Her jaw drops as she gapes at us in silence.

"Get out," he orders her. Then he returns his attention to me. She doesn't exist to him anymore.

I watch the girl in amusement. I would have sent him packing. Yet she nods, and a second later, she's gone.

"It's a women's bathroom," I hiss, but he doesn't hear me. He takes a step closer, hovering over me.

"You haven't told Layla about this? Because I'm sure if she knew, her brother would have known too."

"They don't know," I repeat, stomping my foot and feeling small. He reminds me of Drake a lot. A fucking wall in front of me.

"If I'm an idiot, then you're an arrogant piece of shit." Thompson bends his head down, looking me in the eyes. "Were you too humiliated to tell your best friend how people are treating you? Was it too embarrassing to ask for help?"

I gawk at him in perplexity. Pursing my lips, I ball my fists and dig my nails into my flesh.

"Fuck you." I shout. Then I turn around and stalk into the nearest stall. Slamming the door behind me and pressing my back to it, I close my eyes. Calming myself down is a priority, because if not calm, I'm afraid to even imagine what I might do to him. Or to anyone who tries to talk to me.

I hear his steps and then the door closing. I'm finally alone, but it doesn't bring me any solace. This guy...he's a fucking nightmare. One second, he acts like he cares; the next second, he's insulting me. But I am no saint either. I call him names, even if I know how short-tempered he is.

I take my phone out of my pocket and look down at the screen. I have twenty minutes before my last class starts, so I better get going. I quickly swipe away a message from Layla. Right now, my studies are way more important.

Breathe in, breathe out, Ava. You've got this.

Opening the door, I saunter out of the stall and halt in my tracks. His bomber jacket is lying on the countertop. Did he leave it for me? I hesitate, not sure if I should go for it. Then I brush my doubts aside and put his bomber on. It helps me with my situation, which is the only thing I want. I fix my backpack and head straight to the exit.

People are here and there, hanging out. They still look at me, but at least I don't hear any laughs anymore. Only whispers, murmurs, and curious glances. Did he say something once he walked out of the bathroom? That's a possibility. Me wearing his bomber is a big statement, but will it be enough to change things for me? I truly hope it will.

With each step, as I hold my head up high, my mood becomes lighter. I'm not a fragile little girl. I'm strong and confident. What goes around comes around, and it means Jordan will have her appointment with karma. Sooner or later, but she will. That's how life works.

Chapter 10

Make Things Right

COLTON

I TAKE A SIP OF MY COFFEE AS I STARE OFF INTO THE distance. For some stupid reason, I'm never on time. I'm either early or late. No in-between. Sometimes it irritates me, but now I'm grateful to have a moment to myself. I need to think about my next steps.

When Benson warned me about the consequences of kicking the freshman out of the party, I honestly thought he was crazy. I had a problem with the girl, no one else. I refused to think that someone in their right mind would want to do something to her because of my hatred toward her. And yet, they did.

The scene from Friday still plays in my mind. Slushy, her eyes locked on mine, emitting fire, her vulnerability when she confessed that she doesn't have any friends, and then again, her fury. This girl is something else, I swear. I have never met anyone like her. So stunning and so infuriating at the same time. I wanted to twirl her around and kiss her just as much as I wanted to spank her for her behavior. She's unbelievable.

My phone dings with an incoming message, and I take it out of my pocket. Clay wants to know when I'm going to be back. *Seven p.m.* I answer him and tuck my phone away. I will be home before that; I just want to figure out what to do first. Obviously I need to stop this. The first year in college is nerve-racking enough. To have to deal with loneliness and people pretending they don't notice you in addition?

No one deserves to feel like they don't exist. Especially her.

"Colton?" I turn my head toward the sound of my name and see Dr. Stewart. He smiles at me, and I stroll over to him, throwing my paper cup into the trash can on the way. "It's nice to see you."

"Hey, Doc." I shake his hand and take a step back. "How are you?"

"Everything is fine, don't worry." He nods, and we start walking. "How have you been? Don't regret coming back?"

"No. I made a mistake, skipping a visit for no reason. I'm not going to do that ever again."

"How is your dad? The last time I saw him was..." Dr. Stewart looks thoughtful. "Four months ago?"

"My father is okay. I don't talk with him much." More like never. I can't forgive him, not that I try. I'm tolerating him—that's the best way to describe what I feel for my own dad. Even if he would love for me to change my mind. I'm his only son, and he still has his hopes up about me taking his place in a few years.

"Colt, we have talked about this." Dr. Stewart's voice becomes softer, and I barely hold myself back from rolling my eyes. "You need at least one parent in your life, and without your mom in the picture..."

"He's the only relative I have. I remember." I finish his sentence for him. Every time he has an opportunity, he likes to bring this up. And it always ends with me promising to think about it. Which I never do.

"Okay, I give up," he says. I shoot him a glance, and this time he laughs. "For today."

"Didn't expect anything less from you," I say, watching as he opens the door for us.

"If I remember correctly, you have the first game of the season next week."

"Yeah, on Saturday," I confirm, suddenly realizing that this man knows more about me than my father. Not that it surprises me, but still, how fucked up is my life? "That's why I wanted to be here today. There is no chance I can visit next week."

"Let me guess. Another party after the game?"

I chortle loudly, shaking my head when I notice people glancing at us. "Yup, to celebrate our win, or drown our loss in alcohol."

"I have no idea how you can drink and still play hockey the way you do."

"I don't drink much anymore." My neck becomes hot. "If I go pro, I won't be drinking anything at all."

"At all?" Dr. Stewart smirks, and I nod with a serious expression on my face. "If you're telling me the truth, then I'm immensely proud of you. Honestly."

"Thank you." I drop my gaze, feeling nostalgic. This man is like family already. The family I was robbed of because my father couldn't keep his dick in his pants.

We stop near her room, and I literally hold my breath. What mood will she be in today? Will she remember anything we talked about last time? I put my hand on the doorknob and push. My heartbeat speeds up as soon as my eyes land on her sitting on her bed. I sneak a glance at Dr. Stewart and see him smiling warmly at me.

"You have three hours." He puts his hand on my shoulder. "It was nice seeing you, Colt."

"You too, Doc." He takes a step back and walks away from me. It's time for me to see her. The reason I have been coming here for six months already.

Taking a deep breath, I step into the room and close the door behind me. I slowly stroll to the bed, then I stop and look down at her. She's dressed in a simple floral dress, and her chestnut brown hair is collected into a neat bun. When she finally notices me, she focuses her gaze and smiles, setting the book she was reading aside.

"Hey, Mom."

"Colton." she exclaims as I lower myself onto her bed and hug her tightly. "I'm so happy to see you."

"Me too, Mom," I mumble, leaning away. "How are you?"

"Better now that you're here." She puts a palm on my cheek. "Each time I see you, you look manlier. Bigger. Taller. This stubble on your face. My God, baby, why are you growing up so fast?"

"That's what college and hockey do to you, Mom," I say, and she looks up at the ceiling. If anything, her mood today is the one I love the most. She is exactly herself, without a trace of depression.

Mom shakes her head as I avert my gaze. She was making huge improvements until three months ago, when things declined in just a week. Dr. Stewart is extremely careful with everything he says. I only hope the progress they are making on retraining her brain to help her memory will last. These baby steps are incredibly important for her recovery, so she can start remembering conversations and new people she meets. Hopefully it will keep her from feeling confused and disoriented.

"Colt?" I peer at her, sighing deeply and banishing my gloomy thoughts. "How are you? Tell me about your days."

I smile, taking her palm in mine. She won't remember everything I tell her, only some things if I'm lucky enough. "What do you want to know?"

"I've been in a mood lately," she laughs heartily. "I watched one of my favorite movies, *Serendipity*, with Kate Beckinsale and John Cusack. So I'm all for romance. Do you have a girlfriend?"

I blink long and hard, totally dumbfounded. It's not the question I expected, but okay, I can do that. "Sorry to disappoint, Mom. Hockey is the only crush I have." Not that I'm lying. I have never loved anyone. I didn't get the chance, I guess. Especially looking at my parents' marriage, it was hard to believe in love. Or want a relationship.

"Baby..." Mom looks disappointed. "I can understand you focusing on hockey. It's your life, your passion, and I admire you for that. But you're a young man, and it's impossible for me to imagine you totally alone. Girls have always loved you. Always. You're such a beautiful boy, and I don't believe even for a second there is no one on your mind."

I hate myself for my thoughts. The freshman's image pops into my head instantly and involuntarily. As if she lives there. I close my eyes, and her scent starts wafting around me. I'm momentarily back in the bathroom, bracing myself on the sink and framing her in my embrace. She has a perfect body, but her tits... Damn, her full boobs looked so good in her beige and pink bra that I was literally forcing myself not to stare. Even the glimpse I had was enough to make my dick rock solid. I want her so badly, like I've never wanted anyone in my life.

"Colton?" Mom's voice is quiet, but it's like a slap. It brings me back to my senses. I hate the way I react to that girl. It's new to me, but it's still bothersome. I don't want to feel like that. I need to get it out of my system for good.

I have no idea how, but I need to forget her.

"Sorry, Mom, but I don't have time for anything except hockey. If I want to prove I'm worthy of a place on the California Thunders, that's it." I smile and see her face relax. She pats my knee, looking apologetic.

"I'm sad to hear that, but I understand," Mom murmurs, leaning closer. "Promise me something."

"Whatever you want," I quickly answer, eager to hear her out. It's rare for her to be so smiley and cheerful. I love seeing her like this, because she reminds me of her old self, before shit went downhill. It's precious.

"If you meet a girl you like, one who causes your heartbeat to speed up, who is constantly on your mind, day and night; one who stirs such strong emotions within you that it is hard to control yourself. If you meet a girl like that, promise me you will bring her here and introduce her to me." My face drains of color. I'm speechless. "Please, Colt, it will mean the world to me. Promise me."

I swallow the lump in my throat, blinking a few times to get rid of the state I am in. "O-okay. I promise." No one knows my mom is here. I don't let people get that close to me. Not even my best friend. How am I supposed to bring anyone to meet her? Especially a girl? I cross my fingers behind my back before I open my mouth and say, "I will."

"Thank you so much, sweetheart." She inches closer and plants a kiss on my cheek. I smile, my mind in total disarray. This visit is not how I envisioned it at all. And I'm not sure I like this sudden change. "Hmm, how about you tell me more about your days? How is hockey? Clay?"

I run my fingers through my hair, becoming pensive for a moment. I always need to be extra careful when I tell her about my days. It's best to start with things that happen on a daily basis. A few times, when I reminded her about my previous visits, she almost had another breakdown. Her inability to remember certain things brings her down way more than anything else. It's like a game of Jenga. One wrong move, and everything collapses.

I PARK my car near my apartment building, blinking in surprise when I see Clay, Layla, and her roommate, Grace. When he called me thirty minutes ago, he sure didn't mention Benson's sister. Why the hell are they here?

I climb out of my Lexus RX, crinkling my brows as I meet my best friend's gaze. He shrugs, as if telling me it's not his fault. I lock the car, and stroll in their direction. When I stop in front of them, I see Layla's lips break into a smile. She's literally beaming, while Grace looks moody. She doesn't want to be here—and we're on the same page since I want them gone too. Even Clay if he can't get rid of the unwanted visitors.

"Hey," I say, hiding my hands in my pockets.

"Hey, Thompson," Grace mumbles under her breath.

"Hey, man." Clay nods.

"Hey, Colt," Layla greets me with a smile. "Where have you been?"

"Home," I answer, and whip my head to Clay, looking at him expectantly.

"I was on my way to your place when I ran into them. They were bored and asked if they could join us."

And you said yes?

"I was incredibly busy all week. Catching up on all my assignments took up a huge amount of my time," Layla chirps. "So, I just hoped to have an opportunity to relax. Nothing else."

"I thought Ava would be with you," Clay comments.

Layla becomes sad; her smile fades away. "I've barely had time for Ava the past two weeks. I hoped to spend this weekend with her, but she left yesterday morning." She glances at Clay. "She didn't even tell me she was going home. I found out when I called her."

So, she's lonely. Her best friend is busy with her classes. Maybe now I can understand why she hid everything from her. It's not a conversation she wants to have with her friend when they barely see each other. She probably wants to use those rare occasions to catch up and talk about nice things, not about idiots torturing her.

I need to make things right. She doesn't deserve to be treated this way. Even if we don't get along.

"Colt?" I look down and see Layla waving her palm in my face.

"Sorry. It's been a long day," I mutter, turning my head and peering at a pizza place. I don't want to invite them into my apartment, but I don't want to be rude. "How about pizza?"

"Sounds great." Clay finally smiles. "Let's go."

I clear my head and decide to focus on right now, on walking toward the pizzeria. I can't get rid of Layla and Grace without offending them. I can't fix the situation for the girl and make people notice her. Not right now anyway. Yet a plan is forming in my head, and I can actually use Layla's help. The freshman needs to be at the party next week.

Chapter 11

Too Wild to Handle

AVA

"You don't like hockey?" Grace asks, glancing at me.

"It's not like that," I retort, tossing nachos into my mouth. I take my time finishing them while she keeps staring at me. I expect her to turn her attention back to the game, but she doesn't. *Fuck me.*

"Not like what, Ava?" She laughs, and I involuntarily smile.

Life is so strange. The first time Layla introduced me to this girl, I was more than hostile. I didn't like her, and the feeling was mutual. Little by little, things have started to change. We watch the game together and talk about personal stuff. I mean, discussing your favorite sports can be considered personal stuff, right? Jeez, I'm so out of my element these days that I want to die. Quickly and suddenly.

Rest in peace, Ava Mason. You left this world too young, taking with you your mind-blowing beauty and sexy-as-hell body.

Well, I definitely won't die from being shy.

"I like watching hockey, especially when I can cheer for someone I know," I muse. My gaze follows Drake on the ice. He's an amazing player, really skillful and very attentive to everything around him. I can honestly say the same about the whole team. Even the asshole.

"You spent most of the game reading a book on your phone." Layla nudges me with her elbow, and I grimace.

"It's kinda boring." *God. Ava. You know better. You're a perfect liar, but this? This sounds like a freaking fat burrito full of bullshit.*

Grace and Layla exchange a look and then burst out laughing. Loud and contagious. People start glancing at us, and I'm ready to disappear. This is exactly why I didn't want to be here.

Since I returned to campus on Monday, I have been keeping a low profile. Spending my time in my cocoon, counting the days till I can go back home. How on Earth I let my best friend convince me to stay? I have no clue. It's like she jinxed me or something. There is no other rational explanation for sure.

In all honesty, the game is intense, and as far from boring as possible. The Great Lake Panthers are incredible, and I'm not exaggerating. The players have such an eager desire to win that it's contagious. The whole place is filled with cheers, hoots, and excited chatter. I'm drawn to the rink. I follow all the guys with my eyes and curse inwardly if they lose the puck. It's a home game, the first in the season, and they are ready to rip their rival a new one, literally. A few times, things got a bit violent, but our guys weren't on the receiving end, so I didn't worry much.

I do love hockey...but I hate the ice and all the memories it brings.

Suddenly, Layla drapes a hand over my shoulder and pulls me close. "I'm glad you're here. I know it's hard for you, so I appreciate you agreeing to come." I turn my head, and we lock eyes. "Watching Drake play without you was weird."

"Watching your brother on the ice is highly entertaining. Always," I say with a smile, relaxing into her embrace. "I have no idea where he hides this side of him in real life. A teddy bear turned into a grizzly."

"That's one of the reasons why I was crushing on him," Grace mutters, and I turn my head to look at her. "I bet he's hot in bed."

Layla groans and pushes me away. "Please, not another your-brother-is-great-in-bed talk. I'm still recovering from images Ava planted in my head three weeks ago."

"You're pathetic. You've heard Drake and his friends talk about their girls so many times, so you shouldn't care about it," I tell her, and she narrows her eyes, smacking her lips into a tight line. I poke my tongue out at her and whip my head to look at the ice for a brief moment.

"I wonder..." Grace trails off, and I sneak a glance at her, making her falter. "Um, what it's like growing up surrounded by hockey players."

"Being a hockey player doesn't make them any different. They're just like you and me, like our classmates, like people watching the game," I say, knitting my brows together.

"It's just... I don't know how to act around the guys from the team, you know? You and Layla are used to her brother and his friends, but I have a feeling I don't fit in. They've known me for a year, but not even a single guy from the team has tried to hit on me," Grace mutters under her breath as I lean closer. "I'm hanging out with them because of your best friend, and it's also the reason why I'm as single as a Pringle."

"But Layla is hooking up with Trey, and he's not from the team," I point out, and I instantly realize I made it worse. Like I said it's not just guys from the team who are indifferent to her, but others too. "Oh God. That came out wrong—"

"Nah, I get it." She blushes and looks away. "I'm awkward as hell when it comes to guys. Like, really awkward. I say stupid things, I laugh too loud, and I always pick the wrong guy."

"Moore was definitely an asshole," Layla adds without even looking at us. I slap her knee, and she tsks loudly. I'm trying to get to know her roommate, just like she asked me to, and her remarks aren't helping.

I turn and let my eyes roam over Grace's face. She's got a sprinkle of freckles covering her nose, big hazel eyes with flecks of blue, and a heart-shaped mouth. She's very cute, and I'm surprised to hear she doesn't know how to use that in her favor.

"But you're beautiful." I say, making her cheeks blush harder. "You can have any guy you want."

"You sure you aren't talking about yourself?"

"I'm not interested in dating hockey players—or dating anyone, for that matter."

"I'm not interested in hockey players anymore either," Grace scoffs, moving away from me. "I like my classmate, but it's absolutely hopeless."

"Look." I put my palm on her knee. "Hockey players or not, things are pretty simple. There are dudes like Clay, who will fuck anyone with a pretty face. The ones like Moore, who finds himself some girl to prey on and won't stop until she's in his bed. Then there are guys like Drake, who has a heart of gold but always looks at how hot girls are, not noticing that they are full of crap and want him only because he's a gorgeous hockey player."

"Interesting perspective." Grace scratches the bridge of her nose. "What do you think about Colton?"

I think back to every interaction I've had with the asshole, from the day we met to him leaving me his bomber. I still keep it among my things, tucked away from prying eyes as if it's a treasure. As if I suddenly lost my mind, because I don't have any explanation for my behavior.

I open my mouth as my eyes land on him. "He's closed off, has a small circle of people he lets close to him. He's arrogant, short-tempered, unnecessarily rude, and his ego...God. It's taller than the Empire State Building. I have never met anyone more confusing than him, because one second I think he hates me, but the next it's like all he wants—" I snap my mouth shut, biting my tongue so hard I have to close my eyes from the sudden pain.

Grace is silent, watching me with curiosity. "He wants what?"

To fuck me like there's no tomorrow. I swallow the words and master a smile. "He wants to be friends with me."

"Oh my God." She laughs so loud her whole body shakes uncontrollably, and now I think she might be right. She is too loud. "You're a fucking gem, Ava. It's refreshing to spend time with you."

"You might regret your words later. I'm too wild to handle." I lean in close, peer at Grace, and grin.

"Can you teach me to be wild?" Grace cocks an eyebrow at me.

I didn't want to go anywhere after the game, even if Layla was on my back like some spoiled brat, but now? Now this idea entertains me, even if deep down I don't understand why she wants to change herself. "How about we start at tonight's party?"

"I'm all in. You have no idea how much I want to hang out with you."

"I heard that," Layla whisper-yells, gawking at Grace and me with her brows pinched together.

I curl a hand over my best friend's shoulder and inch toward her ear.

"You wanted me to be friendly with your roommate. This is me being friendly. Chill."

"Fine," she grumbles quietly, and I kiss her on the cheek. "You two should watch the game. It's already close to the end."

"Whatever you want, babe." I move away and return my focus to the ice rink. Our team is up five against one over Boston U, and it's the last four minutes of the third period. Clay is our goalie and he rocks this game, playing impossibly well. He's funny and nice to be around. At the same time, he's not my type. I would love to have a friend like him—a friend. Not a friend with benefits. For that matter, I already have Drake.

I close my eyes and groan quietly. This party is going to be a disaster, right? If the thought of another night with my best friend's brother crosses my mind, then I'm doomed. I don't know what's wrong with me today, but I know this mood too well. If I don't end the day in tears, I will be extremely surprised.

Chapter 12

Stay With Me

COLTON

"You were a fucking thunderstorm." Someone slaps my back, causing me to choke on my beer.

"For real. For a second I thought I saw fire under your skates," another voice adds, followed by another slap on my back. Since when do they think they can be so friendly with me? "Thompson, you're MVP of our team."

"Were you at the game?" Clay snarls, looking over his shoulder. "If it wasn't for me, these fuckers would have lost."

"Rodgers, you're the best goalie our team has. Do you really doubt that?"

I sneak a glance at the guy behind me. He's uncomfortable, and it makes me smile. It's his fault. Why would you praise one player in front of another one if you don't want to be called out on your bullshit? Definitely one of the reasons why I don't engage with anyone outside my closest circle. People are awkward as fuck and full of shit, and I don't need such farce in my life.

"Me? Nah. I know I'm the best, but some of you need a reminder. From time to time," my best friend adds. Then he turns away from the guys and gulps his drink, gripping the bottle so tightly his knuckles turn white. "Jerks."

"Why are you so jumpy? You know your worth. Why let some idiots bother you?"

"Not everyone is like you," he mutters, setting the now empty bottle aside.

"Sometimes it's better to be someone like me, who doesn't give a fuck about other people and their opinions," I tell him, taking a sip of my own beer. I take it slow, as I don't have any plans to get drunk. The party isn't even in full swing. It's barely nine p.m., and the house is just starting to fill with people. "Do you think Benson's sister and her best friend will be here tonight?"

"I think so. Why?"

"I want to keep an eye on the freshman."

"What?" He snickers loudly, standing up and staring down at me. "That's bullshit, Colt. Benson is the one who looks after her."

I shake my head, following him and explaining what happened to the freshman after I kicked her out. Clay listens, balling his fists, the veins in his arms bulging.

"What do you plan to do?"

"Well, I already said loud and clear that I hate bullies after I saw what her roommate did to her." *Loud and clear?* I left my bomber for her to wear so she wouldn't need to walk down the hallway in her ruined T-shirt. I yelled at her stupid roommate in front of everyone once I rushed out of the bathroom. No one tried anything with her this week, but I still want to proceed with my plan. I just hope she will be here tonight. "I will make sure everyone knows there is no bad blood between us."

Clay gapes at me with a serious expression on his face. His hands are still balled into fists. He finally sighs and strolls into the kitchen. "You should have told me about it."

"She didn't want anyone to know," I say, opening the fridge and taking out two beer bottles. "Layla has no idea about any of it, neither does Benson. I didn't think I should be the one to tell her secrets. So I just... I dunno, I was keeping an eye on her."

Clay grabs the beer I offer him. "You just basically said I couldn't be trusted."

I run my palm over my face and look around. Moore offered to throw this party at his friend's house, and it happens to be a fucking mansion. If it weren't for the guys from the team, I would have gone home. I hate Moore, and I'm not sure there is anything that can change that.

"That's not what I said." I clear my throat, noticing Benson and a few guys from the team reclining on the couch in the living room. What's more, Benson has a girl sitting on his lap, some blonde junior. *Interesting.*

"But that's what your behavior says." Clay slides a hand into his pocket, taking a sip of his drink at the same time. "You need to learn how to trust people, Colt. Sometimes I think you don't even completely trust me."

I stay silent because I don't know what I can say. He's right. I'm keeping things from him. And Clay is the only friend I have who knows almost everything about me. Almost.

"Let's go join the guys?" I ask, and he rolls his eyes.

"Whatever you want," he says and heads to the living room.

I count to five and only then go after him. I need to keep my cool for another hour or so. I need this house to be full of people when I make my move. I want everyone to see that the freshman and I aren't enemies. We're just...nobodies to each other? Is that even a thing? It's definitely the shittiest explanation ever. I don't look at her like a nobody. I would love to feel her body pressed up against mine, to hear her beautiful mouth scream my name.

Fuck. Colt, say it with me: we are nobodies to each other.

We are, but it doesn't really help.

I TELL Clay I want to grab some food, and he just waves his hand at me. He's competing with the team's right defenseman, Bailey, to see who can fit more peanuts in their mouth. Walking into the house, I stop by the door and just observe. It's packed with people, and I'm not entirely sure they are all from our school. But it's not my place, and not even my friend's place, so I couldn't care less. Having a friend like Moore is already a catastrophe, so I wouldn't be surprised if his guests turn this house upside down.

I take a step further, and my lips curl into an involuntary smile once my eyes land on her. I don't have any damn control over my own face. What am I going to do if everyone notices? What if she notices? I pinch the bridge of my nose, loudly exhale, and saunter over to her. She's dancing with Grace, Layla's roommate, and they look happy, smiling and singing along to the song. I start to wonder what she does in her free time, what movies she likes, what songs she loves. I want to get to know her, just because she intrigues me. No other reason.

"Hey." I slip an arm around Grace's shoulder. "What are you two up to?"

"Colt-on..." Grace blushes as she stammers my name. "We are just having fun. You? What about you?"

"Hanging out with the team and doing nothing," I say, focusing my gaze on the freshman. It's a mistake. My brain stops functioning properly when I'm near her.

She's wearing a long-sleeved top that exposes her stomach and a short denim skirt. Her clothes are so simple, yet so sexy at the same time. I don't even know how to behave around her.

"Why did you decide to join us?" Grace asks in a shaky voice.

"Dunno. Just because." *Very convincing, Colt. You definitely deserve a medal for being subtle...not.*

"Oh, I need to use the bathroom," she squeals and untangles herself from me. "Ava?"

The freshman opens her mouth, but I cut her off before she can even say a word. "She can keep me company."

"I can?" She quirks an eyebrow at me as I take a step toward her, holding her gaze. All I want at the moment is to bend her over the couch and fingerfuck her until she comes all over my fingers.

The emotions she causes me are stronger than anything I've ever experienced, and that speaks volumes.

"Yeah," I murmur, taking another step in her direction and wrapping my arm around her waist. She gasps at the contact of my skin against hers. "Stay with me."

The freshman blinks but doesn't try to scoot away. She hesitates for a second, then licks her lips and looks at Grace over my shoulder. "I'll stay."

I hear Grace squeal and mumble something close to *oh my God*, but I'm not sure. Not that I care anyway. As the girl focuses her gaze on me, I know we are alone. Alone in the middle of the crowd, exactly as I wanted. But for some reason, it's not feeling right.

Fuck, this emotional shit is playing on my nerves like nothing else.

"What's the matter with you?" she demands, her hands dangling at her sides. "Why are you acting so nice to me?"

"Because I'm nice." I sway to the music a little, urging her to move with me.

"Nice? Not the word I would use to describe you." Her green eyes are dark and full of mischief.

"Handsome? Hot? Well-built?"

"Annoying," she corrects me. But with how the corners of her lips tremble, I know she's finding this whole situation entertaining.

"If you don't like annoying, how come you're friends with Layla?" I press her a bit closer to me. "I spent a few hours with her last weekend, and I was ready to climb up the wall."

"She's not annoying." The freshman shakes her head. "You don't get personal with anyone, so how would you know? Layla is friendly, intuitive, and fun to be around, that's all."

"Intuitive?" I bend down a little, inhaling her scent, and I feel like I've become drunk within a second. Like two beers have turned into a shot of something stronger. "Last year, I told her I wasn't interested, and I needed to repeat it. She never seemed to listen."

"You probably weren't very convincing." The music slows down, and "We Found Love" starts pounding, enveloping everyone on this improvised dance floor. This song is old, but for whatever reason I utterly enjoy it. Maybe because she's with me. "If you tell someone that they are off-limits, it makes them think there would be a possibility otherwise."

My eyes roam over her face. "Are you off-limits?"

She frowns. Her full lips form an adorable pout, and my eyes zero in on it. She blinks long and hard, and her chest rises and falls rapidly. Then she sighs and shakes her head. "I have no idea what's wrong with you tonight, but I need to remind you that you don't even like me."

"What makes you think you know anything about me?" I smirk. My hand travels south, incredibly close to the waistband of her skirt.

"I see right through you, Thompson." She inches her face closer, rising onto her toes. "You and I are not going to happen. Ever. Even if you were the last guy on this planet, I would say no."

"Why?" The question leaves my mouth before I can even think what I'm asking.

"You're not my type." Not her type? What the fuck does that mean? "Besides, you left kind of a lasting impression on me, and not in a good way."

"I can easily change your mind." I wink at her. "And I think you're lying."

"I'm not." She stomps her foot. "I don't like you."

"Are you trying to convince me or yourself?" I chortle. Then I go for it—my hand slides down and cups her butt. It's the biggest mistake, because my dick instantly hardens. I grab her arm and turn her around, her back pressed to my chest. "I can be slow, as you said that day, but I'm not an idiot. You like me."

"I hate you," she hisses, but she makes zero attempt to free herself. I look around the room and notice curious glances. If anything, my plan is working. After this, no one in their right mind will think she's my enemy.

"How many times have you dreamt about me?" I whisper in her ear, feeling her body tense up against mine. God, she's so tiny in comparison to me, and it ignites an unfamiliar desire. I want to keep her safe.

"Zero." Her answer is curt. "Unlike you. Your hard dick poking into my ass kinda says a lot."

"I appreciate beauty when I see it." My hand covers her belly, and her muscles contract. She sucks in a breath, and I know the answer without her saying anything. She likes me.

"Your words about me being plain and boring don't add up. Don't you think?"

"What did you expect? Your roommate was giving me the laziest blow job in the world, and then you came in and ruined even that." I let my fingers play on her skin, and she presses herself closer to me. Instinctively. "I'm sorry for my words. You didn't deserve them."

She stiffens, and then she slowly spins around. I let her, and I look down at her face as she gazes up at me with a deep wrinkle between her eyebrows. "What are you playing at?"

"Nothing," I mumble, not sure I understand her reaction. "I just apologized to you."

"I heard that." She puts her palm on my chest, and my heart starts pounding so hard that it echoes in my ears. She feels it too, as her eyes go wide. "Why are you... Do you really like me?"

The girl sounds so surprised, and I feel uneasy. Does she think I'm such an ass that I can't have feelings like a normal person? Shit. I'm a fucking idiot.

I take a step back, and my hands fall to my sides. She gulps nervously as she tucks her hair behind her ears.

"You're welcome," I say, shoving my hands in my pockets.

"What?" Her confusion increases, just like her nervousness.

"I wanted to make things right for you, so no one would bother you because of me." I gesture around, and her eyes dart between me and people that surround us. "You're welcome."

"That's why you approached me?"

"Why else?" I ignore the growing heaviness in my chest. Her reaction hurt me, and I'm not good at dealing with hurt. "You might be beautiful, but I don't like you. At all. I just hate bullies, and I don't like to be accused of things I never did or wanted."

"Oh. Cool, thank you. I appreciate it." The freshman fiddles with her earring, shifting her weight from one leg to the other. "I wanted to say it before, but, um, I'm sorry for the slap. I should have handled it differently because violence is never an option." She takes a step back, putting more distance between us. "I need to give you your bomber. Can I—"

"I don't care. You can keep it." I wheel around, not letting her finish.

"Bye, Colton." I look at her over my shoulder. Am I making a mistake? My gut is always right about people, and it feels good when she's around. What if... *No.* I silently slap myself in my mind. I shouldn't be here.

"Bye," I rasp and walk away from her. I can't even bring myself to say her name. Not aloud, not in my mind. I'm so fucked up. Pathetic fucker.

Chapter 13

Is It My Karma?

AVA

Colton motherfucking Thompson. I hate the guy, and I can officially say it aloud to anyone who asks. He's the most confusing and irritating person ever. What the hell was that? Coming up to Grace and me, flirting with me, touching me, and then just a stupid "you're welcome"? Is he for real?

I whirl around, trying to figure out where the fuck Grace is. Is she stuck in the bathroom or what? I make my way through the crowd and finally see her. She is standing with her back pressed against the wall, watching people dance. I frown and stomp over to her, feeling my blood boil. Why did she leave me alone with him in the first place?

"Hey," I say, and she looks up, focusing her gaze on my face.

"Hey," Grace echoes.

"Why didn't you come back to me?"

"You and Colton were having a moment." A smile stretches across her lips. "He has the hots for you."

"He doesn't." I sound unconvincing. I better up my game so she believes me. "He just wanted to help me."

"Help you?" Grace grimaces. "With what?"

I explain what happened to me because of Thompson's actions at the last party. My voice is low, and she leans in to listen to me closely.

"You were bullied?" Grace yelps so loud, I wince. "Layla never mentioned it."

"She doesn't know. I haven't told anyone." I lick my lips, looking around, avoiding eye contact with her. "He knew because he saw what my roommate did with her slushy."

"Ava." Grace takes a step forward, wrapping me in her arms. Her hand smooths my hair. "I'm so sorry. That's absolutely horrible." She leans away. "Never do that again. Ever. Why do you have friends if you can't lean on them?"

"It's not that simple," I argue, taking a step back. "I have never been in a situation like that. Usually I'm the one everyone wants to be friends with and—"

"People are different everywhere, Ava," she interrupts me. "Do you *really* expect everyone to like you? That's unrealistic."

I turn around and storm away from Grace without answering. She calls my name behind my back, but I ignore her. I was trying to explain why I kept this mess to myself, and she made me sound like a self-centered asshole with a huge ego. She made me feel worse than I already did after my dance with Thompson. My emotions are all over the place. I blink and suddenly start crying.

Oh God. Is it my karma? Why do I always end up in some shit when I go to parties? Is Drake right when he says I create trouble out of nothing?

I beeline through the crowd, farther and farther away from the living room and all these people. Tears stream down my face. It's like I turned on a damn faucet, and now it's flooding. I hate this place.

"Hey." An arm wraps around my wrist, stopping me. I know it's Thompson without even looking. "What happened?"

"Nothing," I whine, trying to wipe these traitorous Niagara Falls tears off my face.

He slowly turns me toward him, gently taking my chin between his fingers. He makes me look him in the eyes, and I feel myself drowning. His brown eyes are so dark, they remind me of a starless sky. He gazes at me with tenderness, making my knees give in. What is it with this guy? I have no idea what he wants from me, but what's more, I have no idea what *I* want from him.

"Are you going to tell me, or should I guess?" he asks, and I chuckle, still crying.

"Dancing with you turned out to be a big mistake."

"When no one dares to bother you next week, you'll see it wasn't a mistake," Colton says softly, his long fingers tracing my jawline. "I don't like seeing you so upset."

I gulp down the lump in my throat, unable to produce a sound. "Yeah, me either. I look horrible."

"Never. You look like the most—" Thompson doesn't have a chance to finish this sentence, as someone shoves him away from me. I stumble backward, and the back of my head hits the wall.

"Ouch." I whimper. I rub the back of my head in hopes of getting rid of this sudden pain. "Ow...ouch."

"Ava, are you alright?" I center my attention on the person hovering over me and see Drake. His face is tense; his lips are pursed into a thin line. "What did he do?"

"I did nothing." Thompson roars from behind Layla's brother. "You misunderstood the whole situation."

"Misunderstood?" Drake spins around and comes face-to-face with his teammate. "You kicked her out of the last party. Now I find her crying her eyes out right in front of you. Are you going to tell me you weren't the reason?"

"I wasn't, Benson." Colton's voice is an octave higher as he glares at Drake. "I just tried to help."

"Do you think I'm going to believe you?" I take a step closer and put a hand on Drake's forearm. His muscles flex under my touch. When he focuses on me, his gaze is heavy. "What did he do?"

"Nothing." My eyes dart between the two guys. "Colt was trying to calm me down. Promise."

"*Colt*?" Drake's eyebrows almost reach his hairline.

"That's my fucking name, asshole," Thompson grumbles. For some incredibly stupid reason, I find it amusing. He doesn't have anything against me calling him Colt, does he?

"I know." Drake runs his palm over his face. "Sorry if I took it wrong. Just seeing her cry, and you beside her..."

"I get it." He takes a deep breath, sneaking a glance at me. "I'll go.

You're a way better person to deal with all this..." Thompson points at my face, and I instantly feel insecure. I probably look even more dreadful than I think I do.

"Thank you, Colt," I say as he takes a step back. Our eyes lock, and he doesn't look away.

Hesitating, he slowly opens his mouth. "You're welcome, Ava." He finally calls me by my name. For the first time since the day we met.

Drake grabs my hand and leads me to the nearest bathroom, leaving Thompson behind. As soon as we are inside, he closes the door. I decide not to pay attention to his gaze on me and just go to look at myself in the mirror. If he wants to know what happened, he can always ask me. *Nicely.* Right now, I'm far too emotional for my usual poker face.

"Are you going to enlighten me?" he asks when I'm done cleaning my face.

"About what?" I lean my back against the sink.

"Why were you crying?"

"Because people are impossible," I mumble, and he smirks.

"Care to explain?"

"No." I shake my head. "Grace just pissed me off."

"What did she do?"

"She left me alone with Thompson," I explain, and his face darkens.

Drake takes a step closer but stops himself, hiding his hands in his pockets. "I saw you two together. I just happened to go to the kitchen and... Why did you dance with him?"

"Because he asked me to keep him company," I blurt out nervously.

"And you agreed?" Drake laughs. "Just like that?"

"H-he wanted to make things right for me."

"That doesn't make any sense." Another step closer, but this time, the expression on his face is the one that I classify as "worried-and-confused Drake Benson".

"Remember how you thought there would be consequences for me after the last party?"

"Yeah, why?"

I look away and focus on the wall behind him. "Well, you were right. I had two weeks from hell because everyone thinks I'm his enemy."

"How does Thompson know that?"

I suck in a breath and finally look back at my best friend's brother. "Colton saw my roommate being extra bitchy to me one day. He knew his actions at the party started it, so... He was just trying to make sure people know there is no bad blood between us."

I don't mention my talk with Thompson in the bathroom. The less Drake knows, the better. He already looks weird, as if he's on the verge of yelling at me. It wouldn't be the first time that's happened, but usually it's because I do something stupid. Now, there is something else in his gaze too, and I can't put my finger on it.

"Why didn't you tell me about this?" He raises his voice. "I'm always there for you. Always. I could have—"

"I didn't want anyone to know." I swallow hard. "Not even Layla."

"So, if Thompson hadn't stepped in for you...it would have continued happening?"

"Probably." *Oh God. I'm an idiot.*

"Ava." Drake walks up to me and stares me in the eyes. "If something like that happens again, or if what Thompson did today doesn't work...tell me about it. Please."

"Okay," I reply, sighing deeply. I'm ready to leave this room and probably this party. I'm just too wound up. "How was your night?"

"It was okay." Drake's arm slips around my waist. He lifts me and positions me on the countertop with ease, as if I weigh nothing. Now we're on the same level, and I look him in the eyes. "I was worried about you. I need a moment to get myself together."

"I'm sorry," I murmur. "I shouldn't have hidden it from you. You're my friend, just like your sister."

Drake keeps his hands on the counter, not touching me. It soothes my nerves and helps me forget all the bad things that happened tonight. He sure has a calming effect on my fucked-up state.

"Do you want to stay at the party?" His voice is husky as he gently tucks my hair behind my ear.

"Not really. I want to go to my room and watch something."

"Let's go to my place? We can watch something together." Drake grins cheekily and steps back. "I wouldn't mind your company."

"Sounds good." I jump to my feet and give him a smile. "I love spending time with my friends."

Drake holds my gaze for a moment, acknowledging the hidden meaning behind my words. Sex with him is mind-blowing, but I'm honestly not sure we should continue.

"Whatever you want, Ava. I'm up for anything." Drake ambles to the door. He opens it and lets me walk out first.

"That's good to know. I hope you don't backpedal when we start looking for a movie. I have very peculiar taste."

We continue our banter, going down the hallway and straight to the exit. I'm in such a good mood, as if I wasn't just crying my eyes out moments ago. It feels great, right, until I feel someone watching me. I turn my head and lock eyes with Thompson. A strange energy surges right through me, and my heart starts beating faster.

As I leave the house, I'm aware of three things, and they all scare the shit out of me. For some reason, Colton Thompson likes me, and now he's jealous. This leads to another realization: he thinks Drake and I are hooking up behind Layla's back. The third one? I'm a messed-up idiot who likes the guy I'm not supposed to like at all, and he's not the one I'm leaving this party with.

See? The biggest idiot ever.

Chapter 14

The King of Stupidity

COLTON

The door closes, and I lean my back against the wall. I just stay here, not moving. My body is tense, all my muscles rigid, and shivers run down my spine. Not the ones I get from excitement, but the ones that remind me of spiders running up and down my skin. A sticky and unwelcome feeling settles in my chest, and I have no idea how to deal with it.

Music is booming. Laughter and people's voices drift to me, but I don't hear anything; it's no more than white noise. I concentrate on the closed door, and the gnawing starts.

Why did he take her to the bathroom? He could have waited outside while she collected herself. Why did he go inside with her?

I shut my eyes tightly and grit my teeth. I shouldn't be here. It's just that my drunk ass doesn't want to do what is right. It's like I'm dead set on making myself miserable. I'm not her boyfriend. I'm the guy she hates. But she called me Colt, and I finally said her name aloud.

What the hell is wrong with me? I remind myself of a coward.

"You're a way better person to deal with all this, my ass," I hiss under my breath, balling my fists. I hate when girls cry, and I never know what to do, but with her... With her, it was different.

The longer they stay in the bathroom, the harder it is to control my thoughts. The sounds from the party are too loud, and it's impossible to hear anything happening inside the bathroom. Yet I know what I might hear if I press my ear to the door. I bang the back of my head against the wall. It doesn't even hurt, and it doesn't replace the ache in my chest either.

I'm a loser, nothing less.

Pushing myself from the wall, I storm back to the living room. I don't know how to explain what I feel. As if every fucking bone in my body hurts. She's not mine, but all I want is to have her. Is it jealousy I feel? If it is, it fucking sucks. I've never felt this way about anyone.

I grab a beer bottle from the table and gulp down as much as I can. My plan to stay sober is getting flushed down the toilet with each passing second. A girl saunters over to me, talking and talking while I barely listen. My gaze is glued to the hallway I just came from. I'm waiting for them to come out. My anger rises, and I'm ready to set this place on fire. And it's so fucking unusual, it confuses the hell out of me. What is so fucking special about her?

I turn my head just slightly and see Benson and her strolling to the front door. A beast in my chest roars, and a poisonous feeling fills my lungs. He has what I want. Obsessively. It's definitely not healthy, and it makes me want to do stupid things. Things I'm going to regret later for sure.

Suddenly, our eyes lock, and her lips part. There is something in her gaze I can't explain. She's the most confusing girl I have ever met. I have no idea what she thinks of me most of the time, and it irritates me to no end. Just like watching her leave the party with him.

Finishing my beer, I put the empty bottle back on the table and focus on the girl in front of me. She has curly jet-black hair, and her body is very feminine.

"My roommate left and..." She trails off as I look her up and down.

I might as well use sex as a distraction, as I often do. It will help take my mind off what I just witnessed—hopefully it will make me forget it. On the other hand... *No.* No, I shouldn't even think like that. I want her out of my system, and if this will do the trick, then I'm all for it.

"What did you say?" I ask, stepping closer.

The girl shifts a little, arching her back more. My gaze falls on her body, and her full breasts catch my attention.

"My roommate left, so maybe you would be interested in going to my place?" She bites her bottom lip, waiting for my answer. Fuck it. She's exactly what I need right now.

I tip my head, placing my palm on her cheek. Her skin is warm as she looks up and gazes at me with her big blue eyes. "I'm interested."

I tilt her face up and kiss her lips. She opens her mouth, eager to taste me. We kiss, and I slowly wrap my arm around her waist, pulling her closer.

I have kissed a lot of girls, and this kiss doesn't stand out from the others. Did I expect fireworks? Definitely not, but I would have loved to feel something different. At least something that would make me remember it.

Taking a step back, I keep her in my embrace. Her eyelashes flutter as she finally opens her eyes and stares at me. "I'll go anywhere with you if you promise to kiss me like that again."

I chortle, shaking my head in disbelief. I always say how fussy I am, how I try to maintain a certain distance between me and my one-night stands. Tonight proves otherwise. I just need someone. Someone who can make me laugh, make me want to protect them, make me feel... dammit. I'm thinking about the freshman again, and I don't want to.

Plastering a smile on my face, I drop my hands from the girl's sides and hold out my hand. "Ready for a walk?" I ask, and she nods.

We leave the house together, and I feel people's eyes on us. It doesn't bother me, but the girl is timid and struggles to deal with it. She tells me her name—Dylan—and I start asking questions about her major, and little by little words start pouring out of her. I sigh in relief, inwardly congratulating myself. My job here is done. All I need to do is listen to her. As simple as that.

"Can I ask you something?" Dylan stops near her dorm room, leaning on the wall and not hurrying to let me in.

Did I come here to talk to her or to fuck her? Pressing my fingers to my temples, I massage them slightly. I have never had so much trouble getting laid—like, ever. All my problems connect to one person, to the girl who is making me hate my last year in college with every bone in my body.

My agitation rises, and I lick my lips to keep from saying anything rude or stupid to Dylan. She has nothing to do with this storm in my chest.

"What is it?" I try to sound polite, and thankfully she doesn't notice my sarcasm.

"Why did you decide to leave with me?"

What kind of question is that? "Because I love sex."

"I saw you looking at the girl who left the house with Drake Benson. You were dancing with her before." I tune her out as I come to realize that I was more obvious than I'd hoped. Does everyone know I want a girl who doesn't want me?

"She has nothing to do with me being here," I grit through clenched teeth.

"Look, I want to open the door and invite you in. I want you to fuck my brains out. I want that." Dylan takes a deep breath. "But I don't want to be a fix. I don't want to be a girl you fuck because you couldn't have the one you wanted."

I'm silent for a moment, holding her gaze and saying nothing. Either I admit I like the freshman, or I prove that I don't by sleeping with a girl I just met. I close my eyes for a brief moment, allowing my mind to drift back to the party, to me dancing with her, to Benson taking her to the bathroom, to them leaving the party together. Fuck it. I'm tired of it. I'm not in the mood for sex anymore.

I force a smile. "You know, this was a mistake. I shouldn't be here." Her face pales as I take a step back. "I'm going home, but not because I like that girl from the party. I just don't want you."

Tears form in her eyes. I don't fucking care. I never do. All these emotions and feelings are foreign to me, and I prefer they stay that way.

"Colton, I—"

"Bye, Dylan." I whirl around and slowly head to the exit. I don't have any regrets. I should just focus on getting rid of my stupid ideas about the freshman. I need to forget about her. I'm not even thinking about her anymore...or am I?

I'm the King of Stupidity, nothing less.

Chapter 15

The Games We Play

AVA

"Will you go with me?" Layla hovers over my shoulder as I finish stapling my essay. She came to the library with me, and she has been reading a book the whole time.

"Go where?" I shove my essay into my backpack as we both stand up from the table.

"To the get-together with the team." She pops a candy into her mouth, looking at me with curiosity. She has taken my M&Ms.

"Why not? I don't care. You asked me to come, and I said yes."

"Love you." Layla smiles, winding a hand around my shoulder and leaning into my ear as we leave the library together. "Grace has a date tonight."

After the party, things between me and my best friend's roommate got tense. Layla quickly grew tired of it and made sure Grace and I talked things out. We have been on speaking terms since then, but that's all. We aren't friends, but at least we aren't enemies either.

I turn my head to look at her and ask out of politeness, "Who's the lucky guy?"

"He's her classmate. She's been crushing on Kaleb for weeks."

"Good for her." I shrug, and Layla lets out an exasperated sigh. "What?"

"I thought you were warming up to her."

"Look, she's your roommate, and I get that she's your friend. If we have to spend time together, okay. But if not, I'm definitely not going to be sad about it." I lock eyes with my best friend as we walk close to each other. "Actually, I forgot to ask. What made you decide to stay with me?"

"Just wanted to check on you," Layla mutters. I shake my head in disbelief, pushing her away.

When I finally told her about the bullying, she threatened to kill me if I ever hid things from her again. We're good, as always. She will forever be my favorite, even on days when I think I hate her.

"Stop playing mother hen with me. I'm fine." I can deal with her looking after me, but only when there is a reason. "It has been three weeks since the last party, and nothing is the same. All those stupid girls who didn't talk to me now suddenly want to be my friend."

"Even your roommate?" my best friend asks.

"We don't talk about her. She doesn't exist to me."

Layla stares at me in silence and then just nods. If anything, she knows how much I hate Jordan. She didn't even think to apologize for ruining my tee, but then she tried to befriend me once she heard about me dancing with Thompson. Not fucking interested.

"How are things with your classmates? Have you decided about the choir—"

"Benson, leave me alone, or I'll go to my room and stay there instead of going to this get-together with you." Why does she need to be so persistent? We have talked about it so many times already.

My threat works, as she raises her hands in front of her chest as if admitting defeat.

"Why do you even want to go?" I ask. "Don't we have anything else to do?"

"Like what?" She takes my M&Ms from her pocket and pops another one into her mouth. I snatch my candies from her hand and hide them in my backpack. She pokes her tongue out at me. "Meanie."

"How about clubbing? Bowling? A movie?" I throw out suggestions, but Layla shakes her head like a bobblehead toy. "Whatever."

"It will be just the team and those closest to them since they have a game in two days. Usually it's a lot of fun, and I swear to God, I need more fun in my life." My best friend takes a deep breath. "Since I broke up with Trey, things have been weird. So I just need this. I want to unwind, you know?"

"I know." I pat her shoulder. "Let's go to my dorm. If we're going out, I need to change my clothes."

"That's why I love you." Layla jumps on me, hugging me tightly. I hug her back for a brief moment, and I then try to shake her off for what feels like an eternity. She finally lets me go, but only after she gives me a loud smooch on my cheek.

"Love you too, but try not to kill me next time."

I won't say no to having fun. It's been a while.

I SIT ON THE COUCH, sandwiched between Layla and Drake as they compete against each other in Mortal Kombat. It reminds me a lot of our childhood, and a happy smile is stretched across my lips the whole time. It's precious, and I don't have any regrets about agreeing to come.

"That's how you do it, bro." Layla jumps to her feet, looking triumphant. "Do you still want a rematch?"

Drake scoffs, extends a controller to me, and stands up from the couch. "No, thank you. I need a drink to drown my sorrows."

"Suit yourself," she mumbles, plopping onto the couch and glancing at me. "Wanna play?"

"Nope." She's competitive, just like her brother, and I don't take losses easily. My mood is too good, and I don't want to spoil it. I lift the controller for everyone to see. "Anyone up for a challenge?"

"Me."

My stomach drops, and I turn my head to look at Thompson, who's standing behind the couch. He takes the controller from my hand and moves around the couch to sit by my side.

I instantly want to be as far as possible from this place, and from him.

"Ready to be defeated?" he taunts my best friend.

"In your dreams." Layla smirks, focusing on the screen.

"Will you cheer me on?" Thompson asks me.

I swivel my head to see him smiling at me. "Sorry. She's my best friend, and my loyalty to her comes first."

"Loyalty..." He holds my gaze. "It's a remarkably interesting thing, and every person has their own take on it. Right?"

"Probably." *What the fuck was that?* Is he implying something?

"Thompson, are you going to play, or are you just going to sit here and talk to Ava?" Layla rasps, her brows furrowed together. She looks irritated.

"Talking to your friend won't stop me from kicking your ass, Layla." He winks at me.

He's so fucking confusing. My head starts spinning.

The more they play, the more people gather around the couch. Some cheer for Layla, some for Thompson. All I want to do is leave. I need a moment to catch my breath because the atmosphere has started to suffocate me. Every time his hand brushes my bare leg, a horde of tingles spreads across my skin. Any time I notice him glance at me, I feel fire rekindling in my lower abdomen. It's all too much, and I want out.

As Thompson celebrates his third win in a row, I stand up and stroll into the kitchen. I need a drink. I open the fridge, grab a beer, and close the door. Then I lean my back onto it, staring off into the distance. I don't understand myself or what I feel, and that's a pretty new feeling. I always know if I like someone or not, and if they like me or not. Now? I'm so baffled and not sure of anything.

"Hey, look who I found here." Moore stops in the doorway, sweeping his gaze over my body. "How are you, Ava?"

"Good. You?"

"Not so good," he complains, coming closer. "Do you need help with this?"

He points to my bottle, and I nod. I can open it myself, but if it will keep him from hitting on me for at least a minute, I will take it. "Thank you."

The beer slides down my throat, cooling my insides. It's exactly what I needed, because sitting near Thompson almost started a fire within me.

"You're welcome, beautiful." Moore leans in, making me grimace. He's so sleazy. "When are you going to agree to a date with me?"

"Hudson, I think I was clear with you." I push myself off of the fridge and take a step forward. If I expected him to move out of my way, I was wrong. He slips his hand around my waist and pulls me against his chest.

"I'm a very talented guy, Ava." He's drunk. His breath reeks of alcohol, and his gaze is unfocused. "One day, this pretty mouth of yours will be full of my cum."

"Oh. So, if all you want is to fuck me, then why bother with a date?"

"Dunno." His hand moves down, lifting the skirt of my dress and squeezing my butt. "Fucking hell, baby, you're so hot."

"Get off me." I push him away, raising my voice. "Hudson."

"Why are you so stubborn? I'm a good guy; you're just not giving me a chance," he whines as I try to wriggle out of his embrace.

"I think we have very different views on what being a good guy means." I yell, finally able to break free from him. I put my bottle on the kitchen counter. "Touch me again, and you will regret it."

My blood is boiling when I storm out of the kitchen. I'm so aggravated I don't even look where I'm going. Not until I bump into someone, and two strong arms wrap around me to keep me from falling. I suck in a breath and relax at once. It's Drake.

"Hey. Are you okay?" He steadies me while I stare at him in total stupefaction. "Ava?"

"Can you please talk to Moore?" I ask, my voice trembling from my anger. "Tell him to fuck off."

"What did he do?" Drake bends his head down, gaping at me. "Did he hurt you?"

"No." I make my voice firm. "He's drunk and tried to hit on me. Just tell him to leave me alone. Please."

"Sure. I will beat the living shit out of him first, and then I'll tell him to leave you alone." He sounds so serious, but I laugh.

"Just talk to him." I put my palm on his cheek. "And not right now. Maybe tomorrow, when he's sober."

"Fine. Do you—"

"Benson. Come here." A voice rings in the air, and Drake instantly releases me. My hand drops to my side. "You too, freshman."

The fuck? I have a fucking name, asshole. I lock eyes with Thompson, and I don't like what I see. He's seething, even if he is trying to force a smile onto his face. This guy is terrible at pretending.

Pursing my lips, I follow Drake to the couch. Some people sit on the floor, some linger on chairs. I slump onto the couch near Layla.

"What's up?" Drake asks, hiding his hands in his pockets.

"Your sister suggested we play Truth or Dare." Clay is almost bursting with excitement. "We all agreed."

"Are you implying I don't have a choice?" Drake laughs, leaning his back against the wall.

"You don't," a girl giggles. She's dating someone from the team, but I have no idea who. I wasn't listening when Layla was talking about her.

"Bring it on then." My best friend laughs, while I feel uneasy. Not because I don't like this game, but because Thompson's gaze is glued to me.

Layla starts and asks Clay about the most embarrassing thing he has ever done. His story is long and hilarious, and the room erupts with laughter once he finally stops talking. The guy fucked a coach's daughter in high school and was almost caught leaving her house at night.

The game rolls on, and I feel at ease. I think there are perks to all these people being friends since even their dares don't sound nasty. It's like no one wants to embarrass each other.

"Freshman, truth or dare?"

I hold myself back from mimicking him. "Dare."

"I dare you to kiss the last guy you had sex with," he says calmly, enjoying my shocked state.

"Colton, that dare is stupid," Layla chimes, and I feel a pang in my chest. "How do you expect her to do that? Do you want her to go back home to kiss someone?"

"Why?" He takes a swig of his beer. "The last guy she had sex with is here, in this room."

I clench my jaw hard, not daring to look at Drake for even a second. People are watching me, waiting for me to make a decision.

"So if I give you the same dare," my best friend grits through her teeth, "will you go find the girl you hooked up with last?"

I stare in front of me, unblinking. Thoughts are swirling in my mind, making my head spin. He saw me leave with Drake and assumed we fucked. Not surprising, as he already suspected it after the first party. He's challenging me because he's jealous.

What a fucking idiot.

"Kiss the guy I had sex with, you said?" I slowly stand up from the couch, holding Thompson's gaze. He nods, narrowing his eyes. I'm sure he thinks I will chicken out—and he's so wrong.

Heading to Drake, I stop right in front of him. He looks calm, and it helps me to make my decision. I rise onto my tiptoes, put my hand on the back of his head, and pull his face toward me for a kiss. His hands slide down my sides as he slips his tongue into my mouth. Drake doesn't hold himself back, but I don't feel anything anymore. I become conscious of the sounds that surround us. People whistle, clap, and cheer, and I pull away.

Slowly turning around, I meet Thompson's eyes. "I hope you're happy." With that, I storm out of the room, down the hallway, and straight to the front door. There is only one thought in my mind as I leave this place: *I don't like Colton Thompson. I fucking hate him.*

"MASON, get your stupid ass back here." Layla yells.

I continue strolling aimlessly down the street. I don't want to talk to her, and I definitely don't want her to make a scene. I need to take the time to learn my way around this town and campus. Being lost is becoming exhausting.

"Ava."

I take a deep breath and halt in my tracks, not turning around, just waiting for Layla to catch up to me. Why the hell did I go along with his dare? It's not like he was holding me at gunpoint or anything. I could have said no and left the freaking house, but I didn't. I went and kissed Drake, right in front of everyone. Revealing to my best friend that I slept with her brother.

I'm the dumbest idiot on Earth.

Layla walks around and stops in front of me. "When did it happen? And how the fuck does Thompson know and I don't?"

"He's had the idea for a while." I lower my eyes to my feet.

"What? Can you be more specific?"

"After I stormed away from Grace at the party, I bumped into Thompson, and he tried to calm me down. Drake saw us and thought he made me cry. We talked things through, and then your brother took me to the bathroom. Thompson believes we fucked in there." My voice is just above a whisper and incredibly monotonous.

Layla blinks and opens her mouth, but no sounds follow. Then she clears her throat. "Is he right?"

"No." I hug myself tightly. "He saw your brother and me leaving together and assumed it was to fuck. But in reality we ended up watching *The Witcher* till morning, and then I went to have breakfast with you. That time, we only watched TV."

"That time..." Layla trails off. "Ava, how many times, exactly, did you and Drake have sex?"

"Two."

"Two?" And she's back to yelling. Amazing. "When?"

"First time happened last year, when he came home after his team lost a game. We were drinking and got carried away. Next one was after the first party, when Thompson kicked me out and Drake ran after me to make sure I was fine."

"He sure did," my best friend hisses, her eyes emitting fire. I almost feel like she is burning holes in me. I keep quiet, not knowing what to expect. I have thought about this happening a thousand times, and it never ends well in my mind. Is she going to stop being my friend? "You know that you're a stupid cow?"

"I do," I blabber. My vision blurs with tears. "I should have told you, but...it doesn't mean a thing. To either of us, and I was sure you weren't going to like it—"

"Do you even know how many times I fantasized about you and Drake together? About you becoming my sister-in-law?" I blink in total stupefaction. It's exactly what her brother told me she would say. What the actual fuck? "You just went and ruined all of that."

"Ruined? I didn't ruin anything, Layla. Your brother and I are friends. Friends with benefits when we want, but no more than that. I don't even like him in that way." I argue. "He's a great guy, and you're perfectly aware of what I do to guys like him."

Layla looks around nervously. Suddenly, she sighs and takes a step closer, wrapping me in her arms. "You're a dumb bitch, but I fucking love you."

"I love you too." I wind my hands around her waist and hide my face in her hair.

"You could have said no to Thompson," she whispers in my ear, and for some extremely weird reason, I giggle. "Ava, I'm serious."

"He was hinting that he knew about me sleeping with Drake from the moment he saw me leaving your brother's room after the first party. I honestly just wanted him to leave me alone; that's the only reason why I did it." I hug her tight.

"He's an ass. Don't pay attention to him anymore." Layla runs her hands up and down my back, reassuring me and giving me the warmth I crave.

"I hate him, and I probably have never felt like that about anyone."

"Not even Skylar Hayes from high school?" she asks jokingly. "Did Thompson top your hatred for our queen B?"

"Almost." I lean away, my eyes roaming over my best friend's face. A gentle smile plays on her lips, and her gaze is tender. "You aren't angry with me?"

"I'm not angry with you." She averts her gaze, inhales deeply, and peers at me. "But please stop. Whatever is going on between Drake and you, it needs to stop. Because if it keeps happening, he might fall in love. Do you want to be the reason for Drake's broken heart?"

"No," I mutter, suddenly feeling uneasy. Heartbroken Drake is the worst version of him I have ever seen. And me being the reason? I'd need to drop out of college or go study abroad for him to move on. Not on my agenda for sure. "I was already thinking we shouldn't do it anymore after last time."

"Thank you, Ava." Layla kisses my cheek and steps back.

"Thank *you* for being such an amazing friend." I drape a hand over her shoulders as we resume our walk. "The way you decided to defend me is precious. Even if I didn't deserve it."

"Colton shouldn't have outed you like that. It was extremely wrong, and he deserves to be called out," she says. "He should have gone and kissed his last hookup, whoever it was, if he thought that dare was fair."

"Yeah." I force myself to smile, but I yawn instead. "Let's go back to the dorms? I want to go to bed."

"It's a fifteen-minute walk from here."

"Okay."

"What are you going to do about Thompson?"

I pinch my eyebrows together. "Why are you asking me that?"

Her gaze sweeps over my face, and a lopsided grin forms on her lips. "Maybe you're going to plot some revenge."

"No. I just don't want to see him for the foreseeable future." I exclaim harshly. "Until his ass graduates and leaves."

"Didn't know we live in a fantasy," Layla sneers. "Where are my fucking dragons when I need them?"

"They are still eggs, Daenerys. Have patience," I say between fits of laughter. We continue chatting, bickering, and even singing on our way to the dorm. I feel finally at ease when I step into the building, and it's all because of my best friend. I pushed every little memory or thought I had circulating in my head to the farthest corner and locked it there. Thompson belongs in that darkness. For good.

Chapter 16

Liar, Liar, Pants on Fire

COLTON

She hopes I'm happy? I'm fucking furious. I don't hear a thing Benson is saying to me, but I can tell he's becoming angrier by the minute. I blink, and the volume finally returns. "What?"

"Are you fucking kidding me?" he rasps, burying his fingers in his hair. "What's wrong with you, Thompson? Did you even hear what I said?"

"No." I glance over his shoulder and realize that his sister isn't here anymore. Did she leave to follow her friend? "What do you want?"

"Leave her the fuck alone." He takes a step closer and stares at me. "For whatever stupid reason, you chose Ava as your target, and I'm telling you to stop. I mean it."

"My target?" I frown, looking around the room. It's not just Layla who is absent, apparently. Only Clay is still in the room, standing near the door with his arms crossed. Did he send everyone away? I honestly feel lost, and I don't understand what is going on around me. Time froze the moment she decided to proceed with my dare.

"Colton, stop acting like an imbecile." Benson heaves a sigh. "You figured out we had sex—"

"Figured? I freaking saw you leave together." I bark loudly, and he scowls at me. "I fucking knew since the first party, when you gave all of us that bullshit about her being off-limits."

"How the hell does it concern you? It's between Ava and me. No one else." He points his finger at me, poking me in my chest. "Why do you care what she's doing?"

"I can't stand her." I ball my fists. "She lies and then goes on about her loyalty to your sister. It's hypocrisy at its highest level, because if you're loyal, you don't keep secrets from your best friend."

"It was just sex, nothing else. Layla would have flipped. She'd be planning our wedding and suggesting names for our kids. That's why neither of us wanted to share the news with her." Benson's voice drops an octave lower. "And you're the biggest hypocrite of all, Thompson."

"How am I a hypocrite? Don't put your issues on me, Benson. You were fucking around with your friend, with your sister's best friend, while calling her family. Just suck it up and own it."

Suddenly, a grin forms on his lips. He takes a step back, as if he wants to get a better look at me. "Why didn't I notice it before?" Drake chortles, running a palm over his face. "You know I fucked Ava? Well, genius, I saw you dance with her. Throwing a tantrum just because the girl you want chose another guy?"

I start laughing because his words are ridiculous. "I don't want that girl. I don't even like her. She's just annoyed the fuck out of me since the day I met her. Nothing else."

"Keep telling yourself that; maybe you will start to believe it." he exclaims, turning around and heading to the door. He stops near Clay, and they nod at one another. Then, Benson looks at me over his shoulder. "I hope I made myself clear. Leave her the fuck alone, Colton."

I roll my eyes, finding this whole situation infuriating. This party turned into complete shit. Where the hell is everyone? Why did they leave? Did I scare them all away revealing the truth about Benson and his chick?

"Colt?"

I lock eyes with my best friend, and he dips his head in the direction of the exit. "Are we leaving?" I ask, grabbing my phone from the couch and shoving it in my pocket.

"Let's go for a walk. You need some fresh air." I arch my eyebrow at him. "Colt, just—let's go. I'm sure you don't want to stay here any more than I do."

Well, here's the thing. I want to stay. I haven't done anything wrong. My teammates are here, and I was honestly enjoying my time until I saw... The thought sinks in, and my shoulders slump. I growl in frustration and march to the door, walking past my best friend. I need to clear my head and find a way to get rid of everything the girl awakens within me. I can't continue acting how I tend to act.

I have never been a friendly person, always keeping my distance. I have hated almost everyone except the people closest to me and the guys I played hockey with in high school. My family drama has made it worse. Clay, my teammates, and a few people from class are the only ones I get along with. From time to time. Now it looks like this girl's presence makes it impossible to be friendly to anyone. Even my teammates.

"How long have you known?" Clay joins me on the porch, but I keep silent. I hide my hands in my pockets, and go down the stairs. "Colton."

"You said I need some fresh air," I retort, not looking back to see if he's coming or not.

"Why the hell am I friends with such an egocentric jerk?" I hear his steps. A moment later he's by my side, and we're walking shoulder to shoulder down the street. "How long have you known, Colt?"

"Since the first party."

"What? But why did you..." Clay grows quiet, contemplating his next words. "How did you know?"

"I'm observant."

"Nah, man, you've been hiding this shit from me for almost two months. I want answers." He punches me in my shoulder, and I wince, cracking a smile nonetheless. "How?"

"Dunno. Benson's behavior at that first party was suspicious. Like why the fuck is she off-limits? She's just a friend, a neighbor kid, as he said. I watched them together, how they acted around each other. I thought maybe he was just an overprotective friend. But then I saw how he looked at her when she was dancing alone, and it started to make more sense." These memories become vivid in my mind. The sounds and the smells come back to me, and I clench my jaw, wishing them out of my system.

"But it was just suspicions," Clay mutters. "Right?"

"Well, yes and no. When he stormed out of the party after I kicked her out, I asked him if Layla knew about them." Then I tell him everything that's happened since.

Looking around, I wonder how far my apartment is from here. I wouldn't mind going to bed. My head is killing me.

"Colt?" A clap on my shoulder brings me back to reality. I glare at my best friend, but he only grins at me. "We're in the middle of a very intriguing story, but you keep spacing out. You're no fun, bro."

"I just think I'm ready to call it a night."

"Let's go to your place." He doesn't even suggest or ask; he assumes he's welcome anytime. "I'll crash on your couch."

"Whatever you want," I grunt as we trudge down the street.

"Thompson, I swear, you're making it really hard for me," Clay whines loudly, and a smile haunts my lips. "Don't make me feel like I'm pulling teeth while all I want is for you to tell me everything."

"There is not much to tell. They were both giving me mixed signals, like one second I believed them, the other I was sure they were both liars. The last party was a breaking point." I swallow the lump in my throat as an uneasy feeling settles in my chest.

"I didn't expect that from Drake. He's our team captain. Everyone loves him because he's a good guy."

"He is a good one. Fucking his sister's best friend doesn't make him a bad boy all of a sudden." Clay gives me a look. "Dude, consent is a thing. He didn't force himself on her; he didn't manipulate her into sex. She wanted it."

"How can you be so sure?" My best friend grimaces as if he has a toothache.

"Did you see how she kissed him? If anything, those two trust each other."

"I think he likes her," he rumbles. Then he squints at me. "Do you think she likes him?"

Do I think she likes him? Hell, I hope she doesn't, but who am I to say it aloud? I'm the asshole she hates. "I don't know. She's not easy to read."

"Aw, come on, man. Give me something." Clay drapes his hand over my shoulder.

"I-I don't think she likes him in that way."

"Uh-huh. Do *you* like her in that way?" he asks, and I halt in my tracks.

"I don't. The only reason I did what I did is because I hate liars."

"And yet you lie," Clay says, holding my gaze. "I have never ever seen you so riled up over a chick."

"Exactly. I have never met someone who doesn't give a shit about me and isn't afraid to tell me to fuck off or slap me across my face. She's the first one, and I'm not handling the disrespect too well."

Clay looks me over, and then he smirks. "Ava is confident, knows her worth, and keeps her chin up most of the time. I think growing up with Benson taught her not to pee her pants when hockey players waltz into her life. She looks at us like totally ordinary people."

"You sound like a real snob," I say, feeling the tension disappear. He doesn't suspect anything. "We are ordinary people—"

Clay cuts me off, making a face. "Sportsmen are elite: hockey, football, basketball, baseball, soccer, just name it. College sportsmen especially. How you don't notice it is beyond me."

"I just don't care what people think about me most of the time." I yawn.

"More like ever," he snorts, slapping my back. "Even if you're an asshole, I still love you man. You're like the brother I never had."

"Same." I smile at him. We're near my building now. "I have no idea what you want to do once we're upstairs, but I'm going to bed."

"I wonder where Ava and Layla went," Clay suddenly says. "Thanks to the stunt you pulled, Ava has a lot of explaining to do. You're damn well her least favorite person on campus."

"I don't fucking care." I laugh, hiding my uneasiness behind it.

Liar, liar, pants on fire, Colton. You definitely care, and that's a huge problem.

It's Wednesday, and I haven't seen Ava for a whole week. It's like she disappeared and doesn't go to this college anymore. That's not the case at all, since I know Clay is hanging out with her any chance he gets: during lunch breaks, cornering her in the hallways, walking her to her dorm. They are friendly to each other, but nothing else.

Layla, on the other hand, is always in my face. She's everywhere I go, and I don't like her glances in my direction, as if she's plotting something, or just thinks I am a dumbass who screwed up the possibility of her brother and her best friend ending up together. Or both. I'm honestly confused by everything going on around me, so I just go with the flow most days. Like today.

"So, do you think this movie is worth the hype?" Benson asks no one in particular as we wait in line to buy popcorn and drinks.

"Probably," Moore answers lazily, leaning against the counter.

"Good answer, dude," Benson laughs. "You have a real gift for conversation."

"I prefer to use my tongue for other things." Moore narrows his eyes slightly; his gaze drifts around the place. "I'm sure you understand."

"What are you hinting at?" Benson becomes twice as big; a sneer contorts his features.

"Saying your sister's best friend is off-limits so only you can have that little cunt? I didn't expect it from you, Benson." Moore has been trying to find a way into her panties, but so far, he's only succeeded in getting a middle finger from her every once in a while.

"Another word about Ava, and I promise you will regret it." He takes a step further. "I didn't do anything at the party because you were drunk, and she told me not to deal with you there, but I might change my mind."

My gaze flickers between them both, and an awfully familiar feeling forms in my chest. Anger. And it's targeted solely at Moore. Did he try something with her at the party?

"What happened?" I ask before I can even think about what I'm doing.

Drake looks at me as if he sees me for the first time. "Nothing that concerns you, Thompson," he rasps and turns around to order his popcorn. He is treating me like I'm worse than motherfucking Moore.

"What are you getting?" Clay's voice is so sudden I jump away from him, biting my tongue in the process. Fuck. I taste salt in my mouth and just know that I bit myself bloody.

"Ice cream with—"

"M&Ms." My best friend claps me on my back, smiling from ear to ear. "You're such a predictable fucker."

"I'm not even going to argue with that." I order ice cream while thoughts quickly fly through my head. Did something happen at the party between Moore and the freshman? Was that the reason why Benson was holding her?

Just as we are about to enter the movie theater, my phone vibrates, and I stop in my tracks. When I pull it out of my back pocket, I stare at the screen. I have no desire to talk to him now, but I know this man. He will keep calling until he gets what he wants.

"Colt, you're coming?" Clay looks at me over his shoulder as he waits for me.

"Two minutes," I shout back. Then I spin around and go to the nearest corner.

"Hello, Colton." My father's voice is firm and collected, just like he always is. A pretentious fucker.

"Hey."

"How have you been?" *Oh God, just tell me what you want so I can go back to my friends. There is no fucking need for these pleasantries.*

"Good. What do you want?" My ice cream starts melting from the warmth of my palm, and I stare at it as if it's the only source of stability in my life.

"Your games next week will be on Friday and Saturday, right?"

"Yes."

"I want you to come home on Sunday. Your grandma asked me about you a few times, and I promised her you're going to visit." His fucking tone of voice means one thing: I don't have any say in it at all.

"I'll be with Mom."

"I know." *If you know, why do you never join me? Just to talk to the doctors, ask them if she's fine, if she's getting better?* "You can come home right after your visit, and then go back to campus on Monday morning."

"I can...but don't be delusional," I hiss, gritting my teeth. "If I do come, I'll do it for Grandma. Not you."

"Whatever you say, Colt. I'll be happy to have you home whether you want to see me or not." The bastard chuckles, knowing damn well I'm pissed. "Bye, Son."

I don't say anything in return and just end the call. I'm a mess. That fucking human trash can affects me worse than any other shit in my life. I have never felt such anger, even on the ice rink, and that says a lot. I freaking hate that sperm donor more than anyone, and I can't wait to graduate and start living on my own. Without his patronizing desire to rule my life the way he wants.

Staring at my ice cream, I'm not sure I want to watch this movie anymore. Or even be here. This week was strange for me. Maybe my decision to join the guys for a movie was a mistake. Most likely it was a mistake, but I'm here, and I don't want to let the idiot ruin my day. He already destroyed my beliefs in happiness and love. He's the reason I don't want to have any kind of committed relationship. What's the point if you're going to end up heartbroken anyway?

I want someone to slap some sense into me. Life is becoming exhausting. I close my eyes for a second and exhale loudly. Then I open them and breathe deeply again and again. I can always go home if this movie is total shit, or if I realize I can't keep pretending anymore and need to be alone. Yeah, I can always do that.

Determined, I stroll into the theater. The lights are still on, and an ad plays on the huge screen. I notice the guys and head in their direction —then I see her. I freeze mid-step. My foot doesn't touch the stair as my eyes are glued to her smiling face. They are all here: the freshman, Layla, and Grace. Sitting not very far from the guys, a few rows below, they are talking and laughing. And I can't look away.

I stare, watching how her lips move when she says something to her friends, how her head bobs up and down as she laughs. I smile, reminding myself of an idiot. *A hopeless idiot, who keeps ruining his life any chance he gets.*

I finally take a step further, and she notices me. Her eyes go round, then her brows knit together at once. She looks surprised, but it's quickly replaced by a grimace. She hates the idea of us being at the same movie, and I suddenly want to stay. Just to get on her nerves.

I wink at her and continue my walk. Slumping down into the seat next to Clay, I keep my gaze trained on her. I know she feels me watching her. Her neck is slightly red, and her posture becomes tense. She's adorable.

"What took you so long?" Clay asks.

"My dad," I say. He doesn't know the whole truth, but he's aware I have a shitty relationship with my father.

"Did you see..." The lights turn off, and Clay falls silent. He loves watching trailers, and he never misses one. This dude is strange for real. He can easily miss most parts of a movie, but he never misses ads or trailers. A weirdo.

Thirty minutes later, my ice cream is finished, my friends are watching the movie with undeniable interest, while I... I watch her. Don't get me wrong, I tried to get into the movie, but I couldn't. I don't want to leave anymore. Riling her up just by looking at her is entertaining, to say the least, and I enjoy every second of her misery.

Another fifteen minutes go by, and she stands up. She moves slowly, trying not to disturb anyone, and she intentionally chooses the aisle opposite from me, even if it's farther away. A smile creeps onto my lips as I follow her with my eyes. I think back to this boring movie, to the guys, whose faces are trained on the screen. Fuck it. I stand up, climb up the stairs, and see the door close. I'm pretty sure I know where to find her. She can't escape me.

Chapter 17

Not My Jam

AVA

I plop myself down into the seat on Layla's right and wiggle, trying to nestle more comfortably. I love going to the movies, but at the same time I don't. Watching something on my bed suits me better, especially if it means I can cuddle with someone. But my lack of a cuddling partner and Jordan being an annoying bitch made me agree to go to the movies with my best friend and her roommate. I wish I hadn't. I'm not the biggest fan of superhero movies. The only three I liked were *Spider-Man, Doctor Strange and Captain America: The Winter Soldier*, so it's very unlikely this movie will be my favorite.

I shove a spoonful of ice cream into my mouth and close my eyes. It's delicious, and the way it melts on my tongue brings all my taste buds to life. At least it's something to cheer me up and hopefully change my mood.

"Let me try it." Layla points her spoon at me, but I shake my head. "You're being stingy, Mason."

"I'm not. You were too evasive about the movie. You knew I wouldn't come if I heard it was another superhero flick."

"You don't like this genre?" Grace leans forward in her seat and stares at me. I shake my head no, and her hazel eyes round a little. "Why not?"

"Not my jam." I eat another spoonful of ice cream. "It's good for one movie, but no more than that."

"Usually she leaves before it ends and just waits for me in the hall," Layla comments, pointing her spoon at me again. "Are you going to do that again?"

I laugh wholeheartedly, shaking my head. "We'll see. The movie hasn't even started, so who knows?"

"Drake texted me," my best friend says slowly, her eyes glued to my face. "He and a few of the guys are here too."

"Okay." My smile becomes tight. *Just my luck, I guess.*

This week was full of Clay Rodgers, and I think we're close to being friends. He's incredibly nice to be around. Unlike Moore. Drake told him to fuck off, threatening to beat him up if he tried something with me. Did it help? Not really. He just changed tactics. Now he plays the nice guy who is hurt by my rejection. The last time he pissed me off, I gave him the finger, right in the middle of the dining hall. Clay had tears in his eyes from laughter when he walked up to me a few minutes later, telling me it was the most epic thing he had ever seen.

Drake and I... Well, we haven't had the talk that Layla expected us to have. We've just been acting like nothing changed—or more like nothing ever happened. Just like we did after our first time. We are friends. We care about each other. Period.

"Girls." Speak of the devil. I glance over my shoulder. Some guys from the team are heading to their seats. Drake strolls toward us with Clay in tow. They're both smiling from ear to ear, and I involuntarily smile back. "Didn't expect you to pick this movie."

"I love Marvel," Layla grunts. "Mason is the one who's not a fan."

"I'm aware." Drake's gaze fleets to me, and his sister grimaces. "Ava loves you too much, and that's the only reason why she's here."

"Or it's because no one told me what we were going to watch." I plop another spoonful of ice cream into my mouth.

"What do you have here?" Clay reaches out and grabs the ice cream from my hand. "M&Ms. Why am I not surprised?"

"Give it back," I pout, and he hands it back to me with a mischievous smile. "Thanks."

"Do you need a ride back to the dorm?" Drake's gaze rakes over the three of us, and Layla nods. "Cool, then enjoy the movie."

They turn around and find their seats. I quickly scan the room, and tension leaves my body. Thompson isn't here, and my mood drastically changes. I haven't seen him all week. Not because I was avoiding him, but because we were never in the same place at the same time. I can honestly work with that. It's way easier to forget about that asshole when he's not constantly in my face.

"Who's your favorite Avenger?" I shift slightly toward Layla and her roommate.

"Captain America," Grace breathes, a dreamy grin on her face.

"Then it's not surprising that Kaleb is your type." I arch an eyebrow, and she only shrugs, still smiling. Her classmate asked her on a date, then on another one. They aren't officially dating, but I wouldn't be shocked if they started to. "Layla?"

"As if you don't already know." She sulks, her rose-colored lips twisting into a grimace. "Are you even my best friend?"

"Of course I am," I laugh. My head bobs back, and I even close my eyes. God, if someone had told me that the absence of one idiot could improve my day so much, I would have agreed to come here just for that. Opening my eyes, I'm ready to tell her I certainly remember her crush on Thor, but my breath gets stuck in my throat.

He is standing on the stairs, staring at me. Why the fuck does he need to be here?

Averting my gaze, I turn a little to focus my attention on Layla. "You were obsessed with Thor."

"And still am." Her body shakes with laughter, while I basically force myself to smile. The stupid fucker keeps his gaze on me, and my neck feels hot.

"Is there someone you like, Ava?" Grace asks with curiosity.

"Sebastian Stan," I answer curtly. "Winter Soldier."

"I'm aware." She shakes her head as the lights slowly turn off. "You're all for bad guys, girl."

"I am," I assent, my body tense and rigid. I'm uncomfortable and angry. It will be harder to enjoy this movie with that jerk here, and with his eyes on me.

Forty-five minutes later, I'm ready to stomp out of this place. The movie isn't that bad, but I barely hear anything, let alone remember all the characters or what's happening. That stupid idiot has kept his eyes trained on me, and I can't even think straight. What the hell is his problem with me?

"I'm going to the restroom," I whisper to Layla before standing up and taking my purse from the seat.

"Will you be back?" Her gaze is scrutinizing. I lift one shoulder as an answer. "If not, just wait for us in the hall. Drake will give us a ride to the dorms. Okay?"

"Sure."

I move slowly, apologizing for any inconvenience. The place isn't packed with people, so it's pretty easy. I purposefully choose the far aisle to avoid that motherfucker.

The door closes, and I blow out all the air from my lungs. Might as well use the restroom, and then I will figure out what to do. If I'm being honest with myself, the possibility of me going back into the movie theater is highly unlikely. That fucker's attention messed up my mood, and I would prefer to read something on my phone to get back on track.

The guy behind the counter looks up from his book and smiles at me as I pass him. I bet he's bored to death all alone, and he's reading—a point in his favor. Maybe I can hang out with him while I wait for the movie to end. I smirk to myself as I open the restroom door. I head to the farthest stall, close it, and suddenly hear the door open. The water starts running, and I shake my head at my stupidity. When the hell did I become so jumpy?

The moment I'm out of the stall, I lock eyes with the asshole. He stands there, leaning against the countertop with his arms folded across his chest. Is he fucking kidding me?

Chapter 18

Fuck It

COLTON

Seeing her so flustered is precious. She even freezes in the stall's doorway, her hand still on the doorknob. Looks like I managed to surprise her. Well, if the place wasn't so empty I probably wouldn't have done it, but it's the last movie of the night, and it's after ten. No one is going to walk in, and if they do, I will apologize and leave.

"This is a women's restroom," she hisses, coming closer to wash her hands. I keep quiet, letting my eyes wander all over her body. She is wearing a red dress with a floral print, and the skirt ends just above her knees. It has long sleeves and a little cut-out neckline, giving me a great view of her cleavage. Her tits look perfect, and I can't wait to see them without all these clothes. "Did you bite your tongue or something?"

I blink, swallowing my nerves. It's one thing to stay silent to rile her up, but being speechless because of the thoughts I was just having? It's my downfall. Nothing is going to happen between us. I plaster a sarcastic grin on my face, holding her gaze. "I didn't."

She turns on the water, adds soap, and starts washing her hands. "Maybe you didn't notice the sign, but I'm telling you this is a women's restroom. You're not allowed in here."

"Says who?"

"Me." She turns off the water and dries her hands with a paper towel.

"Well, society says I can be whatever I want wherever I want," I say, watching as she turns around and leans against the counter. "Anyone can be anything anywhere."

"That's *Zootopia*, not the real world," she comments, and I notice the corners of her mouth quirk up in the tiniest smile.

"I don't watch Disney movies."

"Then how do you know the quote, about anyone being anything? And how do you know it's Disney?" She's got me. I watch Disney sometimes. Usually after I visit my mom. It gives me a very nostalgic vibe, and I enjoy it. Though I would rather die than admit it aloud, especially to her.

"What quote?" I murmur. "And besides, *Zootopia* posters were everywhere a few years ago. I would have needed to be blind not to notice them, so it kinda proves you wrong. I saw the sign. I just don't care."

"About a lot of things apparently," she mutters. Then she takes a deep breath. "What do you want, Thompson?"

"Nothing."

"It doesn't seem like you want nothing." She pouts. "Do me a favor and fuck off?"

"Can't do that," I say slowly, bending down to look her in the eyes. Such a beautiful dark green. Her gaze is stormy, and I'm mesmerized by her yet again.

"What did I do to you? I said I was sorry for slapping you. It was wrong; I admitted it. If you are still hung up on what happened or didn't happen between you and my roommate—"

"I don't give a shit about that girl. I forgot about her the day I walked out of your room. I blocked her on Instagram after she sent me photos of her boobs." Her nose wrinkles in disgust, and her brows knit together.

"Why do you even..." She grimaces, shaking her head. "I don't really like girls who send nude photos to boys they aren't even dating, but I hate guys who talk about those photos even more. You're horrible."

911? We've got an emergency. Her words are totally on point, and I don't know what I can do to change her mind. She's the only person besides Clay I told about the photos, and I wasn't going to tell anyone else. I deleted every pic her roommate sent to me the second I blocked her.

"I didn't tell anyone—"

"How do you think guys would feel if they knew I showed their dick pics to my best friend and discussed their size, length, smoothness?" She bombards me with questions, and I feel my mind becoming jelly. Dudes send her dick pics? A lot? "I never discuss those pics. I never show them to anyone, and I just block any guy who sends one. While you—"

"Clay is the only person who is aware of the photos, because I wanted to know if she sent them to him too. I deleted her messages and blocked her, and I didn't show her boobs to anyone," I blurt out. In the silence that follows, I say, "I'm not the type of guy to brag about that."

"Dunno, you seem like the type to me." She challenges me, and it changes my mood. I narrow my eyes, leaning closer to her.

"To brag about my sex life, or to send photos of my cock?" She bites her bottom lip when the word "cock" leaves my mouth. She has a very dirty mind, doesn't she?

"The first one." She shifts a little, crossing her legs at the ankles.

"You're wrong. I don't brag, and I never discuss sex with anyone. Not even with Clay." I gaze at her intently. "Ask him if you don't trust what I'm saying."

"So you're an honest person?" she asks, and I nod. "Okay. Then a question: what do you want from me, Thompson?" She speaks sweetly, but a fire dances behind her irises.

"You're not listening." I smirk. "Nothing. I don't want anything from you."

"Then what is this all about? Why are you here? Why were you watching lil ol' me instead of the movie?"

"I think I like our dynamic."

"Our what?" She blinks.

"Our dynamic," I repeat with a smile. "At first, I was irritated with you, but now it's kinda funny. How you react to me; how easy it is for me to get under your skin."

"This is entertaining for you?" She blows out a noisy breath and crosses her arms over her chest. "Do you enjoy seeing me so aggravated? Volatile?"

"A little."

"You're making my first year of college unbearable."

"Don't be so dramatic, freshman." It comes out on its own, without me even thinking about it. Her expression becomes blank, and I have a strange feeling in my gut that I just broke *our dynamic*.

She takes a step to the side, intending to veer around me to the door, but I block her way.

"Get lost, Thompson."

"I thought we were talking." I shove my hands in my pockets to hide my nervousness.

"It's an illusion. I don't talk to people who can't even call me by my name."

"You don't call me by my name either." I remind myself of a big kid.

"Really, Colton? You're looking for excuses, nothing else. I bet you don't even say my name in your head." Is she a mind reader? She sees right through me, and it scares me. "Your face says it all. Do you even know why you're like this?"

"Like what?" I lick my lips, seeing her beautiful eyes narrow even more.

"You're reserved and opinionated. You don't let people in, because you have too many things you don't want to share with anyone. You create boundaries, filter your words and even your thoughts. Calling someone by their name means becoming familiar. Becoming closer. And you're dead-set on being distant." She looks up at me. She's small, but at the same time, she's a warrior. That word suits her perfectly. Just like the way she described me is totally on point, but I'm not ready to admit it.

"And you were fucking your best friend's brother behind her back." I speak in a hushed voice. "Pretending to be loyal and—"

"At least I like the guy I fuck." She takes a step closer, her eyes locked on mine. A question pops in, and I'm having a hard time getting rid of it. "While you—"

"Do you like Benson?" I blabber hurriedly, cutting her off.

"What?" Shutting her down is ridiculously simple, but only because she's stunned by my question.

"You said you like the guy you fucked," I repeat like an idiot. "Do you really like him?"

"Fuck you." She bolts to the door, but I grab the doorknob, not letting her open it. "Open the damn door."

"Is my question so hard to answer?" I whisper in her ear. "Is it so hard, Ava?"

Saying her name has the effect I hoped for. She wheels around slowly and peers at my face. I wait for her to say something, literally anything except yes.

"I certainly do not like *you*." She punctuates every word, and I'm losing it. For the first time in my entire life, I've lost control, and I'm not sure I want to take it back.

"Fuck it," I mumble to myself. I wind my hand around her waist and pull her close to my chest. Without giving myself a chance to change my mind or giving her the opportunity to push me away, I bend down and cover her lips with mine. Just because I want to have a taste, nothing else.

I press her closer, and she gasps in surprise, letting me slide my tongue inside her mouth. The second mine brushes hers, my cock comes to life and my whole body becomes tingly, because she answers my kiss, closing her eyes at once. She has a fucking piercing in her tongue, and it makes this moment even more sensual. More passionate, but at the same time I go slow. I don't want to rush things, not with her. I want to experience every emotion this kiss is giving me, every quickened heartbeat this girl causes me. I want it all.

The scent of her perfume wafts around me, filling my nostrils and sliding under my skin. It's strong, and at the same time very pleasant. She smells of vanilla and coffee. I really like it. Her mouth is soft, and I suck her bottom lip into my mouth and graze my teeth over it. This girl drives me crazy, and I have no idea if I will ever be able to react to her without looking like an obsessed moron.

Lifting her and turning to my right, I put her on the countertop and stand between her legs. Our lips move together, and our tongues play with each other while I let my hands slide down to her hips.

She's so freaking fine my brain stops functioning. I want her, here and now.

I squeeze her butt and yank her to me, until she's sitting on the very edge, and my hard dick pokes through my jeans. I know she can feel it. She moans into our kiss, and it's the sweetest sound on Earth, especially because I'm the reason for it. She moans for me, and I can't fucking wait for her to scream my name. Over and over and over again.

A door closing with a bang makes us both freeze, and I lean away from her. Someone walked into the men's restroom; that's the only other door in this hallway. We are both breathing hard, our chests rising and falling. I just had the best kiss of my life. I have never felt—

"What the hell was that?" Her whisper-yell brings me back to reality. I furrow my brow, gawking at her in bewilderment. *What the hell was what?*

She pushes me away and jumps to her feet, smoothing down the skirt of her dress. Her movements are erratic, proving her nervousness. What is going on? I honestly feel absolutely confused and out of place. It's the first time in my life a girl went from moaning to literally destroying me with her glare in a matter of seconds.

She strides for the door, and this time I just watch her, not moving a single finger. "Don't you dare kiss me." She opens the door and looks at me over her shoulder, halting in her tracks. "Never do that again, Thompson. Ever."

"But you kissed me back, Ava," I reply, amused. It takes two people to kiss the way we just did. I wasn't alone in it, and I fucking know it.

"In your dreams," she stammers loudly, and the next moment, the door slams shut. *Man, this girl is going to be my absolute nightmare.*

I splash some water on my face, then I quickly walk out of the restroom and head back to the movie. I haven't said anything to Clay, so it would be better for me to return and try to watch the movie at least a little. Or watch her again. I definitely like the second option more, and I can't stop myself from smiling once I get to my seat. She likes me. Ava likes me, and for incredibly strange reasons, I'm excited. I'm scared as shit, but at the same time, this new experience intrigues me. It's a very big deal for someone like me, and I...

The thought disappears as I slump down into my seat next to Clay.

Where the fuck is she? Did she take another seat? Did she even come back? My blood boils, and the hair at the nape of my neck stands on its end. I'm a mess, and I can only be grateful for the darkness of this place. I probably look like a total psychopath.

"What took you so long?" My best friend turns to me. "You missed such an awesome moment."

"Another call from my dad," I tell him quickly.

"Sorry he's ruining your night." Clay smiles sadly and looks away, focusing on the movie again.

I take a deep breath, put my elbows on my thighs, lock my hands, and just stare at the screen. If anyone asked me about this movie, I wouldn't be able to tell them what it was about. My mind is occupied with someone incredibly special, and she won't be leaving it. *Fucking remarkable.* I'm stuck in the theater, watching something I don't want to watch and thinking about someone I never thought I would be thinking about.

When the movie ends, Moore and I are the first ones to leave. We walk shoulder to shoulder, not saying anything. When he opens the door, we both blink. The lights are too bright after the darkness of the movie theater. I rub my eyes with my knuckles, adapting to my surroundings as a loud laugh whizzes through the air.

I whirl my head in the direction of the sound and see her. She is sitting on a couch with a guy who works here. I remember him; he was the one who sold me the ice cream. I instantly clench my jaw.

"There you are." Layla's voice behind me is penetrating. "Ava, are you ready to leave?"

She stands up and spins to face the guy. I have no idea what she tells him, but he smiles from ear to ear. *Fuck.* She bends down and plants a kiss on this dude's cheek. *Double fuck.*

"How was the movie?" Her voice is melodic and clear as she saunters over to Layla and Grace.

"Who's the guy?" Grace singsongs. I want to strangle her for the stupid question.

"Alec? He's nice," Ava says, and I'm freaking sure she knows I'm listening. "He kept me entertained; he was way better than the movie."

“Unfortunately, I can’t agree with that.” Layla drapes a hand over her best friend’s shoulder and tugs her close to her side.

They’re almost out the door when Benson jogs over to them. Motherfucker is giving them a ride back to the dorm. I pull my hoodie over my head, waiting for Clay to show up. When he finally does, I’m beyond impatient but also enthusiastic. I know what I should do to get her all alone with me, and I’m pretty sure I’ll be able to pull it off.

Chapter 19

Rides or Rodeos

AVA

Pretending nothing happened doesn't work. Not with me, at least. I forbid myself to talk about it, to think about it, but I can't control what happens when I sleep. He's in my fucking dreams, and I wake up every morning feeling hot and bothered. It's infuriating. I haven't slept peacefully for two weeks now, so I'm edgy and mean. So mean that Layla has started calling me a porcupine.

"Ava?" My dad's voice sounds groggy. No surprise there—it's four a.m. I'm sitting on the kitchen island with a glass of water in my hands, and our cat Smokey is sleeping on the stool. He followed me here from my bedroom and stayed when he realized I wasn't going anywhere. "Why are you up so early?"

"I'm not really up," I mumble and take a sip of my water.

"So you're sleepwalking?" He comes to the fridge and takes out a bottle of grape juice.

"No, I just can't sleep."

"Why is that?" Dad pours juice in a glass while keeping his gaze trained on me. "Is something bothering you?"

"Nope." I look away and focus on the wall. Our kitchen is decorated in white and turquoise, a little project Dad and I did together a year ago. It's one of my favorite places in the whole house.

"Is *someone* bothering you?" My eyes flick to my dad. There is a triumphant smile on his lips. "Who is he?"

"Who said it's a guy?" I whine, making him chortle.

"So it's a girl? Is it your roommate? Is she still giving you trouble?" Dad bombards me with questions, and I sulk, letting my shoulders slump. He comes closer and leans against the kitchen counter. "Talk to me, kid. Please."

"Jordan is Jordan. I don't care about her." I heave a sigh. My dad always gives pretty great advice, but I'm not sure he needs to know everything. "Someone just confuses me."

"Baby, I don't remember ever judging you. You can be honest with me," my father reassures me, and I inch closer and put my head on his shoulder.

"I like someone, but at the same time he brings out the worst in me, and sometimes I hate him. No, most of the time I hate him. Literally can't stand the guy, but I don't know," I fumble. The scent of Dad's aftershave reaches my nostrils and envelops me in warmth. He's my rock, and even if it was incredibly hard for him to raise me on his own, he did an amazing job.

"And what about this guy? How do you think he feels about you?"

"That asshole?" I say sarcastically, and Dad cracks up laughing. "It's totally the same. One second he insults me, but the next he looks at me with puppy dog eyes, like I'm his favorite snack."

Dad coughs, spitting out his juice. I tap on his back, helping him to clear his throat. He slowly turns to look at me, and a deep wrinkle forms between his eyebrows. "You are *not* a snack," he states. "What exactly happened between you and this guy?"

"We kinda had an argument, and he said something rude. And then he kissed me, and I kissed him back." Dad tilts his head to the side, expecting me to continue. "Well, I came to my senses, pushed him away, and told him not to do that ever again."

"What did he do?" he speaks in a calm and soothing voice, showing me I don't have anything to be afraid of.

"Nothing. He let me leave." I press my water glass to my forehead and close my eyes. "I have avoided him ever since."

"That's why you came home instead of going with Layla to the game last weekend?" Dad puts his own glass on the countertop, takes a towel, and starts cleaning up the mess he made.

"Yeah..." I trail off, and my dad straightens his back and grins at me. *What is that about?* He looks so pleased with himself.

"So he's a hockey player." I roll my eyes but nod in confirmation. "Does Drake know?"

"God, no." I yelp. Then I close my mouth and press a palm to my lips. Dad throws the towel he was using into the sink and gazes at me intently. Then he sighs and runs his hands over his face.

"Please tell me you didn't break the rule."

"The rule?" I frown, arching my eyebrow in question.

"The rule of not sleeping with your best friend's siblings." He sets his jaw, while I purse my lips to control the laughter forming in my belly. What the hell is wrong with me?

I lift my shoulders, spread my arms, and just say, "Oops."

"Ava," Dad groans, threading fingers through his short hair.

"It happened last year," I lie, looking him straight in the eyes. "Once."

"Uh-huh, as if I'm going to believe you." He shakes his head but doesn't add anything else, scrutinizing me. Why am I always so open with him? "Okay, tell me about this guy. Not Drake."

"Drake and I are just friends." I sigh, getting up and walking over to the sink. "And in all honesty, there is nothing to talk about when it comes to the jerk. He's arrogant and secretive. I don't like guys like him."

"I don't know, baby, sounds exactly like your type," Dad muses as I turn on the faucet. "You like troublemakers. Like Jefferson."

"Jefferson is a stupid fucker, and he deserves to..." A hand squeezes my shoulder, and I close my eyes, taking a deep breath. "Sorry, Dad, I shouldn't have—"

"That idiot deserves your hatred, little one. You have every right to call him whatever you want." I whirl around and hide my face in his chest. Dad holds me close, rubbing my back. "How about you go back to bed and try to sleep? We can always talk about this mysterious hockey player some other time. When you are ready to tell me about him."

"You don't need to know anything about Thompson, I swear." I lean away. "Is it bad that I would love to stay longer?"

Dad tucks a strand of hair behind my ear and then cups my cheek, stroking it with his thumb. "No. It fills my heart with joy that you can always find comfort in this house and you know it."

"You're such an amazing dad," I murmur, and he bends down and kisses me on the forehead. "I love you."

"I love you too." He steps back, turning to the sink. "Now, shush. Go back to bed."

"Yes, Mr. Mason." I smile, spinning around and heading to bed.

"Ava?" I look over my shoulder, meeting Dad's gaze. "Did you say his last name is Thompson?"

"I... I did..."

"Okay." He gives me his back. "Go to bed, baby. You're going back to campus today, and you need to feel rested."

Blowing air out of my mouth, I go straight to the stairs and climb to the second floor. Next time, I'll brood in my room rather than go to the kitchen, where Dad can run into me. I disclosed way more than I planned to tonight. Sometimes, having a close relationship with your family is a curse. In my case, at least.

"How about a coffee?" The first person I meet once I walk out of the dorm is Moore. He leans against his fancy SUV, palms hidden in his armpits and legs crossed.

"No, thank you, Hudson." I plaster on a smile and walk away. I hear him lock his car, and then he jogs after me. Why can't he just back off? "Listen—"

"I want to apologize for my behavior." He cuts me off, his eyes glued to my face. "For real."

"Okay. Apologize." Not sure I'll believe or trust whatever he has to say.

"I'm sorry for hitting on you, for trying to force myself on you. It was disrespectful, and I shouldn't have done it." He smiles, and my eyes slowly roam over his face. I see the appeal if you're just looking at him. I see why girls like him, but I'm not sure. There is something about him that doesn't sit right with me. "Will you forgive me?"

"Maybe." I look over his shoulder and notice Clay. He's not alone. A woman takes a step back and slides into a blue car. Is that his mom?

"I have a question." I tear my gaze away and focus on Moore once again. "I don't like losing, so is there any chance you'd ever agree to have sex with me?" he asks.

I'm literally speechless, which means one thing: I'm fuming. He's so fucking dumb. "Excuse me?"

"I'm great in bed, Ava. So I'll ask again: any chance you will agree to have sex with me?" He leans in, hovering over me with a suggestive smile on his stupid face.

"I hate cows. And bulls. They scare the shit out of me with their horns, the sounds they make..." I accompany every word that follows with a punch in his shoulder. "But I'd ride the meanest bull at any rodeo before I'd ever ride your dick. Get the fucking memo. I don't like you."

I shout all that in his stupefied face. Then I hurry up and march away from him, heading right over to Clay.

"Hey, Clay," I call out, waving at him as I come closer. He sees me and starts grinning from ear to ear. "How are you?"

"Hey, Mason," he says as I stop in front of him. "I'm good. What about you?"

"Just yelled at Moore. Told him I would rather ride an angry bull than ride his dick." His face changes so drastically, it's funny to watch. He's stunned speechless, but a second later, he bursts out laughing like crazy. "Are you proud of me?"

"More than you fucking know," he lets out between fits of laughter. "Do you have any plans?"

"Not really." Layla and Drake will be back on campus tomorrow morning, and staying in my room with Jordan for a few hours straight isn't on my to-do list. That's how I ended up outside in the first place. "Why? Do you want to invite me somewhere?"

"I do." Clay winks at me, wrapping an arm around my shoulder and strolling us away from the dorm. "Do you like pizza?"

I wrinkle my nose, and his face falls. “Don’t get me wrong; pizza is great, but I already ate at home, and after my dad’s lasagna I’m full.”

“Your dad’s lasagna? What about your mom?” he asks playfully.

“I don’t have a mom,” I say, seeing his eyebrows shoot up to his hairline. “She died when I was six, so it’s been a pretty long time. Since then, it has just been my dad and me.”

“I’m so sorry about that. And about my words...” Clay tugs me closer, hugging me tighter. “God, I feel terrible now.”

“It’s fine. You didn’t know.” I give him a small smile, nudging his side with my elbow. “Was that your mom with you?”

“My mom?” He sounds and looks surprised, and I feel stupid all of a sudden.

“I saw you with a woman when I was talking to Moore. I thought...” I fall silent, noticing Clay’s lips tremble. He’s trying hard not to laugh, and I scowl. “What’s so funny?”

“That’s not my mom. I hooked up with her last night—” I don’t let him finish, untangling myself from him and scooting away. “Hey? What’s wrong with you? Ava?”

Giggling comes out on its own, loud and infectious. Clay cracks a smile too, shaking his head as he watches me with amusement.

“How old is she?”

“Do you think I asked for her ID?” Oh my fucking God. It’s gold. This guy is the best thing that’s happened to me in college. “Sierra is around thirty-four, I would guess.”

“Do you like older women?” I ask as we finally resume our walk. We cross the quad, and laughter and loud voices reach my ears. A few groups of people loiter on the benches.

“You’re younger than me, and I like you,” he points out, making me chuckle. “I just like women overall. As long as she gives me good vibes, then we’re good.”

“You’re full of surprises, Clay Rodgers,” I tell him, and he reaches over and drapes an arm over my shoulders. “I like you too.”

“As a friend,” he adds, and I nod. “Your vibe is different. It intrigues me, and for whatever reason, I don’t want to screw it up.”

“Me either,” I confess, and Clay gazes at me intently. He leans in and kisses my temple. So simple and yet so tender, making my heart flutter in my chest.

"You need to give me your phone number. I'm the kind of friend who will call whenever I want to talk to you, and that shit works likewise for you too. Especially if you need help with something. Or if someone is bothering you. You can rely on me too, not just on Benson."

"Aw, Clay. I had no idea you were such a softie."

"Only for you, babe." He hugs me tight and turns us to the right. I see a pizza place not far from where we are. "Where is Benson? And his sister?"

"Drake and Layla are home. They will be back tomorrow morning," I say quietly. "They suggested I go with them, but I decided to have my dad drop me off. He has to work tonight, third shift, so he won't be able to bring me tomorrow."

"Layla is pretty hot."

I halt in my tracks so abruptly that Clay stumbles forward. His gaze is fixed on me as I observe him with my eyes narrowed.

"Do you like my best friend?"

"I always did." Something in Clay's eyes tells me he's being honest. Maybe that's why I'm so drawn to him? There is no bullshit or confusion when it comes to the guy, and I like that. "Her brother told us right away she's off-limits for the team."

"What if I told you Drake is bullshitting all of you? About Layla, I mean?"

"Can you be more specific?" Clay's brows pinch together, and the pupils of his yellowish-green eyes dilate.

"If Layla ever started dating any of the guys from the team, he wouldn't say a word." He blinks; the crease between his eyebrows becomes deeper. "He's only against one of you fucking his sister like there's no tomorrow and forgetting about her the next day. That's all."

"That sucks," Clay mutters. "It means she's still off-limits for me. I don't do relationships."

"Have you tried doing relationships?" I ask him jokingly, and he shakes his head no. "You have no idea how much you're missing out."

"How so?" He takes his hand off my shoulder and opens the door of the pizza place for us, letting me in first. "I'm getting laid without any real effort."

"Sex is better with someone you can trust. When you have a certain level of familiarity. A comfort." I go to the nearest table, but Clay catches my hand and stops me. "What?"

"I need to order."

"We're not staying?"

"Nope. Do you want something to eat? I'll buy."

I come closer and look at the menu. As I'm not hungry, I settle for a drink. Clay looks at me like I'm wacko but doesn't say anything. Five minutes later, we are sitting at the table, waiting for our order.

"You mentioned trust and familiarity when it comes to sex. Can you explain a bit more?" He gawks at me with such vulnerability, I wonder why he chose hookups over a relationship. "What does that mean to you?"

"I'm going to be extremely upfront, so don't judge," I warn him. "For most men, reaching orgasm during sex isn't a problem, while for women it's often not so easy. We need a connection, the ability to talk openly about things we like or even show a guy what makes us feel good. It's simpler when you know you can trust him."

"It was like that for you with Benson?"

"I trust him like I trust myself. I know he will never hurt me, and I can be honest with him. I can be myself with him." I smile sheepishly, casting a glance to the side. "I'm open to experimenting, and I'm not afraid to try something new, but it never ended well. Until Drake."

"Is our captain the best sex you've ever had?"

"He is," I confirm, holding his gaze. This is not something I can talk about with my best friend, but with Clay I don't feel ashamed to admit it.

"Wow. Who knew Benson was a beast?" he jokes, and I smack him in his shoulder. "What?"

"You didn't understand a thing I just told you."

"I did," he counters, looking over my shoulder. "When you're dating someone, you trust them. You talk to them. You create bonds. So sex is better when it's your permanent partner and not just some random hookup."

"True." I tuck a strand of hair behind my ear, raking my eyes over his face. He has freckles but they aren't pronounced, and his hair is a nice auburn color. His dark green hoodie favorably sets off his skin, making the yellow shades in his green eyes stand out. All in all, Clay Rodgers is a handsome guy. "Why did you decide not to date anyone?"

"Getting personal, are we?" Clay laughs heartily and then looks over my shoulder again. "Our order is ready."

"You're no fun." I stand up and follow him to grab my pop. I have no idea what he has in mind or where we're going after this. I just go with the flow. Strangely, I like it.

"I need to make sure I can trust you before I reveal all my dirty secrets to you." Clay elbows me in my ribs, and I whimper. "So if I ask Layla on a real date, her brother isn't going to kick my ass?"

"I can put in a good word for you," I suggest. "To make sure none of your body parts are broken if you *do* ask my best friend on a date."

Clay looks me up and down and grins. "Cool. I'll think about it." He hands me my drink and takes three large pizza boxes in his hands. "Let's go, Ava. It's time for you to become a part of my gang."

I choke on my pop, barely keeping it in my mouth. I cough, and tears spring to my eyes. He's unbelievable. "Part of your gang? Who are you? Jax Teller?"

Rodgers stops in his tracks and gapes at me with a ridiculously funny look on his face. "You know who Jax Teller is?"

"Um, yeah? *Sons of Anarchy* is my dad's favorite TV show." I lift my shoulder, furrowing my brows. "Why are you looking at me like that?"

"Because you're the most amazing girl I have ever met," Clay mumbles, heading down the street.

"Just remember not to say that in front of my best friend. There is no way in hell she'll go on a date with you if you call me that in front of her."

"Duly noted," he sneers, turning to his right and opening the door of an apartment building. Does he live here?

"Clay?" I follow him inside, even as an uneasy feeling settles in my chest. Something isn't right. "Where are we going?"

He ignores me, climbing the stairs to the third floor and turning to look at me only when we stop in front of apartment thirty-five. "Welcome to the gang, baby." He knocks on the door, beaming at me.

I'm ready to ask the question that's been lingering on the tip of my tongue, but it dies as soon as Colton Thompson opens the door and looks at Clay and me in total bewilderment.

Fuck.

Chapter 20

Fuckity Fuck

COLTON

I flip through Netflix with annoyance. I have no idea what I want to watch, or if I even want to watch anything. I've been in the strangest mood for almost two weeks now. The only person to blame for it is her. She's like fucking water, slipping through my fingers no matter how hard I try to keep her in the cup of my hand. She's everywhere and nowhere at the same time, because I haven't seen her even once since she left the movies with her friends. And it sucks.

I huff and stand up from the couch, heading to the kitchen. I need a beer. And some snacks. Where is fucking Rodgers? He texted me almost an hour ago, asking if he could come to my place to hang out. The dude promised to bring pizza, so I didn't go out and buy anything to eat. Now? I regret it.

I grab a bottle from the fridge and put it on the kitchen counter, when someone knocks. Finally. I stroll to the door, open it, and my heart drops to my feet. What the hell is going on?

"Hey, man." Clay greets me enthusiastically and pushes inside my apartment, ignoring my stunned face and handing me pizza boxes. "I hope you don't mind I brought Ava along. She was lonely, and Moore was bothering her. Again. So I decided to save her from her misery and invite her to join us."

I don't even look at him. I keep my eyes on her. She's wearing black jeans that end above her ankles, a pink knit sweater, and my bomber jacket. I honestly thought she got rid of it, so seeing it on her is overwhelming. In the best possible way. I bring my gaze back to her face and see fire dancing in her eyes. She doesn't like this.

"If being your friend means you don't speak a word of truth, then I don't need it," she exclaims harshly, turning to leave. Clay rushes out of my apartment and grabs her by the wrist. She pulls her hand out of his grip, but he catches it again and drags her inside. "Clay."

"I'm sorry, Ava," he says softly, beaming at her. "I didn't warn Colton about you being with me. I thought if he felt sorry for the evening you're having, he wouldn't object."

She chews on her bottom lip, squinting in my direction. As soon as she sees me watching her, she looks back and focuses her attention on Clay. "I don't think this is a good idea."

"Colt, tell her she can stay." Clay wiggles his eyebrows, staring me in the eyes. I shake my head, close the door, and turn the lock. I give the pizza boxes to my best friend and then shift my gaze to look at her.

"You can stay, Ava." I walk around them and go back to the kitchen where I left my beer.

It's best to act as if nothing is wrong, as if the girl I have been trying to catch for two weeks didn't just show up at my apartment with my best friend. What is she even doing with him? And what about Moore? I need details, but I don't want to be nosy. Clay will become suspicious in no time if I sound too interested in anything related to her.

I saunter into my living room and stop in the doorway. Clay is already sitting on the couch with a slice of pizza in his hand. Ava is near him, holding her drink between her palms. A pizza box sits on the table, while the other two are on the floor. This guy and his habits drive me crazy sometimes.

"Do you want a beer?" I ask, coming closer.

"Yes, please." A grin stretches across Clay's face. I hand him my bottle, and then look at her.

"Ava?" She turns her head slightly, curiosity written all over her face. I bet she wants to know what I'm thinking, why I let her stay and why I'm being so nice.

"I have my drink." She arches her eyebrow, lifting a shoulder at the same time. It's a little shrug, but it's full of meaning. She hesitates.

"Suit yourself." I spin around and head to the kitchen. I grab another beer bottle from the fridge and return to the living room.

Wandering to the couch, I put the beer on the table and slump down beside Clay. I reach over to the pizza box and snatch a slice. My best friend peers at me. "What are we going to watch?"

"I don't know." I take a bite, glancing between my guests. I force myself to not pay her too much attention, because if I do, I won't be able to look away. "Any suggestions?"

"Yeah, how about you don't talk when your mouth is full?" Ava mumbles. A smile lifts her face, but I can tell she's trying to hide it, raising her cup to her lips. *Ladies and gentlemen, it's a sign.* She has started to feel more comfortable if she isn't holding herself back from jabbing at me. One point in my favor.

"I'll try, but I can't promise anything." I hold her gaze. The tip of her tongue slowly runs over her bottom lip, and the thought of kicking Clay out flashes in my head. "What do you want to watch?"

"I'm up for anything," she says and takes a sip of her drink.

"How about something spicy?" *Clay motherfucking Rodgers. You're the dumbest idiot I have ever met.*

My eyes zip to her, and I watch as she slowly gulps her drink. She shifts slightly to face my best friend, and he wheels his head to look at her too. "You're testing my patience, friend. It's like you invited me here only to get me to run away."

"Nah, it's all good. I often crack unfunny jokes," Clay retorts. Then he winds his hand around her shoulders and pulls her to his chest. What the fuck? "Colt, how about we let Ava choose a movie for us?"

I blink, tearing my gaze away from his hand on her shoulder. How did they become so close? He does spend time with her whenever he has the chance, unlike me. I extend the remote to her, grab the beer bottle, open it, and take a sip.

Ava huddles more comfortably on the couch, hiding her legs under her butt and leaning against Clay. I have no right to be jealous, but I'm curious what she's going to put on. Taking another swig of my drink, I focus on the TV screen. The second I see what she's starting, I barely hold myself back from spitting out everything I just gulped.

"*Zootopia*?" Clay asks, taken aback. "Are we going to watch Disney?"

"Why not?" She grins at him, sneaking a glance at me. "Anyone can be anything in *Zootopia*, which means you can watch a Disney movie."

"Colt?" My best friend draws my attention to him. "You don't mind?"

"Nope. I just hope it's good." I've fucking seen it three times already; this will be the fourth.

"It is. You'll like it." Her eyes glimmer with mischief, and I bottle up a snort. This girl is something else.

A FEW HOURS LATER, we're still watching movies. After we finished *Zootopia*, Ava got her hands on the remote again and started *The Falcon and the Winter Soldier*. Forty minutes into the fourth episode, my best friend started snoring.

"Do you think I should wake him up?" Ava asks as we stand in front of the couch, looking down at Clay. He is sitting up straight with his hands locked behind his head.

"I don't think so. He didn't really sleep last night," I tell her, counting in my mind how many beers he had. I had two. Ava caved and drank one. That leaves two for Clay. "Why?"

"It's almost one a.m.," she utters under her breath. "I want to go back to the dorm."

"Bullshit. You're staying," I blurt out in a harsh voice. Instantly, she spins toward me and puts her hands on her hips. "Look, I didn't mean that like it sounded. When is your first class?"

"Eleven."

"Cool. Clay and I will give you a ride to your dorm tomorrow morning. Before your classes start."

"And where am I supposed to sleep?" She narrows her eyes, becoming defensive.

"In my room. I'll take the couch. It's not a big deal."

"Clay is here."

"So what? Don't worry. We will fit. Rodgers won't be happy if I let you go home on your own. He will understand why I'm crashing with him on the couch." I turn away, collect the empty bottles from the floor, and amble to the kitchen.

I quickly clean up, making a mental note to buy some food. I can't continue to roll like this, even if I'm too lazy to cook for myself.

"You have a nice place."

I look over my shoulder and see Ava leaning on the doorframe.

"Thanks." I whirl around and rest my back against the kitchen counter. "You have been avoiding me."

"I'm in your apartment."

"If you knew where Clay was taking you, would you have agreed to come?"

"No." Ava grins. I want to know what she's thinking. Arching an eyebrow, I encourage her to tell me what she wants to say. "Have you been practicing?"

"Practicing what exactly?"

"Calling me by my name," she says, making me laugh.

"Not really. I was just tired of all the 'she', 'her', and 'freshman' I was using when I thought about you. You have a name, and I like it."

"That's nice to hear." Ava takes a step into the kitchen. Her fingers fly to her earring as she avoids looking at me.

"Seeing you in my bomber is nice too. I thought you threw it away." Her gaze dashes to me.

"No one knows it's yours." She shrugs, the ghost of a smile at the corner of her mouth. "Besides, it looks good on me."

"It does." Our eyes lock, and my body warms up. The air in the kitchen becomes charged.

Ava comes closer, stopping by my side and leaning against the countertop. "You have watched *Zootopia* before."

"Maybe."

"I knew it. Totally called it." She elbows me in my ribs, and I shake my head in disbelief.

"I will never admit that to anyone else. Ever." I watch her intently.

"Don't even think about telling anyone. I'm serious. Not even your best friend."

"Not talk about something that makes you more real? More human?" She rakes her eyes over my face and down my body. She is checking me out, and a smug smile forms on my lips. "You're strange. Why are you smiling?"

"You just checked me out, ogled me without even a hint of embarrassment or shyness," I state, staring down at Ava. She grazes her teeth over her bottom lip, turning slowly to face me. There isn't an ounce of resistance in me. Moving on instinct, I press my palm to her cheek and lock my heated gaze with hers. "How come you're friends with Clay?"

My need to know more about her sudden appearance at my apartment is strong, and I hope she will be honest.

"I like him—not in a romantic way or anything. You know that connection when you just click with someone? He was hitting on me in the beginning, but it never bothered me. He's never given me a bad feeling in my gut, unlike Moore."

Speaking of the motherfucker. "What did he do? At the party? Tonight?" My fingers skim along her jawline, enjoying its smooth softness.

"Nothing unusual. He was hitting on me at the party, kinda forcing himself on me because he was drunk. Tonight, he actually stopped me so he could apologize. He even said he was wrong and asked if I could forgive him." She looks away for a brief moment. "I would have, but then he opened his big mouth and asked if there was a chance I would ever agree to have sex with him."

"And what did you tell him?" I force myself not to stare at her lips. My breath quickens, and my heart pumps fast in my chest.

"I told him I would rather ride a bull at a rodeo. And that means never and that he's disgusting, because I'm freaking scared of bulls."

"You are such a feisty girl," I coo, dragging my thumb over her bottom lip. "I have never met anyone like you..."

"Colt." Ava says my name, and the sound is so overwhelming and so powerful, I inch closer and place a light kiss on the seam of her lips. "I don't want to be another random hookup for you."

She could never be a hookup. Absolutely out of the question. The emotions she causes me are unique, and I'm not stupid enough to screw it all up, yet the doubts are loud in my head. I have never dated anyone. I have no idea what it all means. Angst starts to fill my body. Nervousness finds its way under my skin and straight into my heart, and I flip.

"And Drake can be a hookup?" I ask, holding her gaze. Her brows knit together, and anger crosses her features.

"Drake could be a boyfriend, not just a hookup, if I wanted more." She takes a step back, and my hand drops to my side. "You just spoiled everything, asshole."

"Oh, really?" I mutter, watching her head to the door. "So Benson is good enough for you, but I'm not?"

Abruptly, she twirls around and glares at me. "How would I know anything about you? All you do is make me feel like you fucking hate me." she whisper-yells, balling her fists. "You took my words all wrong, and now you are fucking pushing me away."

"I heard you right. I'm not good enough for you, while Benson is exactly what you need."

"No, you're a dumbass. All I meant is that I don't want to be a one-time thing."

Ava spins around, ready to bolt to the door, but I catch her. My hands wind around her waist, and I press her back to my chest. Her body crashes into mine, and a breath catches in my throat. Just a little touch, and I'm completely alive. I feel everything, even shivers on my skin that have never been as real and palpable as they are now. A jolt of electricity runs through my veins and sets my body on fire.

"I'm an idiot. I'm sorry. I fucked up," I utter in her ear, kissing her neck tenderly. "Can I touch you?"

She presses into me; her voice is breathless. "Yes...please..."

I slide my hand under her sweater, moving up and cupping her breast. It fucking fits my palm so perfectly, I groan in her ear. Pulling down her bra, my fingers fly to her pebbled nipple, rubbing it between my thumb and middle finger and drawing a moan out of her. Her skin is velvety to my touch, and my hands slide along, enjoying how it feels under my palm.

My left hand reaches the waistband of her jeans. I unzip her fly, unbuttoning her button next. I could have snuck in my hand without all that, I just want my movements to not be confined or finite. I want to give her pleasure, to indulge my fantasy from the night we danced together, the one about fingerfucking her. I want her juices all over my fingers. I want to taste her, and I want her to come for me. Only for me.

Her underwear is silky, just like her bra, and even if I'm dying to see them, I restrain myself. Ava is not leaving my place unsatisfied, and I'm determined about that. She sucks in a breath as my hand slides down and touches her clit through her panties. My movements are slow and calculated. I press just a little bit, teasing her and circling my fingers over her sweet spot. Her breath quickens and becomes shallow.

Feeling her wetness through the fabric of her panties, I smile and bend down, inhaling the scent at the nape of her neck. Her perfume tonight is not as strong as it was when we kissed at the movies, but I still enjoy it. It suits her, mixing with the aroma of her skin and making her even more alluring.

Ava is fucking perfect.

I bring my lips to her neck and lightly bite her skin, tracing my tongue over it and making her shudder. Her nipples are like points as I rub and pinch them between my fingers, adding pressure. She hisses every time I do this, and she wiggles her ass over my erection. What a greedy little girl I have in my arms. Gliding my palm under her panties, I finally press my fingers to her clit, instantly slipping down to her slick core. She's so fucking wet.

"Colt…" she moans, and there is nothing I want more than my tongue playing with hers.

I massage her clit, increasing the tempo little by little. With my free hand, I grab her neck, squeezing it for a brief moment and then moving my fingers up to her jaw. I force her to turn her head and cover her mouth with mine. Ava welcomes my tongue with eagerness, curling it around mine and arousing me even more. My cock is hard, and it wants to be deep inside her, but that's not what I have in mind. She's my priority now. My pleasure comes next, only when I know she has had her orgasm.

We kiss, tongues dancing in a frenzied motion. I finger her, speeding up my movements with only one purpose: to make her come. To send her over the edge and give her an orgasm she won't forget.

My grip on her jaw tightens. "I want you to come for me," I whisper, and she nods erratically. "Are you close?"

"So close..." she whimpers as my finger slips into her again.

Silencing her sounds, I smash my mouth onto hers and rub her clit faster, until she starts to tremble. Her legs try to close, but I keep them apart, continuing to finger her. Then she orgasms, drenching my fingers in her juices and emptying my brain of its every last thought. I want my dick inside her mouth.

I spin Ava around with my free hand and stare at her beautiful face in admiration. Her usually emerald-green eyes are now closer to black. Her cheeks are flushed, and her lips are parted. She's still rocking on the waves of her orgasm, and I have never seen anyone look more beautiful.

I plunge my fingers into my mouth and lick them clean. "You taste like heaven."

A smile stretches across her lips, and I grab her sweater in my fist, pulling her to me. I'm so ready to devour her mouth—but my world crashes down when Clay's voice rings in the air, and Ava and I freeze. *Fuckity fuck.*

"Colt? Ava?"

A bewildered look crosses her features as she jumps away from me. She zips her fly, turning her back to the kitchen entrance.

I shake my head, knowing the moment is ruined, and go to the living room. Clay is standing by the couch, stretching his arms in the air and yawning. Why the hell did he have to wake up?

"How did you sleep?" I mock, shoving my hands in my pockets to hide my hard-on.

"Not bad." My best friend yawns again. "But my neck fucking hurts. I think that's why I woke up."

I glance at the TV screen and see the last moments of another episode of *The Falcon and the Winter Soldier*. "You're up just in time to see how the season ends."

"I don't fucking care." He rubs his eyes and only then looks around the room. A deep wrinkle forms between his eyebrows. "Where's Ava?"

"She's in the kitchen. The episode was ending, so she offered to help me clean up," I tell him as she emerges. She's collected her hair into a high ponytail, looking absolutely cute. Her still-reddened cheeks are the only sign of how naughty we just were in my kitchen.

"You're up," she says to Clay, avoiding my gaze. "Did you know you snore?"

"Always. Especially after I've been drinking," he chortles, clapping his cheeks with his palms. "Do you want to go back to the dorm? I can walk you—"

"Why can't she..." I catch myself as I notice her eyes rounding. "Why don't you stay? I'll drive both of you to the dorms in the morning."

"Nah, man, my neck is killing me, and I want to crash in my bed." Clay shakes his head, rubbing the back of his neck. "What do you say, Ava?"

"Let's go." She sashays to the couch, grabs her purse, and straightens her back as our eyes meet. "Thank you, Colt. For everything. You made my night a ten out of ten by letting me hang out."

Is that her way of saying thank you for the orgasm? I'm a bit lost, and I'm not sure how I feel about any of it. I don't understand her, and it drives me up the wall. I lean on the doorframe, watching hopelessly as Clay and Ava slowly put on their jackets and shoes.

"See you, dude." Clay opens the door, letting Ava walk out first. She ambles out to the hallway and glances at me over her shoulder.

"Night, Colton." She winks at me and wheels around, heading to the stairs with Clay in tow.

"Night." I close the door, taking a deep breath to dissolve my dissatisfaction.

I go to the living room and turn off the TV and the lights. When I step into the kitchen, my eyes land on a piece of paper on the fridge that wasn't there before. In two strides, I'm across the room. I move the magnet away and take the little note in my hands. My lips curl into a smile, and I dig my phone out of my pocket and save her number in my contacts.

Enemies make the best lovers, Colt. -A

Never in my life have I wanted morning to come so badly.

Chapter 21

Gorgeous Asshole

AVA

Dove Cameron's voice fills my ears, and I lip-synch "Boyfriend" along with her. I smile to myself, continuing my essay. I've been in an incredibly good mood since the moment I opened my eyes this morning. Even the playlist I chose for the day is light; it's filled with more pop than I usually listen to. Just because of the evening I had.

My hand freezes over my keyboard, and I'm again lost in my memories. For the thousandth time today. I'm distracted by everything that happened yesterday, but especially Colton fingering me in his kitchen. Heat floods my veins. My belly twists and knots, and I squeeze my legs together. I need to snap out of it, at least until I'm back in my room. The coffee shop is definitely not the place for my fantasies. Or my clit twitching, or my panties being wet, dripping wet. Oh God. I'm hopeless.

Abruptly, I push myself from the table and lean my back on the chair. I take a deep breath, and release it. Breathe in, breathe out. Over and over. Until my heartbeat becomes even. That's better.

The door of the coffee shop opens, the doorbell dings and Layla strolls inside. She has two cute braids framing her face, while the rest of her hair sprawls over her shoulders. My best friend notices me, and a big, toothy smile spreads across her lips. She saunters up to the barista to place her order.

I turn off my music, take out my AirPods, and put them back into their case, scanning the coffee shop with my eyes. It's small and very cozy, peach colored walls decorated with posters of Hollywood classics. There is also a bookcase with mostly detective and historical fiction books. One guy is sitting at the table near the window with his laptop opened and headphones on. He's nodding his head, while typing quickly on the keyboard. The scent of coffee and cinnamon becomes stronger, Taylor Swift's "Midnight Rain" plays in the background, and warmth spreads through my veins. I remind myself of a big, fluffy toy, happy to have a chance to spend time with my best friend. I want to tell her something very important. Keeping secrets from her is easy, but there are some things I want her to know.

I still have about five sentences to write, but they can wait. I close my laptop and shove it in my backpack, as Layla edges to the table. She lowers herself on the chair across from me, taking off her leather jacket and nestling comfortably into the chair. It's not the first time we have seen each other today, but we didn't really talk when we met on campus. I'm not one to spill my guts in the hallway, surrounded by strangers.

"What did you do once you got back yesterday?" Layla takes a sip of her caramel Frappuccino, and I scrunch my nose. "What?"

"How can you drink that?" I quirk an eyebrow at her as I take a sip of my flat white, enjoying the rich taste of coffee. Fucking perfect.

"No accounting for taste, Ava," she points out with a mocking smile, taunting me. "You've never heard me criticize your love of M&Ms, have you? So please, don't be a judgmental bitch, and leave me the fuck alone with my Frappuccino."

I raise my hands in front of me. "No objections, Your Honor."

"God, why are you so annoying?" Layla scowls, leaning back in her chair. "Did Jordan spoil your return, or did she behave?"

"In all honesty, I didn't see her." My heartbeat accelerates. My best friend's eyebrows knit together. "I left the room immediately, intending to spend some time alone, as far from my lovely roommate as possible. And when I got back, she was already asleep."

"Since when does Jordan go to bed early?"

"She didn't. I came back around two a.m." I sip my coffee, hiding my smile behind my mug and enjoying Layla's shocked state.

"Where were you?"

Averting my gaze, I look around the place. "I was with Clay and...*ahem*...Colton."

Layla's eyes look as if they are popping out of their sockets. She leans forward on her elbows. "At the dorm?"

"No. At Thompson's apartment," I blurt out, preparing myself for an outburst from her side. "Clay invited me to go there with him."

"Wow. You had much more fun than me last night. Playing UNO with my six-year-old cousin was boring."

"Damn, I'm sad I didn't see Cameron." I set my mug on the table. "Does he still have plans to marry me?"

"He does, but now you have competition. Her name is Anna, and she's the princess of Arendelle. You can blame it on his sister. She showed him *Frozen* two weeks ago."

"Nah, he's still too young for me. I prefer older guys," I say, and then I surprise her with my next question. "What do you think about Clay?"

Layla blinks, then huddles more comfortably on her chair and peers at me. "Clay is handsome, and very funny. I feel good around him. Plus, he has always been nice and understanding to me. Why?"

"We kinda decided to be friends." I flash her a small smile, waiting for her reaction.

"He doesn't know what he's signing up for. You're a nightmare." She chortles loudly, almost spitting her coffee all over the table. "Though maybe not. Colton Thompson has been his best friend since elementary school, so I bet Clay knows how to deal with annoying people."

One mention of him is all it takes for my skin to flame up. Dammit, I want control over my body back. I will exhaust myself with this pent-up frustration if it keeps happening so often. Exhausted Ava makes horrible decisions, like going to the ice-rink with her boyfriend when he—

"How was Thompson?" Hearing her question, I suck in a breath and grasp my mug tightly in my hands. It's not the time or the place for memories, especially the ones I'm hoping to forget. After I gulp down the last of my drink, I force a smile onto my lips but instantly drop it. I'm too worn out to pretend.

"I think I like him," I mumble quietly. Layla's gaze sweeps over my face, the wrinkle between her eyebrows becoming deeper. I want to hide what already happened between Thompson and me. Yet I want her to know the truth about my attraction to him. It's only fair.

The longer she keeps silent, the stronger my fear of losing my shit becomes. Why is she so calm? Wait, why is she smiling?

"I should have guessed that," my best friend singsongs. "The dude is exactly your type: a walking disaster, causing an emergency the second you see him."

"He's an asshole," I admit, crossing my arms over my chest. "But he's a gorgeous asshole."

"Do you think he likes you?"

"Maybe, maybe not. It's hard to tell." There is nothing hard about this question. Thompson likes me, while I'm not sure it's the same for me. I'm attracted to him, and the chemistry between us is definitely something else, but it's not enough to make any other assumptions. It's not easy for me to fall in love with just anyone. Especially with a guy who turned my life into a living hell and didn't even say he was sorry. And I let him finger me. I'm an idiot.

Layla downs her drink and sets the empty mug on the table. "All I'm going to say is be careful; he doesn't date anyone."

"Well, I'm not interested in a relationship either," I retort, and we smile at each other.

LATER THIS EVENING, I'm in my dorm and finally done with my essay. Jordan is watching something on her laptop, ignoring my presence, just like I do to her. I change my clothes and climb into bed, grabbing my phone from my blanket. I unlock the screen and open the only unread message I have. A cheeky smile plays on my lips as I read it. I quickly save his phone number, send him my response, turn off the sound, and toss my phone on the bedside table. This guy has no idea what's going to hit him, and that makes everything a thousand times more exciting.

Chapter 22

The Real Me

COLTON

"Dude, you look weird." I shoot a glance in Clay's direction. What the hell does he want? "Before practice, you were checking your phone almost every fifteen minutes. Now you're doing it again, and the more you do it, the angrier you look."

"I'm frustrated." And horny, but I keep that bit to myself.

Clay furrows his brow, eyeing me suspiciously. "About what?"

"About..." I grab my bag from the bench and drape it over my shoulder. "A lot of things."

Clay blinks and immediately snorts. "Such a mysterious asshole."

"Shut the fuck up," I mumble, edging to the door of the locker room and nodding to the guys as I go.

All my muscles are sore because practice was shit. We did drill after drill, focusing on puck protection and maintaining possession skills. It ended with Coach yelling at all of us for being useless pricks. Not that we didn't deserve it. Being a bunch of cocky morons, we let our latest wins cloud our minds, feeling as if we already won the cup. No matter what, we should always keep our eyes on the prize and not let confidence control our actions. The main thing we all need on the ice rink is a cool head and an indisputable desire to win. Nothing else.

"What are you planning to do?" Clay chimes in, interrupting my thoughts. He follows me down the hallway, and I don't even need to ask. He's sure I'm giving him a ride.

"Need to finish my essay, and then I'm going to sit on my couch and do nothing."

"Boring," he mocks, and I show him my middle finger. "It's our last year, Colt. We need to have fun."

"I think we've had our share of fun already, starting with freshman year. Don't you think?"

"Of course not. We're fucking young, and before we graduate, we should enjoy our youth, do—"

"Clay, you have no idea how much I want to be signed by the California Thunders once I'm out of this place. I don't want to risk my chances again."

"You were their first-round pick, and your game has only gotten better with time. Hanging out with your friends, going to parties, hooking up with girls..."

And I'm not listening to him anymore. Her image pops up in my mind, and my skin instantly feels hot. My palms still remember her soft skin under my touch, how fucking perfect her tits felt in my hands, and how sweet she tasted. Why didn't she answer my text? Is she going to avoid me again?

"Thompson."

I wheel my head toward him and pinch my brows together. A stupid smirk plays on his lips as he looks me up and down. "What?"

"You weren't listening," he states mockingly as we trudge to the parking lot.

"Kinda got lost in my thoughts." Or more like memories. Vivid and fucking real—I even feel her scent all over me. As if she's here with me. I'm under her spell, so much even my head is spinning. For the first time in my life, I have no idea what to do with myself, because I'm afraid to ruin everything. "What did you say?"

"Moore is throwing a party in two weeks," Clay says. "It's his birthday, and he expects all of us to be there."

"Not interested." I unlock my car and toss my bag into the backseat. "As soon as he mentioned it would be at his house, I knew I wouldn't go."

"It'll be after our home game on Saturday," he presses, putting his bag into the backseat too. "If you skip, it'll look weird."

"Since when do I worry about other people's opinions?" I scoff as we climb inside my car. "It's not a secret I don't like him. He knows it too."

"Isn't that exactly what Coach said? A healthy relationship between team members is as important as our behavior on the ice. Even Benson is going, and you know they were pretty hostile with each other because of Ava."

Ava. Ava. Ava. She's fucking everywhere and nowhere at the same time. She's definitely not within my reach.

"Benson is free to do whatever he wants, even being friendly with that asswipe. I can't think of anything that would change my mind about this party."

"I know exactly what would change your mind," he says, and I focus on him with a raised brow. "Layla is always at the parties if her brother is, and that means Ava will be there too."

"And what?" My heart pounds rapidly, and my palms get sweaty.

"I saw how you looked at her yesterday." Clay points his finger at me. "You like her. Don't deny it."

"I was being friendly, nothing else." I try to play it cool. Cracking a fake smile, I stop my car near his dorm. "Plus, I can admit she's gorgeous and it's hard not to pay attention to her."

"First, Thompson, you suck. Second, next time the girl you like hooks up with another guy because you were a damn coward and couldn't make a move on her, don't take it out on her. That's a hundred percent on you." My jaw drops. What the actual fuck?

"Rodgers, get your fucking ass out of my car." I shoot daggers at him as he opens the door and jumps outside.

Clay takes his bag from the backseat, slams the door, and then comes back to the passenger side. Our gazes lock, and he shakes his head. As if he's disappointed in me. Is he serious? "Moore hasn't given up, and he's running out of time, Colt. Do you want him to win the bet and hook up with her at his party?"

"The bet is fucking stupid." I state, remembering the uneasiness that spread through my veins when I broke Moore and Rodgers hands when they made the bet. But I don't want Clay to know how I feel about all that. So I do what I do best to keep people away from me: I turn this situation around. "Do you think she'll want to be your friend if she knows you made a bet on her?"

"Colt, you're a predictable asshole." He closes the car door, spins around, and storms inside the dorm.

I don't move for the next ten minutes. I rap my fingers on the steering wheel as my thoughts go in circles, each one stupider than the next. Her radio silence is affecting me in the worst way possible. What if she keeps ignoring me? What if what happened at my place was just a moment of weakness? Her being a bit drunk? My head hurts, and I start the engine. Hoping to take my mind off these thoughts, I drive aimlessly till after nine p.m.

I walk out of my shower, dry my hair with my towel, and then just stare at myself in the mirror. When did my life turn into a fucked-up circus, one I have trouble navigating? I continue to push everyone away, not allowing myself to open up to even my closest friends. I have no idea how to accept when I'm wrong; I always turn things around and put the blame on others. The walls I have built around myself are high thanks to my dear father, who always sees me as his heir and never his son. And anyway, because of Helen's manipulations, my walls are almost unreachable.

Did I think Helen would wreck my life when I met her in my father's office three years ago? Never. She was his new secretary, a sexy twenty-four-year-old with big boobs and a round ass. I wanted to fuck her, and she was more than happy to indulge my games. I thought I was playing her, only to later realize she was playing me. Damaging in the process the only person I've ever loved: my mom.

My phone buzzes, ripping me out of my thoughts. I grasp the countertop with my fingertips to steady myself. My forehead is sweaty, and my damp hair sticks to it. It's hard to breathe, and my heart is ready to jump out of my chest. Fucking rabbit hole. I hate myself for letting these memories back into my mind. I hate everything that woman represents. She wasn't worth even a minute of my time.

I grab my phone, unlock it, and realize I don't see anything. My vision is blurry, and I can't even put letters into words. A fury whirls inside my chest, darkening my emotions. I'm nothing more than a tangle of anger, hate, and bitterness. Do I think anyone will want to be close to me if they see the real me? I'm fucking sure not even Clay would stay. No one. Especially not Ava.

Putting my phone back on the counter, I turn around and stride to my bedroom. I need to get myself together, and the only solution I have is going back to the ice rink. I can always practice getting the puck to the net, or just do rounds on the ice. Hockey is my cure, and I can't imagine my life without it. It has healed me so many times, and one thought about not playing anymore brings me down a peg or two. It's my dream, and I won't give up until I make it a reality. Nothing can stop me.

In my car, I finally take my phone in my hands. I sent her a message around two p.m., and I got an answer at ten tonight. She knows how to rile me up without even trying.

ME:

What else do enemies make better?

HONEY:

To answer your question, we need to test the theory first. Do enemies really make the best lovers, or is that just a myth? Your kisses definitely made it to my list.

I break into laughter, and I can't stop for a good five minutes. This girl is a fucking hurricane, and I'm right in the middle of it. In all honesty, I wouldn't want to be anywhere else.

Chapter 23

Checkmate

AVA

"What is my favorite friend doing?" Clay's voice rings in my ear before he slumps down beside me and drapes his arm over my shoulder.

I've been sitting on a bench in the quiet of the main hallway for almost an hour already, enjoying the peaceful atmosphere and waiting for Layla. We've made plans to go shopping once her classes end.

"Reading." I point at the book, sneaking a glance in his direction. His yellowish-green eyes are full of mischief as he reaches over and grabs it from my lap.

"And what are you reading?" he mocks while I wait for his reaction. The more he reads, the wider his eyes become. I bite the inside of my bottom lip, trying to stifle my smile. I want to laugh so bad. "What is this?"

"A story about a girl falling in love with her stepbrother." Clay's face is long, his gaze heated. I snatch my book away from him and arch my eyebrow. "Boo, you should have told me you've never seen a book before. I would have given you a few of my favorites."

"I have never seen sex in books—"

"Aw, Clay, you're literally ruining my image of you. I thought you weren't judgmental." I pout, enjoying his stunned expression.

He finally clears his throat, and a lopsided grin blossoms on his face. Leaning closer, he inches to my ear. "You didn't let me finish. I have never seen sex in books before, but now? I definitely need to borrow one or two. For research purposes."

"Of course." I snort. "Asking for a friend, right?"

"Something like that." He guffaws, standing up. "God, how am I supposed to go to practice now?"

"Cold shower might help," I suggest, and he instantly narrows his eyes. "Or jerking off. Or maybe a quickie."

"Considering the books you read, I'm not surprised you have such a filthy mouth." Clay falls quiet, zoning out and staring off into the distance. Then he blinks and focuses his gaze on me. "Does Layla like these books too?"

"Why?" I sip my iced coffee.

"Just curious." He bends down and grabs his bag from the floor. "Wanna come to practice with me? It might be a lot of fun. People love watching."

I flash him a smile and take my book in my hands. "I'll pass. I want to finish this story before I go shopping with my best friend."

"Now that I think about it, you always stay away from the ice rink." I hold his gaze, curious to know what he's going to say next. "Are you avoiding someone?"

"Why would I be avoiding anyone?" I chortle. "It has nothing to do with people. I just don't have very pleasant memories of ice rinks. Home games are the only ones I go to, and that's only if I can stay as far as possible from the ice. So..."

"Not going to tell me more?"

"Nope. There is nothing to talk about." I lift my book and open it again. "And you're too nosy."

"Ouch, my poor heart." he whines, pressing his hand to his chest and pinching his brows together. "You hurt my feelings, friend."

"Sorry, Clay." I won't talk about it because I don't want to give the accident power over my life. Again. It happened; I healed. "Aren't you going to be late?"

He takes his phone out of his pocket, glances at the screen, and curses. "Shit. You're right." He threads his fingers through his hair. "I wanted to talk to you about something, and your book kinda sidetracked me. Dammit."

"What is it?"

"Colt made me realize something, and I think you should know—"

"Colt?" My mouth suddenly feels dry, and I hook one leg over the other. I haven't seen Thompson in two days; I've only been texting with him from time to time. I'll be damned if I don't enjoy it. Teasing him feels exhilarating, building the anticipation and making him lose his mind. I have no idea what will happen when he gets me all alone like he wants, but I honestly can't wait.

"Yeah, I did something, and he pointed out how stupid it was." Clay licks his lips, shifting his weight nervously from one leg to the other. "Moore and I—"

A door slams with a bang, making us both turn our heads. Layla freezes in her tracks, standing with her backpack pressed to her chest. I arch my eyebrow, looking her over. Did she run to get here? She heaves a sigh and edges in our direction, moving her hips as slowly as possible. Putting on a show for a guy she doesn't like? I think I need to have a word with her. Setting her up with Clay would be awesome.

"Hey, Clay." Layla grins, lowering herself onto the bench next to me and gazing up at him.

"Hey, Layla," he murmurs, raking his gaze over her face and down to her cleavage. Why does he need to be so obvious? My best friend needs a little challenge. Otherwise, he will be just another Trey, a guy she has sex or goes on a date with if she's feeling lonely. He needs schooling, because as of now, he's hopeless.

"Shouldn't you be at practice?" A playful smirk tugs at the corners of her mouth.

"Fuck. Coach is going to kill me," he babbles, taking a step back. "It was nice to see you, Layla." He shoots me a quick look. "And we need to talk, Ava. It's important."

"You have my number, Clay. Just call me."

He nods and takes off, running in the direction of the ice rink. Layla and I watch him without saying anything. I haven't known Clay for long, but I didn't like the serious look on his face. What about him and Moore is so important? And what does it have to do with Colt?

"Do you think he likes me?" Layla asks, and I slowly turn my head toward her. She still has her eyes glued to Clay's figure in the distance.

If I truly want him to have a chance with her, there is no way in hell I'll tell her what he said. "Yes, I think he likes you."

"Hmm, that could be entertaining." Layla grabs my iced coffee and takes a sip, grimacing at once. "Ew, that's disgusting."

"And that's why you shouldn't have touched it." I steal my coffee back, gulping it down right in front of her. Oh my fucking God. *Ouch, brain freeze.*

Layla observes me in amusement. "You're such a brat, bestie."

"Shut up." I close my eyes hard, gritting my teeth. I need to focus my attention on something, anything. "Why do you look like you ran a marathon to get here?"

"Because I did." She confirms, still giggling. "I thought I was late."

"You were. You always are." I hide my book in my backpack and stand up, hovering over her. "Come on. We still need to drop off our things at the dorm before we go shopping. What do you want to get, by the way?"

"Dunno. Maybe a new tee or a hoodie." She lifts her shoulder in a shrug, joining me as we stroll to the exit. "You?"

"I want a new book, and new...lingerie." I quietly mumble the last part.

My best friend halts in her tracks. "Are you going to see Colton?"

"What does that have to do with him?" I brush her off, but my neck feels hot. I shouldn't have said anything. I won't hear the end of it now for sure.

"Aw, bitch, you're blushing." Layla muses, hauling me to her side and squeezing me tight. "Can I read his messages? Pretty please?"

"Absolutely not." I wriggle to free myself from her grip. "You wouldn't have known about his messages at all if you didn't sneak up on me yesterday."

"Can you blame me? You were smiling like an idiot while typing something on your phone. Of course I wanted to know who you were texting with." She elbows me in the ribs, cackling loudly. "When *it* happens, I want to know everything. And I'm not taking no for an answer."

I shake my head as we walk out of the building. She's impossible, but it's exactly why I love her so much. She's my favorite.

I'm standing in front of a mirror, looking at my reflection. This lightly lined cotton triangle bralette fits perfectly, making my boobs rounder. I spent at least fifteen minutes just picking the right color. Layla grabbed the blue and handed it to me without saying anything. It looks great, but at the same time, it's super simple. Do I want him to see me in this? For the first time?

I close my eyes, inhaling deeply. What has gotten into me? I don't even like him that much. Everything he represents hits too close to home, reminding me of Jefferson. A bad boy. *Check*. A hockey player. *Check*. Assholeish behavior. *Check*. But Colt is deeper. He has so many layers to him, and even glimpses of what I saw at his place intrigue me.

"Ava?" Layla's head pokes into the changing room. Her eyes roam over my body. "I thought you were dead. What's taking you so long?"

"Isn't it too simple?"

My best friend tsks, stepping inside and standing behind me. She catches my gaze in the reflection and slowly wraps her arm around my waist. "You look beautiful. No matter what you're wearing." I smile at her, covering her palm on my belly with my own. "You have plenty of sexy lingerie, from what I remember. Lacy, sultry, slutty. This one is sporty, but also effortless. It gives off the vibe of your confidence. It proves you don't need anything revealing to look like a real queen. Exactly what you are."

My eyes water, and I spin and wind my hands around her neck. "I fucking love you, Layla. So much."

"I love you too, Mason." She clears her throat. "I hope you're not expecting something more? Our first kiss was the only one I can tolerate with you."

I push her away, smiling from ear to ear. "Weren't you the one who wanted to practice before your date with Will?"

"I told you to never mention Will again." She points her finger at me, eyes narrowed to slits. Suddenly, her jaw drops, and she gapes at me in silence. I frown, trying to figure out her weird reaction. What does she have in mind? She dives to my stuff, grabs my phone, and pushes it into my palm.

"What?"

"Send him a photo." Layla beams at me, looking all excited.

"No. That's stupid." I shake my head, remembering my talk with him in the restroom. How would that make me any different than Jordan? The fact that he likes me?

"It's not stupid." She steps closer, inching to look me in the eyes. "The guy wants to see you, but you'd rather taunt him. Didn't I get that from your messages?"

"Maybe." I'm not ready to admit that, deep down, I like her idea.

"Then send it. We'll see what Colton Thompson is capable of when he wants something." She pinches my cheek between her fingers. "Do it, Ava."

"I hate you," I hiss, sounding totally unconvincing.

I strike a pose, trying to find a better angle. Then I finally get the shot and stare at my screen. It's just my boobs, a bit of my abs, and my belly-button piercing. *It's like you're in your bikini.* God, I hope I won't regret this.

ME:

About to buy something nice. On a scale from one to five, how much do you like it?

As soon as I hit send, I lock my screen, turn off the sound, and hide my phone in my purse. "Happy?"

"Me?" Layla's face lights up with a devilish smile. "You should ask Thompson."

"Why am I friends with you?" I shake my head, shooing her out of the changing room. I quickly change my clothes, and when I'm about to leave, I decide to check my phone. Not that I expect anything, since he has practice, but he surprises me.

CT:

a hundred.

And I can't stop myself from smiling. Damn him.

I came to the library this afternoon to finish my homework for my mass media course since I still need to add references. The more I study, the more I'm sure I chose the right path. I don't want to be an influencer, but I definitely wouldn't be opposed to working at a media company, helping celebrities and companies with their social media presence, preparing PR campaigns, and creating content. The last part is my favorite. I have my own bookish account on Instagram where I post reviews and aesthetics I make for every book I read and love. My account is still growing, and so far, I have more than one thousand followers. My goal is to reach at least two thousand by the end of this year. We'll see if I'm successful, if I have enough time for my book-boyfriends.

"What are you doing?"

A horde of butterflies takes flight, doing somersaults in my belly. I slowly turn my head and meet Colton's enigmatic gaze. His eyes are deep brown with gold irises. I'm drowning, trying to reach the shore, but no matter where I look, I only see him.

"Ava?"

Who allowed him to sound so hot? Deep and husky. Like pure sex. Fuck. I forbid myself from sweeping my gaze over his body because that will be my annihilation. Keeping my eyes on his face, I force a smile. "I certainly know what I'm *not* doing."

How did he find me? Did he ask Layla? He couldn't have followed me; I've been at the library for two hours already.

Colton smirks and plops himself down on the chair next to me. "You're not talking to me, am I right?"

"You're a smart boy," I say, looking away and starting to type again. He doesn't say anything, just bends down and takes a book from his backpack. I watch him with my side vision, typing slower and slower by the minute. Thompson sets his book on the table, places his elbow on his knee, and puts his chin on his hand.

I scan the room, sighing in relief once I see how deserted the library is. Not that I'm not used to it. It's almost always like this, and it's one of the reasons why I love coming here to study. Except for me and Colton in the farthest corner, there are only four people on this floor. Two guys are sitting close to the entrance with their noses buried in books, one girl is lying on a beanbag chair with a laptop on her lap and a book in her hand, and then there is Ms. Lewis. The woman is the most apathetic librarian I have ever seen. She doesn't pay much attention to what the students are doing as long as they keep quiet so she can enjoy reading her romance novels. After I saw her with *Den of Vipers*, I don't think there is anything about her that would surprise me.

My hand hovers over my keyboard, and my fingers refuse to move. I suck in a breath and leisurely lower my gaze. Colt's palm rests on my knee, and he slowly drags it up, under my skirt. He inches to my ear; his hot breath on my skin makes my nipples harden instantly.

"On a scale from one to five, how quiet do you think you'll be able to keep?"

And he fucking won. *Checkmate, Ava.*

Chapter 24

Library and O's

COLTON

"What are you planning to do tonight?" Clay watches me intently as I swallow my burger, washing it down with Pepsi. I keep silent, holding his gaze without seeing him.

What am I planning to do? Fuck Ava into oblivion if I can finally corner her somewhere on campus. The girl might be a fucking spy, because she navigates through this place without letting me get my hands on her. Wherever I go, she either already left or wasn't there at all. Of course, I could wait for her near her dorm, or even in her room, but I'm sure as hell she wants to keep this a secret. Especially from her roommate.

"Colt?" I blink, refocusing my attention on my best friend.

"Have you seen Ava?"

He breaks into a smile, eyes full of amusement. He knows I like her, and that I can actually use his help. I don't want to put on another act. "I did."

Do I need to pull every word out of him? "When?"

"Yesterday." Clay sips his drink, enjoying the moment. "Before practice. She was waiting for Layla. They were going shopping."

Shopping, my ass. When I opened her message and saw her boobs in some sporty bra with a glimpse of her abs and yet another piercing, I cursed like a madman. There is something about her that makes me lose my head. It's like a switch flips, and my mind shifts to only one thing: being completely obsessed with Ava. I desperately want to have her, not only in my bed, but in my life, and that's why this shit scares me to death. What if she never feels the way I do? So far, it's been all fun and games for her, and while I'm happy to play along for now, I know myself. With my issues, I need to know she likes me and feels the same way I do. I just need it.

"Do you know where I can find her?" I lick my lips and grasp my drink in my hand. My mouth is as dry as the Sahara desert, so I chug my Pepsi and set it back on the table.

"She loves to read, and she's always at the library. From what I know, she prefers to study there rather than in her dorm room."

"The library? I definitely didn't expect that answer."

"Man, you have no idea what a wild little thing she is." His head falls back with laughter. "Yesterday I grabbed her book to see what she was reading, and it was a sex scene. It was about some dude fucking his step-sister for the first time."

Actually, that part doesn't surprise me. She has a very dirty mind, and a filthy mouth. It's something I gathered about her myself. But the library? A good girl with a wild side, that's who she is. No doubt about it. "Stepsister, huh? That's why you were late to practice?"

"Shut it, dude." Clay instantly becomes defensive, folding his arms across his chest. "It was enough she mocked me, no need to rub it in. Plus, I wanted to talk to her about the stupid bet I made with Moore, and her book screwed up my mind, so I forgot about it. She told me to call her, but I don't want to tell her that on the phone."

"You don't talk about stuff like that on the phone," I point out. "You will need to apologize."

"Exactly." He looks around, twisting his lips. "I hope he doesn't try anything with her, you know? I don't mind wearing a dress and makeup if I lose fairly, but that's not how Hudson operates. Especially when she keeps telling him off over and over again."

"He can always try," I hiss, balling my fists and clenching my jaw. If that fucker touches her, I will destroy him.

"Wow." Blinking, I meet my best friend's gaze, noticing a little twinkle behind his irises. Why is he staring at me like that? "You really like her, don't you?"

"Maybe."

"I knew it. Man, I want to hug you right now," Clay murmurs.

"Fuck off," I scoff, standing up. "See you tomorrow."

He puts his hand on his belly, calming down and staring at me with growing interest. Clay is a nosy asshole, but the truth is, he's the most loyal person I have ever met, and I know I can trust him.

"Are you going to the library?"

"Maybe." I smirk, snatching my backpack. I haven't been in the library for two years, but to finally get to see her? I would go to the end of the fucking earth.

"I still need to talk to her," he says lazily. "Maybe I should come with you."

"Don't you fucking dare," I threaten him with a smile on my face, and he laughs again. "Bye, Clay."

"Bye, *Colt-on*." Clay moans, and I show him two middle fingers. Moron.

I turn around and amble to the hallway. I quickly go to the bathroom, wash my hands, and pop some gum into my mouth. Running my fingers through my hair, I heave a sigh and head to the library. It's highly possible she won't be there, and even if I text her to ask about her whereabouts, she'd never tell me. I don't have any other choice but to go in blindly and hope for the best.

Stepping into the library, I look around until I notice her. *Gotcha.* A smile blooms on my lips as I quietly stroll in her direction. She sits with her back to me, typing on her laptop. She's completely oblivious to my presence, while my body comes to life at just the sight of her.

I'm whipped, aren't I?

I stop behind her, hovering over her and bending to her ear. "What are you doing?" I ask, noticing how she shivers. She slowly turns her head and meets my gaze. Her lips part, and she looks at me as if she's in daze. "Ava?"

She blinks, allowing her mouth to curl into a smile. "I certainly know what I'm *not* doing." With how she keeps her eyes glued to my face, I know she's controlling herself. And that's something I want to fix. I want her to lose control and let her guard down. For me.

Smirking, I move a chair next to her and plop myself down on it. "You're not talking to me, am I right?"

"You're a smart boy." Ava averts her gaze and continues typing on her laptop. It's just a pretense; she's watching me. I take my book out of my backpack, put it on the table, place my elbow on my knee, and lower my chin onto my hand, opening the book with my other hand. I don't care whether others think I'm studying or not, but I will put on this act for her.

I watch as she turns her head to the right, observing what people in the library are doing. She is still trying to type, and that's adorable. So much determination. I drag my gaze down her body, taking in all the details. Her red tee sculpts her chest like a second skin, making her boobs look big and her waist narrow, and a black skirt ends way higher than her knees.

I inch slightly toward her and put my hand on her knee. Ava stirs. Her typing becomes slower, and she looks down. As I lean into her ear, I slide my palm up under her skirt. "On a scale from one to five, how quiet do you think you'll be able to keep?"

Ava whips her head to me. "A hundred," she rumbles.

Our eyes lock, and neither of us looks away. My palm reaches her panties, and my finger brushes her clit through the fabric. Once, twice, circling with calculated slowness. She slides further down in her chair, spreading her legs apart a bit more and giving me a better angle. I want her to lose her mind, but so far it looks like it will be me doing that all over again. She holds my gaze, stubbornly staying quiet.

I smirk, shifting and leaning my elbow on the table. Facing her, I slide my fingers down, feeling her wetness. She's fucking dripping. *Jesus Christ.* My breath becomes heavy and shallow. My cock is hard, straining against my jeans.

Adding more pressure, I massage her clit through her panties, eyes glued to her face. Her eyebrows knit together, and she bites her bottom lip. A blush grows on her cheeks, and a few wild locks fall out of her bun. It's getting harder and harder for her to keep quiet, and I'm loving it.

I move her panties aside. My finger dips into her core, sliding inside her without any problem. Her eyes grow wide, and she swallows with difficulty. "Why did you stop typing, Ava? Is there a problem?" I ask, taking my finger out of her. She shoots me a glare but keeps silent. "Is there anything I can do to help you?"

Ava shakes her head, closing her eyes. I press my thumb to her swollen clit, massaging it. She pants; her hips rotate with the movements of my finger. She's desperate in her desire to come, and I decide to indulge her, making her break her promise at the same time. Her breath quickens, and her palm absentmindedly flies to her breast. She squeezes it, shutting her eyes harder, and finally lets out a quiet moan. It's more like a whimper, but I'll take it nonetheless.

I double down in my efforts, and she shudders in no time, exhaling loudly with her orgasm. Her legs shake, and I'm so damn proud of myself.

Her eyelashes flutter, and she timidly opens her eyes, meeting my gaze. I fix her panties, move away, and just admire the flushed look on her face. Her bun is messy, her cheeks are red, and her chest is rising and falling rapidly. She rakes her eyes over me. I have no idea what she sees, but she heaves a sigh, runs her palms over her skirt, and sits up straight.

"I think that was a two," I say, laughter in my voice. "From one to five, you keeping quiet was a two. Not a hundred for sure."

"I hate you," she hisses, but it's so unconvincing that I laugh again. *No, baby, you don't.*

Gathering my things, I hide my book in my backpack and drape it over my shoulder, rising to my feet. It's funny how her eyes instantly drop to my crotch. Ava licks her lips, eyeing the bulge in my pants. I want to tell her that she's the only one who has this effect on me, the only one who gets me off like I did when I was younger, a horny teen. I want to tell her so many things, but I can't. It's not the place and not the time. At least for now.

"Are you...leaving?" she asks, her voice trembling.

I lower my head, boring my gaze into hers. "Even though I want to stay and fuck you, bend you over this table, I need to go. I have some errands to run."

She twists her lips, looking angry. With me? Or herself? I frown, watching her in confusion. I played my part to a tee, but what if it was too much?

"Okay."

Okay? My dignity just waved me goodbye. Disappearing into the midst of Ava's chaos. "How about you come with me? I need to drop off my stuff in the locker room."

"To the ice rink? No, thanks," she snaps at me, grasping her laptop in her hands and pulling it toward her. Her attention is on the screen, as if I no longer exist.

I thread my fingers through my hair and take a step back. "See you around then."

"Uh-huh." Fucking perfect. *What did the girl you like say to you after you gave her an orgasm? Uh-huh.*

Veering around the table, I edge to the door. My shoulders are squared, and my head is high, but my heart is heavy, so each step takes a toll on me. It's hard to breathe, and I almost suffocate. For the first time in my entire life, I met a girl who turned my world upside down. Fucked up my head and made me brainless. I feel alive around her and empty when she's not with me. Her behavior is confusing and irritating, and it is totally driving me crazy.

The door slams behind me, and I trudge to the ice rink. Ten minutes, and I will be free to go home and throw myself a pity party. I definitely need it.

Just as I'm about to enter the locker room, I feel my phone vibrate. I take it out of my pocket, unlock the screen, and take a deep breath. She sent me three new messages, and I'm not so sure I want to know what they say. Fuck it.

HONEY:

I kinda didn't expect you to leave.

HONEY:

But sorry for snapping at you. You didn't deserve it. The ice rink and I aren't friends anymore, so...

A lopsided grin forms on my face, and it feels as if I can breathe freely again. Her final message makes me laugh so hard, I have to press my forehead to the wall to steady myself.

HONEY:

Thank you for the O in the library. Not sure whether to be mad at you or feel grateful. How about going to the movies tomorrow? It's dark, and there's more privacy.

I need to calm down before I reply. There is no way in hell I will fuck her for the first time anywhere except my bed. It's absolutely out of the question, and I won't change my mind no matter what.

ME:

I'll buy tickets and send you the details. And we're not fucking in the movie theater.

HONEY:

Sounds like a challenge.

Chapter 25

It's Not a Date

AVA

What the hell is wrong with me? What was I thinking? Letting him finger me—again—and where? In the fucking library. I totally lost my mind allowing Colton to do whatever he wants with my pussy. And he wants fucking everything.

"Ava?" I turn my head, meeting Grace's gaze. She smiles at me, arching her brow quizzically. "What are you thinking about?"

"Nothing. School stuff."

Liar. Thompson sent me a message a few minutes ago, and since then that's all that's been on my mind. I want to find a way to snap out of it. Desperately. Hopefully going to the movies with him will help. I need to find reasons to keep my distance, and if I get to know him better, that might just happen.

"Really?" Layla chimes in with a mischievous glint in her eyes. "What are your plans tonight?"

"Staying in, doing nothing," I lie.

My best friend smirks but doesn't push for more. She shifts her attention to her roommate. "What about you?"

"Kaleb and I are going on a date. He wants to go to the movies, but I'm not really up for it." Movies? I don't want anyone to see me with Colton. It's absolutely out of the question.

"What does he want to see?" I ask innocently, feigning interest. The second she says the movie title, I start sweating. *Fuck.* That's the exact same movie we're going to see.

"He said he wants to have dinner together, and then go to the movies since it isn't playing until later...but I don't know."

"It's supposed to be an awesome movie," Layla comments, biting her banana and continuing with her mouth full. "Have you seen the cast?"

"We have seen Layla Benson being a hamster." I frown, narrowing my eyes. She snorts and pokes her tongue out at me. I avert my gaze and focus on Grace. "The cast is great, but I'm not sure about the story. It might be something like *Star Wars*, and I'm not a fan."

Please say no.

"Really? That's the most iconic series ever." Grace beams. "You actually made it a hundred times easier, Ava. We're definitely going to the movies."

"Yay." I laugh it off, trying to figure out what I can wear so she won't recognize me. But the more important question, the one I should be asking: what is he going to wear so no one recognizes him? Colton Thompson is pretty well-known, and him showing up with any girl at the movies will cause a scene.

"Mason, as two hot and single bitches, why don't we go somewhere together?" Layla playfully cocks her eyebrow at me.

"Actually." I grab my things and dump them into my backpack. "I have a date."

"What?" Layla stares at me wide-eyed, shock etched on her face.

"With who?" Grace's expression mirrors Layla's, but she raises her voice, literally screaming like a banshee.

I roll my eyes. "You're so gullible." I stand up from the chair and look at them. "I've got an advance reader copy of a book I've been dying to read, so tonight I have a date with my new book boyfriend," I lie nonchalantly, doing my best to keep my smile at bay.

"When I die from boredom, I'll come back as a fucking ghost and haunt your lazy ass, Mason. Mark my words." Layla points her finger at me, then stands up as well and stretches. "Maybe this is a sign I should call Trey?"

"No." Grace and I exclaim at the same time. Then we timidly smile at each other. We aren't friends, and we're not really close, but we both want what is best for Layla.

"Why not?" my best friend whines, gaping at us in confusion, her big eyes almost popping out of their sockets.

"Because you don't like him, and he has a girlfriend, duh." I take my leather jacket from the back of the chair and put it on.

"And the last time you saw him, before your breakup, you spent an hour arguing instead of watching a movie together." Grace zips her jacket and takes her books from the table, pressing them to her chest. "You never promised him anything. You weren't official, but he acted like an ass. A jealous ass."

"You two are no fun." Layla takes her backpack from the floor. I get to go home because I'm done with class, but she's not. She still has two classes left. "Next party, I'll officially be on the lookout for someone else."

Hopefully it will be Clay. I'll try to help them get together because I think they would be perfect for each other. If I need to, I'll talk to Drake —even though that might be awkward as hell. All my interactions with him recently have ended with him falling quiet. It's like I pluck the electricity out of him and he doesn't have the energy to continue the conversation. Or sometimes he wants to talk, but it's me who isn't interested. Or I'm busy. I don't like it, and I want to fix it. He's my childhood friend. All this tension isn't healthy.

"*We* will be on the lookout," I correct her, wheeling around and heading to the hallway. "I'm just as single as you are."

Layla lines up with me, sneaks a discreet glance at Grace, and then leans into my ear. "Single? Or smitten with Thompson?"

The corners of my mouth tremble; a tiny smile haunts my lips. I shake my head and say nothing as Grace joins us.

"Bye, Ava." She waves at me, then steps closer to Layla and plants a kiss on her cheek. "See you later."

"Bye," I say, watching her turn around and leave Layla and me alone.

"You're going to see Thompson, aren't you?" Layla says, a smug smile on her face. I heave a sigh, twirl around, and make my way to the exit. I'm not talking about it. "You're fucking boring."

"Love you too, bestie." I wave my hand without looking back at her. I do have plans to read, but also? I need to prepare for my date with Thompson.

It's not a date. It's not a date. It's not a date.

I keep repeating this to myself in hopes that I'll believe it, but so far it's not working. I suggested this outing myself because I want to know more about him. I need to find reasons not to like him. To keep him away from me. I don't like to be in debt, and I owe him an orgasm—two actually, but we'll see how it goes. *We're not fucking in the movie theater*, flashes in my head, and I chuckle. It definitely sounds like a challenge.

I notice him from afar, and my eyes roam over his form. Relief washes over me instantly, because he is wearing a pair of black sweat-pants and a hoodie paired with white sneakers. Sporty and comfy, as if he doesn't care what he looks like. I quickly scan the cars parked near the building and notice his Lexus RX.

"Hey." I walk up to him and stop.

Thompson rakes his gaze over my face and down my body. I watch him intently, wanting nothing more but to see his reaction, and he doesn't disappoint. His pupils widen, making his eye color close to black. I always know what I'm doing when it comes to my clothes, and today is no exception. I am wearing a red dress, black tights, and a black leather jacket with black boots. My hair is collected into a high ponytail, and I let a few locks frame my face on purpose. No lipstick, just lip balm and mascara on my eyelashes.

"Hey, Ava." He smirks. "When you said you would be late, I didn't think we were going to miss the first ten minutes of the movie."

"Grace should be here with her boyfriend. I didn't want them to see me with you." I expect him to smile back at me, but he doesn't. He hides his hands in his pockets, at once becoming broody. What's wrong with him?

"Well, let's go then." His voice is dull, and shivers like tiny ants spread across my skin. We saunter inside, and he lets me in first as we proceed to the concession stand.

The girl who works here smiles at us politely. “Can I get something for you?”

“An ice cream,” I mumble, standing on my tiptoes to get a better look. “With M&Ms.”

Colton’s lip twitches, as if he’s trying to fight the urge to smile. Then he averts his gaze and buys two ice creams with M&Ms. We wait in silence, and nervousness finds its way under my skin. Nothing is how I imagined it. How am I supposed to get to know him if he keeps silent and avoids looking at me?

Fuck it. I can take matters into my own hands. “Do you always order ice cream at the movies?”

“Most of the time,” he answers, taking the ice creams from the girl and handing one to me. “Not that I’m a frequent moviegoer. I prefer the comfort of my place.”

Me too. Damn him. “I kinda noticed that.” Our gazes lock as we walk to the theater. “A Netflix lover, and a secret admirer of Disney.”

Thompson laughs curtly, shaking his head. “I have to be in the mood for Disney. It doesn’t happen often, and only under very specific circumstances. While Netflix? Never regretted buying a subscription.”

As I grab the door handle, a question lingers on my tongue. “What is your favorite TV show recently?”

“Why does this sound like an interrogation?”

“Since we’re here, why not get to know each other?” His gaze slides to my mouth, and my heartbeat accelerates. The ice cream in my hand is the only thing that stops my skin from heating up. “So?”

He taps on my nose and leans away. “*You*.”

Me? I blink, and he opens the door to the theater. It takes one second for me to realize he meant one of my most favorite TV shows ever. *Houston, I think we have a problem.* Instead of finding reasons not to like him, I find things that draw me to him. What the hell am I supposed to do with that?

Suddenly, he grabs my hand and drags me inside. I spaced out.

“Sorry,” I whisper as he edges to the back row. We sit down, and I finally sweep my gaze over the place. There are barely twenty people here, and we're pretty far from all of them. It's like he chose these seats on purpose, to have me all to himself.

"For someone who didn't want to be seen in my company, you sure put us on full display," he comments quietly once we settle into our seats.

"Didn't expect *You* to be your favorite TV show," I sass back, taking a spoonful of my ice cream. "Should I be worried?"

"Nah, I'm not a serial killer." He shoves a spoonful into his mouth. "What's your favorite TV show?"

Should I tell him the truth? Is it even a question? "Actually..." I trail off, and he turns his head to look at me.

"*You*?"

I nod, and he chortles, hanging his head low. When he finally calms down and looks at me, a playful smile sprinkles over his lips. "Should *I* be worried?"

"Who knows?" I smirk. "I can easily quote Joe if you want."

"You're that kind of a fan? Knowing the quotes by heart?" He glances at me. "A bit geeky."

"I'm a nerd. I love reading books, annotating them, and saving my favorite moments in highlights. So I quote things I remember from a TV show? It's not a big deal."

"Yeah, Clay told me about the books you read." He doesn't sound judgmental, but he does sound mischievous. "What was the one he saw about? He mentioned sex between stepsiblings."

"Maybe one day I will read you that moment. Aloud." I wink at him, and he cracks another smile. Taking a spoonful of his ice cream, he focuses his attention on the screen, and I do the same. We always have time to talk later.

The movie has been playing for a little while, but it's been hard to focus. I didn't lie to Grace when I said I never liked *Star Wars*, so I can't get into this movie either. Even if the actors are fucking perfect together, it doesn't save me from boredom. I tried to sit upright, then leaned forward, then put my feet on the row in front of me. Nothing has helped, and I'm incredibly annoyed. Unlike Thompson. He's totally immersed in the movie, and he's ignoring everything I do. Or so I think.

His palm on my knee stops my leg from swinging back and forth. I look at him, knitting my eyebrows together. "You don't like the movie?" he asks.

I shake my head no. "Usually I leave and wait for my friends outside, but I'm still here."

"You should have told me." His voice is quiet and soft. "We could have left, gone for a walk, or done anything but be here."

"It's okay." I lick my lips, and his gaze drops to my mouth. "You seemed into it."

Colton shifts in his seat and faces me. He gently cups my cheek, and I part my lips, holding his gaze. My skin is tingling; the pounding of my heart quickens. I inch forward and gently press my lips to his, closing my eyes the second his hot breath envelops me. Our kiss is slow, but for some reason, it takes all my emotions to the next level. I nibble on his bottom lip, and he opens his mouth for me, letting me slip my tongue inside. I shuffle in my seat and press my palm to his chest. Even through his hoodie I can feel his rapid heartbeat. The simple realization of how much my presence affects him overwhelms me. The guy who's had countless hookups wants me, as if I'm the only girl in the world. As if I'm the only one he has eyes for.

The moment I allow myself to think like this, my mind goes overboard. I barely know him. I'm making assumptions. Colton Thompson doesn't date anyone. He doesn't even sleep with anyone more than once. I'm just another hookup, a girl who owes him two orgasms, nothing else. I already made this mistake once, letting myself believe that a guy can change for a girl. They never do. Not when they are still young, anyway. It's all in my fucking head, and I should remember that.

I glide my palm down his chest and to his groin. His dick is hard, and I feel him through his sweatpants. Colton groans into our kiss, and I take it as a sign of approval. I run my fingers up and down, and his hand reaches to my ponytail, tugging on it and making me hiss. His other hand lands on my chest, caressing my boobs. This roughness combined with gentleness is new to me, but I find myself really liking it.

Breaking our kiss, I move my lips down his chin and lower, to his throat. His cologne is woodsy and has notes of ginger. My skin warms up from our closeness, and I suck on his neck, leaving a hickey. His cock becomes thicker under my touch, and my clit pulses. I'm so turned on, I don't even care where we are anymore.

As soon as I press harder on his dick, Colton freezes. He grabs the back of my neck and forces me to look him in the eyes. I gaze at him intently through blurry vision. "I told you, Ava. We aren't going to have sex in the movies."

"And I told you that sounded like a challenge." Why is he so stubborn? He wants it just as much as I want it, so why restrain ourselves? "Let me make you feel good."

"Kissing you feels good," Colt hums huskily, and my breath hitches in my throat.

His gaze is heavy, as if he's looking into my soul. He sees right through me, and it shouldn't be like that. I don't want a committed relationship. Being fuck buddies suits me damn well, and I don't have plans to change my mind. At least not in my freshman year. And not for someone who won't be around after the school year is over.

"Please, let me make you feel good," I whisper, my words scattering over his lips as our eyes lock. I don't do anything, just wait for his decision. I won't take it further if he doesn't want it. "Please, Colton..."

He watches me in silence, his brows knitted together, and then he just shakes his head no. My skin flames up, and I fidget in my seat. His rejection stings, and I scrunch my nose, trying to do anything to keep myself from crying. I take my hands off his lap, turn away from him, and stare straight ahead, not seeing anything. I have no idea what he wants from me, because what I've heard about him contradicts how he is with me.

"Do you want to stay?" he asks me, and I lift a shoulder in a shrug. I don't care.

"Do you?"

"Not really," he mumbles, standing up. "Let's go."

We silently head to the exit, and an unsettling feeling forms in my chest. He is keeping his distance. His hands are hidden in his pockets. He was incredibly affectionate when we walked into the movie theater, and now his posture radiates coldness. Whatever it is, it doesn't matter. This is not a date. He's not my boyfriend, or even my friend. If he wants to part ways, he's free to do just that.

Sashaying out of the movies, I reach up and take down my ponytail. My hair cascades over my shoulders, and I tuck a few strands behind my ears. I keep my head high, watching Thompson with my eyes narrowed.

"Where are we going?" I ask, bracing myself for his answer. Somehow, I'm certain I already know.

"I'll give you a ride to your dorm." He brushes past me and edges to his car. I stay still, frowning more and more with each breath I take. Fucker. Predictable fucker. Nothing else.

"You know, Thompson, I'll walk." With that, I whirl around and stomp away from the movies, making a mental note that he's not doing anything to stop me.

Chapter 26

Nothing Special

COLTON

"Colt, stop being such an ass," Clay snaps at me as I pass him.

There is no need to be a crybaby if your game sucks, loser.

"Stop being a pussy," I hiss, skating away from him, gripping my stick tighter.

It's Tuesday, and with each passing day my mood has worsened. I spent a few hours with Mom on Sunday, and it gave me a short breather. Once I was back in my car, my smile faded away, and the shittiest mood I've ever been in returned. I'm not sure I've smiled even once since fucking Thursday night. Everything became insignificant and frustrating. And I hate it. Hockey is my only salvation. As long as I'm on the ice, that's it.

Our practice is about to end, and so far, it's all good. Coach certainly knew what he was doing when he gave us hell the other day. Everyone is motivated, collected, and devoting a hundred percent of their attention to the game. I'm the same, and my bottled-up anger doesn't hurt. I hit as hard as I can again, sending the puck flying into the net. If anything, my fury is my fuel. All my shots today are powerful and well-paced. I didn't hear a word of scolding from Coach, unlike the rest of the guys.

I'm one of the fastest players on our team. I feel the game. I'm attentive to details, and I don't let myself lose focus for even the slightest moment. I live for hockey; it is my whole existence. My purpose. Something I'm good at, and dear God, how much I need this validation after that disaster with her. Never in my life have I felt so miserable after being with a girl.

"Thompson." I wheel around and focus on Benson. He eyes me with his brows pinched together and his stick lifted, ready to pass the puck to me.

I scan his posture to figure out the angle, nod curtly, and skate to where the puck is going to be. Cutting across the ice, I speed up just in time to see the puck lift into the air and land within my stick's reach. I shoot and watch as it goes into the uppermost part of the net. I lift my fist in the air, content. "And that's where mama keeps the peanut butter, man." I burst out laughing, skating over to Clay. "Don't sulk. It doesn't suit you."

Clay gives me a nasty look and keeps silent, his nostrils flaring in anger. Then he grabs his water bottle and storms away from me. He's such a child sometimes. It's not my fault he let me score so many times today.

I notice guys gathering around Coach, and I join them. Another pep talk. He does one after every practice. This time, there's a bit of praise for our hard work, but he reminds us again to always stay focused and motivated, because otherwise we will lose the game.

I'm barely listening. I look around the arena and notice the cheerleading squad is practicing. All the girls are attractive, and some are even fun to hang out with, but they aren't her. *Congrats, moron, you let your mind go into the loop again.* This is a fucking shit show. I have no idea what I can do to change her mind about me.

"You did great, Thompson." I turn my head toward the voice and lock eyes with Moore. He leans on his stick, and a smug smile illuminates his face.

"Just did my usual," I say, averting my gaze.

"Nah, man, that was not your usual." He laughs, shifting to face me. "You looked like a madman for most of today. I have never seen you so aggravated during practice."

"What's your point?"

"Just observing. Like I always do." Moore edges closer. "Rumor has it you were at the movies last Thursday. With a delicious-looking piece of ass."

"Do you believe all the rumors you hear?" I smirk, not showing even the slightest change of my emotion.

"Not really." He sweeps his eyes over my face. "You don't date anyone, so hearing about you on a date with some chick felt weird. She must be someone special, Thompson, if you decided to break your own rules."

Coach dismisses us, but I don't move. I hate this fucker. If anything, he reminds me of my father—manipulative, believing that his money can buy anything and anyone. I want to prove him wrong.

"I didn't break any rules because I have none." I move closer, standing up to him. We're almost chest to chest. "And it wasn't a date."

"But you were at the movies with a girl, and you never do that." *Shit.* She's fucked me up in the head. I've become brainless. "How about you introduce her to me? You usually don't mind sharing, right? At least, it never was an issue between you and Rodgers."

"What I do doesn't concern you." I take off my helmet, my sweaty hair falling into my eyes. "I tolerate you only for the sake of the team."

"Aw, I love it when you're honest, Thompson," Moore snorts. "It's such a pity you don't want to tell me who she is. It would save me a ton of time, but whatever. I will figure it out myself. I want your special girl too."

I shake my head, leaving him alone as I edge to the locker room.

Hopefully he will back off. I don't want him spying on me. Hudson Moore is the last person on Earth who needs to know about Ava. It would only double his determination to win the bet. The fucking stupid bet she still has no idea about. *Dammit.*

Walking into the locker room, I notice Clay with a towel wrapped around his hips. He's broody and doesn't look at anyone, focusing instead on getting dressed. He goes through phases when he silently hates everyone, including himself. When he's like that, I give him space and don't try to cheer him up.

I take off my gear, quickly hop into the shower, and then put on my clothes. Benson and I are the only two guys in the locker room. We talk about practice, discuss Friday and Saturday's games, and joke. I'm glad things have gone back to normal between us. I like the guy, and being his enemy isn't something I want.

My phone buzzes, and I pick it up from the bench. My father wants to talk. About what this time? I hope it's not another shitty excuse to lure me home.

"Are you leaving?" Benson lingers by the door, and I shake my head no. "Okay. Bye."

I press my phone to my ear. "Hello?"

"Colt, hey." *The fuck?* "It's Helen."

I keep quiet and hear her heave a sigh.

"Can we talk like adults for at least five minutes? It won't take long."

"I was pretty clear with you last time. I don't want to talk to you."

"Oh, I remember." She pauses for a second, clearing her throat. "Yet this is my job, and there are some things I need to do, no matter what I want myself."

Fucking asshole kept her close, and when things calmed down, he brought her back. Promotion, new job title, big paycheck. He gave her everything. At the same time, he ghosted my mother, never paying attention to her needs or her current state. He pays her bills, nothing else.

"I'm calling you from your father's phone because I knew you wouldn't answer if I used my own. It's important."

I zip my bag, grab it from the bench, and drape it over my shoulder. The room suddenly becomes small, as if the walls are closing in on me. My forehead is sweaty, and I thread my fingers through my still-wet hair. "What?"

"Your dad is throwing a big party next month. He will need you there—"

"Not interested." I cut her off, taking an apprehensive step toward the door.

"All your future partners will be there. You need to make acquaintances." I shut my eyes, because listening to her voice brings everything back. All my memories are bubbling to the surface, as if I haven't spent all these months trying to erase them. "You are graduating soon, and if you think it will be easy to just dive into your responsibilities, you're wrong. You need to start now—"

"There's a good chance I'll go pro, Helen," I grit through my teeth. "If that happens, my dad can kiss all his plans about me inheriting his empire goodbye."

"Eric is sure you're going to join him. He has no doubt."

Chuckling to myself, I shake my head. That's the thing about my dad. One second, he assures you he wants you to go pro, but the next he shows you his plans for the next five years, which include your active participation. He's delusional if he thinks I will give up on my dreams. Even if worse comes to worst and the California Thunders don't sign me, I can be traded to another team or become an unrestricted free agent. I will do anything to land myself a contract.

"Well, I don't share the sentiment. As soon as the school year is over, I'll be out of this state."

"Don't bite off more than you can chew, Colton," she fires back, losing her patience. "I will send you the details. Make sure you mark it on your calendar. You *must* be there."

"Only if it's not the same day as a game."

"Don't worry about that. Your father knows your schedule." *I highly doubt that*, I want to add, but I keep the words to myself. I want this call to be over with.

"Anything else?" I put my hand on the doorknob.

"She has grown so much...she misses you."

"Bye, Helen." I end the call and shove my phone into my pocket. I refuse to play her games. Not anymore. Not ever.

I trudge out of the locker room and down the hallway as my thoughts race in a vicious circle. That woman added another pinch of frustration to my anger, making me unmotivated. Your relatives are supposed to be your biggest supporters, but mine knock the air out of my lungs. My father pretends to care about my future as a hockey player, but in reality? He's already planning my involvement in his business because he doesn't believe in me. Sadly, it doesn't even surprise me.

Opening the door, I saunter out of the building and inhale deeply.

Everything is going to be alright. It's just an unfortunate coincidence. Nothing else. I just need to go home and—

I freeze when I realize what I'm staring at. My blood boils, my skin becomes hot, and a vein in my neck pulsates so hard it's deafening. She's here. Ava is here, and not for me. She's here with Benson. They stroll to his car. He is carrying two cups from a local coffee shop, and she has what looks like a box of donuts in her hands. They are going to his place, aren't they?

Storming to the parking lot, I keep my gaze trained on my car. She doesn't exist anymore. She's just like everyone else. Nothing special.

I open my car door, jump inside, toss my bag on the backseat, and start the engine. My whole body is tense, and my hands are trembling. I curse, grip the steering wheel hard, and take off. My eyes meet hers for just a moment as I pass Benson's car. Her lips part, and she frowns. I look crazy, but I don't care. She's no one, and there is no way in hell I'll let myself think about her again.

Chapter 27

Where Is Your Room?

AVA

"I don't know who pissed Thompson off, but he's acting like a damn psychopath for the second game in a row," Kaleb, Grace's boyfriend, chortles out loud, his eyes locked on the ice. I'm sitting with him and Grace, as Layla went to sit with her parents a few rows below us. "But it doesn't matter. We're winning, and that's the most important thing."

"Yeah, I have never seen him so intense and violent," Grace adds, not taking her eyes off the game. "He's gotten into two fights already. Usually he stays away unless it involves the whole team."

I'm curious. If I told them it was me who pissed him off, what would their reaction be? I obviously don't think the world revolves around me, but in this case, I'm certain I'm the reason. I didn't see him for a few days after the movies, but on Tuesday night, the look he gave me said it all. He hates me. Again.

On Friday, I decided to admit a few things to myself. First, even if his rejection at the movies hurt me, I missed texting him. Our exchanges were the highlight of my day, even if I didn't realize it then. Second? No one has ever kissed me the way he did. So I swallowed my pride and sent him a quick message. Just to test the waters. I wished him luck at his games this week and asked how he was. What did I get in return? Nothing. He didn't even read it. *Lovely.*

I let my gaze follow his every move on the ice. Growing up with Drake, hockey has been a part of my life. Layla and I played with him more than once, having too much fun and getting scolded by him. So I know talent when I see it, and Colton Thompson is a great player. He moves effortlessly, and it's constant. I've never seen him stand around on the ice. And don't even get me started on how intelligent he is when it comes to the game. He feels it, as if it's a part of him. He's alive when he's on the ice, and it's so attractive that I have a hard time not watching him.

I tap Grace's knee, and she turns her head. "Yeah?"

"I'll wait for you outside."

"There's only ten minutes left; why don't you stay?" Kaleb asks, earning an eye roll from me.

"Because I don't want to," I retort and instantly cover it with a smile. "See you in the parking lot."

"Sure." Grace nods and focuses on the ice rink. Kaleb's eyes stay glued to me for a moment longer, and then he looks away too.

Slowly, I stand up and move to the exit. The Great Lake Panthers are beating Massachusetts State, and people are excited. They don't appreciate me getting in their way, but I don't care. I need some fresh air and perspective. Thinking about being at a party with Colton later is already freaking me out. For a lot of reasons.

Just as I get to the stairs, I hear a commotion. When I look over my shoulder, my eyes land on Thompson. He and Drake are storming toward Massachusetts's net at full speed, both focused and resilient. Drake passes the puck to his teammate, and the next thing I know, Colton scores another goal. Six to two. I fiddle with my earring, eyeing our center. I feel so many emotions. Already forgotten. Somewhat forbidden. And, most importantly, inappropriate because of what I want him to do to me. Of what I want to do to him.

Even the thoughts in my head grow silent the second our eyes meet. Colton holds my gaze for what feels like an eternity, and then he looks away, skating back to the team. *Whatever.* I'm not letting him get the reins of my life in his hands. Not him, not any other guy. Setting boundaries to create a healthy atmosphere around myself is something that I do perfectly now.

Walking out of the building, I take a deep breath. I'm not sure what I want from tonight's party, or if I even want to go at all. Maybe just for Clay. I want him to make a move on Layla, and without my encouragement, he will definitely be a pussy and go screw some random girl yet again. I don't want my efforts to go to waste. My talk with Drake wasn't the easiest, so I'm not letting Rodgers ruin my plans for him and my best friend. Not on my watch for sure.

What are you going to do if you see him with someone else?

I lean against the wall, hearing my inner voice loud and clear. What am I going to do? I have no idea. It would be a sign that whatever was between us is over. If anything, it would allow me to move forward and continue to live my life as I did before he suddenly decided he was interested in me. I mentally pat myself on the back for not getting carried away, for keeping my guard up around him. I was just another hookup for him. Shaking my head, I walk to Grace's car. Colton Thompson is not allowed in my mind. Not anymore.

I HEAD to the table full of different drinks, trying not to collide with anyone. The place is packed, and it slows down my movements. The Panthers' won and for Moore's birthday partygoers have turned his parents' house into a mosh pit. If it survives without any broken furniture or other damage to the property, I will be utterly surprised.

"Where are you going, gorgeous?" A hand wraps around my waist, and someone hauls me to their chest. "How about wishing me a happy birthday?"

"Sorry, Hudson." I twirl around and rake my gaze over his face. "I'm leaving," I lie.

"What? That's bullshit." He raises his voice, grasping my hand and dragging me with him. I wriggle my hand, trying to pull it out of his grip, but nothing helps. "You've been hanging out with the wrong people. Now I'll teach you how to have fun."

Teach me? Is he insane? I don't need anything from him. "Hudson. Stop."

"Come on, baby, don't be so stubborn. It's my fucking birthday, and I want to have fun with you." He pulls me to him, and my body crashes into his side, knocking the air out of my lungs. "Have a drink with me? Just one drink."

I grit my teeth, calculating my options. The house is full of people. He won't try anything unless we're alone, somewhere private—which means I need to stay where everyone can see me.

"What do you prefer?" He stops near the table, motioning toward the drinks. I grab a beer can and open it under his gaze. "I kinda thought you'd like something heavier."

"Nah, this is all good." I fake a smile and take a sip. It cools my insides and helps me to calm down. I'll be back with my best friend as soon as he lets his guard down. I should have waited for Layla to finish playing beer pong with Grace and Kaleb instead of going off to find a drink alone. "What about you?"

Moore winks at me, and a toothy grin lights up his face. He pours a shot of tequila, downs it, and drapes his hand over my shoulder again, pulling me close. He nuzzles my neck with his nose, and I shiver.

"Baby, you smell so good." He sucks on my neck, and my face twists into a grimace. I put my beer on the table and elbow him in the ribs. When he releases his grip on me, I instantly jump back, putting my hands on my hips. "What the hell?"

I open my mouth, but someone shoves me back and hides me from Moore. I realize at once it's Clay. "Leave her the fuck alone."

"Are you her new knight in shining armor?" I take a step to the side and see the look on Moore's face. He's pissed, fists balled at his sides.

"I'm her friend," Clay warns, his voice thick with anger. "And when I tell you to leave her alone, you'll do just that. Understood?"

"Friend?" Moore snickers loudly. "More like a dude who doesn't want to lose a bet. Are you going to do whatever it takes to keep me from winning?"

"It has nothing to do with the bet. She's not comfortable around you, and I don't like it."

I blink. Then I blink again. And again. A bet? They fucking made a bet on me? I stomp forward and stop right in front of them. Clay and Moore both focus their gazes on me. "What is he talking about? What bet?"

"Ava, I'm so sorry," Clay pleads, his shoulders slumping. "I tried to tell you earlier, but something was always in the way. And I kept telling myself that I had time but—"

"The bet was about me?" Anger fills my every pore. "With him?"

"Yes, but it was before—when I didn't know you."

So not knowing me gives you the right to play with my life?

"He said he would fuck you, and I told him it was never going to happen—"

I can't listen to him anymore. It's all just white noise. "What does the loser have to do?"

"Wear a dress and makeup the last day before winter break," Moore muses, enjoying Clay's misery.

"And the winner?" I demand, not giving a shit that everyone can hear me.

"Dunno..." Moore taps his finger on his lips, pretending to be thinking. "I kinda forgot. Let's ask Thompson. He was the one who broke our hands."

My world spins, becoming blurry. Did someone jinx me? Because I don't feel the ground. I'm levitating, drowning in my emotions. The fucker knew about the bet too? He fucking broke their hands?

"Colton, tell the lady what the winner gets." And that's how I know he's here. I turn around, and my eyes find his. His body language is solemn, unbothered, but his gaze betrays him. There's panic there.

"A bottle of their choice," he breathes, and I'm ready to crumble.

Closing my eyes, I take a deep breath. I feel him move closer to me. His body warms my skin, and I become all tingly. But as soon as I let everything sink in, I'm furious. I want to punish them all, and I know exactly what to do.

I snap my eyes open, twirl around, and extend my palm to Moore. "Where is your room?"

"Upstairs." He beams, taking my hand and lacing our fingers together. I feel nauseous, but I still proceed. I have a punishment for each of them. "Let's go."

"Ava." Clay yells, wrapping his hand around my wrist. "Don't do this."

"What? Are you worried about the dress thing?" I taunt through gritted teeth.

"I don't give a shit about that. I don't want him near you." He's frustrated, not knowing what to do to stop me.

"Should have thought about that before. Now? I expect to see you in a dress and full makeup on Monday." I turn my head away, letting Moore drag me upstairs.

Before I disappear from view, I look over my shoulder and find Colton. He doesn't blink. His gaze is focused on me, and his jaw is hard. He's furious.

Serves you right, asshole. I'm so fucking done with you.

Chapter 28

I Thought I Liked You

COLTON

I sip my beer, pretending to be listening. Clay is talking with Benson about the game, discussing the crucial moments and goals. I lost interest in their conversation the second I saw her with Layla, Grace, and Grace's boyfriend. It's not the first time I've seen her tonight, but it is the first time she's been so close. And I can't look away.

I've been trying to convince myself to ignore her, to not notice her. It took all my willpower not to read the text message she sent on Friday before the game. Seeing her on the stairs after I scored sent all my emotions into turmoil. Thank God the game was almost over, because I had an incredibly hard time concentrating after that. She's all I want, and it gnaws at me that I'm pushing her away. Ava is the first girl I've ever really liked, and I'm letting her go without putting up even the tiniest fight. Without trying to make her understand I want more than just one hookup. I'm sure I'm making a mistake.

I frown, leaning forward, hoping to hear what she's saying, but it's useless. The music is blaring all around me. Ava says something to Layla, wheels around, and goes over to the drinks. I keep my eyes trained on her and see Moore sneaking up behind her. When he puts his hands on her, I ball my fists. What the hell is wrong with him? Why can't he leave her alone? I'm ready to jump out of my chair when I hear Clay's laughter. He still hasn't told her about the bet, and she has no idea what Moore is capable of when he wants something.

"Clay?" I meet his gaze and nod in Ava's direction. "Don't you want to step in?"

My best friend looks uncertain, his eyebrow arched in question. As soon as he realizes what I'm hinting at, he curses under his breath and stands up from his seat. "See you later, Drake. I need to fix something."

"Sure." Benson shrugs and wraps an arm around some girl's waist.

I follow Clay, keeping my distance. But as soon as I see her step closer to them, I speed up. Just in time to hear her question.

"What is he talking about? What bet?" Her voice is trembling with barely hidden fury.

"Ava, I'm so sorry," my best friend says quietly, becoming smaller. "I tried to tell you earlier, but something was always in the way. And I kept telling myself that I had time but—"

"The bet was about me? With him?" she shrieks.

"Yes, but it was before—when I didn't know you." Clay digs himself deeper with each word. He's going to make her think the only reason he feels bad about the bet is because they are friends now. "He said he would fuck you, and I told him it was never going to happen—"

"What does the loser have to do?" Ava demands, and I step closer. She's losing it, and it makes my heart swell with ache. Clay should have told her earlier. He should have found the time and told her everything. She shouldn't have found out like this.

"Wear a dress and makeup the last day before winter break." Moore grins, noticing me.

"And the winner?"

"Dunno..." He taps his finger on his lips, staring at me with a strange glint in his eyes. What is he planning? "I kinda forgot. Let's ask Thompson. He was the one who broke our hands." *Fucking asshole.* "Colton, tell the lady what the winner gets."

She wheels around, her gaze boring into me at once. As if she felt me behind her. I try to keep my cool, but it's hard, and my nervousness starts showing.

"A bottle of their choice," I mutter, and she shuts her eyes. I step closer to her, wanting nothing more than to hold her in my arms.

Suddenly, she opens her eyes, whirls around, and extends her palm to Moore. What is going on? "Where is your room?"

"Upstairs," he murmurs, taking her hand and lacing their fingers together. My gaze locks on their hands, and it becomes hard to breathe. What the fuck? She's not going to sleep with him, is she? "Let's go."

"Ava." Clay raises his voice, grabbing her wrist and holding her back. "Don't do this."

"What? Are you worried about the dress thing?"

"I don't give a shit about that. I don't want him near you." my best friend begs.

"Should have thought about that before. Now? I expect to see you in a dress and full makeup on Monday." She spits it out, letting Moore walk her further from us.

Neither of us looks away, watching as they climb the stairs. She glances over her shoulder, and our eyes meet. She's perfectly aware of how pissed I am. She just doesn't care.

"Fuck. Fuck. Fuck." Clay bellows, fingers flying to his hair. "What the fuck is she thinking? Sleeping with that dimwit? Just because she wants me to feel miserable?"

"You should have told her—"

"Go fuck yourself, Thompson." He turns around and stomps to the front door. When it closes with a bang, I know he's left. *Typical Clay.* I heave a sigh and hide my hands in my pockets. Waiting for her will be pure torture.

Thirty minutes forty-five seconds later, I see her walk down the stairs. She looks serene and incredibly calm. There is no sign of the disturbed state she was in when she found out about the bet. I drag my eyes down her body, taking in every detail, as if I haven't done it a thousand times tonight already. She is wearing a white skirt, which ends way above her knees, a black pullover that hugs her chest like a second skin, and a leather jacket. No matter how much I try not to look, it's useless. She's the only girl I see in this fucking place. The only one.

So many feelings rise as I watch Ava free her hair, letting it spill down over her shoulders. She tosses it a little, her fingers threading through her locks. She seems lost in her thoughts. There's not even the hint of a smile on her face. Her anger is gone, just like mine. Now I feel only two emotions: relief because I know she's safe, and jealousy. The latter continues to grow as I keep my eyes on her. Of all people, why did she have to sleep with Moore? Why did she even decide to go upstairs with him? I don't get it.

Layla rushes over to her, throwing her arms around her shoulders and whispering in her ear. They stay in each other's embrace, and suddenly Benson's sister starts laughing. Ava takes a step back and presses a finger to her lips, urging her best friend to keep quiet. I frown, my eyes glued to her face. This is not the reaction I expected. They chat some more, and then she points to the front door. Her best friend nods, whirls around, and hurriedly walks further into the house.

Ava heads to the front door, and I go after her. I don't care if she slept with Moore; that won't change how I feel about her. I just try to understand why...unsuccessfully. I feel like I need an instruction manual, a how-to guide. How to win over a girl without pissing her off every damn minute? I need a book for dummies, because I feel hopeless when it comes to her.

"Where are you going?" Someone puts their hand on my shoulder, stopping me in my tracks. I furrow my brow, turn my head to the left, and meet Benson's gaze.

"Out," I grit through my teeth, brushing his hand off my shoulder.

"Just like Ava," he counters. "Leave her alone."

"I'm not your pet, Benson. You have no right to tell me what to do."

"Haven't you done enough damage? Making a bet—"

"Clay made the bet, not me." I'm losing my patience. My temples start pulsing, and my vision blurs.

"Does it matter? You knew about it and did nothing to stop them. Moore was groping her, forcing himself on her, all because of the damn bet. Was it worth it to watch him try to get into her panties?"

"Is it really that hard? To get into her panties? I mean, you did it pretty easily."

The second the last word leaves my mouth, Benson punches me in the face. I stumble back slightly and bump into someone. Some people gasp, some hoot, and some clap. What's a great party without a fight, right? I quickly wipe the blood from my bottom lip and stare at him icily.

"What's your problem?"

"My problem is assholes like you, who think they are all-powerful and can do anything they want," Benson hisses, balling his fists. "Don't you dare follow her. She's not your toy to play with."

"Because she's yours?" *Mental note to self: Colton Thompson, you're a fucking idiot.* "I saw her getting into your car the other day."

"She's my fucking friend." he shouts. He's ready to charge at me again, but someone steps in front of me and stops him. I lower my gaze and recognize his sister. "Layla, move."

"Why was Ava in your car? Are you still screwing her behind my back?"

"She wanted to talk. We're just friends."

I use this moment to twirl around and dash out of the house, coming to a stop instantly.

Ava is standing on the porch with her phone in her hands. Once she looks up and our eyes meet, she pouts. Then she shoves her phone into her purse and pivots to the stairs, striding down without even a glance in my direction. I heave a sigh and go after her, matching her steps.

She keeps silent for a few minutes, then stops and turns to face me. "What do you want?"

"To make sure you're safe."

"You're like a week late, Thompson." She narrows her eyes. "I don't remember you giving a shit about my safety when you let me walk back to my dorm alone after the movies."

"I'm sorry about that." I take a step closer, hovering over her and looking her in the eyes. "I'm sorry about the bet—"

"I don't care." Ava averts her gaze from me and resumes her walk. I do the same, strolling down the street with her.

"Clay wanted to talk to you about it—"

"I don't care," she repeats, louder this time. "Anything you want to tell me, I'm not interested."

I sigh in exasperation, trying to calm down my fired-up nerves. "He felt bad about the bet, and he knew it was wrong."

She doesn't try to stop me this time, and I feel hopeful. But it doesn't last long. She covers her ears with her hands, shutting out any sounds.

I reach up and tear them away from her ears. Her eyes widen at once, and her mouth gapes open. "Stop acting like a child." I say.

"Me?" Ava pinches her eyebrows together. "When was the last time you looked in the mirror? You're the biggest kid I've ever met."

And the award for the most awkward apology goes to me. "Ava, I didn't mean..." I lean forward, trying to grab her arm, but she slaps my hand away.

"Fuck you," she scoffs furiously.

"I'm just trying to say I'm sorry." I manage to grab her hand and hold her wrist in a steady grip. "I should have told you about the bet myself. Moore didn't deserve you—"

"That's what you think of me?" Ava gasps, wriggling and trying to free her hand. "That I'm so easy? That I'll fuck anyone?"

"I didn't mean it like that. I'm not judging you—"

"I fucking hate you, Thompson." I let her pull her hand free. Breathing heavily, she opens her purse and takes out her phone. A moment later, she shoves it into my hand. I bend down to look at the screen, and suddenly my insides are frozen.

The photo is colorful and clear. A blindfolded Hudson Moore is lying on his bed with his hands tied to the headboard. He's naked, with only his hockey glove covering his dick. She never planned to sleep with him. She just wanted him to pay for making a bet about her.

"I don't fuck just anyone, Thompson. And I definitely don't fuck someone who has zero respect for me." Ava snatches her phone out of my palm, hiding it back in her purse.

"You were upstairs for more than thirty minutes, and I—"

"I needed him to let his guard down. I needed him to think I wanted him. That's the only reason it took so long." My palms are sweaty as I wait for her to say something else. She takes a deep breath and tilts her head to the side. "I can't believe I thought I liked you."

My heart stops for just a moment, and then it speeds up and thunders in my ears. She thought she liked me? *Liked?* As in past tense? No. That's bullshit. I refuse to accept it.

I invade her personal space, wrap my arms around her waist, and haul her to my chest. She puts her hands up, creating distance between us. "You're lying," I tell her, holding her gaze.

"Nope." She shakes her head. "Physically? You're my type. But your personality? A hundred percent no."

"You don't know me."

"I'm a very attentive person, Thompson. I notice everything." My skin is already on fire. Her closeness is making me go crazy.

I lift her, making her lock her legs behind my back. She licks her lips, her breath hitching.

"What are you doing?" Ava whispers, all her bravado gone.

"Kidnapping you." I head in the direction of my apartment building. It's about twenty minutes away from here, but I'll carry her the whole way without any problem. "Looks like that's the only way to make you listen to me."

Chapter 29

Because I Want To

AVA

Just a second. Just a second is all it takes to lose my shit and turn into a submissive idiot.

What is so special about this guy? He's the only one who affects me like this. The only one who gets under my skin with such ease it scares me to death. The only one whose kisses keep me awake at night. Just kisses, nothing more. It's so fucked up. I can't even think straight when he's around.

"Put me down," I tell him like a thousand times, and he only shrugs. "Colton, I'm serious. Put me down right now."

"Why?" he asks, meeting my gaze for a moment.

What does he mean? He has been carrying me for ten minutes already, and he's absolutely unaffected, as if I'm lighter than a feather. I didn't notice even a drop of sweat on his forehead, and he hasn't shifted his hands. He is acting as if it's the most natural thing in the world. I hate him.

Or maybe not. I don't know how I feel about him anymore. He's giving me whiplash, being hot then cold, whichever suits him better in the moment. Plus, there's his reputation and everything I already know about him. Why is he so fixated on me? Why is he here when he can have any girl he wants? It doesn't make any sense.

I sneak a glance at him, raking my gaze over his face. He's so stunning I get tingles all over my skin just looking at him. Deep brown eyes with long, thick eyelashes, a straight nose, and full lips above a strong jawline. He must spend a lot of his time outside, I notice a scattering of freckles on his nose. It's cute somehow, like it's something that makes him real and down-to-earth. I get them during the summer, just because I'm not a homebody. I love going places, and I prefer outdoor activities over spending time indoors. Is he the same? Or not? I know almost nothing about him, and I did nothing to change that. Miscommunication is a bitch, and it's our fault we let it happen.

"Colton, I'm not going to run away." Hearing this, he focuses his attention on me, slowing down just a bit. "You can put me down."

"Do you think that's the reason I'm carrying you? That I'm afraid you'll run away from me?" His voice is full of amusement, and I pinch my brows together.

"Why else?"

"Because I want to." His eyes are glimmering with mischief. My heartbeat accelerates, and the butterflies in my belly decide to throw a party. That's the only explanation I have for the flutters I feel. It's insanity.

I sigh, tightening my grip around his shoulders. I lower my gaze to his mouth again, admiring the lopsided grin that's still playing on his lips. He's even more attractive and carefree now, not the usual broody and moody Colton Thompson I know. He's different when he's with me. As long as I don't say anything that makes him cringe. Or angry. At least that's something I've gathered about him. Why does his bottom lip look puffy?

Without thinking, I trace his bottom lip with my thumb. He grimaces when I touch the puffy spot. "Did someone punch you?"

"Your friend did."

"Drake?" I ask, and he immediately snorts. "What's so funny?"

"You guessed it right away." Colton smiles, drawing me closer. "You really are just friends, aren't you?"

"Duh, of course. Hooking up with him was great, but..." I notice him furrow his brow. He's jealous, and my mood suddenly improves a ton. "I don't want to lose my best friend over something that doesn't mean anything to me."

The corners of his mouth quirk a little as he tries to fight his smile. "Good to know."

A moment of silence passes between us as my body fills with warmth and happiness. It feels so good, I decide to tell him the truth about Layla's brother and me. "I didn't sleep with Drake that night you saw us leaving the party together. We just watched *The Witcher* in his room till morning."

His face lights up with a smile as he gazes at me. "Geralt is a great character. I watch it too," he chimes in softly. He doesn't question my words, he simply chooses to trust me.

Colton takes a few steps forward and lowers me to my feet. He fishes his keys from his pocket and meets my gaze again. He doesn't say a thing, just carefully takes my palm and pulls me to him. I stumble, placing my hand on his chest to steady myself. Who am I kidding? Touching him feels like a dream come true.

"Come with me." And now my panties are a hot, wet mess. Damn him. I suck in a breath, my lips parting as I stare at him from under my eyelashes. Colton grins and leans to my ear. "Come *for* me could be arranged too. But only later. First, I want to talk to you."

"Sure," I mumble, licking my lips. "Talk."

He sighs, raising his eyes to the sky for a brief moment. "If I wanted to fuck you, I would have done it already. I wouldn't have brought you to my place. And I definitely wouldn't have carried you here. Any dark alley would have worked. Or a car."

"Who said I'm interested?" I arch my eyebrow, keeping my face impassive.

"Your pulse." I slide my gaze to my wrist, only now noticing that his hand is wrapped around it. "And probably your panties."

Smart-ass. I push him away and saunter inside his building as he holds the door open. I walk up the stairs, heading to his apartment as if I've been here a thousand times before. He stays behind me, and I'm sure he's enjoying the view. His gaze is on my back, and it truly affects me more than any physical contact. Just the knowledge that he's watching me...

Once we're inside his apartment, I take off my boots and my jacket, putting it on a hanger. I hesitate for a second, and Colt presses his palm to my lower back. "Do you want anything to eat?"

"No, thank you."

He ushers me to the living room, turning on the lights as we step in. Last time I was here with Clay, I thought he would be my friend. I shake my head, trying to get rid of my memories. Only when he fulfills his part of the bet will I think about forgiving him. I'm too revengeful to let it slide just because.

"What about a beer?"

"No. I had enough at the party," I tell him, edging closer to the couch and plopping myself down onto it. Colton joins me and turns to have a better look at me. I have a question for him, and without waiting for him to take the lead, I push the ball into his court. "What happened at the movies?"

"Meaning?" Colt leans on the couch, propping his head on his hand.

"Why did you say no? You were into me just as much as I was into you. Then you pushed me away. Whatever you want to call it, the result is the same. You were cold and distant."

"Didn't I tell you I liked kissing you?"

"You did," I agree, shifting a little to take a hair tie from my purse. I collect my hair and twist it into a bun. "But you could have handled it differently. You didn't have to ditch me the second you rejected me, without any explanation."

"I realized you were with me because you thought you owed me something. Because you wanted to reciprocate."

"Colton, you need to know one thing about me." I point my finger at him. "I *never* do anything I don't want to."

He watches me, his fingers tapping on the back of the couch. I wait, letting my words sink in. I wanted to return the favor, it's true, but I also wanted to make him feel good. He's smart; it shouldn't take him long. When he finally starts smiling, I know he understands.

"I'm sorry. I should have explained myself. Now I feel like a complete jerk."

"You should." I lift my shoulder. "Why didn't you read my message when I texted you on Friday before the game?"

"Because I saw you with Drake," he admits quietly.

"And?" I press, trying to figure out what that means in the long run. Do I want to believe what he's saying? Does it mean he likes me? Because if yes—oh my fucking God.

"I thought you were going to hook up with him again." His voice drops an octave lower, and I want to laugh. His words from earlier come back to me, and they start making sense.

"Did you say something to Drake about that? About me being in his car? Did you call me names?"

"That's what I always do. Say something mean and offensive—"

"To push people away. To keep them from getting closer, to not let them see the real you." Colton swallows soundly, shifting in his seat. "You need to do something about this habit of yours. Not everyone has the patience of an angel. I definitely don't."

"You have no idea how sorry I am. For assuming you slept with Moore, for not telling you about the bet, and for being a fucking moron who can't handle his emotions. Your college experience wasn't a nice one because of me and my actions." It means a lot that he says it. The first step in fixing things is to make sure we understand our mistakes. I only hope the honesty I hear in his voice and see in his eyes is real.

"Thanks." I speak softly. "I'm not a saint either. I can be mean and vengeful too—"

"You're a tornado. That's what Drake called you not so long ago."

"That's what my dad says," I confirm with a smile that all at once breaks into a yawn. What time is it? It was past two a.m. when I last checked my phone outside Moore's house.

"If I knew you were so sleepy, I would have kidnapped you earlier." Colt stands up from the couch and extends his hand to me. And just like that, I'm nervous. What does it all mean? "You're not sleeping on the couch."

I take his outstretched hand, letting him pull me to my feet. "I can go back to my dorm and sleep in my bed."

"No." It's firm. With a pinch of finality. Steely. Colton doesn't expect objections. He's sure I will stay.

"I don't really take orders."

"It's not an order." He takes a step forward, still holding my hand in his. "Please, Ava, stay."

That's better...or not. He makes me doubt my feelings. My cravings. My usual likings. His roughness at the movies turned me on more than anything else, and that's new for me. I prefer to be in control, to be the one who orchestrates everything. But Colton Thompson turns me into someone very different without even trying, by just being by my side.

"Okay." I lace my fingers through his, and his Adam's apple bobs up and down. Finding his weak spots is exhilarating and invigorating. I want to know more about him, about his habits and addictions. I want to know him. The real him.

Colton slowly ambles to his bedroom, and I follow him. Once he opens the door, he lingers in the doorway and looks at me. "Just to be clear: I'm not taking you into my room to have sex."

"Should I be offended?" I tease him, cocking an eyebrow in question.

"You look tired." He cups my cheek with his hand, bending down to meet my eyes. "Even though it would be flattering if you passed out while I was fucking you, that's not how I want our first time to be."

Colt kisses my nose, leans away, and walks into his bedroom. I step inside, thinking about everything he just said. My mind drifts back and forth between his words, and the more I absorb them, the more my amusement grows. *Our first time*. He doesn't want it to be a one-time thing. He doesn't want it to be his usual, but what does that mean for me?

"Here." Something soft is pushed into my hands, and I return to reality. "You can sleep in this."

"Thanks." I head to his bed, but he's retreating to the door with a blanket under his armpit. "Where are you going?"

"I have zero self-control when you're around." He puts his hand on the doorknob, holding my gaze. "I'll sleep on the couch."

"That is the shittiest excuse ever."

"Well, shitty or not, it's the truth." Colton winks, taking a step outside the room. "Breakfast is on me."

He closes the door behind him, leaving me alone. I understand where he's coming from, and I do want to sleep, but that doesn't make his behavior any less confusing. What will happen in the morning? After breakfast? Are we going to talk? Is he going to fuck me then? Or send me home?

I put his T-shirt on the bed and quickly find the bathroom. The rest of the apartment is plunged into darkness and quiet. I try to move without a sound. He can't already be asleep, but I don't want to draw his attention to me. I'm a mess, and I'm yawning nonstop. It will be way better to face him when I'm rested.

Closing the door, I trudge to his bed and quickly change my clothes. His tee is long and soft, covering my ass completely. Not that I'm surprised—he's way taller than me. I slip under the covers and nestle comfortably, huddling like a baby. I feel secure when he's around, protected, and that's something I feel even being in his room. Alone. I drift off to sleep way sooner than I thought.

QUIETLY TIPTOEING out of the bedroom, I hope to catch him off guard. It's nine a.m., and I honestly don't expect him to be up, but I'm wrong.

The sound comes first, followed by a delicious aroma. He did say breakfast was on him, so that explains why he's already cooking.

Stepping into the kitchen, I smile to myself and then freeze. This is not what I expected for sure. Colton is making breakfast for us, wearing only his briefs. Suddenly, I have lost my appetite—but my infatuation with him is only growing.

Chapter 30

Enemies Make the Best Lovers

COLTON

I'M SITTING UP STRAIGHT ON THE COUCH IN MY LIVING room, having a hard time calming down. What the fuck was that? Why on Earth was I dreaming about Helen? About her kissing me in my car? I haven't had a dream like that for a while now, and I didn't see it coming.

I rub my face with my palms, shooing away the remnants of sleep. I raise my arms, stretch them over my head, and stand up, grasping my phone from the table. Eight forty a.m. I listen to the quiet of my apartment. She's still asleep, and I don't want to wake her up. Not until breakfast is ready. Maybe I should just admit to myself I would do anything to get her to stay longer? To persuade her to spend the day with me?

I've never been as whipped as I am right now. It's ridiculous.

I smile to myself and silently head to my bathroom. I close the door and quickly wash my face. Drinking yesterday was a bad idea. The stubble on my cheeks has become more visible, and I'm not sure if I like it...because I'm not sure if she likes it.

Jesus Christ. Someone needs to help me navigate my shit. So far, I feel like I'm stuck in the middle of the Bermuda Triangle—which in my case is Ava's Triangle. For the first time in my twenty-one years of life, I feel like a lost puppy. A very lost and hopeless puppy.

Once I'm in the kitchen, I open the fridge and scan what I have in here. Fried eggs with toast will do. Hopefully she likes that. I don't want to ruin my chances with her by cooking something she'll refuse to eat.

For the next fifteen minutes, I'm busy preparing food for us. The kitchen is filled with different sounds, but I hear her. She tiptoes from the bedroom and then stops in the doorway. I feel her gaze on me, and my lips involuntarily stretch into a smile. My skin warms up, and my heartbeat accelerates. The effect she has on me is just...wow. I never thought it could be possible for someone to affect me like she does.

"Good morning," I say without looking at her. It's almost time to place the eggs on the plates, and I don't want to wreck them.

"Good morning," Ava echoes and walks up to stand by my side. "Smells delicious."

"Hopefully it will taste good too." I squint at her. Ava has this look on her face, one I struggle to interpret. Mischief, happiness, and...*damn you.*

As soon as I lower my gaze to her chest, I know she wants me. Her pebbled nipples poke through my tee, and I suddenly don't want to eat. At least, not the eggs I just fried. I breathe out through my nostrils and clear my throat. "Can you please grab two plates from that cabinet?"

"Sure." She moves away, brushing her fingertips over my hand. It takes all the strength I have not to send everything flying and toss her over my shoulder. I have a plan, and I desperately want to stick to it. I can always fuck her later...or now?

"We got to bed pretty late. I didn't expect you to be up so early. Or are you always an early riser?" she asks.

"Depends. If I need to be somewhere, I'll be up way earlier than I need to be. But if I get a chance to sleep in, I will." I turn the burner off, round the kitchen island, and edge to the table. I serve the eggs and then go back to grab the toast with Nutella. I want to pat myself on the back for buying all this stuff. This morning would have been disastrous if I didn't have anything in my fridge. "Do you want coffee or tea?"

"Coffee would be great." Ava takes the plate with the toast from my hand and puts it on the table. "Do you need help?"

"Nope." I expected her to want coffee, so it was the first thing I made once I got to the kitchen. I pour some into two mugs and return to her. "Do you need—"

She waves a fork, and I chuckle. She's always one step ahead of me. I plop myself down on the chair and take a fork in my hand, holding her gaze.

"Enjoy your meal," Ava murmurs, taking a bite of toast.

"Thank you. Enjoy your meal too."

We eat and talk. About college and our majors, about movies we watched recently. Small talk with her is easy and effortless. She doesn't pretend, and I enjoy the conversation to no end. I'm not playing anyone as well; I'm just being myself around her. I ask her questions about her hometown and realize it's thirty minutes away from my own. If she were older, I probably would have met her already, just like I already knew Drake before we got to college. Our high school teams played against each other more than once.

"My dad is the coolest man I know." She takes a sip of her coffee, cocking her eyebrow. I put our empty plates in the dishwasher, so there is only a bowl of M&Ms cookies left. "He set my standards pretty high."

"I'll try to live up to your expectations." I take a bite of cookie and wash it down with my coffee. "Never thought I would be competing with someone's dad."

Ava pauses, and her eyes round slightly. She sets her mug aside, puts her elbows on the table, and lowers her chin into her palms. Her gaze is intense and penetrating, but I don't look away. I let her see me. "I have a question for you, but you have to promise not to lie."

"I never lie."

"Everyone lies." She rolls her eyes, and I clench my jaw.

"I keep things to myself when I think they don't concern anyone but me. I'm not really open with people or talkative," I say simply, placing my mug on the table and leaning in. "But I'm not a liar."

"And you've never lied?"

"In the past, but not anymore." My body relaxes, and I sigh. "My lies led to something horrible. Someone incredibly dear to me suffered because of it. The consequences of my actions will haunt me forever, and I don't have it in me to lie ever again. It's not worth it."

She's silent for a moment, gawking at me without blinking. Then a hasty smile stretches across her mouth. "That makes me wonder how many people know the real you. Because something tells me I wouldn't even need all the fingers on one hand to count them."

"No one," I confess, and her lips part. I'm sure she thought I would at least say Clay, but that would be a lie. Even my best friend doesn't know everything about me. "But you're getting dangerously close to the ugly truth, the one I hide from everyone."

"There is nothing ugly about you, Colt."

"You don't know—"

Ava interrupts me, grinning. "True, but I intend to fix that."

I laugh, shaking my head. "Looking forward to it." I lick my lips. "What did you want to ask?"

"Do you like me?"

Do I tell her the truth or laugh it off? If I want her in my life, there is only one option.

"Yeah, I do. I like you. I thought I'd made it embarrassingly obvious."

"And confusing," she utters, smacking her lips together. "I like you too, but—"

"But?" I pinch my brows together.

"You don't date anyone," Ava blurts, grabbing her coffee mug between her palms. "And before I went to college, I promised myself I'd do the same. Hookups are the only thing I'm interested in right now. At least in my first year."

"It's my last year here."

"And that's another reason why I don't want anything serious." She brings the mug to her lips, but instantly lowers it to the table. "Can you imagine falling for someone and then saying goodbye as soon as they graduate? I don't know about you, Colton, but my feelings can't be changed with a remote control. I can't turn them on and off whenever I want."

"No one can." The weird feeling in my lower abdomen whirls and grows, filling my insides with sorrow. "After graduation I plan to sign a contract with the Thunders and go to Cali. Or any other state if I can find another team."

"And I will stay here. For the next three years."

We both fall silent, and I feel the wheels in my head turning. They're painfully slow, but that's exactly what I need to find a solution. If my past taught me anything, it's that everything can change. Nothing is set in stone. Except for one thing: I refuse to accept her not being in my life.

"Then how about being my enemy with benefits?"

"Why enemy?"

"Because they make the best lovers, don't they?" My smile blooms, and I wink at her. She's far from my enemy, but teasing her feels amazing.

"We haven't tested that theory." And that's how I know she's back in the game. Her emerald eyes are full of amusement, but with how dark they are, I know her desire is there.

"We have the whole day ahead of us." I stand up from the table and take a step closer to her. "To test the theory." She lets me pull her to her feet, and I lift her, wrapping her legs around my hips. "Besides, I'm still hungry."

"And what are you going to eat?" she breathes, winding her hands around my neck.

I ignore her question, wheel around, and saunter to my bedroom. We still have one thing we need to settle before I'll answer her.

"Colt?"

"Being enemies with benefits means being exclusive. I'm only yours, and you're only mine," I muse huskily and feel her shudder. "Are you okay with that?"

Her gaze is feverish, and I feel my skin becoming hotter with each second. I slam the door to my bedroom closed and lower her onto my bed, standing up between her legs. I put my palms on her thighs, moving them up along her skin and taking off her panties in one swift motion. Spreading her legs apart on the bed, her knees wide, I groan seeing how wet she is. I swallow hard, boring my gaze into hers.

"Are you okay with that, Ava? Ready to be mine?"

"Yes," she purrs, and I kneel, hauling her ass to the edge of my bed.

"Then get comfortable. I'm going to eat my dessert."

Chapter 31

You Are Perfect

AVA

Colton places a light peck on my inner thigh, causing a wave of goosebumps to break out across my skin. The tenderness of his kiss and his soft lips send my mind into overdrive.

"Such a beautiful little cunt," Colt says gruffly against my clit. Then he sucks it into his mouth. I clutch the blanket, digging my fingers into it. All sense of time and place dissolve into nothingness. I feel only him, and it's intense and heart-stopping. I'm losing my mind from how good it feels.

He sucks and licks, circling his tongue over my clit gently and slowly. It's not aggressive or rough like some guys do it. He's into this, roaming his hands over my thighs and higher, hiding them under the tee. Colton cups my breasts, playing with my nipples and drawing a moan out of my parted lips.

I catch his darkened eyes and see that he's watching me. He wants to own every emotion, every moan, and every breath he pulls out of me. His tongue slides lower, teasing my lips, and I arch my back and spread my legs wider. I hold his gaze—a fire dances behind his irises. He's turned on just because he's giving me pleasure. I am a hot, wet mess, my body coated in sweat and my heart racing in my chest. He makes it all about me.

Colt plunges a finger inside me, and I whimper, covering my eyes with my hand. He pumps into me but stops working his magic on my clit. "Ava."

I take my hand away and focus on him through blurry vision.

"I want you to look at me. I want to see you come, taste you on my tongue. Can you do that for me?"

"Yes," I breathe. "Keep going, please, I'm so close..."

A cheesy smile flashes on his face, and the next moment his head is back between my legs, his tongue lapping over my clit. It's wet, and his breath is hot, and I'm enjoying every second of it.

Suddenly, Colton curls his finger inside me while sucking on my clit, and I moan, fisting his hair in my fingers. "Oh, fuck." I cry out, lifting my hips in sync with his movements. Up and down, in and out, lips and tongue. He speeds up, feeling my urge and driving me toward my limit without stopping. I come hard in no time, letting the feeling overwhelm me. I'm floating and absolutely blissful, curling my toes and making my body quiver.

"You taste so sweet," he murmurs, kissing my knee. "Like honey."

Grinning from ear to ear, I prop myself on my elbows and look at him. My body is still shaking from the orgasm. It feels euphoric, and I'm not sure if it has ever been like this before. "Never heard that."

"Really?" His hands grip my hips firmly. "Then the guys you've been with are morons."

"Or you're just a sweet-talker."

"Me? A sweet-talker?" Colton laughs heartily, standing up. "I'm the grumpy one. The grumpiest of the grumps."

I eye his bulge in his briefs, a fire rekindling in my lower abdomen. He's aroused and hard, and my memories bring back the feeling of his thickness. The girth of his cock is probably like nothing I've ever been with before.

"You're not grumpy," I retort. "You're just...different."

"In a good way, I hope." He smirks, placing a hand on his dick, and I suck in a breath. "If you don't want to have sex, that's okay."

Colton reads me with ease, and I sigh, sitting up straight and moving closer to him. I look up, meet his gaze, and place my palm on his cock.

"If you promise to go slow and be gentle." I move my hand up and down, feeling him tremble. "You're probably much bigger than I'm used to."

He narrows his eyes, brows knit together. Pondering my words, he slowly lets them sink in. A satisfied grin crosses his lips. I just gave his ego a huge boost. As if it wasn't big enough already.

"Take the shirt off," he orders, pushing down his briefs. "Ava. Do it."

If he thinks I can properly operate when he's totally naked in front of me, he should think again. His body is absolute perfection. His ripped abs and the defined lines of his chest and shoulders make my mouth water. His muscular arms feel heavenly around my body, and his long, sculpted legs make my imagination run wild. Colton Thompson is a panty-dropper; just the sight of him sends me into orgasmic oblivion.

Nice to meet you, I'm Ava "Brainless" Mason.

"Ava, you're still in my T-shirt." Colt moves closer and steps between my legs, placing his knee on the bed. "Take it off."

I roll my eyes, a bit confused by my own reaction. Since when do I like to be bossed around? Since when do I enjoy being obedient? Since Colton fucking Thompson, goddamn it.

He grasps my chin and forces me to look at him. I swallow hard, my nipples pebbling instantly. He bends down to look me in the eyes.

"Wh-what?"

"If I tell you to do something, you do it," he states, and I stubbornly want to argue. I'm not his toy, I'm— "If you don't want to do it, you tell me. Don't stay silent. Please."

And just like that, I'm ready for anything with him. Every little damn thing.

"I want you," I hum, dragging his shirt up and tossing it aside. I put my hand on his cock, jerk it off once, twice, and then slide lower and palm his balls. He hisses, stepping back abruptly and reaching to his bedside table for a condom.

"Lie down and spread your beautiful legs. As wide as you can," Colton tells me, shielding his cock in a condom.

I crawl back, nestling into the middle of his bed while he stalks over to me and settles between my legs. He teases my opening with the tip of his dick, feeling my wetness. Our eyes are locked on each other, and I feel as if I'm staring into a dark vortex. Unknown and tantalizing. Bewitching and mysterious. He's unique and striking, and something strange forms in my chest. For a split second, I wonder if I will be able to escape this without falling in love with him. Oh God, I hope I'm—

My thoughts die as soon as Colt enters me, moving in carefully and out almost instantly. I seek his lips for a kiss, winding my hands around his neck and pulling him to me. His mouth hovers over mine as he continues to slide in and out, going deeper each time. I run my tongue over his bottom lip and catch it between my teeth.

"Kiss me," I demand, and Colton obeys, covering my mouth with his. His kisses and thrusts are all I feel, all I can think of. I don't want to be anywhere else, only with him.

He slides inside me to the hilt. I'm full. I'm so fucking full, and I love it. His mouth glides down to my jaw, then lower, to my neck, leaving light kisses all over my skin. My head bobs back, and I close my eyes just as he sucks on my skin.

"Does that feel good?" Colt whispers, meeting my gaze.

"You feel incredible," I mumble as he speeds up his movements. My moans are loud, while his breath becomes shallow. I'm close to my second orgasm, so close that I know it's going to hit at any moment.

Colton flicks his tongue over my nipple, sucking it into his mouth and grazing his teeth over it. My eyes roll back in my head. My mind is fuzzy, and I'm not sure I have it in me to hold it together any longer.

"Such a good girl you are, taking me so well..." And, hearing this, I orgasm. I've never come because of something my partner said. Until now. "Fuck...Ava...your pussy feels—"

Colt chokes on his words as I spasm around him. His strokes are fast and hard. My ass slaps against him, and the sound fills the room. He kisses me, taking my breath away, and that's how he erupts too. A guttural groan scatters all over my lips.

Colton stays inside me as we kiss. He caresses my body with his hands, and I use this moment to feel him. His ass, his muscular back and broad shoulders. I love touching him. The feeling of his hot skin under my palms is tempting, and it lights my fire yet again.

He places an affectionate peck on my nose, and then he moves away.

Colt takes the condom off, throws it into the trash can, and gets a new one from the bedside table. I grin, seeing him come over to me with his cock wrapped in another condom. He plops himself onto the bed, looking at me. I know what he wants without him saying anything.

Straddling his legs, I take his dick inside me, and he lets out something close to a moan. *Oh my fucking God.* He will be the death of me. His reactions are so open and honest, it sends my feelings into total overdrive, multiplying my arousal by a thousand. Why? Because I never thought this guy could be like that.

"Your tits are perfect," Colton drawls quietly, palming my breasts and fondling them softly. He rubs my nipples between his thumbs and middle fingers, and my skin is burning. My clit aches, and I'm dripping again.

"What else is perfect?" I ask jokingly, but he shoots me a look, and my heart beats faster.

"You. You are perfect." He puts his hand on the back of my neck, pulling me to him roughly. Our foreheads meet, and we stare at each other, both panting. "Fuck me, Ava. Now."

And with his words, I lose myself in him. Again.

Chapter 32

The Deal with the Devil

AVA

It's three p.m., and I'm still at his place. We continued going at it in his bedroom until we both realized we were hungry. After we had lunch and showered, we went to the living room to watch *Sherlock*. I like that show, but not as much as I enjoy cuddling with Colton.

"What do you usually do in your free time?" he asks, his breath hot on my skin. His arms are wrapped around my waist from behind as I nestle comfortably between his long legs.

"Read books." My gaze flies to a little bookcase near the door. There are a few comics and three really thick books on the shelf. I know nothing about them, but based on the titles, they seem like detective novels.

"And what is your favorite genre?"

"Romance, of course." I sneak a glance at him over my shoulder. "Fictional men never disappoint me, unlike real ones. My book boyfriends set the standard, and it's really high."

"Can your book boyfriends do this?" Colt coos, gliding his hand up my chest and lightly pinching my nipple. "Or this?" He nips on my throat, and a quiet moan slips out of my mouth. "Can they make you come even when you feel like you've had enough?"

I shiver. My clit pulses, and tingles spread all over my skin. The memory of my last orgasm is vivid, and it makes my heart go insane. It's not enough to feel him. As my body grows warm, I want to look at him. Colton lets me turn around, and now I'm sprawled on his chest, my eyes locked on his.

"They can't," I tell him as his hands slip down to my ass. "But books are my safe place."

"Just like hockey for me. Always," he says, tracing my cheekbones with his fingertips. "And sometimes movies. I love a good mystery, and psychological thrillers."

"I think you're lying, Colt. Disney is your favorite." I'm pushing my luck, but after I saw his watch history, I've been dying to comment.

"A very funny joke, Ava. Just like the one about the three-humped camel." He took the bait.

"That's one of the best scenes. Flash's reaction was adorable." I shrug, barely bottling up my excitement. He frowns, as if he can't believe what he's hearing.

"The best scene? That's when they fool Bellwether," Colton argues. I hold his gaze and then break into giggles, hiding my face in the crook of his neck. "What?"

"It's called a hustle, sweetheart," I murmur, my body shaking with laughter. "Ever since the movies, I knew *Zootopia* was your favorite."

He blinks, and then a sly smile crosses his face. "You hustled me, and I didn't even notice it. But it's true. Of all the cartoons I watch, I like that one the most."

"Me too." I lean forward and plant a light kiss on his lips. "But it's not my all-time favorite."

"And what is that?"

"Who knows?" I tease him, closing the distance between us. Colt smirks knowingly, wraps his arms around me, and kisses me again.

A few hours go by. We talk, we kiss, we laugh, and the more we do it, the more normal it starts to feel. As if it's something we do all the time.

"Is that your phone?" Colt whispers in my ear, and I freeze for a second, listening to the sound. Someone is calling me. My purse is in his room, so I untangle myself from him and go get it.

The second I see the name on the screen, I answer. "Hey, Layla."

"Hey hey," my best friend singsongs. "I'm in your room and you're not here."

"Yeah."

"Can we meet?"

"Of course. When? And where?" I saunter over to my clothes and grab them from the chair I put them on last night.

"At our usual coffee shop." I'll need about thirty minutes to get there. "What time works for you?"

"Forty minutes?" I offer.

"Cool. I'll be waiting."

"See you."

I hang up and quickly change my clothes. Colton lingers in the doorway, staring at me nonchalantly. It slipped my mind what I had been doing just minutes ago.

"Leaving already?"

"Uh-huh." He steps aside to let me out of his room. As I head to the bathroom, I hear him follow me. "Layla called. She wants to gossip."

"About us?" he asks with humor in his voice.

"Probably," I tell him, washing my face.

"Do you need a ride? I can drive you."

I flash him a tiny smile in the reflection of the mirror. "No, it's all good. I can walk."

"Okay." He whirls around, strolling to the front door. I turn off the faucet, dry my face with a little towel, and go after him.

I put on my boots and my jacket, and only then do I really look at Colton. His gaze is intense and focused on me. I step closer and curve my hands around his torso.

"Thank you for today. I had an amazing time with you."

The corners of his mouth quirk up, and he beams. "Is there anything I can do to make you stay?"

"Nope."

"Thought so." He hugs me tightly, bending down and capturing my lips with his. I'm melting. Literally. His kisses arouse all sorts of feelings inside me, from happiness to longing, and I don't know what to think about it.

"I need to go, or I'll be late," I murmur as he kisses my jaw.

"Then let me give you a ride."

"No. I'll walk." I put my hand on his chest and gently push him away. Colt releases me and walks up to the door.

"Bye, Colt."

"Bye, Ava." But neither of us moves, enveloped in our own bubble. The world outside his apartment didn't exist not long ago, but it can't be like that forever.

I wave and edge to the stairs, feeling his gaze on my back. Getting all tingly when he looks at me is my new normal. I have no idea what's going to happen next between us. Something is telling me I made some kind of deal with the devil when I agreed to this enemies-with-benefits arrangement. But in all honesty? The devil never looked more attractive than he does right now.

"Hey. Sorry I'm late," I say, sitting down on the chair across from Layla.

I would have been on time, but I decided to stop by my dorm and change my clothes. Showing up in yesterday's clothes wasn't an option. I put on my favorite washed-out jeans, pairing them with a red hoodie and Colton's bomber. It still smells like him, and it quickly has become my favorite article of clothing.

"I ordered you an almond milk flat white." She pushes a mug in my direction.

"Thanks." I take the coffee between my palms. It's a bit colder than I'm used to, but that's because I am late. "How was the party?"

"The party? You want to talk about the party?"

"Yeah, why not?"

"Bitch, you better be joking," Layla huffs. "I created a distraction, made sure Thompson had a chance to follow you when Drake confronted him, and you want to know how the party was?"

"What did you do?"

Layla tells me what happened after I walked out of Moore's house, and I instinctively want to smile. Colton has a problem with putting his foot in his mouth, having no control over his words when he's angry or stressed. He should start doing something about it. I'm not that patient.

Once she's done, she looks at me with her eyebrow raised. I put my mug on the table and lean back in the chair, stretching my legs and allowing my mind to go back to Colton's place. I tell Layla about the time I spent with him, watching movies and talking, but I keep the details about our sex to myself. That's between him and me.

"You hit the jackpot," Layla comments.

"Maybe. For all I know, it could be a one-time thing." I'm such a pathetic liar.

"Yeah, of course." Her voice drips with sarcasm, and she looks at me. "The guy is whipped, and he truly has *never* dated a girl in all the time he's been in college."

Has he ever had a girlfriend? Or a relationship? Has he ever been in love? We spent a lot of time together, but I still know very little about him. Only some glimpses. Some small pieces. It's not enough to get the whole picture. I want to change that. I want him to open up to me. I feel that he needs it, to have someone he can trust and talk to. About anything.

"Okay, Ava, let's change the subject." I meet her gaze, which is full of mischief. "I want you to focus on being here with me and not in Colton Thompson's oblivion. Turn it off."

"Only for you," I utter. We spend the rest of the evening drinking coffee and chatting about college, books, and our plans for the holidays. It feels like heaven.

Chapter 33

Then Prove It

COLTON

"Shit, man, I can't even concentrate when you look like that." I laugh, glancing at Clay. He's wearing a long black dress and a full face of makeup, with red lipstick on his lips and shimmery eyeshadow on his eyelids.

He tightens his grip on his backpack. "Ten more minutes, and I can finally get rid of it."

"Why can't you get rid of it now?" I ask, stopping near the door of the locker room.

"Because Ava said so." My best friend sighs, leaning against the wall. "I still don't get why she needed to sleep with him to make a point."

"She didn't."

"She didn't?" He blinks, his brows knitting together. "Then why the fuck am I wearing this?"

"Because you want to be her friend, and she wouldn't have forgiven you otherwise."

Clay groans and storms inside the locker room. I follow him, watching as he takes off the dress and tosses it to the floor. After only a few seconds, he's back in his black jeans and white hoodie. While I sit on the bench waiting for him, he heads over to the sink and returns with a clean face.

"Your ten minutes wasn't up."

"I don't care. I've embarrassed myself enough. For nothing." He grabs his backpack and takes a step forward, but then he steps back and slumps onto the bench beside me. "How do you know?"

"Know what?"

"About Ava and Moore."

"She showed me a picture she took of Moore naked and blindfolded, tied to his bed with his hockey glove on his dick. Ava wanted to punish him, not sleep with him." I drum my fingers on my thigh, fidgeting in my seat. "She was furious when she realized I thought she'd slept with him."

"Did she slap you again?" Clay snorts loudly.

"No. Even if she had slept with him, I wouldn't have judged her. She knows that. We're good."

"Awesome. I still kinda ship you two together."

"You what?" I say, staring at him like he's crazy.

Clay shrugs and flashes me a smile. "You're like twin flames. So much alike, it's scary."

Suddenly, I'm lost in my memories. In her scent. Her touch. Her sounds. The feeling of her in my arms. Of me inside her. They are the most colorful memories I've ever had. I spent an hour this morning lying in my bed, surrounded by the scent of her perfume on my pillows and in my sheets. Absorbing it, taking it in till the last drop and still feeling that it wasn't enough.

"Can you stop Ava-dreaming?" Clay's voice rings in my ear, and I almost jump out of my seat.

"Stop what?"

"You're Ava-dreaming, obviously. The look on your face says it all." My best friend wraps his arm around my shoulders, pulling me to his side. "When are you going to ask her on a date?"

"She doesn't want to date anyone," I mutter, and Clay frowns. "Ava isn't interested in a relationship."

"And you're okay with that?"

"Why not?" I'm not okay with that. I want her to be mine, but I can't do anything about it right now. I only hope my persistence will help me change her mind. "I'm not a relationship type of a guy either."

"Ava said I'm missing out on a lot of good stuff when I mentioned I prefer hookups over dating." He looks me up and down. "You sure she doesn't want to date anyone? Maybe it's you she doesn't want to date?"

I nudge him with my shoulder, and he moves away. "It's her first year in college, and she wants to enjoy it, to be single and carefree." I lick my lips, standing up from the bench. "Besides, I'm a senior. We don't have a future together."

Clay joins me, and we both trudge to the door. "When you put it that way, I guess it makes sense." I open the door, but I stop in my tracks once I hear his question: "Friends with benefits then?"

"Why put a label on it?" I dodge his question and head to the dining hall.

When the idiot jumps on my back, I know I screwed up. I didn't openly tell him anything, but I left him enough breadcrumbs to figure it out. He knows Ava and I hooked up.

"How was it?"

"I don't brag. Did you forget that?" I brush him off my back with ease.

"Man, just this once?"

"About her?" I shake my head. "No fucking way."

"Looks like our girl has a magic pussy." Clay's laughter dies in his throat when I clutch his hoodie in my fist. "It's a joke, Colt. She's my friend; I don't think about her that way."

"Then don't talk about her that way. Ever." I stare him down, and he gulps nervously. Then he nods, and I let him go. The beast inside my chest slowly calms down.

"If you're so protective of her, maybe you should worry about Moore." He speaks in a quiet voice as we resume our stroll. "Who knows how much time he spent waiting for someone to untie him? Ava made fun of him, and he's not going to let that slide. He's going to want to make her pay."

I keep silent as we enter the dining hall. Clay has a point. Moore has an incredibly big ego, and what Ava did to him was humiliating. He might try to get even, hurting her in the process.

"Colt?" I focus my attention on Clay and instantly furrow my brow.

He is staring at something ahead of us, and he is seething. "See what I mean?"

I follow his gaze, and I only need a second to register what I'm looking at. Ava and Layla are sitting at a table, and Moore is standing directly across from them. Both of his hands are on the table, and he's hovering over the girls. Everything in his posture screams anger. Without giving it a second thought, I storm over with Clay in tow. We aren't the only ones, as Benson suddenly appears on my left, his eyes glued to the table where Ava and Layla are sitting.

"Do you think the fucker threatened them?" Benson asks, glancing at me.

"Looks like it," my best friend chimes in, lining up with us.

"I never should have helped him. I should have left him tied to his bed." Benson mutters under his breath, and I shoot him a questioning glance. "After you and Ava left, Layla told me to go check on Moore. She knew what Ava did to him. And, well, it was hilarious, but he obviously didn't agree. I told him to calm down and think before he did anything, but it seems like he didn't listen."

"...think it was funny?" Moore hisses as we stop behind his back. He senses our presence and twirls around, his face contorted with rage. "What the fuck are you doing here?"

"Haven't I told you she's my friend and I don't want you near her?" Clay says.

"*Friend?* A friend who made you wear a fucking dress—"

"I deserved it," my best friend grinds out, flexing his muscles.

"Did she leave you naked, tied to your bed on your own birthday, at your own house? Did she take a picture of you like that?" He spits out the words. "This ho—"

"Call her that again..." Benson and I say at the same time, stepping closer to him.

"Or what?" Moore demands, but his face pales.

"You will regret it." I hold his gaze, ready to do anything to take him down. "If you don't want anyone to see a picture of you with just a hockey glove on your dick, you will back off and leave her alone. If not, I'll make sure you pay for it."

"*We* will make sure you pay for it," Benson corrects me, and at this very moment I know he will be my friend. A real one. Not just a teammate.

"Whatever," Moore utters, stomping away from the table.

Hopefully, what we just did will be enough for him to drop it. No one is going to use the picture unless he tries to get back at Ava. I'll need to keep my eye on him, just in case. He's not her number one fan.

"Wow. That was hot." Layla shifts her gaze to her brother with a mischievous smile on her face. "But not you."

"Thanks." Benson rolls his eyes and plops himself down next to her. "Are you okay?"

Clay and I both join him, sitting down across from Layla and Ava. I finally look at her, and the beast in my chest purrs. She's so beautiful. Her hair is in a high ponytail, and there's no sign of makeup on her face. Her eyes are locked on Benson, and for the first time in all these months, I don't care. They are just friends.

"No. He definitely annoyed the fuck out of me," Ava mutters, grabbing her Pepsi from the table. "He was going on and on and on about me being an ungrateful bitch, for at least ten minutes for sure. He's the amazing Hudson Moore, and I dared to reject him. Humiliate him. Make him a laughingstock."

"What are you going to do with the picture?" Benson asks.

"Nothing. I'm not a complete idiot. It's just for leverage, if he still tries anything with me."

"He won't. Not after today," Clay reassures her, but I still think it's too early to make such assumptions. I'm not going to let my guard down around him any time soon.

"We'll see," Layla mumbles, looking at Ava. Benson's sister lowers her head onto her best friend's shoulder. "I kinda lost my appetite. He's so gross; I feel dirty after that."

"Are you backing out?" Ava speaks quietly. "You promised you'd go shopping with me after your classes. I need to buy a gift for my dad."

"Is it his birthday?" I ask, and they all fix their gazes on me. Did I say something stupid?

"Christmas is in two weeks," Clay chortles, clapping his hand on my back. "Dude, you really need a calendar at your place."

Shit. I stare off into the distance. They will all go home in two weeks. To their loving and caring families. To the warmth and happiness of their homes. And me? I will stay here, visit my mom on Christmas Eve.

The buzzing of my phone rips me from my thoughts. I pull it out of my pocket, not even trying to listen to what they are all talking about. I'm zoned out and still in my own misery dimension.

HONEY:

You look lonely.

HONEY:

I can fix that. You in?

I lift my head and look at her. Her phone is on the table; her palm covers it. She wears a polite smile, listening to her best friend talk about her plans for winter break. She doesn't care that they all can guess we're texting, does she? I smile and type my answer.

ME:

I have practice in 25 minutes.

HONEY:

Your loss then.

I lock my phone and shove it back into my pocket. Looking up, I meet her gaze. It's full of mischief and fire. She has something on her mind, and I want to know what it is. She intrigues me beyond anything that is normal, reminding me of an obsession. I want to know everything about her, every little detail.

"I'm gonna go to the library. It's my place of zen. A place where no one disturbs me." Ava stands up, taking her backpack from the bench. Layla coughs, and I hear the name—Jordan. Is the roommate still causing her problems? "Yes, the library is way better than my room if I want to concentrate. See you at five, Layla?"

"Yup. I'll find you there. Just text me if you decide to go back to your dorm."

"Sure." Ava bends down and kisses her best friend's cheek. "See you guys, and thanks for standing up for me."

She waves and strolls away. I give myself five minutes. Five minutes, and I'll follow her.

Who am I kidding? Only myself. I stand up from the table so abruptly they all turn their heads toward me.

"I'll see you at practice."

"But we were going to eat." Clay blurts out, his brows pinching together. "Aren't you hungry?"

"It's fine. Dad wants to talk. He just sent me a text."

"Oh, okay. See you later," Clay mutters and focuses on Benson.

I'm not listening to them anymore. I wheel around and saunter straight to the library. As soon as I step inside, I realize it's even more deserted than last time. Only the librarian is here, reading a book and ignoring me. Not that it doesn't suit me. I scan the room and lock eyes with Ava. She holds my gaze, then turns the corner, hiding behind the rows of books.

At the table where she left her stuff, I put my backpack on the floor and follow her. She's leaning on a bookshelf, a seductive grin spread across her lips. She knew I would come.

I stalk over to her, wrap an arm around her waist, and pull her into my chest. "I missed you."

Ava leans forward, standing on her tiptoes. Her mouth is an inch away from my own. "Then prove it."

I smirk, then I smash my lips onto hers. Damn. Being on time for practice will be extremely hard. I have no desire to let her go.

Chapter 34

Say My Name

AVA

I walk out of the dining hall smiling like the Cheshire cat. Turns out I can't be angry with Clay for too long. As soon as I saw him this morning, making his way over to me dressed in a long, black dress with a full face of makeup, my annoyance disappeared. He didn't owe me anything, but he still did as I told him. He's determined to be my friend, and I appreciate him for that. People like him are rare and should be treasured.

As for Moore, I need to be on the lookout. Jerks like him have no idea how to be forgiving; they believe in their exclusivity and think everyone should bow their heads to them. But he chose the wrong person to bet on. I have way too much self-respect to let myself be fooled. And knowing that Clay, Drake, and Colt have my back makes me more confident that I will be able to stand my ground and defend myself.

Once I reach the library, my mind empties except for one thing: Colton Thompson. Sauntering inside, I greet Ms. Lewis, who has her nose buried in another romance book, and go to the farthest table. I put my things on the chair and hear the door open. When I look up, I'm captivated by his enigmatic eyes. The fire behind his irises revives, and I feel hot. My skin is scorching, and the only thing I want is him.

I veer around the corner and disappear into the stacks. I lean back on the bookshelf, waiting for him to join me. It only takes him a few minutes.

Colton edges around the bookshelves and walks toward me, his eyes never leaving my body. Winding a hand around my waist, he pulls me close to his chest. His scent hits my nostrils, and I'm not okay. Absolutely not okay. It's overwhelming and incredibly familiar.

"I missed you," he whispers, and I try to chuck away the urge to touch myself. The feelings he ignites within me are shattering, throwing me off balance.

I stand on my tiptoes, letting my gaze wander over his face and pinpointing my attention on his lips. "Then prove it."

Colton bends down and steals all of my coherent thoughts. His kiss is like a glass of cold water during the summer heat. It's full of need, passion, and also demanding. He's claiming me, marking me as his, and it's so fucking addictive I cave in.

His hands slide down to my butt and squeeze it firmly. My eyes roll to the back of my head, and I moan. Colt smiles in our kiss and lifts my skirt up, digging his fingers into my skin. Oh God, this feels so good. I press myself to him, my desire for him growing with each second. I have no idea how I'm going to study once he goes to practice. My panties are already ruined. I pant, kissing him back with everything I have.

"How do you expect me to be focused on practice after something like this?" Colton murmurs against my lips, inching closer to my ear and sucking my earlobe into his mouth. He drags his teeth over my earring, and I shut my eyes as the pain courses through my body. The strangest thing? It excites me. I love how the pain mixes with my arousal, intensifying my need.

"I don't. I'll need a cold shower instead of studying."

"But you hate studying in your dorm."

"It's not that I hate it, but studying in my room makes me uncomfortable."

"Is your roommate still causing problems?"

"Sometimes." I whimper as he sucks on my neck, leaving a hickey. "We don't get along."

"Do you want me to talk to her? I can make it better." And give her our secret on a silver platter? No, thanks. It's been three months, and I've gotten used to her antics. It's not something I can't deal with.

"No, that's okay." He palms my breast while his lips leave a trail of light kisses down my neck. His other hand finds its way under my skirt and tights, and the next thing I know, he's pressing his thumb to my clit through my panties. "Colt."

"I don't have any condoms with me, but I can still make you feel good."

"You don't have to," I argue as he massages my clit in slow and gentle circles, sending my emotions skyrocketing into my own universe. A universe I named after him. "I didn't mean it that way...you just looked lonely, and I—oh my fucking God, Colt."

I dig my fingers into his forearm, steadying myself because my legs are about to give out. He's no longer just circling his thumb over my clit, he's already pushed my panties aside and slid two fingers inside me. When I catch his gaze, I drown. He has the most beautiful eye color I have ever seen.

"Say my name."

"Colt."

"Again."

"Colt." My vision is blurry. My eyelashes tremble as I struggle to keep my eyes open. "Colt-*on*."

He smashes his lips onto mine, silencing my moans. I cling to his shoulders, because if I don't, I will fall. The possibility of us getting caught is thrilling. It's even more intoxicating than when he fingered me here the first time. One fleeting thought about that, and I'm gone. I come hard, all over his fingers, with his name on my tongue in a barely audible voice.

Colton fixes my panties and retracts his hand. I grab his wrist, stopping him. I'm curious to see his reaction. I pull his hand back, but he brushes me off and sucks his fingers into his mouth. "It's mine, and I'm not sharing."

I straighten my skirt, smoothing it down with my hands. I need a shower, and to change my panties. Studying can wait.

He fishes his phone out of his pocket and smiles, looking up at me. "I have ten minutes before practice, so I have time for a shower."

"Lucky you," I say, walking past him, but he grabs my elbow, stopping me.

"Lucky me is when your pussy is clenched around my dick, wetting it with your juices, and my palms are on your perfect tits. That's what lucky me means."

"Kinda hate you right now," I murmur as he gently kisses my forehead.

"Because you want me again?" he chortles. Then he lets me go, and we both stroll back to the table to get our things.

"Because I want you again," I scoff grumpily. He laughs, pulling me to his side and kissing my temple. This affectionate side of him needs to go away, or I could fall in love.

"Come to my place later."

"I can't." I pick up my backpack, suddenly feeling a heavy weight on my soul. I want to go to his place. I want to spend time with him, and it's not about sex—maybe a little bit about sex, but not really. Even just watching something with him sounds perfect. "I'm going shopping with Layla. See you around, Colt."

"See you, Ava." He winks, turns around, and ambles out of the library. I follow him, dragging my feet purposefully slow. I'm still floating on the waves of the pleasure he gave me, and don't want to come down.

"Ava?" Ms. Lewis calls out as I pass her desk. I halt in my tracks, wear a polite smile, and turn to her. She's around forty, and she's actually very nice. She's one of the reasons why I like coming here. We have talked a lot about books we both like, always adding more to our endless to-read lists. She even follows my bookstagram now.

"Yes?"

"Try to be quieter next time."

My skin is sizzling with embarrassment. She laughs, shakes her head, and picks up her book. "You were distracting me from my date with Damon Torrance."

She's reading *Kill Switch*? I wonder who her favorite character is. *Oh my goodness. Ava. You're unbelievable. The woman just heard you getting fingered in the college library, and you're curious about the book she's reading?*

"Sorry. It won't happen again," I mumble. Then I scurry away, hearing her tinkling laughter behind my back. She definitely won't say a word if we do that here, but I'm not sure I want the library to be our place anymore. I don't want anyone to pry.

On my way to the dorm, I pull my phone out of my pocket and notice one new message. When I read it, I grin like an idiot and instantly type my answer.

CT:

How about Wednesday?

ME:

Yes.

I'm loving our agreement more and more. I just hope I won't get burned.

Chapter 35

Hopeful

COLTON

Two weeks have passed at lightning speed. It's Thursday, and tomorrow everyone is going to leave for winter break. Except me. Usually I don't mind. I'm happy to spend my time alone, with no one bothering me, demanding my attention. Now? I fucking hate the idea of her leaving. It's probably going to be the longest two weeks of my life.

Between exams and hockey, Ava and I have barely seen each other. We hooked up twice after our moment in the library, and that's definitely not enough for me. I miss talking to her, watching movies with her, doing anything with her, because she makes even the shittiest things better. But we have been texting a ton. We joke, we flirt, we talk about school, the books she reads, the shows and movies we both want to watch, new songs to listen to. I feel carefree and happy when she's around, and I talk. I *really* talk. I tell her things I usually keep to myself.

"Thompson, ready to go?" I turn my head and stare at Benson as if I'm seeing him for the first time in my life.

"What?"

He fixes the bag draped over his shoulder. "I asked if you're ready to go. Everyone left already."

I look around the locker room, and my eyes go wide. I was so lost in my own head I didn't even hear the other guys leave. Ava's presence in my life has screwed up my mind. Or is it her absence? I stand and pull up the hood of my hoodie. I pick up my bag from the floor, zip it, and walk over to Drake. He smirks, pushes the door open, and I follow him outside. I have a very strange feeling, like he stayed behind on purpose because he wants to talk.

"What are your plans for winter break?" Benson asks as we stroll down the hallway to the exit.

"No plans. I'm staying here."

"Must be lonely."

"I've gotten used to it. Summer breaks are the only ones when I go home."

He glances at me, looking me up and down. There is no need for his pity. I'm totally fine with not seeing my family. I actually feel way more content when I'm alone. Or when I'm with Ava, but that's not going to happen. She already told me how much she misses her dad, and how happy she is to finally go home for longer than a weekend.

I open the door, and cold air hits my face. I shiver, and goosebumps spread all over my skin. It's too fucking cold.

"Colton?"

I stop in my tracks and spin to my right, looking at Benson.

"Listen, I'm not the prying type, and I'm most definitely not a fucking gossip, but I'm attentive. I see things, hear things, and make assumptions." Benson shifts, suddenly becoming serious. "Is something going on between you and Ava?"

The honesty of my answer depends on one thing only. What does he want to know? "Maybe."

"No matter what you think right now, she's just my friend," he says, straightening his back and squaring his shoulders. "We had sex, but that's in the past. I have no feelings for her. I'm asking you this because I care about her, and I don't want her to get hurt."

"Why would I hurt her?"

"Um, because it's you. Thompson, I've known you since our first year here, and your reputation precedes you. Have you ever had a girlfriend? Or any type of committed relationship?"

"What does that have to do with anything?" I ask, feeling perplexed.

"Everything. Two years ago, her ex did a number on her, and she hasn't had a boyfriend since." Benson licks his lips, looking away and staring at something behind me. "She was ready to lose herself in that guy, but now she refuses to be with anyone. So if she lets you get close to her, it means something. And I don't want you to fuck her up even more than her ex did."

"I'm not going to hurt her." He opens his mouth, but I don't let him interrupt me. "She's different, and I—I like her."

Benson is silent for a moment. Then he breaks into a smile. "Good to know."

Shoving my hands in my pockets, I hold his gaze. A question lingers on the tip of my tongue. "What did he do?"

"Ask her yourself. We'll see if she trusts you."

"Great," I huff, my fingertips itching. I suddenly want to smoke, badly—I haven't done that in months. But the possibility of her not trusting me scares the shit out of me.

"Look, that breakup affected her way more than she thinks. Ava naively believes she's over it, but she's not." Benson takes a deep breath. "Her refusal to be on the ice proves it."

"Wait. She told me that she and the ice rink aren't friends anymore. Is it because of her ex?"

He nods. "Ava loved being on the ice. You have no idea how many times she and Layla would play against me when we were kids. Helping me practice, skating with me, or just dancing and singing, having fun and being her usual easygoing self. That idiot ruined it for her. Games are the only times she gets close to the ice."

We both fall silent, looking at each other and saying nothing. The wheels in my head work fast, and only one possible conclusion comes to my mind. "Is he a hockey player?"

"You are quick." Benson grins, chuckling. "He plays for the Gladiators."

Our worst rivals. I know every guy from that team. "Who is he?"

"Jefferson," Benson snarls, grimacing. "He's a fucking douche."

"If he hurt her, he's more than just a douche." I vaguely remember him since he's two years younger than me, but I will make sure he remembers me after our next game.

"Oh, I know that look, and I don't feel sorry for him."

"You shouldn't." I laugh quietly, step closer, and extend my hand to Drake. He takes it and pulls me in, hugging me briefly before stepping back.

"Thank you for being honest, Colt."

"You too." I give him a smile. "Now I know something new about the girl I like."

"You make it sound as if she's..." Benson's jaw drops, and he eyes me like I've turned into Shrek. "Is she the first girl you've ever liked?"

I fix my hood in annoyance, furrowing my brow and looking away. "Yes."

"Dude. Are you for real? That's amazing."

"It's embarrassing."

"No, you dumbass. It means she's special. Maybe even *the one*."

I blink. Is he fucking serious?

"I'm done with this conversation." I turn on my heel and storm away from Benson, who is choking on his laughter. Unlocking my car, I toss my bag in the backseat and slide in behind the wheel. Only now do I realize I'm smiling.

As I start the engine, I think about her last text. She's leaving as soon as her classes end, and I won't have a chance to see her at all.

Two weeks without Ava? I'm doomed.

What time is it? I breathe heavily; my whole body is covered in sweat. Being alone isn't good for me. This is the third time this week I fell asleep watching *Sherlock* and woke up because I dreamed about my past. The image of pregnant Helen talking to my mom pops into my head, and a nauseating feeling forms in my throat. I'm getting dangerously close to memories I want to forget, ones that I tried to erase, to destroy because they bring only pain and sorrow.

I grab my phone from my bedside table and stare at the screen. Four a.m. It's earlier than the last time. I climb out of bed and head to the kitchen. I need a glass of water to chase away this sticky feeling of hopelessness.

Things have started to come back, and I'm not okay. I'm not ready to face the demons of my past, not when Christmas Eve is in four days. Not when I need to be at my father's stupid party next month. If I survive it without punching him in his face, it will be a miracle. He shouldn't have asked her to call me.

He would have made things more tolerable if he'd called me himself. I would have argued, would have cursed, but I would have come and played the role of the perfect son. But after Helen's call? I'm ready to kill him with my bare hands and kick her out of his company. He shouldn't have kept her close, not after everything. He could support her, give her money, anything—just put her in her place. But that's not what the great Eric Thompson does. Pathetic douche.

After chugging two glasses of cold water, I drag myself back to my bedroom. I'm yawning, so maybe if I hide under the covers, I will fall asleep? That would be great, because I'm having headaches almost daily now, all because of my lack of sleep. My apartment is dark, and hardly any sounds from the street reach it. I feel so alone, more alone than I have ever felt in my life. Because now I know the difference. What it means to have someone who makes my days brighter. Someone who makes me feel alive, who makes me smile a thousand times a day, even if usually I'm grumpy and hate everyone.

Ava isn't compelled to like me. She isn't tied to me by any bonds except her own desire to spend time with me. It's something that turns my world upside down, giving me hope and filling me with happiness and warmth. I only pray I won't fuck it up.

Back in bed, I close my laptop, put it on the floor, and slide under the covers. Her scent is no longer here, and I miss it. I miss everything about her, and it is driving me crazy. I can't touch her, kiss her, or be with her. Winter break chose the worst time ever to start.

I unlock my phone, intending to turn off the alarm I had set for eight a.m., but I have two unread messages. They came in after midnight, when my "do not disturb" mode started. One is from Ava, the other is from...Benson? What the fuck?

I open her message first and freeze when I read it. Then I open

Drake's text. I quickly type responses to both of them, put my phone on the bedside table, and close my eyes. Drifting off to sleep happy and hopeful isn't something I'm used to, but it feels amazing.

Chapter 36

You Know Each Other?

AVA

"Call him," Drake says in my ear and then quickly moves past me.

"Who?"

"You know who." He smiles, slumping down into the chair in front of me. I came here to spend some time with Layla but ended up with her big brother. My best friend is being her usual self and forgot to tell me about her dentist appointment. Of course, I could have gone home after Drake told me where she was, but I was bored to death there, so it wasn't an option.

"Actually no, I don't." I frown, taking my mug from the table and holding it between my palms. He made me a hot chocolate, as he has a thousand times before. It's always incredibly good.

"Thompson."

I bring the mug to my mouth and take a sip, using this moment to buy myself some time. Since fucking when does he know anything about me and Colt? Putting my hot chocolate back on the table, I narrow my eyes. "Why should I call him?"

"Maybe ask him to visit."

"Why?" I press, and Drake snaps. Driving him crazy is the best way to find out what I want.

"Because you and him have something going on."

"Who told you that?" I smirk, a lopsided grin on my face. *Making assumptions, Drake? I thought you were better than—*

"He told me."

"When?" My voice sounds hoarse. I absolutely didn't expect that.

He leans back, staring at me with a smile playing on his lips. "Last week."

I huff, pouting and looking away. Why did he do that? It doesn't make any sense. "We're just...um...we're hooking up. That's all."

"Kinda figured that out." Drake snorts. "You have it bad."

"Excuse me?" I narrow my eyes.

"Layla told me you were all worked up yesterday. Your itch is strong, and you need your fix. Your best friend's words, not mine."

My itch? My fucking itch? Layla fucking Benson. I will strangle her as soon as I see her. "She has no idea what she's talking about."

"But I do. I know how you look when you—"

"Another fucking word, and I'm out." I say through gritted teeth, and he bursts out cackling. These fucking Benson siblings will be the death of me. Why on Earth did my dad think it was a good idea to buy a house near their family?

"Ava, your reaction only proves my point," Drake mumbles between fits of laughter. "Call him."

"Do you think I haven't talked to him since we left for winter break?" We talk. A lot. Texting him takes up a huge amount of my time when I'm not with my dad or Layla. Colton wants to know everything about my day, barely telling me anything about his. It's frustrating, but he justifies it every time, saying that he is staying at home and doing nothing. Isn't he hanging out with Clay? The last I heard from his best friend, he was spending almost every night partying.

"You do know he didn't go home, right?" My jaw drops, and Drake notices it. "He's by himself in his apartment. I think it's probably pretty lonely."

Uneasiness spreads throughout my body. How didn't I figure that out myself? The answer was there, and I was too self-absorbed to notice. When he said he was staying "home" he meant his apartment.

Dammit, Colt. I thought you'd started opening up to me.

"He told me the only thing he does these days is watch movies," I mutter under my breath, avoiding looking at Drake. "I assumed he wasn't in the mood to party with his friends. Fuck."

"You obviously like him as more than just a hookup."

"Drake Benson, you are trying to get me to hurt you today," I hiss. Then I grab my phone from the table and stare at it hopelessly. What can I do? Christmas is in four days, and I'm not going to leave my dad alone. Should I go visit him before that? It could work, but I don't know.

"You could invite him to stay with us." I look up from my phone, locking eyes with Drake. A playful smirk illuminates his face, and he arches his eyebrow at me. "Our parents are barely home, and we definitely have spare rooms. They won't say a word if he comes and stays at our house for a few days."

The idea of having Colt here is appealing. Even if I have no desire to admit it, I do miss him. I miss our time together, our talks, and the sex. He is the only person who can fix it, because after sex with him, I can't imagine myself with anyone else.

"Ava?" Drake calls my name, and I collect myself, pushing aside all my dirty and disturbing thoughts. I grab my drink and take a sip. "Do you want me to invite him?"

Yes or no? Simple, right? Unfortunately, not exactly. I need to talk to my dad first, because if Colton's here, I will be spending way less time at home. "I do."

"Cool." He pulls his phone out of his pocket, but then he notices my gaze on him. "What?"

"I need to talk to Dad first, just to give him the heads-up and see if he's okay with it."

"Your dad never says no to you."

"You're wrong."

"Yeah, okay, maybe you've heard 'no' once in your life. But sure. Ask him and tell me what to do."

"Thanks, Drake. I appreciate it. A lot." We smile at each other. The house is quiet, so when the door closes with a bang, we both jump in our seats. My best friend is back.

Drake stands up and edges to the door, lingering in the doorway. I watch him as he shuffles his feet. He obviously wants to say something, and he's trying to find the right words.

"Yes?" I nudge him.

He rolls his eyes, and a grin tugs at one corner of his mouth. "If Colton does come, I don't have any problem with you two hooking up here."

Who the hell does he think he is? I grab a towel off the table and throw it in his face. No luck. He catches it in the air, shaking from laughter. "I hate you, Benson."

"Nah, babe, you love me." With that, he winks and walks out. A minute later, I hear him talking to his sister, telling her I'm waiting in the kitchen. I'm blessed to have friends like them, even if they drive me insane sometimes.

I lie on my stomach, reading a book about a younger sister who falls in love with her oldest sister's husband. It's a taboo romance with a healthy dose of smut, but everything in this story is exactly how I like it. Characters who are realistic and flawed, a plot that tears my heart to shreds, then repairs it with the happiest ending. The vibe this book gives me is what I'm looking for.

Sometimes I listen to music while I read, but not tonight. I'm waiting for my dad to come home. I want to talk to him about Colton. It's important.

The sound of a door opening pierces the air, and I squint at Smokey. His ears are perked up, and he slowly lifts his head. It must be Dad.

It's past midnight, and the house is dark. I slowly tiptoe down the stairs with my cat in tow. Smokey is like my shadow, and I'm sure he misses me when I'm away at college. He barely leaves my side when I'm home.

"Dad?"

"Why are you still up?" His soft voice sounds tired, and a rush of tenderness swirls through my veins. I love this man so much, and it always pains me how exhausted he is after work.

"I was reading," I confess as he turns on the lights.

"Uh-huh." Dad walks up and kisses my forehead.

"I left mac and cheese for you. I can heat it up."

"It's been a long day, Ava." He smiles at me affectionately, and I shake my head, grab his hand, and drag him to the kitchen. With how much he works, he needs to eat. "Baby, I'm not hungry."

"When was the last time you ate?" I cock an eyebrow, pushing him to sit in the chair. Ambling to the fridge, I take the plate I left for him and put it into the microwave. I set the timer, then I wheel around and peer at my father. He's barely hiding his smile, and I know I won. "When, Dad?"

"Around five?"

"And it's twelve thirty." Smokey rubs his head against my ankle and then goes to drink his water. I smile and focus on Dad.

"What would I do without you, huh?"

"You'd probably starve yourself to death," I joke, and he laughs heartily. "How was your day?"

"Good. Just had too much paperwork to do." Dad sighs, running his hands over his face. "What did you do?"

"Nothing. I hung out with Drake and Layla at their place."

The microwave dings, and I take the plate out, set it in front of him, and plop myself down on the chair across from him. He starts to eat, but his eyes are full of suspicion. He knows me too damn well.

"Do you want me to choke on my food?"

"What?" I mutter, and my brows pinch together.

"You're looking at me so intently, like you're waiting for me to choke on my mac and cheese."

"Dad." I groan, dropping my forehead onto the table.

"As you rightly noticed, it's already past midnight, and I'm exhausted. Spill, young lady."

Taking a deep breath, I sit up straight and stare at him. "Do you remember the guy I mentioned a few weeks ago?"

"Drake's teammate. Thompson." Why does he always remember everything? "What about him?"

"We are kinda...seeing each other," I blurt out, suddenly realizing my palms are sweating. Why am I so nervous? I've never been like this.

"Okay. So he's your boyfriend?"

"No," I say, falling quiet for a moment. "We're just...having fun."

Dad puts his fork on the table and narrows his eyes. "Define 'having fun'."

"We talk a lot. Text all the time. Spend time together when we both have a moment to spare." Honesty is the fucking holy grail. It's the foundation of my relationship with my dad. If I ever lie to him, it would be for a very solid reason. "He's nice to me, and he has never forced me into anything I don't want to do."

Dad watches me without saying anything. He's calm and collected, and it soothes my nerves. "Do you want to invite him here? What about his family?"

"He's kinda closed off, and it's hard for him to open up. So I honestly don't know a lot of stuff about him. Yet." I weigh my next words carefully. "Drake told me Colton didn't go home for winter break. Apparently I was too dumb to figure it out myself."

"You're not dumb. You often look at things from your own perspective, and that doesn't always work. That's all."

"Maybe." I sigh, twisting my hair around my finger.

"Do you miss him? Or is this just an act of compassion because you feel bad for him and want to cheer him up?" I feel my cheeks warm. I'm so fucking deep in my shit for this guy. "Ava?"

"I miss him," I admit. "And I feel sorry for him. No one deserves to be alone on Christmas."

"You can invite him," Dad tells me, cupping my cheek with his palm.

"Drake suggested Colt could stay at their place."

"Good." He chuckles, eyeing me with a smile on his face. "Something is telling me if I want to see you at home, I'll need to prep a room for your new guy."

"He's not my guy."

"But I'll still need to prepare a room," my father counters with laughter.

"You're the best dad in the whole world." I say, throwing my arms around his neck and kissing his cheek.

"I have a few days off coming up, so if he agrees to come, it would be great to meet him."

"He'll say yes. I'm a hundred percent positive." I jump to my feet, taking Dad's empty plate from the table and waltzing to the sink. "Go to bed. I'll take care of the dishes."

Dad stands up and heads to the living room, glancing at me over his shoulder. "I know no matter what I say, you will find an opportunity to sneak him into your room."

"Dad."

"I want you to be careful. That's all." He doesn't wait for a response, just saunters further into the living room. "Night, baby."

"Night, Dad." I can't stop smiling. I'm fucking hopeless.

WHEN I WAKE up at eleven a.m., the first thing I do is grab my phone to check for new messages. Why was he up at four a.m.? Was he partying? Or clubbing? It doesn't matter. What is more important is his answer.

ME:

So how about spending some time in my hometown? With me :)

CT:

Send me your address?

I fall back on my bed with a big, radiant smile on my face, holding my phone in the air and sending him the details. His reply comes a few minutes later.

CT:

Will be there around two p.m.

I toss my phone aside, grasp my pillow and hide my face in it, yelling at the top of my lungs. Someone needs to slap me upside my head. Something that was just supposed to be fun is turning into something incredibly serious. All these butterflies need to be murdered, or I'm afraid to even think about how I'll feel at his graduation. I'm setting myself up to be heartbroken.

I'm in the living room, reading a new book, as I already finished the one about the sister's husband. Rom-coms aren't usually my thing, but this one is amazing. Plus, it's a hockey romance with a friends-with-benefits trope—I can kinda relate to it.

"Looks like your guy is punctual." Dad's voice rips me from my thoughts. He's staring out the window, and I stand up from the couch. My heart flutters in my chest. It's so loud it's almost painful. The hardest part? Hiding my current state from my dad. I don't want anyone to know how much I like this guy.

"Let's go. I'll introduce you." I put my book on the couch and stroll to the hallway.

When I open the door, my eyes instantly lock on Colton's. He smiles, and I'm a fucking puddle already. The guy is too handsome for his own good—or maybe my own misery. I still haven't decided.

"Hey."

"Hey." He steps inside. His scent wafting around him makes my butterflies go crazy. It's a fucking punk concert in my stomach. I close the door and whirl around, ready to introduce Colton to my dad and—I literally freeze. The look on his face is extremely weird. There's confusion, and also fear.

My father gazes at him with a tender smile. "Hey, Colt."

I honestly feel like I'm drowning. Does he know him? It's the only way to explain this strange reaction.

"Hello, Dax," Colton mutters. His voice is barely audible.

I step closer, looking at both of them in turn. "You know each other?"

Chapter 37

The Bridge

COLTON

One year ago

Why the hell will no one tell me how she's doing? I'm her fucking son, and all they are giving me is a line of crap: "Your mom is in the ER; we're doing everything we can." I need to fucking know what happened. How severe are her injuries? What is the prognosis? What are the chances of her making a full recovery? Answers. I need fucking answers, and they are giving me none.

I take my phone out of my pocket and see missed calls from my grandparents, from Clay and other guys from the team. Even my coach has already called me, but not him. My asshole father is pretending that nothing happened, that nothing is his fault, while in reality? It's on him, and on me. I should have told her everything the second I found out the truth. I shouldn't have listened to him. I shouldn't have lied to her.

I shove my phone back into my pocket and rub my palms over my face. I'm so fucking drained, I feel like I'm going to pass out. I lean against the wall and close my eyes. I just want to go back in time and fix everything. I want to save her from this, from this knowledge, from how she found out about her husband's infidelity. It shouldn't have come to this.

"Hey." A deep and soothing voice snaps me out of my thoughts. I open my eyes and see a man I have never seen before. He's tall and big, with broad shoulders and a toned chest. He's close to my father's age, but he looks different. The vibe he gives me is the exact opposite of the one I feel near my dad. It's like this man's calm demeanor affects everyone around him, including me.

I keep silent, gaping at him. I'm not in the best mood, and I'm afraid I'm going to flip out any minute. It's always hard for me to communicate with people I don't know, but tonight it will be impossible. It took all my strength not to yell at the nurses earlier. This man doesn't look like he works in the hospital, so I honestly have no desire to engage with him.

"My name is Dax," he tells me, and I narrow my eyes. What does he want from me? "I was on my way home when I saw your mom's car hit the railing of the bridge."

I push myself away from the wall. My whole body is tense, and I ball my fists. My heart thunders hard against my chest. The world around me stops existing, and I focus my attention solely on this man. Is he the one who saved her? Someone told me she was lucky—a firefighter was on the bridge. Is it him?

"Did you..." I clear my throat. My mouth is dry, and I sound hoarse. "Did you save her?"

"That's what I do. I'm a firefighter." He smiles gently at me, the corners of his eyes softening. "The second I saw her car go over the bridge and into the river, I knew what to do. I just hope I made it in time and she will have a chance to recover."

"No one will tell me anything," I blurt, choking on my own words. "I know nothing about her injuries."

"I'm sorry, son. Being in the dark is always hard. Sometimes our imaginations draw pictures that are much worse than reality," Dax says, hiding his hands in his pockets. And just like that, I know he speaks from experience. Not just the kind he gained from his work, but something way more personal.

"You need to have hope. To hold it close to your heart and pray for the best. It's bad right now, but it won't be like that forever. Keep that in mind, and try to focus on good things. Thinking positively is hard, but it's worth it. Trust me."

I stay quiet for a moment. If only I didn't feel so guilty, it would be easier; it would be the only thing on my mind: is my mom okay. Now? On top of feeling nervous and scared of her future, I'm drowning in my own ocean of regret. I failed her. I betrayed her trust, her faith in me. I broke her when I agreed to keep quiet. Fuck.

"Where is your father?"

I clench my jaw so hard my teeth hurt. Dax notices it and frowns, his brows pinching together.

"My father is a jerk."

"Should have guessed," he mutters under his breath, looking around. His gaze lingers on my gym bag and my hockey stick on the floor, and then he stares me in the eyes."You play hockey?"

"Yeah." I gradually relax because he doesn't push the issue. Telling a complete stranger the truth about my father and why my mom ended up on that fucking bridge is not something I want to do. "I was on my way to the dorm from practice when I got the call from the police. Rushed here without a second thought. I have no idea why I grabbed my stuff from my car."

Dax chuckles, flashing a little grin. "You were stressed, and in a state like that we don't think clearly. It actually means something."

"What?"

"Hockey is important to you. It's something you love. And when you felt like your world was falling apart, you grabbed your stuff because it's a stable element in your life. Am I right?"

"Maybe," I chortle. I was tense, and now I'm fucking smiling?

"I've probably seen you play. My friend's kid is a hockey player too. If they played at home when he was in high school, I was there with his family and my daughter. Can't say I love hockey, though."

"No? Hockey is the best thing ever, along with soccer."

"Arguable." He laughs, looking at something over my shoulder. "I think the doctor is waiting for you."

I hurriedly whip my head and see a young doctor eyeing me from a distance. He's the one I already tried to talk to, and he brushed me off. Maybe he has some news for me?

"Thank you so much for saving my mom, Dax. She's the most important person in my life, and losing her..." I fall silent, taking a deep breath to steady my heartbeat. I shut my eyes for a moment, and then center my attention on Dax. His eyes are emerald green, and they are full of warmth. He said he has a daughter, and I honestly envy her. Having a father like him must be great. I'm sure he's not a douche like my sperm donor is. "Thank you."

"You're very welcome..." He arches his eyebrow, and I realize I still haven't introduced myself.

"I'm Colton Thompson. Colt."

"You're very welcome, Colt." He extends his hand to me, and we shake. "I hope to see you on the ice one day. I promise to cheer for you."

I glance over my shoulder. The doctor shifts uncomfortably, and shivers run down my spine. "I gotta go."

"Of course." Dax takes a step back. "Bye, Colton."

"Bye," I mumble. Then I whirl around and storm over to the doctor. If it wasn't for Dax, I probably would have had a breakdown already. His presence and conversation helped me a ton. I will forever be grateful to him.

The second my eyes land on Ava's father, I'm lost in my memories. I can't back away without looking like a moron. I don't have any other choice except to step inside their house and relive all the things I tried to forget.

What the fuck is this? How is it even possible that the first girl I've ever liked is the daughter of the man who saved my mom's life?

"Hey, Colt," he says with a smile. My heart contracts. It feels like someone is keeping me underwater, not letting me take a breath. Not letting me fill my lungs. I want to disappear, because I'm afraid of the talk that is coming.

"Hello, Dax."

Ava walks up close and steps between us, glancing at me and her father in turn. "You know each other?"

Dax smiles at me. "Yes."

"How?" She puts her hands on her hips, confusion evident on her beautiful face.

I lock eyes with her father, and I instantly know he won't say more. He's letting me make this decision. "Your dad knows my mom."

"Really?" The wrinkle between her brows becomes deeper and more visible.

"Yeah." Dax nods. "Met once, but I still remember her. A woman like Avery is hard to forget."

"Did my dad hit on your mom?" she asks, and he cackles. "Dad."

"Do I look like a man who would hit on someone's wife, Ava? You definitely know better."

"Sorry, Dad. I just...didn't expect you two to know each other."

"The moment you mentioned he was a hockey player named Thompson, I knew I'd met Colton already." Dax meets my gaze, and I have no idea what to say. He's not angry with me, is he? He understands why I'm not telling her the truth. But why?

"You should have told me," Ava says. Then she freezes, and her mouth falls open. "Oh, you asked me for his last name, but I didn't figure out why."

"Sorry, sweetie. You called him an asshole, so I wasn't sure if I should mention it."

"I am an asshole," I state, seeing her blush. She huffs, shifting her weight from one foot to the other.

"She also said you look at her like she's your favorite snack." Dax slips his hands in his pockets, hardly keeping himself from laughing.

I run my fingers through my hair. My skin is itching. All this freaking tension is keeping my body hostage, and my mind goes blank. Is this how meeting your crush's parents for the first time always goes? So easy and so fucking nice? Something is telling me it's not usually like this at all. It's just Dax and his personality. And how much he loves his daughter. It's contagious.

"Dad." Ava says, and her father bursts out laughing, unable to contain himself anymore. She grasps my hand in hers and drags me upstairs. "I'm going to show Colton to his room, and then we can have lunch together."

"Whatever you say, honey," Dax murmurs, still shaking with laughter.

I follow her in silence. Thoughts circulate in my head like a swarm of bees. My room? Wasn't Drake's message about me staying at his house? I don't understand a thing, but I'm happy nonetheless. The more time spent with Ava, the better.

She opens the door to a room, and we step inside, heading straight to the bed. Ava lets go of my hand, and I sit, watching her. Every time I look at her, I fall harder. Sometimes it scares me, but sometimes, like today, I feel blessed. With how fucked up I was, I didn't think I'd ever feel anything close to how I feel now. It's a fucking miracle she likes me back.

Ava's long brown hair is in two braids. She wears no makeup and is still absolutely gorgeous. She doesn't have even an ounce of pretense in her, and I'm pulled to her and her honesty like a magnet. She's my kind of orbit, and I revolve around her every damn minute of every day.

I put my hands on her hips and draw her closer, so she's standing between my legs. She's wearing a white crop top and blue cotton shorts. She's cute and sexy as hell. Her flat midriff with her belly ring makes it hard for me to concentrate on anything else, because every new thought that comes to mind is dirtier than the last.

I squeeze her butt and peer into her eyes. "My room?"

"Do you like it?" she asks with a tiny grin on her plump lips.

I rake my gaze over the place and nod. It's simple, in navy blue and gray colors, without any obnoxious decor like my family's house is full of. There is one full bed, two nightstands with two white table lamps, a wooden closet, and a full-length mirror. Nothing superfluous, and I like it.

"Yup. It's nice, and the bed is soft."

"Cool."

"I'm a bit confused," I go on, and she arches her eyebrow at me. "Drake sent me a message too, saying I could stay at his house."

"That was the plan." Ava places her hands on my shoulders, then locks them around my neck. "But once I talked to my dad about your visit, he was sure if you stayed at the Bensons', I would constantly be over there. With you."

"Is that so?"

"Uh-huh." She speaks softly, bending down and hovering her mouth over mine. "Why didn't you tell me you were staying at your apartment alone?"

"You were excited to go home and spend time with your dad. I didn't want to take that away from you."

"And you didn't want me to feel sorry for you?"

"A little," I confess. Her hot breath sends a rush of energy right to my cock.

"Stop having ideas, Colton." She quickly kisses my lips and pulls back. "My dad is downstairs, and he's waiting for us to have lunch together."

I drop my hands from her sides, and Ava steps back. She turns around and edges to the door. "The bathroom is next door. You can use it whenever you need. I'll wait for you downstairs."

The door is almost closed when I hop to my feet and race after her. She halts in her tracks, glancing at me over her shoulder. "I don't want you to wait for me, and I'm kinda tired of being alone."

"Do you need to get your stuff from your car?" Ava asks, lacing our fingers together. "I can go with you."

"Yes, please." I grin as we go downstairs.

LUNCH WITH DAX and Ava was great. They made me feel welcome, as if I belonged in their little family. The conversation was flowing, with lots of jokes and funny stories. Dax never asked me anything about my mom, and I was honestly grateful to him for that.

But I know it will be impossible to leave this house without talking about her.

It reminded me so much of lunches with my mom before shit went down, so much that my heart was aching. Those memories tear me down, bring me to my knees, and make me feel hopeless. I would trade everything I have for even a minute with my mom as her old self. I would do anything to heal her, to take back what she suffered. She didn't deserve to have her future stolen. My father was the one who needed to pay for his sins, not her. Yet destiny proved again how unfair life is.

"What do you want to drink?" Benson's voice is so loud, I curse. Being so deep in my head, I didn't even notice him coming closer. "Day-dreaming in the middle of a party, Thompson?"

"More like getting lost in my memories," I mutter, and he chortles. "When I came here today, I didn't think I would end up at a party."

"Neither did I." He takes a sip of beer and grimaces. "It's as warm as pee."

"Talking from experience?" I kid, and he freezes, staring at me as if he doesn't recognize me. "What?"

"She's rubbing off on you. In a good way."

"You make it sound like I never joke," I scoff, hiding my hands in my pockets.

"Oh, you do, but not like that." Benson smiles, jokingly punching me in my shoulder. "Glad to see you here."

"Me too." I flash him a smile, chuckling. "Rodgers wants to tag along."

"I saw his Insta. He's having the time of his life at home, partying and clubbing. Why the hell would he want to come here?" Benson pinches his brows together, eyeing me with curiosity.

"I think he likes your sister."

"Not going to happen. Out of the question." He shakes his head, setting his beer on the table. "He's even worse than you when it comes to girls."

"Wow." I whistle. "I thought my reputation preceded me."

"Rodgers is a manwhore, and you're not. I stopped counting the girls he slept with during our freshman year, and we're fucking seniors now." Drake gives me a pointed look, and I can't argue with him. He's a big brother; he wants the best for his sister, and Clay is definitely not suited for that role. "I can invite him, and he can stay at my house since you're staying at the Masons', but I will never ever approve of him having a relationship with Layla. What am I even talking about? He doesn't do relationships."

"There are always exceptions," I say quietly, and we lock eyes. I'm talking about Ava, and he understands it right away. "Someone who will make you forget everything and everyone else."

"Colt, I know he's your best friend and you mean well, but unless I see a difference in the way he treats my sister as opposed to all the other girls, I will say no."

"I respect that." We smile at each other, and then I turn around to search for Ava in the crowd. No luck. She went to the bathroom with Layla, and I haven't seen her for at least ten minutes.

"Oh, fuck no," Drake mumbles, taking off without another word. I follow him with my gaze, and my body becomes rigid. Ava and some dude are arguing in the middle of the crowd. He's tall and as big as a fucking bull, and I finally recognize him. It's Jefferson. Her ex.

I storm over, and I only have time to notice the movement of her hands. She pushes him away with all her might, making him stumble back and almost fall on his ass. I'm proud of her, but at the same time I'm scared as shit. If he tries to hit her, I won't be able to make it in time. I speed up as Ava twirls around, marches to the front door, puts on her jacket, and then slams the door behind her. I pass Drake, who's holding the guy back, and then I notice Layla. She points at the door, and I nod. I've got this.

Chapter 38

Bend Over

AVA

"You two are so cute. Never in my life could I imagine Colton Thompson being so affectionate. It's like he can't keep his hands to himself when you're around," Layla murmurs in a breathy whisper while I wash my hands. She's so dramatic sometimes. "Did you expect him to agree so easily? I mean, once you told me you wanted to invite him, I wasn't sure he would come."

"Why?" I turn off the faucet and lean against the countertop. Layla turns to her right and looks at me, her eyes glimmering with warmth.

"Because it meant he would meet your dad. And I wasn't sure he would want that. It's kinda serious for just hooking up." She grins at me, and I can't help but smile too. "The boy is smitten; it's hard not to notice."

"I'm happy he's here." I scan the room without seeing anything. I didn't expect my dad to know him. Dad can obviously tell me more about how they met, but I want Colt to open up to me himself. It's important to me.

"I kinda noticed that," she chortles, draping a hand over my shoulder and pulling me into her for a hug. "How do you feel about him?"

"I like him," I confess, and she hugs me tighter.

"What if he wants to date you?"

"No. We're just having fun, no obligations."

Didn't you promise to be exclusive, Ava?

I wonder if I can turn off my inner voice, because recently it has been saying things I don't want to hear.

"But what if—"

"No." I don't let her finish. I step back abruptly, frowning like a kid. "I have no future with him, and I don't want to drag myself into another shitty situation that will break my heart."

Aren't you already too deep in your feelings for him?

I grit my teeth, turn around, and saunter to the door and out of the bathroom. I want to find Colt and go back home. I have no desire to be at this party any longer, and I honestly regret coming here in the first place. It was a stupid idea, and I should have said no when Layla suggested it.

The first person I see once I step into the living room is Jefferson. Our eyes lock for a moment, and then he checks me out. My skin is burning hot under his gaze—not from desire, but from shame. I hate that fucking asshole, and I despise myself even more for how I feel in his presence. As if I'm still the same girl I was when we were together. As if I'm still someone who allows a guy to treat her like an object. His fucking property.

"Wow," he murmurs, ambling closer and blocking my way. "Stunning, as always."

"Bye." I try to walk around him, and of course his fucking wall of muscles won't let me. "What the fuck do you want, Levi?"

"To talk to you." He steps into my personal space, towering over me and instantly making me feel like less than I am. Physically and mentally. "I saw you earlier with another hockey player. It looks like your type hasn't changed, babe."

"You're definitely not my type," I sneer, balling my fists.

"The guy is well-known in our circle. He's just as much of a player in real life as he is on the ice rink. Thompson is no better than me—actually, even worse. The dude has fucked almost every girl there is. I can't believe you fell so low and became a slut."

I suck in a breath, a sudden coldness hitting my core. "Go fuck yourself, Levi. No one wants you."

I push past him, heading to the front door as quickly as possible considering all these people dancing around me. What I always forget is my size. I need to push through the crowd, while that fucking idiot just takes a step, and people automatically get out of his way.

"You need to drop the fucking attitude, Ava," he hisses through his teeth, grabbing my elbow and stopping me in my tracks.

"Fuck off." I pull my hand out of his grip, turn around, and push him away as hard as I can. Surprise crosses his features as he stumbles back and almost trips over people in the crowd.

"You're a fucking bitch." Jefferson yells. His shocked state holds him back for a moment as he tries to steady himself.

I don't wait for him to stand up. I wheel around and march to the front door, put on my jacket, and stomp out of the house. I just want out. I don't hear a sound. I don't see anyone or anything. I want to have at least a moment alone. To get myself together and erase that fucking jerk from my mind.

"Ava." I hear my name, but I refuse to stop. I'm not in the fucking mood for talking. "Ava."

"What?" I freeze on the spot, not looking at Colt. Why can't he take a hint? I don't want to talk to him. I don't want to talk to anyone. Even Layla.

He jogs over and stops in front of me. His gaze is tense, but he seems lost. He has no idea how to handle my anger, and it only proves how little we know about one another. *Isn't that what you want, Ava? Just sex, no strings attached?*

"What happened?"

"Nothing."

"Who is that guy?" Colton asks.

Jefferson's words ring in my ears, sounding louder and louder with each passing moment.

"No one."

"What did he say to you?"

"Nothing."

"Why did you push him?" His tone becomes lower, and the wrinkle between his brows deepens. His annoyance is rising, and it won't be long before he loses his patience and snaps at me. And honestly, I want it. I want him to leave me alone.

"He deserved it."

"Why?"

"It has nothing to do with you." Only it does. I didn't like what Jefferson said about him, what he insinuated.

"If it has to do with you, then it concerns me." He raises his voice. My chest is ready to explode, so much it hurts. I bite my inner cheek, eyeing him from under my eyelashes. He cares, and I don't fucking need that.

"Bullshit," I mumble and spin around, intending to leave him.

Colton wraps his arms around my waist from behind, crashing me into his chest and lifting me. He stalks to his car, unlocks it, and opens the door of the backseat. He pushes me inside, and I fall flat on my face. Tears spring to my eyes, and I dig my fingernails into the seat. Why can't he leave me alone and give me time to calm down? That's the only thing I need.

"I'm taking you home," he rasps and slams the car door. A second later, he's starting the engine and driving away from the party. I'm seething, and it increases with each beat of my heart, with each turn his car takes. I'm not one to keep silent, and I explode.

Sitting up straight, I meet his gaze in the rearview mirror. "Stop the car."

"No."

"Stop the fucking car, Colton."

"No."

"Stop it." I hit his seat with my hand. A fury fires up my whole body, and I have no control over my emotions anymore. Tipsy Ava always makes bad decisions, no matter the consequences. "I want out."

He grimaces, as if from a sudden toothache. "No."

I slide to the door and yank it, trying to open it. It's useless, and I know that, but if I'm wound up, I never know how to stop. "Stop the fucking car and let me out."

I hear him curse, and the car begins to skid. I bang my head on the window, and my vision blurs from pain. I pissed him off so much, he almost lost control of his car.

The vehicle stops abruptly, and I look out the window. We're about ten minutes away from my house, close to a local park.

Colton jumps out and comes to my door. The next thing I know, I am staring at his face, which is contorted with anger. "What the fuck are you doing?"

"Let me out." I put my hands on his chest, pushing him away.

"No." he shouts, not budging even an inch.

"Let." I push more. "Me." And more. "The fuck." And more. "Out." My legs are on the ground, and I look up, meeting his cold stare. "Move."

Rage is the only emotion I recognize. He rakes his gaze over my face, his nostrils flaring. My heart skips a beat, and my mouth falls open. What the fuck is this? Oh my God. I'm sick in the head—my fucking pussy is wet.

Colt inches closer, grabbing my throat with his palm. He lowers his face; his mouth is less than an inch away from mine. "Stop being a fucking brat." His tongue traces my bottom lip, and my nipples pebble from the contact. "Get in the car and bend over."

"Wh-what?"

He lets go of my throat, winds his hand around my waist, and spins me around. His other hand on my back pushes me facedown into the backseat. Colton lifts the skirt of my dress and drags my tights down, still not touching my panties.

"How wet am I going to find you, Ava?" he asks huskily, unzipping his fly. "How wet are you for me?"

And my fucking brain stops functioning. I lift my ass higher, hearing him tear the condom wrapper. I look over my shoulder and meet his gaze. "I'm dripping."

Colton glides my panties down and presses the tip of his cock to my opening, wetting it with my juices. I want him to fill me. I want him so bad, it's the only emotion I still have. My anger and frustration have dissolved, replaced by primal desire. I'm a fucking goner already.

He slides into me, and I shut my eyes tighter. This time, he doesn't give me any opportunity to adjust to his girth. Fire surges through my veins, and my clit throbs. I love how he makes me feel. I love the feeling of him inside me, how he stretches my pussy until he's balls deep. I feel complete as he slides deeper, slamming his hips into mine and digging his fingernails into my ass. There is no tenderness, no slowness like there was before. It's wild and unpredictable, fulfilling and emptying at the same time. As soon as he moves away, I want him back.

Sex is unique. It depends a lot on your partner. I can't say I have a lot of experience, but I know what gets me off, and I know what cools me down. I know my body and how I like to be touched. I'm all for trying something new, but except for a few times, sex was pretty ordinary. With Colton, it's blissful, driven, and sensual. He doesn't need to ask about the things I want him to do to me. It's like he knows everything about my needs, like they are his own. It's pure passion and infinite lust, but there is something else too. Something else is forming between us, and I'm definitely not ready to acknowledge it.

"Does it feel good?" Colt pumps into me steadily and without holding back. I whimper as he slaps my butt. My legs are shaking, and the peak of my orgasm builds up.

"Yes," I breathe, and he pulls my hair, fisting my braids. "Oh God, please don't stop."

"Maybe I should—wasn't that what you wanted? For me to stop?" His movements gradually slow down, and I feel my orgasm fading away. "I don't think you're ready to come just yet."

I look over my shoulder, glaring at him. He smirks, slaps my ass, and picks up the pace again. As he slowly rams me from behind, pleasure builds in my lower abdomen. He's going incredibly deep. The sound of our bodies slamming against one another is spellbinding. It makes me forget everything around me. Except him.

"You feel so good inside me...please don't stop...don't fucking stop, Colt..."

But he does. He slows down, and my almost-there orgasm slips away from me again. I hide my face in the seat, shutting my eyes tight. I fucking hate him for that. It's pure torture already, and him depriving me makes me see red.

"Please, Colt...I need to come...please..." I whine, admitting defeat.

He tugs on my braids as he starts to move again, his thrusts long and hard. I rotate my hips, meeting him halfway, desperate in my desire to come.

"Anything for my little brat."

Colton fucks me so deep, I see stars. I bring my hand between my thighs, find my clit, and rub it fast. My legs give out, and my toes curl as I come, moaning his name. "Choke my dick, baby...just like that..."

His grip on my ass intensifies, and he groans, spilling cum into the condom. He continues fucking me, prolonging our orgasms and making me feel like I'm on cloud nine.

Colt steps back, helps me fix my clothes, and then takes the condom off. He hides his dick in his pants and looks around for a trash can. Once he has gotten rid of it, he returns to the car and climbs into the backseat with me. He pulls me onto his lap, circling his hands around my waist and looking into my eyes.

"Let's try this again." He smiles as I wrap my arms around his neck. "What happened?"

I snicker, licking my lips. "I saw someone I can't stand."

"Who was that guy?"

"He's my ex. Jefferson. Levi Jefferson." I take a deep breath and exhale loudly. "I think you know him. He plays for—"

"The Gladiators," he tells me. "What did he say to you?"

"He saw us together and said I must have fallen really low to be seen with someone like you."

"Someone like me?"

"He said you've fucked almost every girl ever."

"I don't fuck just anyone. I'm not Clay."

I punch him in his shoulder, and he laughs. "You just called your best friend a manwhore."

"I'm stating the obvious." His hand slides lower, and he palms my butt. "What else did he say to you?"

"I hate when he touches me. I hate how he makes me feel, bringing back all the bad memories. I can easily brush off what he says, but all that combined with what he said about you...it made me lose my shit."

"You pushed him good," Colt murmurs, cupping my cheek with his palm. "But I honestly freaked out. I was afraid Benson or I wouldn't make it in time and he would do something to you."

I press my forehead to his and gaze deep into his eyes. "Thank you, Colt, and I'm sorry for my behavior. I was being irrational and reckless."

"What did he do to you? It must have been pretty bad for you to react to him like that."

I keep quiet, but then inch toward his lips. "Can we talk about it some other time? I don't want to get into my past right now."

"Promise to tell me everything?"

"Yes."

"Do you want to go home?"

"I want you to kiss me," I urge him, and he grins.

"Whatever you wish, Ava." With that, he pulls my face to his, and our lips connect.

This guy is like my own reflection and a total stranger at the same time. It's like someone cursed me, and other people cease to exist when he's around. And honestly? There is nothing in the world I love more than losing myself in him.

Chapter 39

Winnie-the-Pooh

COLTON

Waking up, I lie on my back and stare at the ceiling with a smile on my face. I've been at Ava's house for two days already, and I honestly can't remember the last time I was so happy. Her invitation was the best Christmas present I have ever received. Though I have two dilemmas now. First, I need to buy gifts for her and her dad, and I need to do it without her knowing about it. The second is way more complicated. I want to go see my mom on Christmas, and I'm not sure I'm ready to talk to Ava about her.

I feel my blanket move and sit up straight, locking eyes with her cat. Snooping little monster—that's what she called him yesterday, when he barged into her room at full speed while we were in the middle of something. Just kissing, but it felt like he was interrupting. When she's with me, I don't want anyone to interfere, and her reaction proved she feels exactly the same way. I hope it's real and not just in my head.

"What are you doing here?" I lean forward and grab the cat, press him to my chest, and fall onto my back. I caress his fur, and the purring sounds don't take long to surface. "I thought you were glued to her."

The cat closes his eyes while my fingers run back and forth over his fur. It's short and soft under my touch, and I smile thinking about the name she chose for him. Smokey. Because his fur is gray. As predictable as possible, but for some reason it suits him. Maybe because he's like smoke, disappearing whenever he wants and showing up when he feels like it.

My phone rings, and I snatch it from the bedside table. Smokey walks away from me and jumps onto the floor. I look at the screen and roll my eyes. My best friend is an impatient fucker. I answer the call and press my phone to my ear.

"Yeah?"

"What do you mean 'yeah'?" Clay demands as I toss aside the blanket and swing my legs over the edge of the bed.

"You want me to get pom-poms and chant your name?"

"Of course not. Just...try to be a little more enthusiastic, you know?" He huffs grumpily. "Going to see Ava and the Bensons without me is not okay—"

"They just invited me. I had no idea I would be here when I talked to you about my plans for winter break." I tell him, standing up from the bed and moving to my clothes. "Besides, Drake invited you too, and I kinda need you here with me."

"I'm intrigued."

"I need to buy presents for Ava and her dad," I say, putting on my sweatpants.

"Could you say that again?"

"Why?" I ask, grabbing a tee from the closet.

"Because I honestly think I'm losing my shit. My best friend wants to buy gifts for his girl and her dad. For *his* girl and *her dad*. Colt, are you shitting me?"

"No." I pull on my T-shirt. "She's not my girl. We're just...seeing each other."

"*Seeing each other*? Thompson, can you tell me the truth for once?"

"What do you want from me?"

"Tell me this: if you're just seeing each other, what happens if some guy decides to hit on her? Ava is gorgeous. It's easy to imagine."

"I'd break his neck."

"That's what I thought," Clay chuckles, and I hear a horn honking. "I'll be there around noon. Hope Benson didn't change his mind."

"He didn't," I say and hang up. It's time for me to go downstairs. I've been sleeping way too long.

I make a quick detour to the bathroom and wash my face. I thread my fingers through my hair. It's longer than I'm used to, but it's closer to how it was before. Before shit hit the fan and I became the loneliest of loners. It's like life has come full circle, and I have returned to the point where my world turned upside down. Trying to understand what it means is like solving an ancient riddle. The fear of making the wrong decision, of giving myself a glimpse of hope and then being disappointed, is stronger than ever. Shattered dreams and plans are normal for me, so it's always good to keep myself in check.

Taking a deep breath, I head downstairs, straight to the kitchen. I step inside and freeze—Dax is here, and he's alone. Our eyes meet, and he gestures for me to come further. I flash him an awkward smile. Does this feel like a trap? No, but I'm nervous.

"Morning," I mumble, edging closer and plopping myself onto a chair.

"Morning." Dax grins and pushes a plate of pancakes in my direction. "Ava made them before she left."

My hand hovers over the plate, and my eyebrows raise. Where did she go? I don't remember her mentioning anything about plans this morning.

"Layla called her and asked to go shopping." He answers my unasked question and stands up from the table. "Do you want coffee?"

"Yes, please." I grab a pancake, take a little bite, and instantly break into a smile. It's delicious.

"She's a good cook," Dax tells me, correctly interpreting my reaction. He pours coffee into a mug and places it in front of me. Then he leans against the kitchen counter. "I often felt guilty, since she always had to cook for herself, for me, and for us when I would come home late at night. She made it clear she was doing it because she liked it, and because she wanted to help me. At least with something."

"Sounds like Ava to me," I mutter with my mouth full. "She's very selfless, and she's always there for her friends and family."

"And for you." The pancake feels hard as I swallow. My throat contracts, and I cough. Dax slides onto the chair across from me. "Didn't mean to scare you."

"It's not that." I take sips of my coffee to ease the lump in my throat. "I'm not used to people giving a damn about me."

"Something tells me you're not open with people either, that you mostly prefer they keep their distance."

"I've been told I'm a closed-off, judgmental asshole."

"Nah, you're not. She wouldn't like you if you were." Dax lifts his mug and takes a sip. "Being open with only certain people isn't a bad thing. From my experience, keeping your circle close is way better than letting in everyone. You're saving yourself from disappointment."

"Maybe."

"It can also be very lonely. Without giving people a chance, you'll never know if they were good for you or not." He gives me a pointed stare, and uneasiness seeps into my veins. "Some people will try to break through your walls because they see something in you, like my daughter does. But most people? They will think that's too much trouble."

"It never was easy for me to open up to strangers. I didn't become like that all of a sudden." I look away and then bring my attention back to Ava's dad. "I think you noticed that a year ago."

Dax sighs, reclining in the chair. "I did. My first thought was that you were too wound up to talk to anyone, but the more I watched you from afar, the more you reminded me of a caged animal. One who used to live wild in nature and was suddenly trapped. You're a loner, Colt, but it doesn't mean you need to stay like that forever."

"The old version of me wouldn't believe what I'm about to say." I shake my head, heaving a sigh. "I don't want to be a loner anymore."

"That's nice to hear, because my daughter definitely wants you around."

"I don't plan to let her go," I confess, and Dax's eyes widen. "I-I didn't mean—I won't be trying to...I just want her to be with me."

"Then be honest with her." He folds his arms over his chest. "She said you're not dating, that you're just having fun. But, watching how affectionate you are with one another, I don't think I agree with her. You talk a lot, but you're comfortable with each other in silence too. What you have is deeper."

"It is deeper, but I don't think she's ready to be open with me. Jefferson was at the party, and it didn't go well, but she told me she didn't want to talk about him yet when I asked."

Dax purses his lips. "She didn't tell me he was at the party."

"She handled him pretty well herself. As usual. She pushed him so hard, he almost fell on his ass."

Ava's dad blinks, and then he bursts out laughing. I smile, realizing how much I enjoy spending time with him. It feels right, and so familiar. As if I have known him my whole life.

"That's why I call her a tornado. Emotions brew inside her, pushing her to act faster than she thinks. She'll destroy everything in her way and then calm down a second later, as soon as she lets out her anger." He narrows his eyes. "You said 'as usual'."

"I, too, often say things I don't mean when I'm angry or can't handle my emotions. I paid for it the first time we met."

"My daughter definitely knows how to stand up for herself. Even if I don't always approve of her methods," Dax murmurs with a gentle smile on his face. "I would have preferred you control yourself, because she doesn't have the patience of an angel, and you're risking something way more precious than you realize."

"Duly noted."

His phone buzzes, and he takes it from the table. After he quickly checks the message, Dax stands up and hides his phone in his pocket. "Sadly, I need to go to work. It was nice talking to you, Colt. I'm glad Ava invited you to spend Christmas with us."

"Me too." He walks to the door, and I blurt out my next words, afraid I'll change my mind if I don't. "I'm going to visit my mom on Christmas."

Dax turns around, eyeing me in agonizing silence. Then he finally says, "I'm sure she will be happy to see you. It must be lonely where she is."

And that's how I got confirmation. He knows what happened to my mom. "Do you..."

"Sometimes people leave a lasting impression on you. It was my day off; I was going home after meeting a friend. It was pure coincidence I happened to be on that bridge at the same time as your mom. Of course

I have kept my eye on her. I know what that car crash caused, and I'm very sorry about it, Colt."

His phone buzzes again, and I clench my jaw so hard, afraid to move a muscle. I hold my eyes wide open, feeling them tear up. I don't want to cry, especially not in front of Ava's dad.

"Son, your emotions are valid. You shouldn't be scared or embarrassed of them. You lost someone very important to you without losing them. This pain you're holding on to...it is eating you alive, and you need to let it out."

"I know." I avoid looking at him, and he doesn't push it.

Dax exhales loudly. "Ava won't be long. Make yourself at home."

"Thank you, Dax. Have a good day."

"You too, Colt."

With that, he exits, and my shoulders slump instantly. I need to let it out, he said. Exactly the same thing that Dr. Stewart has been telling me. What my grandma told me. I need to open up and be honest about my mom's trauma and her diagnosis—and about my fault in all of it.

"Why are you here?" I ask, stepping aside and letting Clay walk into Ava's house.

"The Bensons are on their way home from the mall. Drake told me to come here."

"Is he with Ava and Layla?" I furrow my brow, pulling my phone out of my pocket. She's been texting with me for an hour already, telling me she would have never agreed to go shopping if she knew how long Layla's list was.

"He went to pick them up," Clay answers, looking around with his mouth half open. "Ava has a nice place."

"Yeah." I head to the living room, plop myself onto the couch, and toss my phone aside. Dax left for work two hours ago, so I am honestly happy to see Clay. "Why were you so adamant about coming here?"

"Dunno. I felt like an outsider when I found out you were hanging out with Ava, Benson, and Layla." By how he lowers his voice when he says Layla's name, I know she's the main reason his ass is here.

"Benson doesn't want you near his sister."

"Why?" He looks at me in confusion.

"Because you're not a relationship type of guy."

"You're not a relationship—"

"We're talking about you and Layla, not about me and Ava," I interrupt him, and he huffs in irritation. "Show him how much you like her, that you can be different for her."

"But I have no idea if I can be different."

"You can. For the right girl, you can."

"Aw, you fucker." He lunges at me, taking me into a bear hug. "Can I be your best man?"

I push him away, hearing my phone buzz. "Get off me, Rodgers."

"Only if you promise to make me your best man." His face lights up with a huge grin as he stares at me in silence. He's about to say something stupid, I have no fucking doubt. "Make me the godfather of your firstborn. Please."

"Fuck off, Clay." I wriggle out of his grasp, grab my phone, and read her message.

HONEY:

two minutes.

"Is it from Ava?" I turn my head and see him eyeing my phone with a curious expression.

"Yes."

"Why honey?" Just fucking great. He saw how I saved her number. "Because she tastes like honey?"

"Fucking nosy moron," I hiss, standing up to hide my phone in my pocket, and my jaw drops open. Ava is standing in the doorway, leaning against it. Her long brown hair is spilling over her shoulders, and snowflakes are slowly melting on her hair. Her black jacket is half zipped, and she's holding her hat in her hands. She's so cute, so I can't help but smile at her.

"Ava, baby, so happy to see you." Clay jumps up from the couch and strolls straight to her, wrapping his arms around her and hugging her tightly. She giggles as he whispers something in her ear before he puts her back down and steps away from her.

"Layla and Drake are waiting for you on the porch. They'll show you your room."

"Great." Clay claps his hands together, glancing between Ava and me. "See you later?"

"Absolutely." She steps aside to let him out. "We're planning to hang out at the Bensons' tonight. Just us."

"Sounds good." My best friend follows Ava to the hallway, and she closes the door behind him while I wait for her. How much did she hear?

When she comes back, I see she's wearing a white hoodie with a howling wolf and black jeans. She walks up to me, and I look her in the eyes. "Can I see your phone?" she asks.

"Why?"

"I want to see how you saved my number in your contacts."

"Why?"

"Because I want to." How am I supposed to say no to that? Shaking my head, I take my phone out of my pocket, unlock it, and hand it to her. A second later, she gives it back to me. "Honey?"

"Honey," I confirm, draping a hand around her waist and pulling her to my chest. "Because you're the sweetest girl I've ever had."

She sucks in a breath and stands on her tiptoes to bring our lips closer. "Can you keep a secret?"

"Yes."

"I want you between my thighs so bad."

"Say please." I lift her, wrapping her legs around my waist.

"Please, Colt...I'm so wet already."

I turn around and rush upstairs. Once we're in her bedroom, I put her on the bed and tower over her. My eyes roam over her beautiful face. "When will your dad be home?"

Her eyes sparkle with mischief as she slowly takes her phone out of her pocket. She types something and then tosses it on the bed. "Around six."

"We have the whole house to ourselves for six hours?" I unzip her zipper and pull down her jeans, along with her panties. Her pussy is dripping, and I feel as if I'm starving. For her. "Ava?"

"No. Drake and Layla are expecting us at four."

"Okay, I still have time to eat my girl out—" I'm ready to dive in, but she pulls my hair, stopping me and making me groan. "Ouch. Never do that again."

"Or what, Winnie?"

Realization dawns on me at once. She called me Winnie because I named her Honey. "Did you change how you saved my number?"

"Maybe, Winnie-the-Pooh," she teases, and I'm losing my mind.

Abruptly, I pull her to her feet. Ava's eyes go round, and her eyebrows knit together. "I changed my mind," I tell her, plopping myself down on her bed and nestling comfortably, until I'm lying on my back with my head on her pillow. "You're going to sit on my face."

"I'm going to do what?" Her shocked expression is honestly adorable.

"Sit on my face."

"No."

"Yes."

"No." And yet she takes off her hoodie, keeping on her black sports bra. "I've never done that before."

"Then I'll be your first." I extend my palm to her, my dick twitching with need.

"And last." Ava hesitates, but then she climbs on the bed and straddles my legs. I put my hands on her hips and pull her to me. "What if I suffocate you?"

"Then I will die in fucking heaven." Her brows raise; her eyes are still round like saucers. Taunting her out of her wits is the best way to both calm her down and push her buttons. "Come here and give me what I want."

Ava's chest rises and falls rapidly as she finally makes her decision. Moving slowly, she lowers her pussy onto my face. I maintain eye contact while I suck her clit into my mouth, and she sighs. A blush spreads over her cheeks as she takes off her bra and cups her breasts, rubbing her nipples between her fingers. Those perky little points belong to my goddamn mouth. I don't like seeing her touch herself—because I want to do it myself.

"Grab the headboard," I murmur against her clit, and she does as I tell her. "Ride my mouth, Ava. I want to hear you moan."

The moment she rolls her hips, gliding her pussy over my mouth, I know I will do anything to give her pleasure. She's so fucking addictive. I won't be able to even look at other girls, let alone touch anyone else. She gets under my skin like no one ever has, and I love it. Ava makes me feel alive. She's my favorite type of sweet. She's my honey.

I lap my tongue over her clit and down her folds. I tease and suck as her breath becomes heavier. Ava rides my mouth, moving slow and deep, and the headboard starts to hit the wall. I watch her face, taking in everything. Her pupils darken, her brows knit together, and she chews on her bottom lip to stifle her sounds. And that's not something I want. I nibble on her clit, drawing a long, loud moan out of her. She moans my name, and I come a little just from the sound of it leaving her lips. My cock is throbbing in my pants, begging me to fuck her.

"That feels so good, Colt...I'm gonna come so hard...make me come...please," Ava pleads, staring me in the eyes. "Please, Colt..."

I palm her ass, not letting her move, and I feast on her as if I haven't eaten in weeks. She's the most delicious dish I've ever had. I lick and suck, fucking her with my tongue and devouring every inch of her pussy. She shuts her eyes, her head bobs back, and she comes, trembling and rocking on the waves of her orgasm. I lick her dry, kissing both of her thighs before helping her to lie on her back. She turns her head to her left, peering into my face. Her lips tremble, and the cutest smile plays on her lips.

"That was incredible."

"What can I say? I love the way you taste."

She chortles, hiding her face in her palms. It's such a simple gesture, but I can't stand her not looking at me. I gently lower her hands, and our eyes lock. "What do you want to do next?"

Ava rakes her gaze over my face and sits up on the bed. I mirror her, feeling my heart thunder in my rib cage. Whatever she wants—I'm in. She inches closer, pulls my tee over my head, and throws it onto the floor, letting her eyes wander all over my chest. She presses her fingertips to my pulse, feeling how wildly my heart is beating for her. My skin is burning under her touch, and it takes everything I have not to pounce on her.

"Do you have a condom?" she asks breathlessly, and I pull one out of my pocket.

Ava takes it from me, tears the wrapper, and watches me in silence. I take off my pants and add them to the pile of clothes on the floor, not averting my gaze for even a second. She rolls the condom over my cock, moving to my ear and grazing her teeth over it. "Sit."

I push her pillows aside and sit up straight, leaning my back against the headboard. She straddles my legs, taking my dick inside her pussy. She loops her hands around my neck, presses her tits to my chest, and rotates her hips in the slowest possible motion. *Fuck.* My girl is perfect.

"Kiss me," I demand, grabbing the back of her neck. The faintest smile crosses her lips, and then she covers my mouth with hers, taking away all sense of the world around us. Our tongues dance, her piercing stimulating my growing desire and setting my skin aflame. I never thought I could feel something like this, something so consuming and overwhelming. It warms my lower abdomen and makes my heartbeat go crazy. "You feel so good."

Ava settles more comfortably, putting her knees on my thighs as she rides me slowly, leisurely almost. I bend my head to her breasts, whirling my tongue over her nipple. A breathless moan escapes her lips. I cup her ass, filling my hands with her. There is no rush. I want to savor every moment of this.

She fucks me slowly. Our bodies are covered in sweat, and her hair sticks to her forehead. I reach over and gently tuck strands of her hair behind her ears. I smile as I hold her languid gaze. I never liked looking into the eyes of the girls I had sex with, but with Ava? I don't want to look away. I feel like myself when I'm with her.

"Roll your hips deeper," I tell her, gripping her ass again and helping her to speed up her movements. Her moans become louder, and her breath hitches in her throat. So fucking stunning. "Just like that, baby... just like that."

I grab her throat with one of my hands and squeeze it lightly. She loves this roughness, letting me be in control, even when she's on top. I add more pressure, and she jerks forward, her hips moving wildly. She's on the brink of her second orgasm, and I'm ready to fucking explode too. A wave of heat envelops my body when I feel her walls close around my dick. Her body trembles, and she cries out my name. My release comes right after hers. I let go of her throat, only to pull her into me for a kiss, losing myself in her.

"WHAT ARE YOU THINKING ABOUT?" Ava asks quietly as we walk out of her house, heading to the Bensons'.

"I've been thinking..." The time we spent together in her bed, and her dad's words, helped me figure out what I want to do. I'm ready to make a decision I wasn't ready to make this morning. "Will you go with me to visit my mom?"

"Visit?" She halts in her tracks, and I stop too.

"It's complicated."

Ava reaches my hand, entwining our fingers together. "I'll go with you."

"Really? I mean, I want to go on Christmas."

"We can always celebrate later. My dad will understand."

I hoist her to my chest and gaze down at her. "Thank you, Ava." I kiss her hard. Her hands fist my hoodie, and her lips part, welcoming my tongue with hers. I pull away only when I feel the need to breathe. Lowering my forehead to hers, I smile. "I will explain everything on the way."

"Promise?"

"Pinkie swear." After a light peck on her lips, I let go of her, taking her palm in mine. "Let's go spend some time with our friends."

"It should be fun," she comments with a smile as we resume our walk.

I honestly believe this is the first time since my mom's car crash that I've enjoyed my days.

Chapter 40

The Way You Look at Her...

COLTON

"So, where are we going?" Ava asks as soon as she climbs into my car. I try to suppress my smile—to no avail. She's like my personal source of vitamin D, surrounding me with her light and soaking me in her warmth. A little sunshine to my grump. "Colt?"

Her palm on my knee gets my attention, and I lock eyes with her. "To visit my mom."

She fastens her seat belt and nestles in comfortably, leaning back in the seat. "Thanks for stating the obvious, genius."

I chortle, finally starting the car and driving slowly away from her house. Dax is standing on the porch with a mug of steaming coffee, watching us leave. He was incredibly supportive when Ava told him I wanted to take her to go see my mom. I'm beyond grateful to him for that. She's lucky to have him in her corner. A dad like him would turn the planet upside down and make it rotate in a totally different direction for his kid.

"It's just that I've never ever introduced any girls to my mom. This is all new to me, Ava, and sometimes I feel like I need some guidance."

"Dating for dummies?" She giggles as I tighten my grip on the steering wheel. That word detonates a bomb inside my chest, spreading hope and fear throughout my bones.

"Are we dating?"

Her laugh dies in her throat, and her eyes go round. She looks like a deer in the headlights, and I don't know what I want to do more: laugh or be upset. The answer to my question is written all over her face.

"No, we're just... I don't think 'enemies with benefits' suits us anymore. Maybe 'frenemies', or 'friends with benefits'?"

"Do you hate me?"

Ava narrows her eyes. "Sometimes I do, when you act like an asshole." Fair. She drives me crazy sometimes as well. "But in all honesty? No. I really like you, Colt."

"I really like you too, Ava." A moment of silence passes between us, and then she slowly takes my hand in hers, entwining our fingers together. My breath evens out, and I smile, feeling my tense muscles loosen. What we have is so much more, but I'll never push her. I want her to admit it on her own, not under my demands or pressure. She's a free spirit, and caging her in would only break her wings. I love the way she is, and I don't want any other version of her.

"What happened to your mom?" she asks in a quiet voice, her thumb caressing the skin on my wrist. It's soothing my nerves, helping me navigate through my most hurtful memories to find the ones I'm ready to share with her. For now, it's better to leave some things in the darkness.

"My mom is the most important person in my life. Every happy memory I have is connected to her. How much she cared, how much she loved me, how much she always wanted to be there for me. Even hockey. She was the one who took me to my first game, bought my first puck and stick, and even taught me how to skate. She's the reason I fell in love with the sport. She's the reason why I'm so good at it. Her encouragement, her excitement when I'd score, her presence at the arena even when she didn't have time to come to practice." I take a deep breath, needing it in order to continue. I've never talked to anyone about this, and now I'm having trouble putting my thoughts into words. "She was my everything, and my lies took her away from me."

"What happened?" The torment in Ava's eyes is noticeable, and it leaves no doubt how much she cares about me.

"My father was always in meetings and on business trips. He never seemed to find time for Mom and me. It was always her who was making the effort, pushing me to go to his office to spend time with him. I never felt loved by him, you know? It seemed like he couldn't care less about my life, and especially hockey. He was distant, indifferent, and incredibly toxic. His mentality that everyone should obey him because he has money made me sick to my stomach, but because of Mom I never said anything. He was 'her Eric', the guy she fell in love with years ago... her husband. The father of her child." I fall silent. Anger rises in my chest, because the images in my head are becoming more vivid. "While he—"

"Did he cheat on your mom?" Her question catches me off guard, but I simply nod, grateful I don't need to say it aloud. She's silent, but I feel her fingers tremble. Ava always comes to the right conclusions, and I have no doubt she already knows what happened. "Why didn't you tell her?"

"Because I was an idiot. A little over a year ago, I came home during a break, went to visit my dad, and overheard a conversation. Apparently, he knocked up his secretary, a young girl who had worked for him for three years. She was with him in his office that day, sitting on his desk. His hand was on her growing belly. Idyllic picture, but not what you expect from your father."

I gulp down the lump in my throat and set my jaw hard. "He saw me, and there wasn't even the slightest change in his face. Nothing. As if I didn't just find out that my father was a cheater. A liar. Not even a trace of embarrassment. I turned around and stormed out of his office, and he didn't try to stop me. He just stayed put. With her."

"What did you do?"

"I went home. Mom instantly noticed the state I was in. I couldn't even look her in the eyes. Shame was the only emotion I had, and the realization of my own stupidity. All the years Helen worked for my father, I would joke that I had no idea how he could keep his dick in his pants. But he couldn't, and I failed to see it."

"Why did you hide it?" she asks again, her voice louder. "If you loved your mom so much—"

"She had the perfect life, Ava. A husband who was a successful businessman, a son who was the rising star of his college's hockey team. She was happy, and he convinced me the truth would break her. He came home twenty minutes later and barged into my room. He gave me a long lecture, told me he made a mistake months ago, and she got pregnant. He assured me he was only supporting her because she was carrying his child, and I agreed to keep quiet. On one condition—he needed to fire Helen. He promised to do it, and I believed him. Later, when Mom came to check on me, I lied to her about my mood. Gave her some bullshit about problems with classes. She brought M&Ms with her to cheer me up—my favorite treat—and I lied right in her face."

"How did she find out?"

"He fired Helen, but he didn't stop seeing her. A year ago, my mom was on her way to the gallery when she saw my father pushing a stroller with his secretary by his side. She figured out everything and had a breakdown." Tears burn my eyes, and I try to steady my breath. "She called me, but I was at practice and missed it. She didn't know where to go because her whole world fell apart. She was driving aimlessly, probably crying, and I'm sure she barely saw where she was going when her car hit the railing of a bridge at full speed and fell into the river."

Ava presses her palm to her mouth, tears brimming in the corners of her eyes. "It was my dad, wasn't it? Who found her? I remember hearing about it, but he was vague. He didn't tell me right away, because I would have thrown a fit if I'd known he risked his life, out there alone with no equipment or help from his guys. I think I actually overheard him talking to someone about it. Otherwise, he never would have told me."

"Yeah, he saved my mom. He even went to the hospital, where he met me. If it weren't for your dad, my mom would have died, and I would have spiraled that day. I'm not sure I would have ever recovered from it. He gave me hope, and I held on to it even when the days were dark and depressing. Even when my life was shit, I still had hope. I wanted to believe that things would get better, and they finally are."

"Colt..." Ava utters, tears streaming down her face. Her eyes darken, their emerald color becoming deeper, and I'm spellbound, unable to look away.

I stop the car on the side of the road, unfasten her seat belt, and pull her into my lap. I just want her warmth, her closeness. I want to absorb her scent and drown myself in her. I need her way more than she realizes.

She wraps her arms around my neck, pressing herself close to my chest. She whispers my name again and again, her hands massaging my shoulders, bringing me much-needed peace. I'm ready to tell her something I've been hiding from everyone, all my friends, including Clay. The truth about my mom's state.

"Her heart stopped beating during surgery, but the doctors were able to start it again. They were very cautious about their prognosis, but eventually they thought she'd be okay. She was forty-four, and things were looking up for a while. There was no price too high for my father, and he ended up spending tons of money on doctors and physiotherapists. She was doing well, and it even looked like she'd forgiven him. Until one day I realized she didn't remember the things I was telling her. She couldn't remember what she was doing. She'd become restless and agitated, confused with her own reactions. I approached my father a few times, sharing my concerns and hearing that it was all in my head. It wasn't, and later she showed signs of apathy and depression. Mom lost interest in everything in life, including me. She was a shell, just existing on the fine line between the real world and her memories."

"What does she have?"

"She had a stroke and a severe brain injury, causing anterograde amnesia. She doesn't remember anything about the car crash. She has problems remembering things about her days, the conversations she had. Mom lost control of her life, and it caused her depression. It got so bad that it started to interfere with her daily life. She needed constant care, someone to look after her. And my father, along with my mom's parents, decided to put her into a facility. They told me it would be for the best, because a calm and predictable environment with an established daily routine could reduce her apathy and help with her amnesia. She's been there for almost ten months already, and I go visit her every Sunday. Sometimes she doesn't remember my visits, the talks we had, but sometimes she's herself. Dr. Stewart told me she has been really good the past two weeks. There is no sign of her depression, and the strategy he chose to help improve her memory has shown progress. I honestly can't wait to see her, and I want her to meet you too."

Ava leans away. She presses her thumbs to my cheeks and brushes away my tears. A gentle smile tugs at the corners of her mouth. "And I can't wait to meet her. She sounds like an absolutely amazing person, Colt."

"She is. Unlike my sperm donor dad."

"Are your parents divorced?"

"No."

"What about Helen?"

"She's still in his life, working for his company as if nothing happened."

"Are they together?"

I sigh, not knowing what to tell her. There is still a lot she doesn't know. "They aren't. It's just complicated."

"You're not telling me the whole story, are you?"

"No. That's another long-as-fuck conversation, and we don't have time for it," I tell her, and she pinches my cheeks slightly. "I'll tell you everything some other time..." An idea flashes in my head. "Actually, I have a question for you."

"Go ahead." Ava slides back into her seat, buckling her seat belt.

"My father is hosting a party for his partners at the end of January. He expects me to be there—"

"I'll go with you," she interrupts me, as if it's the simplest question in the world. No hesitation, no holding back.

"Really?" I start the engine again.

"Yeah. Your father is clearly a real piece of work, and I don't want you near him alone." Ava tilts her head. "Will Helen be there too?"

"Yes."

"Well, can't wait to meet the bitch."

"Something is telling me I might regret asking you to come."

"Nah, you will love having me there." She pokes her tongue out at me, and I laugh heartily and gradually relax. I would love to have her anywhere, not just at the stupid party, but I keep those words to myself. Scaring her off is not on my agenda.

I first go in alone to see Mom. Considering her fragile state, it's important not to stress her out. She smiles and hugs me tighter than usual. I give her my present, and she can't help but laugh. I got her an avocado pillow and a few more paperbacks, all romance with lots of fluff. When Ava saw the titles, she huffed so loud I thought she was going to make me drive to the bookstore and buy something different. She didn't, but she warned me that next time she was going to choose books for my mom herself. To say I was stunned is an understatement. It means the world to me that she's thinking about coming to see my mom again, and that she cares so much about someone she has never even met.

"You look mysterious, Colt," Mom comments. "Is there something you're hiding from me?"

"Do you remember when you said to bring a girl with me if she was constantly on my mind? If she caused such strong emotions within me it would be hard to ignore?"

Mom smiles apologetically and slightly shakes her head. "Sorry, baby. I don't, but I can imagine myself saying that to you." She pats my knee with her hand. "Is she here?"

"Yeah, and I want you to meet her. Can I invite her in?"

"Of course." Mom jumps up from the bed, looking excited as she tucks her hair behind her ears and smooths her palms over her dress. "Where are your manners, Colton? You've been here with me for an hour already."

I stand up and head to the door, unable to hide my smile.

"Hey." I open the door and peek outside. Ava is sitting on a chair with a book in her hands: *Twisted Love*. I read the title and frown. I think I need to keep tabs on what she reads—Clay's words from before come into my head, and my dick swells in my pants. Oh, man. This is definitely not the right moment. "Come in."

She gives me a smile, hides her book in her backpack, and stands up from the chair. She walks up to me, and we stare at each other for a minute. I'm not sure either of us understands how crucial this moment is, because I'm about to share something really private with her. I step aside, and she moves into the room, lingering by the door to wait for me. I join her, take her hand in mine, and we move toward my mom. Her eyes are sparkling, and the biggest grin plays on her lips as she lets her eyes wander over Ava.

"Mom, this is Ava." I speak quietly, my heart booming in my chest. "Ava, this is my mom, Avery."

"It's very nice to meet you, Avery." Ava untangles herself from me slowly and takes a step forward, extending her hand. Mom sucks in a breath, and a worry instantly crosses my mind: what if this is all too much for her?

"It's very nice to meet you too, Ava." Mom moves closer, hugging Ava briefly. "Thank you so much for agreeing to keep him company, and I'm very sorry he made you wait for so long. My son didn't tell me he brought you until just now."

"It's totally fine. We agreed I would wait for him in the hallway." Ava glances at me over her shoulder. "Besides, I brought my book, so I definitely wasn't bored."

"What are you reading?" Mom sits down on the bed, patting her palm on the covers. Ava joins her, while I stay planted.

"It's called *Twisted Love*. It's a brother's-best-friend romance, and I'm loving every chapter so far."

"You read romance? It's my favorite genre."

"I figured that out once I saw the books Colt got you." Ava says, and they both smile at each other. "Can I pick some out next time? I don't think I approve of his taste."

"That would mean everything to me." Mom clasps Ava's hands in hers, an excited look on her face. "I love my son, but he definitely has no clue when it comes to romance novels."

"Hey!" I say, coming closer and sitting in the chair near the window. They both focus their gazes on me and then laugh wholeheartedly. "I don't remember you ever complaining."

"I didn't have a choice, baby." Mom shrugs and winks at Ava. They chat about books for the next fifteen minutes, while I just sit here in silence, shocked to the core. I had no clue what to expect when I decided to bring Ava with me, but I honestly couldn't imagine it would be like this.

Ava and I stay with Mom for three more hours, until her nurse, Beth, comes to remind us about visiting hours. It's time to leave, even if I have no desire to do so. We say our goodbyes, and Ava walks out of the room first, but only after my mom gives her a very long and hard hug.

I come closer and wind my hands around my mom's waist, hauling her into my chest and holding her tight. "I'm gonna miss you so much, Mom."

"Me too, Colt. Thank you so much for coming to see me, and thank you for bringing Ava with you. Watching you two together...it gives me hope that you won't make the same mistakes as me and your dad, that you will never hurt the person you love." I lean away and peer at her, my eyebrows furrowed. "The way you look at her says it all, baby. You love this girl."

"I *like* her," I clarify, and my mom just shakes her head. I swallow the lump in my throat, finding it difficult to concentrate. "I just..."

"Just be yourself. I'm sure she's the one for you. Call it mother's intuition." She stands on her tiptoes and kisses my cheek. "Merry Christmas, Colton. See you next week."

"Merry Christmas, Mom." I give her one last squeeze and step back. My thoughts are all over the place as I amble out of the room. I notice Ava and Beth down the hall. My eyes are glued to her, and she smiles at me. It's hard for me to figure out what it all means. Today exceeded all my expectations, but there's one thing I know for sure: I told Dax the truth. I'm not letting his daughter go.

Chapter 41

We Aren't Dating

COLTON

"Whatever you say," I grind out as I stand up from the couch.

It's been a month since winter break ended, and it's almost time for my father's stupid party. It's definitely not something I've been looking forward to. I walk to the window and look out at the street.

It's peaceful and quiet outside my apartment. A little nighttime snowfall makes it even more beautiful, reminding me of my childhood. I'm tempted to go out, especially since it might help to calm my annoyed ass down. My father chose the worst time ever to call me. Like he always does.

"Not whatever I say, Colton." He sounds as if he's losing his patience as well. "This party needs to be perfect."

"Then why do you need me?"

"Because this business will be yours one day."

"Why? Have I ever shown even the slightest interest in it?" I bark, pressing my forehead to the cool glass and closing my eyes. "Helen is a way better option. She will be—"

"She's just my fucking employee; you're my son. What the hell are you talking about?"

"Fine." I barely hold myself back. "Choose Chloe. She's your daughter."

"Officially, she has no right to be considered my heir," he snarls, and I clench my jaw. "Her mother signed all the papers. You know that. Everything I have is yours."

"Should have thought about that before you knocked up your secretary."

"My secretary that you, not so secretly, were drooling over? My secretary that you fucked too?" And here he goes again. Whenever his arguments are flimsy or weak, he tries to put the blame on me, and it never works.

"I fucked her once. It was the worst sex of my life." I turn around and lean against the window. "I said I would come to your party. I said I would play the role of your perfect son. Leave me the fuck alone till then."

"Who are you planning to bring?" he asks, breathing hard. Usually we continue arguing until one of us ends the call, but that's not what I want today. Even if he pisses me off. "Rose said you asked her to add a plus-one to your name."

"I did," I confirm, feeling my phone ding with an incoming message. It should be from Ava, but I don't want to check it now. I have no desire to mix my happy emotions with the ones my dad is causing.

"Who is she?"

"It doesn't matter. You'll meet her next week."

"I need to know who the slut is that you're planning to bring to my party—"

"Call her that again, and you will never see me. Am I clear?"

He's silent, and it makes me smile even if my fingers are itching. I want to punch him in his face so bad. That man thinks he has the right to call her names, when he's the biggest manwhore I have ever met. He's a fucking hypocrite.

"Don't be late. It's important." Then my father finally ends the call.

I stand still, mindlessly playing with my phone, throwing it up in the air a few times. He ruined my mood like he always does. Now I don't want to do anything, and I don't want to see anyone. I heave a sigh, push myself off of the window, and stalk to my bathroom, leaving my phone on the table in the living room. I want to take a bath, soak my body after practice and wash away the repulsion I feel toward my father. It's sickening how much he affects me.

Once the bathtub is full, I close my eyes and lean back. The feeling is amazing, emptying my mind and helping me to relax my sore muscles. The water is hot, and my apartment is quiet. I slowly nod off. Just for a few minutes.

"Colt?" I snap my eyes open in total bewilderment and see Ava sitting on the edge of my tub. She's wearing a red knit sweater and jeans. Her hair is collected in a high ponytail, and her cheeks are still a bit red from the cold and windy weather. Where did she come from? "Did anyone ever tell you that falling asleep in the bath is dangerous?"

"No." I sit up straighter, coasting my eyes over her beautiful face. Since winter break, things between us have progressed a ton. She has a key to my apartment and comes over whenever she feels like it. We haven't had a single argument; we just spend time together and enjoy each other's company. She still says we're not dating, but honestly? I don't care. I know she's mine, and I'm hers. Labels don't mean a thing. "What are you doing here?"

"If you'd read my text, you would have known I was coming over," she murmurs, trailing her eyes down my chest and biting her bottom lip. My horny girl is back. Not that I'm any different. I'm insatiable when it comes to her—and only her. She's my personal addiction, sweet and spicy at the same time. An explosive cocktail, but I'll be damned if I stay away for even a day. "Layla and I went shopping, and I wanted to show you what I bought for your father's party."

"You bought a dress?"

"I didn't say I bought a dress," she corrects me. But then she beams. She's so cute. "Fine, it's a dress. I love it."

"Will you show it to me?"

"Nope. Layla took it with her to the dorms." Ava narrows her eyes slightly. "Should have read my text."

I watch her intensely. Then I leap forward, grab her around her waist, and pull her to me. She shrieks as her body smashes against mine and water starts spilling out of the tub. Her shocked expression is worth all the hassle of cleaning up.

"Colton. What the hell?"

"It's called a hustle, sweetheart," I tease her, happy to catch her off guard. I press her to my chest. Her clothes are soaked, and her ponytail is wet. "Will you stay?"

"I don't have any spare clothes with me. Now I have to stay," she breathes, winding her hands around my neck. "Not that I had any other plans."

"Good." I inch closer and kiss her full lips. She's wearing lip gloss, and before her I hated kissing girls who wore it. With her? I don't think there is anything I will ever not like about her. I can't get enough of her. Wanting more, demanding more, and she's happy to play along. This is quite the submissive little kitten I have in my arms, and sometimes she turns into a tigress. It's better if she doesn't know it, but being at her mercy is my favorite thing.

"You're sure you wanna do this?" I've asked her a thousand times, and she rolls her eyes.

"Yes, Colton, I wanna do this." She pouts and looks at me from under knitted brows. "I bought this dress to make a lasting impression on your dear father and his bitch. I'm not going to back out now."

"This dress definitely has left a lasting impression on me." I rake my gaze over her body, wetting my lips. It's a sleeveless light-blue dress with a low neckline, and it hugs her body like a glove. A glove I want to take off. "You'll be the only girl I'll have my eyes on, that's for sure."

"Good. I don't want you to look at or think about anyone else."

I burst out laughing as I press the elevator button. "You think there is space for anyone else in my head? You corrupted every brain cell I have." I slide my hand around her waist from behind and pull her back to my side. "Can't wait to tear this dress off you."

"The words 'tear' and 'this dress' shouldn't be in the same sentence, Mr. Thompson. I spent way too much money on it for you to ruin it," she says, leaning her back against my chest. "Aren't we already late?"

"I don't care."

"Colt, you said yourself that your douche of a father told you not to be late." Her voice becomes softer. "I know this party isn't where you want to be, so why make it even worse for you?"

"Why are you always right?" I kiss her neck, my fingers flying all over her skin, making her shiver.

"You would be surprised at how many times I have been wrong." She glances at me over her shoulder. "Let's go. I'll keep you company."

I tug her to my side, lacing our fingers together as we step inside the elevator. "Better keep me sane. The things this man does and says make me go crazy. If I don't hold myself back, it could get really ugly."

"Whatever you want, Colt." Ava gives my hand a squeeze and pushes the button for the sixth floor.

Stepping into the big and spacious room, I feel a lot of eyes on Ava and me. Pleasant music plays in the background, but the murmurs and whispers grow louder. It doesn't look like they were expecting me to show up. I'm sure my dad fed his guests some fairy tale about his son being a successful hockey player who couldn't join his marvelous party because of his responsibilities. Maybe hockey finally came in handy for the asshole.

"Should we go meet your father?"

I scan the room, meeting his cold stare. I did as I promised. I showed up. I smirk and slowly stroll in his direction with Ava. "He probably won't be nice. Don't pay any attention to him or anything he says, okay?"

"Sure." She singsongs the word, and I'm more than certain she's not going to behave. Ava is a spitfire, and she always does what she wants. Tonight is the first time I can only hope it will end well.

As soon as I near my father, I want to get out of this place. Helen is by his side, with a flute of champagne and a predatory smile playing on her lips. Her eyes are glued to my face, and I feel uneasy. I should have told Ava the whole truth about that woman.

"Is that Helen?" Ava asks when we are only a few steps away from them. They are with my father's partner, Mr. Kavano, talking business and making salacious jokes. Like always.

"Yeah." I swallow the lump in my throat and square my shoulders. *Please, God, give me the strength to pull this off.* I don't want Ava to see me at my worst.

"Colton? Is that you?" Mr. Kavano sees me approaching and turns to greet me, extending his palm for a handshake. "It's so great to see you again."

"It's very nice to see you too, Jacob." I shake his hand and step back as his eyes instantly land on Ava. A sparkle flashes behind his irises as he allows himself to check her out. Stupid motherfucker. He's twice her age, and he still looks at her as if she's his prey. "My my. What a beautiful girl you have here. Eric, your son definitely won a prize with this one."

"Not sure she's his girlfriend," my dad mutters under his breath. "He barely has time for his studies; he spends all of his free time on the ice. No girl will ever replace hockey in his heart."

"Depends on the girl," I blurt out, and I notice my father's eyes grow round. I definitely didn't plan to say that out loud in front of everyone. "Ava is my friend. We aren't dating."

"Such a pity," Helen purrs, still smiling like the Cheshire cat. "You always needed love and affection; it's sad you can't find it with girls your age. Or younger."

"He's perfectly fine without a stranger telling him what to do or how to feel." Helen's smile fades as soon as Ava's words leave her mouth. Then she focuses on my father. "I'm Ava. It's nice to meet you, Mr. Thompson. I've heard *so many* things about you..." She holds his gaze, and a big, radiant smile illuminates her face.

"I bet," he says lazily, but his eyes are betraying him. He's surprised by Ava's behavior and her choice of words. Totally defiant and forward. Her presence at his party intrigues him, because he knows I would have never asked her to join me if she didn't mean something to me. "It's nice to meet you, Ava."

"Someone lacks manners, and—" Helen hisses, but my father interrupts her by handing her his empty glass. What a nice way to point out her place in his life: a servant.

"Thank you, Helen. You can go and relax," he growls, and she turns around and saunters away from us. She doesn't try to argue with him or stand up for herself. She accepted his decision immediately when he told her he wasn't going to acknowledge her daughter as his and asked her to sign a carefully prepared agreement. With one signature, she left Chloe without the right to any of my father's money unless he gives her some himself. She gets child support, but she definitely could have gotten more. "So, Ava, tell me about yourself. My son has never brought anyone with him. That makes you the exception."

"Because I am." She grins at my dad, and I see his right eye twitch. Oh man, I'm going to enjoy this party way more than I thought. Bringing Ava with me was the best decision ever.

The more time passes, the more at ease I feel. Ava and I are inseparable, talking to guests, trying new food. With how often I notice my father's eyes on us, I know he's watching. The smile on his face creeps me out. I hate seeing him so pleased with himself when I know what happened to Mom because of him. He ruined her life, and he continues to live as if nothing happened. It shouldn't be like that.

"Do you mind if I use the bathroom?" Ava murmurs in my ear, and I nod as I continue talking to Mr. Nichols. He's one of my father's oldest partners, and he's a smart guy. I enjoy talking to him; he makes everything more interesting. Debating with him about oil prices and how they affect the world's economy is always a challenge. He knows so much, and he isn't afraid to share his knowledge. I have often wondered how he could be partners with my dad, and I honestly still question it. It's hard to find two people more different than they are.

"Your girlfriend is gorgeous, Colton," he tells me with a smile once Ava has left us. He looks excited, like a kid, and I break into a lopsided grin myself. My girl *is* gorgeous.

"She's perfect," I confirm, hiding my hands in my pockets. My palms have suddenly started sweating. I deliberately don't correct him. I keep it to myself that she's not my girlfriend because his words are like music to my ears. I want her to be mine, for everyone to know. I want to be with her in the open.

We talk some more, until I realize Ava has been gone for an awfully long time. "I need to get going, Mr. Nichols."

"Of course."

We shake hands, and I walk away from him, hoping to find her right away. It's the first time since my mom's car crash that I've stayed this long at one of my father's parties. And I've even enjoyed myself. All because she was with me, and now I don't want anything except her in my arms. She's my lifebuoy, and I'm drowning without her.

I take another step forward, and Ava blocks my path. The first thing I notice is her eyes. Their color is deep and stormy, not even a hint of her playful mood. She's trying not to show it, but by how her chest rises and falls rapidly, I know she's angry. I frown, my brows pinching together. What happened in the bathroom?

"I was looking for you."

"And I was looking for you," I echo and extend my hand to her. The slightest hesitation flickers behind her eyes, but she still lets me take her hand in mine. Even if it's limp. Her mind is elsewhere, and if I've learned anything about her already, I know I can't do anything to make her open up if she doesn't want to. "Ready to go back to the room?"

"Yes." She smiles, but it's fake. What the fuck happened to my girl while she was gone? "Do we need to say goodbye to your father?"

"No." I whirl around, dragging her away with me. "He should be happy I agreed to come at all. He doesn't deserve a proper goodbye."

When she doesn't say a word in return, a cold sweat breaks out all over my body. I only hope she will talk to me, because if not, I'll have no idea how to fix whatever happened. Discovering the truth about Egypt's pyramids sounds easier than cracking Ava.

Chapter 42

Your Punishment

AVA

As I head to the sink, my steps are light. I even sway a little to the quiet music coming from the main hall. I'm loving it here, mostly because I have seen Colton smile and enjoy himself. His father is a nightmare. Everything I knew about him made me despise him. It made me want to protect his son from him. Or at least show that pretentious jerk he has no power over his son's actions anymore. That he's no one. A sperm donor, as Colt calls him.

Mr. Thompson was bombarding me with questions about me and my family. Some honestly sounded like he was trying to figure out how smart I was. With how often he smiled, I know I didn't disappoint him. And that threw me off. I didn't care if Colt's father liked me, but I think he did. He looked happy for his son. Was there something I missed?

"The feisty little girl finally left her knight in shining armor." I look over my shoulder and see Helen standing near the door. I was so deep in my thoughts, and the water was running while I was washing my hands, that I didn't even hear her open the door.

I turn off the water, take a paper towel, and dry my hands. She comes closer and leans against the countertop. I throw the paper towel into the trash can and turn to look at this woman. She's beautiful and sexy—I'm not one to deny the obvious. But with what I know about her and her actions? She's disgusting.

"A woman with no dignity or self-respect followed the feisty little girl to the bathroom? Why?"

She shifts a little, her lips forming a snarl. "Don't you think you should be more careful with what comes out of your mouth?"

"Why?"

"Because of societal norms," she hisses, and I just can't help myself. She's adorable.

"Do societal norms say that it's okay to sleep with someone else's husband? To spread your legs for your own boss?"

Her face contorts in anger, and she digs her fingernails into the countertop. I hit a nerve for sure.

"Looks like Colton let the cat out of the bag." Helen's voice drops an octave, and she narrows her eyes. "Did he tell you everything?"

"Everything? What else is there to say except 'my father had an affair with his secretary'? How do you even live with yourself knowing what you did to Colton's mom?"

Just for a second, I see her mask slip. She's surprised I know so much. She didn't think he would tell me about his mom. Her eyes roam over my face, and a deep wrinkle appears on her forehead. I can tell my words really affected her. I not only showed her that I have zero respect for her, but I also let it slip how much Colt trusts me. And I'm not sure it was the right thing to do.

"I never wanted Avery to know. I never wished for anything bad to happen to her."

"Kinda controversial statement, don't you think?" I frown slightly. "How can you not wish for anything bad to happen to someone and then go and fuck their husband?" *Is she insane or what?*

"We were out of town, on a business trip. I got drunk, he helped me to my room, and I invited him in. He's a handsome man, powerful and in great shape. The next morning, he told me it was the first and last time." She lets her eyes wander around the room before she focuses on me. There is another emotion in her gaze, but I can't put my finger on it. Is it regret? "Eric and I apparently have mind-blowing compatibility.

The only time I had sex with him, I got pregnant, and it changed everything."

I continue to stare at her while Colton's image pops into my head. He's in his car, revealing the truth about his mom's health, and then admitting he didn't tell me everything. "So what? If you didn't want to—"

"No. That never was an option. I have only one ovary, and the doctors weren't sure I would ever get pregnant. I made the decision on my own, and only later told him the truth," she says bitterly, wrapping her arms around her waist. I feel my heart beating violently, so loud and fast it's ear-piercing. "To say he was unhappy is an understatement. He demanded a paternity test once the child was born; he wanted to make sure I was telling the truth. I didn't have anything against doing it, and it was never about money, even if Colt was sure I got pregnant on purpose. He was furious with me when he came to see me after he found out the truth."

"Why would he come to see you?"

Helen's lips part, and she gawks at me in silence for a moment. Nervousness settles inside my chest, growing bigger with how she keeps looking at me.

"When Colton found out about my pregnancy, he promised to help me. And you should know how he is if you two are so close—if he promises something, he does *everything* in his power to make it happen." She smiles at me, her shoulders relaxing.

"You could have left the city, could have kept your distance from their family, gotten financial support from Colt's dad. That way, Avery would have never endured what she went through. All because of you."

"Shut up. You have no idea what you are talking about." she snaps, taking a step forward. "My daughter is Eric's, but he refuses to acknowledge her. He made me sign papers that left her totally at his mercy. If he wants to give her money, he gives it. If not, then he doesn't. Everything he has is Colton's."

"What do you mean 'sign papers'? No parent in their right mind would ever do that to their child." My fingers are trembling from anger. She's a fucking shit show. "Just be honest and admit you wanted to be Mrs. Thompson, because if it was just about you having a child, you would have done things differently. This mistake could have been fixed. You're a greedy piece of shit."

I veer around her and stomp to the door. I see red, I swear. Even the debacle with Moore wasn't anything compared to how she made me feel.

"If I wanted to be Mrs. Thompson so much," Helen says as I swing the door open, "I would have chosen the son, not the father. He's a stallion in bed."

"You're sick," I tell her and slam the door behind me. I probably look like I'm fucking crazy; no trace of my light and good mood is left. The worst part is, I am having a hard time bottling it all up. Making a scene in the middle of the party isn't an option. And besides, what can I say to him? That he should have told me the whole truth before bringing me here? That he should have warned me he screwed his dad's secretary too? What the fuck is wrong with all of them?

I barely see where I'm going when he comes into view. I take a step further and block his path. "I was looking for you."

"And I was looking for you." Colton extends his hand to me, and I realize I don't want him to touch me. I just need a moment to myself to figure out how I feel. But I let him take my hand in his, even if it makes me uncomfortable. Only because I don't want to push him away and hurt him on a whim. My talk with his father's mistress made my head spin.

"Ready to go back to the room?"

"Yes." I force a smile, but it doesn't reach my eyes. It's the fakest smile I am capable of, and he knows it too. "Do we need to say goodbye to your father?"

"No," he says, dragging me away. "He should be happy I agreed to come at all. He doesn't deserve a proper goodbye."

I'm no longer listening to him, trying hard to keep my emotions at bay. My breath is labored, and my heart rate accelerates. The noises around us turn into whispers, barely audible sounds. Helen's words reverberate in my head, and I clench my jaw. I feel dirty after talking to her, and I'm mad at Colton. Not because he slept with that woman, but because he failed to understand how important it was to tell me the whole truth. He should have done it before we came here.

His hand on my skin brings me back to reality. My eyes land on his car. It will be one hell of a ride for sure, because he reads me so well, and he knows the state I am in. He just doesn't know my reasons.

"What's on your mind?" His deep voice goes right through my ears and spreads throughout my body. It's like a soft coat, surrounding me with warmth and the most pleasant scent in the world: his scent.

"Just stuff," I answer, opening the door of his car and climbing inside. He sighs, and then closes the door. He moves to his side, slips inside, and starts the engine. My eyes are on the building as I keep my hands on my knees. They're balled into fists. Digging my fingernails into my skin, I hope to chase away this sick feeling flowing through my veins.

"Please let me in." My chest is aching seeing the look on his face. His misery and sadness are palpable, and that hurts me to no end, because my behavior is causing it. "Let me in your thoughts."

Tears treacherously sting my eyes, and I close them. I bang the back of my head against the seat. Punishing him for the mistakes of his past is pathetic and wrong, but I need time to process all this and prepare my questions. I want answers.

"I will talk to you when we get to our hotel room, okay?" I mumble quietly, and his hand covers mine, gently but at the same time firmly. He worms his way in, unclenching my fist and threading his fingers through mine.

"Of course."

The ride is short because he booked a room in a nearby hotel. Was I surprised when he told me we were going to stay at a hotel instead of his family's house? A little. I didn't expect him to hate the place so much, because even though it's hard for him to admit, he was happy there once too. That house holds memories of his childhood, of time with his mom when she was healthy and loved spending time with her little boy. I hate that his relationship with his father took that away from him. I hate how that man made him feel and how he still affects him.

I'm the first to climb out of the car, and I instantly regret it. The weather has gotten much worse, and the coldest wind wafts around me, scattering shivers over my skin. I hug myself, running my palms up and down my arms, hoping to give myself some warmth. I take a step forward, and his leather jacket suddenly covers my shoulders. The corners of my mouth tremble as I glance at him. The smallest grin plays on his lips as he shrugs.

"I told you we would need this later."

"Who knew it would be *this* cold?" I mutter, heading into the building.

"It's the end of fucking January in Michigan, Ava, not May. This is normal weather for this time of the year."

"Thank you for the geography lesson, Mr. Thompson. I would have never known."

"You're so charming, Little Miss Sarcasm."

"Fuck you." I give him my middle finger as we step inside the foyer. I bite my bottom lip, at once acknowledging that my anger has dissolved into nothingness. *Ladies and gentlemen, let me introduce you to the Colton Motherfucker Thompson Effect.*

Our elevator ride is silent, but we keep smiling at each other, feeling at ease. His care and little jokes did their thing and helped me to get rid of my explosive thoughts, at least for a little while. Because we can't avoid talking about everything I found out—it's too big to ignore. I only hope this change in my mood will prevail.

Once inside the room, Colt unbuttons his white shirt, putting it into his travel bag. I kinda wasn't ready to have a serious conversation with him half naked. It will be way harder for me to form words if my panties are dripping.

He knows I'm watching him as I stand still in the middle of the room. Does it bother him? Not really. Colton is one of those people who could watch a house burn down with no emotion on his face. He's mastered his poker face to a tee.

"So...what happened in the bathroom?" He sits down on the bed in front of me, his gaze glued to my face.

"Helen wanted to talk." As soon as I say it, his jaw hardens.

"What did she want from you?"

"I think she wanted to teach me a lesson. To put me in my place." I shrug nonchalantly. "Too bad I don't care."

He breathes through his nostrils. "What else did she say?"

"Her side of the story." I lift my gaze to his face, and an intense wave of different emotions overwhelms me. "Why didn't you tell me you were helping her?"

"You don't understand."

"Help me understand, Colton, because I'm truly lost here. How—"

"I promised to help her with her pregnancy, and I always keep my promises." I have no idea what goes wrong with me when I'm with him, but his anger turns me on so damn much, it feels as if my skin is on fire. It's burning hot, and I desperately want to touch myself. To relieve this tension and my overwrought nerves. "That's the only reason why I stayed in touch with her. Chloe doesn't deserve my hate."

I shift, and one of the straps of my dress falls off my shoulder. Colton's gaze zeroes in on it. The desire in his eyes is so fucking addictive, I slowly reach over and push it lower, until it's totally off my shoulder.

"She was just your father's employee."

"I don't think she ever planned on telling me about her pregnancy. I just happened to be there when she was at her lowest, crying her eyes out on her way home from the office. She literally bumped into me, and I offered to give her a ride home." I take off the other strap and see his Adam's apple bob up and down. "I was helping her with everything, even after I knew my father was the one who got her pregnant. There were times when I took her and my sister on a walk, just to keep her company." I cup my breast, squeeze it hard, and drag my dress down, exposing my strapless bra. "Ava, what are you doing?"

"Listening to you," I tell him, gliding my hands over my boobs and down my belly. "Were you helping her even after what happened to your mom?"

Please, say no, Colt. "Yes, but it wasn't about her. It was about my sister."

I push my dress down and step out of it. Colton licks his lips, leaning forward and putting his elbows on his knees. I edge to the chair and slump down into it, noticing a crease between his eyebrows. Confusion is written all over his face, while all I want is to cast away my fucking agitation. I understand where he's coming from, but this knowledge combined with the fact that he had sex with Helen leads me astray. I want to punish him for that, and not allowing him to touch me is the best way to make it extra hard for him.

"Are you still helping her?"

"No. When Mom's state worsened, I couldn't bring myself to continue helping Helen. Any time I'd go over, pictures of my mom in that facility would pop into my head, and I couldn't...I haven't seen Chloe in six months."

I stay silent, press a palm to my breast, and start circling it over my nipple. It pebbles instantly, as I feel it through the fabric of my bra. I do the same to my other boob, needing only one circle to make it pointy. His eyes are on me, following my every move. I reach around and unclasp my bra, throwing it to the side. His breath is heavy and shallow. I hold his gaze as I suck my index finger into my mouth, wetting it.

"Why didn't you tell me," I sigh as I swirl my wet finger over my nipple, imagining his tongue doing the same, "that you fucked her too?"

"It was just once; she was already pregnant." His voice is hoarse as he moves his hand to his dick over his black pants.

"I didn't ask how many times you fucked your father's secretary, Colton." I sink into the softness of the chair. Spreading my legs further, I slide my fingers to my clit, massaging it through my panties. I could come just from the intensity of his gaze on me. "Why did you hide it from me? It wasn't the right time when we...oh God," I moan, and my eyes roll back in my head. I need to gather my thoughts before I finish. It's imperative he knows why I'm doing this. Why I'm going to deprive him of something he loves.

"Ava." A low growl escapes his mouth as he rises to his feet.

"It wasn't the right time when we went to see your mom. I get it." I move my panties to the side, slipping a finger inside my pussy and then adding another one. "But you could have told me. She made me feel like a fool."

"When I saw her today, I knew I made a mistake. I shouldn't have kept it to myself, I'm sorry." He steps closer and gradually lowers himself to his knees. "Please, let me taste you."

I say nothing, fucking myself with my fingers faster and deeper. My orgasm is building inside me, skyrocketing with the feeling of his eyes on my body. He devours me without touching me, without laying even a single finger on my skin. I play with my nipple, rubbing it between my fingers and then pinching it. I moan loudly and shut my eyes, feeling a tingling sensation in my lower abdomen. I'm so fucking close.

"Ava, please..." I snap my eyes open, staring at him through clouded vision. I pull out my soaked fingers and press them to my clit, spreading my legs wider. "Please, let me do that. I want to taste you, please."

"No," I whimper, my brows pinching together as I rub my clit over and over, as waves of pleasure ripple through my bones. My abs contract as I come. My legs are shaking from the fervor of my orgasm. "It's your punishment."

Our eyes stay locked on each other for a few seconds, but then he abruptly stands up. Wheeling around, he storms to his travel bag, grabs a hoodie out of it, and pulls it on. The next thing I know, the door is slamming behind him. I have never seen a sex-deprived Colton, and it amuses me.

Getting up, I head to the bathroom. I need to take a shower before I go to bed. As I step into the stall, the image of him on his knees reappears in my mind. Colt is not one to forget me misbehaving and not letting him do what he wants. I'm going to pay for it, for sure, and I can only imagine what he's going to do to me. A smile blooms on my lips. I honestly can't wait.

Chapter 43

Get On Your Knees

COLTON

It's your punishment.

I get that she's upset I didn't tell her about Helen and me. I get that she's angry because that woman probably told her one or two very nasty things. I get all that—but saying no to me? When I was on my fucking knees? When I begged her to give me what I wanted? What the hell is that?

I've been pacing back and forth, for thirty minutes for sure, in the lobby. I pat my pockets, perfectly aware I don't have cigarettes with me. And I need it now. I desperately want to smoke. Even one drag would help. I need to release some tension.

Heading out of the building, I stroll to my car in the parking lot. Quickly unlocking it, I slide inside. I reach the glove compartment, find a pack of cigarettes with only one inside, and exhale loudly. Tonight was too eventful for my liking, but it wasn't as disastrous as I expected. Ava makes everything better.

I definitely met my match in her. She's everything I want. She's my fucking sun, and I revolve around her. Without her, I feel lost, as if the law of gravity isn't working. I'm freaking Winnie-the-Pooh who can't stay away from his honey—so why the fuck am I out here in my car?

Oh, Ava, you have no idea what you have dragged yourself into.

Spanking that fucking attitude out of her sounds way too good; the opportunity can't go to waste. Smirking, I climb out of the car, lock it, and saunter back into the hotel, throwing the cigarette into the trash can on my way. Who needs nicotine when I have Ava? She's my own drug, the only one I need.

OPENING the door of our room, I cautiously step inside and close it behind me. It's silent and dark since she pulled the curtains closed while I was out. I smirk, walking further and taking off my hoodie. I toss it onto the chair and strip off my pants and my boots, keeping my eyes on the prize. Ava is already asleep, curled into a ball in the middle of our bed with a blanket squeezed between her thighs. No wonder I always wake up without any blankets when she stays the night. I heard this joke about guys, how girls sometimes call them keepers. I have my own keeper now—a blanket keeper, to be precise. Only her face and her long brown hair are visible on the pillow. She looks so peaceful and so cute when she's sleeping.

I will be twenty-two in April, but before her, I'd never spent the night with a girl. Sex, yes, but no one ever stayed the night, and I never stayed for cuddles either. Clay used to make fun of me, calling me "Mr. Bang Bang and Gone". Not that it wasn't the truth.

I climb into bed, slip under the blanket, and slowly wrap myself around her. My skin is colder than hers, and she shifts uncomfortably, still asleep.

Sorry, baby. Going to sleep without me was a bad idea. Especially after the stunt you pulled.

"Ava? Wake up, baby."

"Colton..." she murmurs sleepily, eyes half open. Wiggling, she turns to face me. "What do you want?"

"You," I say, holding her gaze. We've talked about things we like and don't like when it comes to sex, and I know she doesn't mind if I wake her up by going down on her. But right now, I want her to give me permission. Especially after she denied me what I wanted before. "Do you want me to make you feel good?"

She looks me in the eyes and then closes hers again. "Yes..."

Skimming my fingers over her skin, I put my palm on her belly, moving over her belly ring and then lower, to her tiny shorts. I drag them down to her knees and leave them there for now. Then I dive under the sheets, pull off her shorts completely, and force my way between her legs, making her open them for me.

I close my eyes for a moment and then bury my face in her pussy, teasing her clit with my tongue. I circle it slowly, kissing and then sucking on it lightly. I lick her cunt, lapping my tongue faster and then slowing down. Ava spreads her legs wider, her fingernails digging into my scalp. I slide my hands around her ass, keeping her still as I nibble on her clit. I feast on my girl, and nothing tastes sweeter than her.

Ava breathes louder and heavier as I start licking her faster. She's soaking wet, and I can't get enough of her. I kiss her pussy, worshiping every little part. Sliding my tongue deeper, sucking her clit harder. She arches her back, forcefully grabbing my hair in her fist and tugging. She comes loud; her legs are wobbly as I continue licking her dry. No way in hell will I let it go to waste.

"Colton..." She whispers my name as I toss away the blanket and sit up straight. I see the cutest smile playing on her lips as we lock eyes. "I was kinda punishing you."

"My punishment is long overdue, Ava," I snort, swinging my legs over the edge of the bed and jumping to my feet. "Come here."

"Um, why?"

"Because we're going to discuss your punishment for making me beg and still saying no." I narrow my eyes. "Come here, Ava."

She rolls her eyes but climbs out of bed. The only piece of clothing she has on is a tiny top, and dear God, it makes her breasts look amazing. She's so fucking gorgeous in it, I quickly start losing my focus.

"What's next?"

"Take it off." I point at her top, and she obeys, tossing it on the bed. In the darkness of the room, her eyes are mesmerizing and inviting. I take a step closer, hovering over her and holding her gaze. "Get on your knees."

Her lips part, and her eyes round. I'm not sure what she expected, but it definitely wasn't this. She sucks in a breath and then slowly gets on her knees, looking up at me. Sweet baby Jesus, I could come right now. The view is fucking divine.

I push down my briefs, kick them away, and inch one step closer to her. I bend down and take her chin between my fingers, stroking my dick with my other hand. "Now open your mouth, baby. I want to see my cock deep down your throat. I want to hear you choke on it until I fucking come with your full lips wrapped around me."

Ava licks her lips, and for a second I wonder if I'm taking it too far. But then she puts her hands on her knees, keeps her eyes on my face, and slowly parts her lips. Fuck, she's perfect.

Carefully, I slide my cock inside her warm mouth, closing my eyes from the contact. Oh God, I'm definitely not going to last long. Ava swirls her tongue over the head of my cock, giving me light sucks and then squeezing my dick harder between her lips. She works magic with her tongue, grazing her teeth over it and drawing a hiss out of me every time she does. I fist her hair, adjusting myself and fucking her mouth. I don't go deep at first, but the more pressure she adds, the more I'm tempted to give in.

"Right there, baby," I groan. She cups my balls, massaging them and then tugging them down. I'm losing my mind from her caress, from her fucking lips and tongue. It's the best blow job in the world because she's the one giving it to me. "Fuck, Ava...you're such a good girl..."

She squeezes my balls, and I dive deeper, deepthroating her. She chokes on my cock; her slurping sounds become louder. Tears form in her eyes, but she doesn't stop. She doesn't lean away. She lets me fuck her mouth as she massages my balls more and more. I fucking come in no time, filling her mouth with my cum. She swallows every drop I give her, and only then do I take a step back.

Ava bites her bottom lip, staring at me in the eyes. I want to experience everything with her. I pull her to her feet, grab her chin, and smash my lips onto hers. I can taste myself on her tongue, and it sends a rush down my dick, making it hard again. It wants to be in her pussy so bad.

I leave a trail of kisses down her throat as she reaches for my cock and wraps her hand around my shaft. *No, baby, that's not what I want.* I twirl her around and push her onto the bed. Ava looks at me with her eyebrows knitted together. I bend down, quickly take a condom out of my pants, sheath my cock, and stalk over to her. "Get on all fours. Face-down. Ass up."

"Oh my God," Ava murmurs, doing as I say. She holds herself on her elbows and knees, giving me that sweet little cunt of hers. "You sound so bossy, and I want to call you daddy...and oh my fucking God. I'm sick in the head."

Smiling coyly, I shake my head. Her dirty mind comes not only from the books she reads, but from the videos she watches. Her remark about it left me speechless the other day, while she was absolutely unaffected, telling me she and Layla were just curious. What a nasty little girl she is, and she's all mine. I angle my cock and bury it in her pussy. "Call me whatever you want, Ava." She feels amazing around my dick—a bit tight, just how I like it. "I'm going to stretch this pussy so fucking damn wide..."

"Fuck yes..."

I fuck her from behind, going steady and slow, as I want her to adjust to my size. She moans, her face hidden in the sheets. With each thrust, my cock goes deeper inside her, and I'm ready to proceed with my plan. I lift my hand and slap her ass, leaving my handprint on it. So fucking good. Ava whines and fists the sheets.

"Next time you want to punish me..." Another slap rings in the air. "Do whatever you want..." Another slap, a bit lighter this time. "But never forbid me from tasting you."

My handprints on her skin look absolutely mind-blowing. She's fucking mine. Only mine. I need her to tell me this. I need her to tell me she understands. "Am I clear?"

"Yes." She props herself higher on her hands and catches my gaze over her shoulder. "Yes, Daddy."

Fucking little brat. I wrap my arm around her waist from behind, helping her to stay on all fours, and fuck her harder. I'm balls deep inside her, and it feels better than anything. Better than anyone else. Ava arches her back and tilts her head up, and I wind my hand over her throat from behind so I can kiss her. She's flexible, and I enjoy it to no fucking end.

"Who's my fucktoy tonight?"

"Me." She moans loud, and I see veins bulging in her hands as she grips the sheets tighter. "I'm your fucktoy, Colton."

"Just for tonight?"

"Always."

"Ready to come?" I'm on the verge, but I need her to be with me. I need her on the same wavelength. "Ready to swallow my cock?"

"Yes...fuck me, Colt. Harder...please."

I cup her boob from behind and play with her nipple. I move faster, and she rocks her hips too, meeting me halfway. Greedy little brat, desperate for my cock. My body is covered in sweat as I fuck her harder, right until I feel her walls wrap themselves around my dick. Her orgasm is strong, and it pushes me over the edge too. I groan, spilling my cum in the condom as I grip her ass.

I slump down onto the bed, catching my breath. Ava climbs up further and pulls the blanket to cover herself. I smile at her, and she smiles at me in return. "I'm sorry for not telling you about my involvement with Helen."

"Thank you, Colt. I hope you know I wasn't angry because you slept with her. I just didn't like looking like a fool in front of her. That's all."

"I know." I gently run my fingers over her ankle and then stand up. "You have a few minutes."

"Before what?"

"I'm not done with you yet." I go to the bathroom and stop in the doorway. "Not sure we're getting any sleep tonight."

With that, I close the door behind me and hear her groan. She might be tired and want to sleep, but I know she wants my cock more. I'm going to make her ride me like only she can. I'm so full of lust for her, it's maddening.

Chapter 44

The Ice Rink

AVA

"Ava?"

I hear Layla's voice, but I don't pay any attention to her. I need to finish these damn aesthetics and finally post them. My engagement these days is shit, and I'm trying to find new ways to make it better. A beautiful picture is a must, but reels also help.

I chose the worst time ever to try to become a bookstagrammer. I spend way too much time reading, annotating, writing reviews, and then juggling my social media. All because of my hobby.

"Mason."

"What?" I save the picture and finally look at my best friend.

"I've asked you three times already, but now I'm wondering if you heard anything."

"I didn't. What?"

Layla examines me, her fingers threading through her blonde locks. She and Clay got together during winter break, and they've been a couple for two months already. She's literally shining these days, always getting pretty and trying on new clothes. Rodgers is always by her side, ready to worship the ground she walks on and shower her with compliments. He's whipped, and he isn't afraid to show that to anyone. The whole college already knows Layla Benson did the impossible: she made Clay Rodgers settle down.

"Will you go to the next game?" she asks cautiously, and something in her tone of voice throws me off.

"Probably. Why?" I hide my phone in my pocket and pick up my backpack from the floor. Colt should be at practice, and since I already finished all my assignments, the thought of going to his place resonates in my head. I've been busy this week, so I didn't have an opportunity to see him. It's the worst. "It's a home game, right?"

"Yeah, against the Gladiators." The look on my face says it all, and she sighs. "Sorry. I kinda figured you wouldn't know, since you don't pay attention to the schedule. I thought I should warn you."

I want to go to the game. I want to cheer for Colt. For Drake and Clay. I don't want to feel like an outcast—but I don't want to see Levi. All my nightmares will come back at breakneck speed.

"Ava?" Layla smiles at me, stepping closer and taking my hand in hers. "Have you talked to Colt about it? About that night and Levi?"

"No."

"Why? I know you trust him."

"I do, but it's not about trust." I shrug. "That shit is still in my freaking head, and talking about it is too painful. It brings back all the bad memories."

Layla pulls me in and wraps her arms around my shoulders. I let her, snuggling closer and hiding my face in her hair. "You need to talk about it with him. The more you hold on to it, the worse it will get. Don't you miss the ice rink?"

"I do."

"Then talk about it with Colton." She leans away, her eyes coasting over my face. "It will help. I've never seen any guy be as in tune with you as he is. He will know what to do."

I fight a smile, but it still blossoms on my lips. She's not wrong. The level of understanding between me and Colt is absolutely mind-blowing. "And if his father's party taught me anything, it's keeping secrets is a bad idea. They will be playing against each other, and Levi never plays fair. Plus, he already saw us together. He could try something on Colt."

"He could try." Layla guffaws, letting me go. "Your guy knows how to stand up for himself. His fights are always epic."

"He's not my guy," I correct her and fix my backpack.

"And I'm not your best friend," she mutters in annoyance. "I'm just some random chick who decided to talk to you about some random guy."

"Layla," I warn her. Her attempts to put a label on me and Colt's relationship are ridiculous. We're just having fun, exclusively. I might have used the word "relationship," but I still avoid admitting the obvious, and I don't want to make it public.

"Don't 'Layla' me." She points her finger at me, takes a step back, and puts her books in her backpack. "You two are always together in your free time. He only has eyes for you, just like you have eyes only for him. You're basically living together a few days a week, and you're not dating? Bullshit. You're deluding yourself, Ava."

"He's okay with it. If he wanted to date me, he could have asked."

"And what would your answer be?"

Nothing. I would run away. As fast as I could. My fear of losing my freedom is still tangible. Jefferson did a great job of ruining relationships for me. Asshole.

"Let me guess...asshole?" she asks.

"Asshole," I confirm as we saunter toward the exit, smiling at each other. "Dating Levi traumatized me, and I'm still not over it."

"That's why I say talk to Colton."

"I will." I zip up my jacket and push the door open. "I'm going to his place right now."

"Sounds amazing." Layla nudges me with her elbow as we go down the stairs. "Call me if you need anything. Like encouragement."

"Go to hell," I mumble as she smacks my ass. "I hate you."

"Love you too." She blows me an air kiss, whirls around, and heads to her dorm.

I watch her go, and then I resume my walk. Hopefully this little stroll will help me to sort out my memories. The parts of my past I buried deep inside my head after only one attempt to forget. Not surprisingly, it didn't work.

What Levi did to me at the end of our relationship is about more than physical pain. More than trauma and pills. It took some time for me to heal and recover. But the mental pain is the worst. The fear that experience caused me is absolutely hindering. It lives rent-free in my head, especially when I step close to the ice. The darkness. The coldness. The unconsciousness. I remember every one of these feelings as if it was yesterday and not two years ago. It's raw, and it alters my whole life and my future. It prevents me from doing things I love, from being with someone I like, from letting him call me his. Even if he desperately wants to, because even if he doesn't say it, I know it's on his mind.

Inside Colt's apartment, I go to the fridge. Quickly rummaging through it, I take out everything I need for banana pancakes. They are his favorite, and I secretly love spoiling him. Giving him what he loves and seeing him smile and enjoy himself. It's the best version of him, the one I love the most.

Thirty minutes later, I'm in my crop top and cotton shorts, dancing as I wash the dishes. A pile of pancakes is on a plate, and a mouthwatering aroma fills the kitchen. Music swims around me, as Zayn blasts through my AirPods. His music and his voice often mesmerize me, and tonight I can't help myself from humming along and swaying to the rhythm.

Suddenly, an arm wraps around my waist, a big, calloused palm covering my belly. A second later, one of my AirPods is out of my ear and in Colt's hand. I spin around slowly, my eyes finding his face. Amusement is easily recognizable behind his irises—so is happiness. If it were up to him, I would already live at his place. He wants me here all the time.

"I've never heard you sing before."

"I don't usually do that when people are around." I stop the music, take the other AirPod out of my ear, and put it on the countertop.

"Why? Your voice is melodic and pleasant, but it's also strong. As if you learned how to use it."

"High school choir." I step closer, wanting his warmth again. I'm not addicted to anything—except maybe him. Just a little bit. "I quit, if you were wondering."

"Why?" he asks, bending down and quickly kissing my forehead.

"Someone made it impossible for me to enjoy."

"Who did that to you?"

"A girl, and I already made her pay for it." I inhale his scent, recognizing notes of his shower gel. He needs to know about Levi. Soon, before I have time to change my mind. I don't want him to feel the way I did when I met Helen. I wouldn't wish that on anyone.

"Still, I hate that someone took it away from you." He hides his nose in my hair, and I'm melting. His ability to be this sweet catches me off guard every damn time. Being rude and dominant is how everyone else sees him, but I see him as he is: with all his flaws and imperfections, with all his rough and soft edges. I see the real him, and it's the most precious view in the world. "How did you get here?"

"I walked." I push him away slightly so his hands drop from my sides. I take the pancakes from the countertop and edge to the table. "Can you grab two glasses and—"

"Apple juice." I look over my shoulder and see him with everything I just asked for.

"Apple juice," I repeat as he sets everything on the table. Then he joins me, sitting across from me. "Why are you looking at the juice like that?"

"Because I'm sure I didn't buy it."

"I bought it on my way over. It's way better than Pepsi."

"Healthier, yes. Better? Not so sure," Colt snorts, taking a bite of his pancake. "Damn, baby, this is delicious."

Warmth spreads through my veins, cruising through me and making my cheeks blush. His praise always gets me in bed—so does a simple compliment. Sometimes I wonder if he can read my mind. The things he does to me are totally astonishing; they make me doubt if he's real. Colton Thompson is way too good to be true.

"Glad you like it," I murmur, watching him.

"Like it? I'm ready to fucking marry you if you promise to make these for me every day."

"I'm not wife material, Colt." His eye twitches, and I instantly regret my words. *Dammit, Ava, way to ruin everything.* But it's Colt. This guy is honestly my personal undoing.

"You're confident and independent, yes. But the way you purr when

I'm taking care of your needs, and how submissive you can be...I would say you're wife material—in the right arms."

I hide my silly smile behind my juice glass, taking a sip.

"You mean your arms, I assume?" His eyes darken. I'm playing with fire, and I should be careful. I need to talk to him about Levi first; that's more important than him fucking me to oblivion.

"My arms. My cock. My fingers. Everything about me is a perfect match for you. Try to remember that, Ava."

The wetness in my panties doesn't surprise me anymore. In all honesty, it's nothing in comparison to how wildly my heart beats for him. How much my chest swells when he's around and showing me affection. His apartment is our safe place, and there are days when I don't want to leave it. Not even for a second.

"Layla told me about the next game," I blurt, and his eyebrows shoot up to his hairline. "I totally missed that it's against the Gladiators."

"If you don't want to go, I understand."

"I want to go." I put my glass on the table, staring him in the eyes. He's frowning, a bit confused, and I go for it, not leaving myself a chance to overthink. "I'm ready to talk to you about Levi. You're going to see him again, and I want you to be prepared. He loves to play dirty."

Colton is silent for a few seconds, and then he smiles. "He has zero chances against me, Ava. Trust me. The only person he's going to impress on the ice is his mother. Everyone else will know what a loser he is."

"You have no idea what he did, but you're already making assumptions." I shake my head and take another bite of my pancake. My nervousness has disappeared. His ability to set my mind at ease is amazing—everything is exactly as Layla said it would be. I have never met anyone more in tune with me than him.

"He lost you—he's a loser. He hurt you—that only proves the weakness of his character. Real men make their women cry from happiness, not pain."

Oh my fucking God. I hate him. I hate him for being such a perfect guy. Good thing I have some clothes at his place already; I will definitely need to change my underwear. My pussy is acting like a lovesick imbecile, soaking wet just from his words. And these fucking insects in my belly... *Please, kill me. I'm a fucking mess.*

Colt and I are in his bed, hidden under the heavy blanket. My head is on his chest, and he keeps his arm draped around my shoulder, securing me in his warmth. We're silent, and it feels great. He lets me gather my thoughts, not rushing me, allowing me to go at my own pace.

"My relationship with Jefferson was odd." I falter for a moment. "My feelings for him made me brainless. I ignored every red flag—in fact, I was drawn to them instead of running away. The shittiest thing? He made me believe I needed to change myself to make him happy, because we definitely had very different views, not only on our relationship but on everything else."

"Like what?"

"He was allowed to do anything, to go anywhere, to spend time with his friends whenever he wanted. Me? I needed to be available to him twenty-four seven. No matter what I was doing, I needed to drop it and run to him as soon as he summoned me." I speak quieter. "I love going out, spending time with my friends, but with Levi, I barely got to see Layla. I rarely hung out with my other friends. He was the only person I wanted to be with, and eventually that was exactly what he expected from me."

"Are you putting the blame on yourself?" Colt asks in surprise.

"Colt, it is my fault. I gave him way too much power over what I did and how I felt. He thought of me as his property, and in my head that meant he loved me, so I put up with it for two years," I confess. "No other guy was allowed to talk to me when he wasn't around, and later he expanded that rule to include my friends as well. One of the biggest fights we had was when Drake came home for spring break. Levi threatened to break up with me if I hung out with Layla and her brother without him. I should have broken up with him right then and there, but I let it drag out for a few more months, until shit hit the fan before his graduation. It was the final straw, and I will be damned if I ever let another guy treat me that way."

"What did he do, Ava?"

"I probably made it way more dramatic than it was, but the whole situation sowed a seed of fear in my chest and in my head. It's palpable, and it's strongly associated with the ice rink. No matter what I've tried, it doesn't go away."

"What happened to you?"

"It was a party. Someone's birthday. I honestly don't remember much, only little parts. Some bits of conversations I overheard." I close my eyes. "Layla and I were hanging out with Levi's friends, drinking and playing some stupid games. It was a fucking dare, and I cheered along with everyone once I heard it. Why would it be difficult for a hockey player to do a few laps on the ice, even after he was drinking, right? Levi definitely didn't make it a big deal, laughing it off and saying he could do it with his eyes closed."

I lick my lips and shut my eyes harder, the memories of that night now flooding me. It's overwhelming, and my head is spinning. I'm struggling for fucking air, and it shakes me to the core.

"Did he do it?" Colt helps me out, asking the right question.

"He did. He actually did pretty good; people couldn't stop cheering for him. I was incredibly proud of my boyfriend." He presses me to his chest harder, giving me the strength I need to continue. "Soon, everyone was gone except him and me. We were fooling around, kissing, and I made a mistake. I challenged him to do a few laps again. Holding me. He said okay. The first lap was good, but the next one took away my love of the ice."

"He couldn't hold you, could he?"

"Nope. He twirled me around once, then twice. The third time, he lifted me, but he was able to put me down. Unlike the fourth time. The only thing I remember is him lifting me over his head, and then it was darkness. He fucking dumped me on the ice because he was too drunk to be able to hold me." My breath hitches as I dig my nails into my palms. "It was my fault. I let him do it knowing how drunk he was. I knew the risks, and I still went for it. He couldn't hold me; he dropped me on the ice, and then he fucking left me. He got scared because I lost consciousness. He couldn't wake me, so he left me on the fucking ice, alone, in the middle of the night."

Tears are burning my eyes, and I howl. It hurts everywhere, just like it did when I finally woke up. Alone. In total darkness. In the silence and the cold.

"Ava?"

"Levi didn't tell anyone what happened. He returned to the party, continued drinking and having fun. He told Layla I went home. Meanwhile, I crawled to the bench I left my phone on. My head was spinning any time I tried to stand up. My dad got there ten minutes after my call and took me to the hospital. I had broken my left arm, and I had a concussion. It's nothing that didn't heal." I sniff, hiding my face in his chest and wetting it with my tears. "But I'm afraid to be on the ice since then. I'm afraid to even set foot on it; my vision blurs, and I become nauseous. He took away my love for skating. He took away the joy I felt playing hockey with Drake and Layla. He took away everything I loved about being on the ice, and I don't know how to deal with it."

Colton is silent. His heart is steady and calm. Only his trembling fingers in my hair reveal his state. He's furious. Carefully lifting my head, I catch his gaze. A moment passes before he opens his mouth. "I will help you fall in love with the ice again."

"Colt..."

"I know what it means to be afraid. I know what it feels like to not be able to even look at the thing that brought you pain and misery. I know about all of that, and I know how to fight it. So, if you let me, I would love for us to try. Okay?" He gently tucks my hair behind my ears. Cupping my cheek with his palm, he holds my gaze. It's intense and penetrating, and he sees right through me. "But first, I'll make him pay for what he did. I promise. He's going down next Saturday."

A thousand different emotions swirl around my head, but one is louder than the rest.

It's called love, and I'm a fucking loser.

Chapter 45

Her Last

COLTON

Standing in the kitchen, I wait for my coffee to brew. It's game day, and I woke up at six a.m. I couldn't sleep. I'm literally buzzing to be on the ice, even if my reasons are not at all professional. Bringing that motherfucker down is just as important as beating the Gladiators. I will do anything to make it happen.

I hear her tiptoeing from the bedroom, and my lips stretch into a giddy smile. She stayed the night even though I told her I would be up way earlier than usual. She said that would never stop her from being with me.

Little by little, she's opening up to me. Talking nonstop about things she loves, her favorite books and movies, telling me stories about her childhood, sharing her dreams and plans for the future. I could listen to her for hours without getting bored. I talk to her too, not hiding even the tiniest thing. She knows about my childhood and my school years, about my fuckups and my little victories on and off the ice. Me taking her to visit my mom and her finally opening up to me about her ex changed everything.

"When you said you would be up early, I thought you were exaggerating." Ava walks over to me, wraps her arms around my torso from behind, and presses her cheek to my back. She's warm and smells like her favorite vanilla shower gel. The kind she bought and left in my bathroom, claiming more and more space in this apartment. Some guys would freak out, but I'm not-so-secretly loving it. I need her by my side every minute, because she completes me and makes me feel desired. "Do you want me to help you with breakfast?"

I glance at her over my shoulder, raking my gaze over her face and her disheveled braids. She's still sleepy, and my heart swells with happiness. The way I feel about her overwhelms me and throws me off every damn time. She's the best thing that's happened to me in my entire life. "Nope, I'm taking care of you this morning."

"Sounds promising." Ava winks at me and steps back, ambling to the table and sitting down. "We have a few hours to spare before the game. What are we going to do?"

"Don't you need to study?" I ask, pouring coffee into two mugs.

"Nope. I finished all my assignments on Thursday."

"You definitely came prepared." Turning around, I edge to the table and put our mugs on it. Then I go back, grab two bowls of oatmeal, and return to her. The second Ava sees what we're having, she pouts.

"It's not my favorite breakfast."

"I know," I laugh, grabbing a pack of M&Ms from the countertop. I rip it open and toss a few candies into our bowls. "Better?"

"M&Ms make everything better," she tells me pointedly. She eats a spoonful, and when she starts smiling, I know she enjoys it. "Are you excited about the game?"

"I am, but I don't want to talk about it. Not on game day. Consider it a superstition," I state, and she eyes me with her eyebrow raised. "We all have our weird habits, Little Miss I Love Judging Others."

Her mouth falls open, and her eyes round. She grabs a napkin from the table and throws it in my face. "I'm not judging you."

"I know you aren't; I'm teasing you." I lick my lips, taking my mug in my hand. "How about we watch something?"

"Like what?"

"We can always watch something new, or continue with *Game of Thrones*." The other day, she told me she hated me because I made her watch all the episodes from the beginning, while she wanted to skip everything till season four. "What do you say?"

"I say you love torturing me, Colton." Ava shakes her head with a smile. "But okay, *Game of Thrones* it is. Jon Snow and Daenerys will always be my favorites."

It's a perfect morning. I'm hyped up about the game, anticipating our win and taking Jefferson down. That is, until I get a call from Dr. Stewart. He asks me about my plans to visit Mom tomorrow. He says she wants to talk to me, and it's incredibly important.

"YOU OKAY?" Clay asks during our break before third period. I shake my head no, breathing through my nostrils. Pulling myself together has never been so hard before. I let my worries overwhelm me. It's getting out of hand, even if we're winning. "Anything I can do to help?"

"It's fine. Thanks," I mumble, gulping down my water.

Closing my eyes, I picture Ava's beautiful face. She's a wildfire that is out of control, intensifying with each heartbeat, with every breath she takes. Or she's a small but gentle bonfire, spreading through every bone, blanketing me with her warmth. She wants to spend time with me, while she doesn't need me at all. For some, it may sound like nonsense, but Ava helped me to draw a line between being wanted and being needed. It's a huge difference, and my heart aches in my chest any time I realize she wants me by her side. And now I'm betraying her. The mess in my head is preventing me from thinking clearly, and her ex continues skating around the ice like a fucking star.

"Is this about Ava's ex?" Clay leans closer.

"It has nothing to do with him."

"Then what? Did you get into a fight with her?"

"For fuck's sake, Rodgers. We're good," I hiss, standing up from the bench and towering over my best friend. "I got some news today about my mom, and it kinda turned my day to shit."

Clay purses his lips, probably deciding if he should be angry with me for my outburst or not. I know the fucker like the back of my hand, and he's too curious for his own good. "How is she? Is there any chance she's getting better?"

What the fucking hell is this? Is this a prank? Or maybe I'm still sleeping? How on Earth does he know anything about my mom's state? Ominous and oppressive thoughts take over every spot in my mind, and this never ends well.

"She's okay. Her usual." I pivot to the door as Coach motions us all back onto the ice. At least Clay's questions did one thing: there is no way I'm letting that fucker Jefferson off the hook. I'm too wound up to play nice.

"Colt?" I meet Clay's gaze. I only pray he won't make things worse for me...unsuccessfully. He skyrockets my feelings to a level I never thought they could reach. "Just because I don't say anything doesn't mean I don't know. I always loved Mrs. T, and I wish her only the best."

He gets up from the bench and walks past me. I stay frozen. Never could I have imagined this day would be so bizarre. Failing on my plans to avenge Ava would be the final nail in my coffin. And hell no—that's not happening.

The last period goes fast. We're leading three to one, so we're playing defense, planning ahead our moves and tactics, and it definitely works out. Our defensemen are doing their jobs to a tee, battling in the corners, making clean, crisp outlet passes and blocking shots. The support from the stands is like another player in our favor.

I watch Jefferson like a hawk, and once I finally see an opportunity, I go over, passing by Coach and getting his approval. Only three minutes left, but I want us to score. It will be epic if I can pull it off, taking him down and rubbing our win in his face. *Dear God, please, after the morning I had, I definitely deserve some luck.*

Skating over to Jefferson, I easily win the face-off, sending the puck flying in Benson's direction. *Gotcha. I'm back in my game, baby.*

To say Ava's ex isn't happy is a major understatement. He puffs out his cheeks and slips away from me in silence. *Really dude? Not even a word?*

I stop him once again, snatching the puck and passing it to Moore. I hate the guy, but right now, he's my teammate, and I need him.

"What the fuck do you want from me?" Jefferson growls as I glide past him.

"To make you pay for what you did to Ava."

"It was her fault; she was just as drunk as I was. She shouldn't have suggested we skate together."

"It's so easy to put the blame on a girl instead of admitting you were a coward. Would it have been that hard to call an ambulance?" I follow him while still keeping my eye on the game. If everything goes right, we'll have a chance to score one more time.

"I was drunk as shit, and it could have jeopardized my career." Good, he's totally distracted. He isn't paying attention to how close we are to his team's net. I just need someone to pass to me. "You wouldn't have called an ambulance if you knew your future could be stolen either."

Forty seconds. Once I see the numbers, I feel my body surge with adrenaline. I desperately want to score, right in front of his eyes. I scan the place and see Benson. Our gazes lock, and he hits the puck rigorously, right into my stick. *Man, you're the best.*

Moving like a flash, I maneuver among the players, and a second later I send the puck into the net, making the final score four to one. I lift my fist in the air, my eyes locked on Jefferson. His lips are curled into a snarl as he breathes hard. He's pissed at me, and at himself for letting me play him.

Scooting over to him, I nudge him as discreetly as possible, and the dude lands on his ass. Hitting him in the face is tempting, but risking my career is not something I can afford right now. I can agree with him there.

"She must have fucked your brain up good if you're so whipped," he scoffs, standing up. "You should thank me though."

"Thank you?" I smirk, seeing the guys celebrating our win and listening to the crowd cheering.

"Everything she does in bed, I taught her. I was her first."

Stupid fucker, never knows when to keep his mouth shut. I step closer. Now we're chest to chest. "Good thing I intend to be her last."

Just as his eyes go wide in surprise, I hit him in his abdomen with all my might. Jefferson gasps and presses his hands to his belly, crumpling onto the ice.

"Try talking to her again, or touching her with even one damn pinkie, and I will ruin you. I promise."

Chapter 46

Sin-Bin

AVA

His head is not in the game. Even watching him from the stands, I know it. He's still on the ice, he is scoring and passing, but it's not his usual play. He's somewhere deep in his thoughts, and I can't put my finger on what it could be.

It's the final minutes of the game. The score is three to one, but with how the Panthers continue to dominate on the ice, I wouldn't be surprised if they score again. I have no idea what happened in the locker room before the third period, but Colt is acting differently than he was at the beginning. He's more focused, and not just on the game. He is watching Levi.

I clasp my hands together, my fingers threading through each other. They are both on the ice now, and Colton is stalking Levi. He blocks his passes, steals the puck away, and sends it flying to Drake. My eyes are glued to Colt as he skates after my ex again. His moves are graceful and calculated; he's in total harmony with himself and his teammates, even Moore. What amazes me the most? The guy still has time to chase Levi, as if it's absolutely normal. Is he a fucking machine or what?

Colt said he would make Levi pay for what he did to me, and I'm afraid he'll let it go too far. I don't want anything to happen to him or his career—especially not because of me.

Colton doesn't let Jefferson out of his sight, following him everywhere and distracting him from the game. When I see him glance around, my mouth falls open. Is he going to try and score? Right in front of Levi? Sweet mother of God, it will be epic if he does. Jefferson will be insulted big time.

There is the quickest moment when Colt and Drake lock eyes, and then Drake shoots the puck in his direction. I hold my breath, watching it land right in front of Colt's stick. I'm biting my nails, my heart thumping in my chest, silencing all the sounds around me. I impatiently tap my foot as he rushes to the Gladiators' net. He lifts his stick, and the next thing I know, he fucking scores. What's more, I know he did it for me.

The final score is four to one, and the whole place erupts with people cheering and clapping, celebrating their favorite team. I continue to sit, my eyes trained on him. He's not done with Levi yet, and I just hope he will be careful. Colt can't take risks right now.

He stalks over to Jefferson and trips him up so he lands on his ass. I press my palm to my mouth, barely holding myself back from laughing out loud. Levi stands up and says something to him, and I hold my breath for a second. He must feel humiliated; his team lost. That can't be nice.

Please, Colt, the jerk isn't worth it. I notice him shake his head, as if he doesn't believe what he's hearing, and then he just punches Jefferson in his abdomen, making him press his hands to his belly.

A player from the Gladiators scoots over to them, and I honestly want to close my eyes. I'm freaking out, afraid he will be benched—or worse. I rise to my feet, and for a brief moment, Levi catches my gaze. His brows are furrowed as his eyes roam over my face, and then he turns around and skates off the ice.

What the hell just happened? Is he not going to make a scene? I'm confused, but also happy. The butterflies I feel stop playing on my nerves, spreading warmth through my veins and pumping my heart louder and stronger. I want Colton to be mine even if I'm scared to be heartbroken. I want to go all in and risk everything I have for him.

"Are you going to the party?" Layla asks, turning around to look at me.

"Not sure." I know what I want; I just need to figure out how to get it. "I want to spend time with Colt."

"Of course you do." She winks at me, taking my hand in hers. "I'm really proud of you for coming to the game. Your talk with Colton did wonders."

"It did." I give her hand a gentle squeeze, a tingling sensation in my fingertips. "Thank you so much for encouraging me to open up to him."

Layla flashes me a smile, and we head to the exit. She's going to wait for Clay so they can go to the party together and celebrate the win. For me, Colt is the only person I want to celebrate with, and I have a perfect place for that in mind.

After I part ways with Layla, I go to buy myself a coffee. I have some time to kill before I'll have Colton all to myself so we can talk. I need to know what happened to him, because he was more than just off in the beginning of the game. Hopefully he'll open up to me.

My phone dings with an incoming message, and I take it from the bench. I already talked to my dad, so it should be Colt. As soon as I unlock my phone, I see I'm right.

WINNIE-THE-POOH:

Where are you?

ME:

At the ice rink. Come and find me.

WINNIE-THE-POOH:

Not fair.

ME:

Be quick, this offer doesn't last 4ever.

I smile, watching as three dots appear and then disappear. Colt is not a man of words, but of action, and I'm not surprised he doesn't send me anything more. If he wants to spend his time with me—he will. He would change his plans, adjust them for me, and I would absolutely do the same for him. That's how our relationship works. We don't need to look for reasons to explain our behavior. And I prefer that to pretense and honeyed lies.

As I wait for him, I read my new book. It's twisty and dark, and lately that's all I want. I'm in my dark romance phase. I enjoy it, often finding myself mesmerized with the stories, not wanting to go back to reality—except when my reality looks like Colton Thompson. Makes it easier.

"Why did you decide to come back?" I lift my eyes from my phone and look at Colton. He's wearing a simple white tee, black jeans with sneakers, and a leather jacket. Classy bad boy.

"I didn't." Locking my screen, I quickly hide my phone in my bag. "I never left. I got a coffee and came right back."

"How come no one kicked you out?" He lowers himself onto the bench beside me.

"Kick *me* out? I'm the cutest girl in the world. I have a way with people, especially older men." I bat my eyelashes at him, and he snorts. "But we don't have a lot of time. Frank said we have to leave by midnight."

"He told me the same." He pulls his phone out of his pocket, checks it, and then slips it back in. "We have an hour, and I don't think he will bother us until then. All the cameras are off too. Frank often lets me practice after hours."

"You work hard."

"I plan to go pro, and I want to be ready for that. In a month or two, I'll know if my contract still stands, or if I'll need to look for another option," Colt mutters huskily, and the white noise in my ears intensifies. *He's going to leave when the summer comes, Ava.* He will be gone, and I will be left with the ruins of my broken heart. "So, why are we here? Why did you wait in the penalty box? Aren't you cold?"

"I'm not cold. And Drake always calls it the sin-bin," I murmur. Colt takes off his leather jacket and puts it next to him on the bench. "I like that more."

"Sure you do, my little sinner." He wraps his arm around my waist and hauls me onto his lap, making me straddle his legs. "Why are we here, Ava?"

"What happened to you? You weren't yourself when the game started."

"I got a call after you left. From my mom's doctor."

"And?" I lock my hands behind his neck. "She's been doing well, hasn't she?"

"Yes, she is, but Dr. Stewart told me she wants to talk to me. And I have no idea what it's about. It freaks me out."

"You're worried, and that's understandable. But you don't know anything yet. What if it's nothing serious? Why is the first thought you have a negative one?"

"Because I'm scared." Colt sighs and presses his forehead to mine.

"Colt—"

"You didn't hear how he sounded, Ava. I was going to visit her tomorrow anyway, but now it's even more important."

"Do you want me to go with you?" I rub my nose against his and feel his arms wrap tighter around me.

"No, but if you can, I would love to have you at my apartment when I get back."

"Didn't have any other plans, actually." I smile at him, and then I take a deep breath. "What happened on the ice? Between you and Levi? You hit him."

"He got what he deserves. I warned him, if he ever talks to you or touches you again, I will ruin his career."

"Thank you so much for that, Colt." I hum against his lips. "What happened after you tripped him?"

"He said he taught you everything you do in bed, that he was your first." I roll my eyes, not impressed in the slightest. That's typical Levi Jefferson—nothing has changed. "I told him I intend to be your last."

Mission abort, mission abort. But my mental alarms are not working. I am a fucking puddle, and my desire for him rockets to infinity and beyond just from his words. I press my palms to his cheeks and kiss him hard. Our tongues move around each other like a slow dance. He lifts his hips, and I feel his hard-on through his jeans. Wiggling on his lap, I rub my pussy over his dick. Oh God, it feels amazing.

"Damn, baby, this is not the fucking place for that." His lips slide down my neck as I roll my head back, enjoying his caress on my skin. "I don't have a condom with me."

I hesitate for just a second, and then I lock eyes with him. "Promise to be careful?"

"You sure?" He's searching my face as I reach my hands under his tee, feeling him up.

"More than ever. Take me right here, Colt." I climb off his lap, take off my panties, and push them into his jacket pocket.

"For motivation?" he asks teasingly, pulling out his cock. He leans back, propping himself on his hands. *Ladies and gentlemen, Colton Thompson has a perfect dick, and I'm not taking any objections.*

Whirling around, I turn my back to him and slowly lower myself down on his lap. I'm so wet already, he slides inside me to the hilt. I sigh, feeling his fingers dig into my skin. I put my hands on his knees for balance as I bounce up and down on his cock. He grows thicker, and his breath hitches. Then he groans, and his hand glides lower, to my clit. I close my eyes when he starts rubbing it between his fingers. A rough tug on my hair makes my head bob back. I moan louder, circling my hips and letting him go deeper.

"Tell me when you're close," he demands, and my knees give in.

"I'm so close...oh my fucking God, Colt..."

He lifts his hips higher as I lower myself onto his dick over and over again. My head is spinning, and I don't see anything. My mind has turned into jelly. His movements on my clit become faster, and I can't hold it together anymore. My body tenses, and my pussy contracts around his shaft. A few more strokes, and then he growls breathlessly, lifting me off his lap and having his own release.

We spend a few minutes just catching our breath and steadying our heartbeats. As I help him clean up his jeans, I can't stop myself from smiling. I never thought I would be the one to suggest bare sex, but the opportunity was too good to let it go to waste.

As soon as we are done, I take a step forward, but he hauls me back to his chest, twirls me around, and cups my face with his big palms.

"How about we go skating tomorrow evening?" Colton asks, and I immediately feel a lump in my throat. "I thought you coming to sit in the sin-bin, so close to the ice, meant something."

"I feel safe here," I mutter under my breath. "Maybe I'm not ready for skating, but just stepping onto the ice at first?"

"Works for me. We can ask Frank to let us in; he has a shift tomorrow too."

"You're the best guy I've ever met," I confess without thinking, and his eyes darken.

I try to take a step back, but he doesn't let me. His palms on my face produce maddening heat, and it sets my whole body on fire. Colt inches closer to my lips; his gaze is intense and piercing. My mind is in such a state that I'm having a hard time deciphering him, at least until his next words leave his mouth.

"Tell me you're mine." His voice cracks. "Tell me you're all mine, Ava."

"I'm yours, Colt." All the tension leaves my body with my words. "I'm only yours."

He takes a long and shaky breath and covers my lips with his. This kiss is full of desperation, filling us both to the brim with passion and longing. He takes possession of my mouth, of my tongue. He claims me, and I let him.

When I step back I'm shaking, watching him. I'm in an absolute daze. Colt smiles, bends down, and takes my things, along with his leather jacket. He grasps my hand and makes me follow him up the stairs and to the exit. He says goodbye to Frank, while I nod timidly in his direction.

He helps me into his car, and we drive away from the arena. Once we're parked near his building, he unbuckles his seat belt and jumps out. I join him a second later, and we walk into the building holding hands.

The second he slams the front door shut, our mouths collide. Hungrily, as if we're both starving for each other. Intensely, as if we weren't together just thirty minutes ago. It feels right, just how it should feel.

My hand finds its way to his groin, and I stroke his dick through his jeans. It grows bigger and harder within a few seconds. "I want your cock in my mouth," I whisper, and he wheels me around.

My back crashes into his chest. Colt sneaks his palm under my dress.

He circles my clit as I start grinding my ass over his dick, following his lead.

"Ava," he groans, sucking my earlobe into his mouth.

"Colt, please. I want your cock in my mouth," I beg, panting. His hands drop away from my sides, and I turn around and get on my knees in front of him.

I unzip his fly, unbutton his jeans, and push them down with his briefs. His dick springs free, and I take it into my mouth. Colt closes his eyes and puts his hand on the back of my head, keeping me positioned in the right spot. I stroke his shaft, sucking the head of his dick and swirling my tongue over it. He pushes me to take him deeper, and I go for it.

"Don't stop, baby. Don't stop." I suck his balls into my mouth as my hand moves up and down his shaft. "Fuck."

I smile to myself and take him as deep as I can. Tears spring to my eyes, but I try not to gag. I suck the base of his shaft, tonguing him and slowly grazing my teeth over his skin. Light sucks, gentle bites, and a lot of tongue, along with my hand to add more pressure. He trembles in my mouth and lets out the softest sound I've ever heard from a guy.

Deepthroating him, I gag but keep going. He pumps his cock inside my mouth, his hips thrusting in and out until he finally erupts and comes hard. I suck him dry and slowly stand up.

"I love the way you taste," I tell him sweetly, and he smirks, draping a hand over my waist and spinning us around. My back hits the wall, and I hold his gaze.

Everything in his moves is pure seduction—he makes me feel wanted. He makes me feel seen. He tugs on my dress, pulling it off in a swift motion. I unclasp my bra and toss it on the floor, and he does the same with his clothes.

I take a step closer, pressing my finger to his chest and dragging it down. "I want your dick inside my pussy. Now."

Colt chuckles, quickly dashing to the living room. Once he's back, I see a condom on his cock. "Any particular wishes, baby?"

"Fuck me from behind, please." I turn around, pressing my hands to the wall and bending over slightly to give him access to my pussy.

He sneaks his hand over my hip and pulls my ass to his groin, teasing my opening and then grabbing my hair with his other hand. "Say my name."

"Colton," I breathe as he slides inside me.

"Tell me you're mine," he demands.

"Yours," I moan as he fucks me, burying his cock in my pussy. He moves steady, with no rush. "I'm yours, Colton."

"You like that?" He winds his hand around my throat from behind and squeezes. "Ava?"

"Yes, go deeper, please. Please, Colt."

Fucking me harder, he slaps my ass, intensifying my moans. Then he inches forward, grabbing my hair and pulling me closer to him. "Your fucking pussy feels incredible. I love the way it swallows my cock and empties my cum."

"I'm gonna come, Colt," I whimper loudly, and my walls are squeezing around him. He continues fucking me, prolonging my pleasure until he comes too, spilling his cum into the condom.

"God, woman, you make me extra horny when you tell me what you like and what you want me to do," he says quietly, and I look at him over my shoulder.

"Really?" I straighten my back.

"Really."

"We're going to take a shower," I state, edging to the bathroom, where I linger in the doorway and stare him in the eyes. "And later, I'm looking forward to sitting on your face, Colt."

Chapter 47

Him and I

AVA

I'm reading a book on the couch in Colton's living room. I can't focus on anything new, so I chose one of my all-time favorites. It's helping distract me from thinking about his talk with his mom.

The front door opens, and then his footsteps follow. The second Colton walks into the room, I know something is wrong. Despair. Confusion. And anger. His brown eyes are almost black. The sorrow in his gaze gets under my skin so easily and so strongly, it feels as if I were the one who got some news about my parent.

He comes over, lays his head in my lap, and closes his eyes. "Talk to me." I thread my fingers through his tousled hair. "Colt."

"My entire ride home I had only one thought: my parents' marriage was like a fucking butterfly effect. The tiniest thing changed everything. Every fucking damn thing."

"It's never like that, no. It's like chess. Certain pieces during the game allow certain combinations. The king is always a king, just like the queen is not a pawn. People's behavior defines what happens to them in addition to their life circumstances," I retort slowly, and he shifts a little to peer into my eyes.

"How we react to situations depends on our personality, on our inner strength. Take Layla and me, for example. We have a lot of things in common; we have similar interests, and we have known each other for years, so we've had time to get used to one another. We almost got arrested once. Her reaction? Screaming and crying. Me? Racking my brain for a solution. And I fucking got us out of that shit—the police officer even gave us a ride home, letting us out a few blocks early so we didn't get in trouble with our parents. The same situation, but a totally different reaction. It's not one thing, Colt. It's never just one thing."

He smiles weakly and sighs, sneaking one of his hands under my tee and pressing it to my belly. "You're too good for me."

"Nonsense." I ruffle his hair gently, massaging his scalp with my nails. "What did you find out?"

"I told you before, my father has never been a nice man. Strict. Authoritative. His business success made him harsher, more scheming, more distant. While Mom...she's the total opposite. You couldn't find two more different people, and yet they loved each other. It wasn't a marriage of convenience; she didn't accidentally get pregnant and he felt obligated to marry her. They fell in love and wanted to start a family. They both wanted me."

Colt falls silent, and I don't rush him. I wait, giving him my warmth for as long as he needs it. "The busier he became with his business, the lonelier she felt. I was growing up, and with hockey and my friends, I needed her less and less. My mom always loved art, and Dad gave her an art gallery. He felt guilty for being absent, and he wanted to make her happy. To help her find something she wanted to do. Ironically, that place ruined everything."

This time, his pause is longer. His eyes are on me, but I doubt he sees me. He's lost in his memories, trying to find things he failed to notice before. All the details, the tiniest signs, everything went overlooked. I know how Colt feels, even if I hate that he's experiencing it. Having your world fall apart is one of the worst feelings in the world. Especially when the people you love are the reason it happens.

"Leo waltzed into my mom's gallery, laughing and charming everyone on his way. He is a funny, easygoing, and incredibly compassionate man. Everyone loved him. I admired him because he was so different from my always busy and stern father." Colton sighs louder and shuts his eyes again. "As I got older, I noticed *how* Leo looked at Mom. The guy had a crush on her, but she wasn't interested."

I see the direction his story is taking, and I close my eyes too. His hand on my belly spreads warmth across my skin. My fingers slide to his cheek, absentmindedly drawing little circles with my fingernails.

"She went with Leo on a trip to New York, to meet with the owner of a local gallery. They had some drinks to celebrate closing a deal. He was always nothing but nice to her—as opposed to her own husband, who barely had time for her. So she gave in. She spent the night with Leo and left first thing in the morning, realizing what she had done." His voice is low, so I lean in to hear everything. "A month. She kept it to herself for a month. She talked to Leo, told him it could never happen again. And then she went and confessed everything to my dad. The guilt was eating her alive, so she decided to be honest with him. Hell, Ava, I have no idea what she was thinking."

"She was lonely—"

"Don't." Colt cuts me off, snapping his eyes up and boring his gaze into mine. "Loneliness is not a reason for cheating. Ever."

"You're right. Sorry."

"You shouldn't be sorry." He smiles at me, taking a deep breath. "I mean I have no idea what she was thinking telling Dad about it. I get it; she felt guilty. I get it; she didn't want to lie to him, but Dad is Dad. You can't hit a rabid dog and expect it not to bite you in return. It wasn't a fucking fairy tale. She opened herself up to his anger, to his wrath, and she still decided to stay. Knowing who he was, she still stayed."

"Because she loved him."

"Because she loved him," Colt confirms bitterly. "And he cheated on her with Helen. As payback."

I look away. My thoughts are like a hurricane, speeding up and becoming wilder with each passing second. As payback... Helen getting pregnant must have been a huge surprise to him. "But why didn't he say anything to your mom? Why did he keep Helen by his side?"

"I have no idea, Ava. He doesn't love Helen, and he never did. He doesn't have any other women in his life either." His tormented eyes find mine, and neither of us looks away. "I need to talk to him. I want to know his reasons. More than anything."

"When?"

"When I am ready." He sits up and instantly hauls me to his chest. "I would have never been able to process all this without you. I would have lost it, for real."

"You're exaggerating." I wrap my arms around his neck, staring into his enigmatic eyes. My very first thought about his eye color comes to mind—*as if he's a demon himself.* Alluring and tempting. All these months later, and I still think the same. Colton Thompson is my own Hades, and I'm his Persephone. The addiction is strong and unwavering.

"I'm stating facts, Little Miss Lover of Arguments."

"A new nickname?" I quirk an eyebrow as he winds his hands around my waist and stands up from the couch. I cross my legs behind his back.

"I have a ton of new nicknames for you," Colt murmurs, inching closer to my face. "But Honey is still my favorite."

"Oh, I have no doubt, Winnie-the-Pooh." I kiss his lips. "What are we going to do?"

"Take a bath." He carries me to his bathroom as a question pops into my head.

"Why did your mom decide to tell you about this now?"

Colt stops in his tracks, eyes on my face. "She feels better these days. Dr. Stewart's approach is working, and her depression is gone. She started keeping a little diary. It helps to train her memory, and she reflects a lot on her past." He gives me a little smile, but it quickly disappears. "Dad came to visit her, and she decided to open up to me. I honestly don't know what else they talked about, or why he suddenly cares, but I want to talk to him."

As we undress and get in the bath together, I know I was right: his father liked me, and he was happy for Colton. No matter how fucked up things are, Eric Thompson loves his son.

THE FIRST GAME of regional semifinals will be held next week, so the hockey team is spending most of the mornings and evenings practicing.

I barely see Colton these days, but at least I always know where to find him. I don't usually go to the rink when he has practice, but I have some news to share today, and I can't wait to know what he thinks about it.

It's been a month since the game against the Gladiators. I've made good progress, working through my fear with Colt's help. My steps are light as I go down the stairs. I smile; my eyes are glued to him on the ice. No one except our friends knows Colton and I are together, but I don't care about that anymore. Layla is right; it's ridiculous to continue hiding it.

I'm right on time. Guys skate in my direction, leaving the ice. My phone dings with an incoming message, and I take it out of my purse. The next thing I know, someone snatches it out of my hands. *What the hell?* I look up and see Moore staring down at me with a smirk.

"Give it back."

"Why would I? You have something very important to me saved on your phone; I want it gone." His eyes, which are narrowed to slits, speak volumes about his intentions. The guy hates me. He's still not over the prank I pulled on him.

"I won't use the picture against you as long as you stay away from me." I try to grasp my phone but fail miserably. "Give it back, Moore."

"Hell nah, that's not how it's going to be." He leans into my face, his nostrils flaring. "You're going to tell me—"

"Leave her the fuck alone." A familiar voice rips through the atmosphere, and Colton snatches my phone from Moore's fingers. "Didn't I tell you to stay away from her?"

"It's none of your business, Thompson." Moore yells. He grabs my elbow forcefully, and I wince from the sudden pain. "She's—"

His words die in his throat as Colton's fist connects with his abdomen, making him let go of me and stumble back. I gasp, and someone rushes past me, pulling Colt back. It's the team's right defenseman, Bailey, but other guys are here too, watching the scene with surprise on their faces.

"What the fuck is wrong with you, Thompson?" Moore's face is pale, and he presses both of his hands to his stomach. "Does that bitch have such a magic pussy that you've totally lost your mind? Attacking your teammate—"

"She's my girlfriend." Colt bellows, and everyone goes silent at once. Even Bailey lets go of him. "And you don't get to lay your fucking hands on her or her stuff. Back fucking off, Moore, and this picture will never see the light. But keep at it, and I will fucking destroy you. Am I clear?"

"Fucking jerk." Moore mutters angrily. Then he turns and storms away from us.

There is an awkward pause, but then everyone around us starts whistling cheerfully. Apparently, Colton Thompson having a girlfriend is a big deal for the team, and they are all happy for him. Hockey guys are such goofballs sometimes. You never would have guessed it by watching them on the ice.

One by one, they leave Colt and me alone—even Drake and Clay, who can't stop blabbering about how proud he is of his best friend and his accomplishments.

"Make sure to celebrate your big news with your *girlfriend* since you finally found the balls to say it aloud," Clay laughs, walking away.

"What news?" I ask, circling my hands around my boyfriend's shoulders.

"It can wait. I'm more interested in what you wanted to tell me. You sounded too mysterious for me not to be curious," he murmurs, his strong arms wrapping around me. Before I know it, he lifts me, and my legs lock behind his back. "Let's get you onto the ice."

He walks toward the ice, stepping on it gingerly. My grip around his shoulders becomes tighter. Colt catches my gaze, and a soft smile curls his lips. "I've got you, baby. I've got you. You can trust me."

"I know." I flash him a little smile.

When he's with me, I notice way less than I do when he's not. He invades my thoughts, just by being himself. He makes me feel safe and secure, even on the ice. The more time we spend together, the more I see how much the color of his eyes changes depending on his mood. With me, they're always deeper and warmer. And the hints of gold are more noticeable when he smiles. It's like he wasn't used to smiling a lot before, but now he does, and new shades appear as old layers peel away. His eyes look softer, not as dark and rough as they were when we first met.

Colton puts me on the ice and turns me around. My back is now pressed to his chest. The last time he tried to convince me to put on ice skates, it didn't go well, so I'm not surprised he's letting me wear my sneakers. His arms are around my waist, and warmth spreads through my veins. Colt makes me feel like home, like I belong, and I forget where we are. He starts slowly gliding across the ice, and I allow him to take the lead.

"What did you want to talk to me about?" he asks, his hot breath warms up my skin.

"You know I have my bookstagram," I say, and I feel him nod. "I love creating stuff for the stories I've read and loved, or just chatting about them with the community. The thing is, I like what I'm doing, and, considering my major, I thought about making this more than just a hobby."

"What did you decide to do?"

"I love one author in particular; I literally devoured all her stories. What's more, she's always nice and ready to talk about her books, or about other books I read. She publishes all her work herself. I told her about my idea to use my bookstagram to spread the word about indie authors."

I take a deep breath, needing it in order to continue.

"She suggested I work for her. Like an intern, sort of, to see what it means to help an author, to know all the pitfalls of the business. She even wants to pay me, as a thank you. I'm so happy, Colt. This opportunity is like a golden ticket. I've never been more excited than I am now, and I feel like this could be *it*. It's something I'd like to do in the future. Helping authors promote their work, preparing promos and info campaigns for book releases. I always wanted to have a job I'd be excited about, and this one fits that requirement to a tee."

I continue talking, adding more and more details about my collaboration. It's a future I can see myself in. One I can totally enjoy, doing what I love, and this way I won't be tied to one place. I can go where he goes—but only if he wants me to.

Colt stops and slowly turns me around, and I wrap my arms around his torso. I'm happy and content, feeling overwhelmed with the news I got, with him telling everyone we're together, with him spending his time helping me love the ice again.

"I'm so proud of you, Ava. You're so thoughtful and caring, and you give so much of yourself to others without wanting anything in return. I admire you, and I honestly believe you will do amazing." He dips his head down, taking my chin between his fingers. "You deserve the world, baby. And I want to hand it to you all the damn time."

"I don't need the world," I tell him, standing on my tiptoes. "I need my boyfriend to kiss me and make my head spin."

"Your boyfriend, huh?" A light peck on the corner of my mouth.

"The best boyfriend I've ever had." And I finally get the reaction I'm hoping for. Colton's possessive side makes my heart go insane.

"If you're going to even hint about the other guys you've been with, I'm going to fuck that attitude out of you." His lips are hovering over mine, and my whole body comes to life. "Am I clear?"

"Yes."

And the world stops existing, disappearing into a vortex of nothingness. No sounds. No scents. No feeling of time or space. Just him and I, and I don't want it any other way.

Chapter 48

Well...Fuck

AVA

Okay, ten lined-up posts should be enough for this week. Aesthetics and reels. I contacted a couple of other bookstagrammers, and they all seemed interested in collaborating. I'm so excited about all this, I can barely sleep these days. My desire to be the best in class is also keeping me up—I'm trying to be on top of everything, and it often turns into the biggest disaster. Having high expectations, I end up disappointed when I don't reach the goals I set for myself. Or I do, but everything is rushed, and I'm still unhappy.

I put my phone down and look up, meeting Layla's glare. I lean my back in the chair and arch an eyebrow at her. "Any particular reason you are watching me like you're trying to jinx me, little witch?"

Her jaw drops, and her eyes go round. The shocked expression on her face is priceless. She quickly gets rid of it and smacks her lips in an annoyed frown. "You definitely deserve to get *jinxed*, bitch. I hate how much of a smart-ass you are, Mason."

"If I weren't, you wouldn't have wanted to be my friend, bitch." I wink at her, and Layla cracks a smile. "What's up with you? You're way too cranky for just being annoyed with me for being on my phone."

"I have my period, and it feels like I'm dying. And flooding. I fucking hate it," she huffs and lowers her chin into her hands on the table. "Clay made fun of me. He said he loves it when I get so irritated because it's so easy to tease me."

"You sure he made fun of you? Looks like your guy tried to tell you it's okay to be in a bad mood; he still likes you no matter what."

"Maybe." She sighs. "What are you going to do this weekend?"

"Dunno. I've been thinking about going home tomorrow. I miss Dad and Smokey. I haven't talked to Colt about it yet. He's too busy practicing for regional semifinals next week. I don't think it's a big deal if we spend some time apart."

"I'll go with you. I hope you'll find time to chill with me too. It feels like we haven't done anything crazy in an eternity."

"We're dating two best friends who were known for never dating anyone. Sounds crazy enough to me."

Layla bursts out laughing and sits up straight. "That's why I love you, Ava. You're a gem. You always know what to say to lighten my mood." She coasts her eyes over my face. "Have you figured out what you're going to give Colt for his birthday?"

"Have no clue." I shake my head and put my books in my backpack. I'm going back to the dorm since I have a little break between my classes. "His birthday is on April eleventh, so I still have four weeks."

We both stroll down the hallway, parting ways when she goes to the bathroom and I head to the exit. I'm preparing a list of things I need to do on this two-hour break: clean my room, read one of my assignments, and—

I stop in my tracks just as I get to the stairs. Layla's words ring in my ears, and my heart sinks to my feet. I hurriedly take my phone out of my pocket, launch the calendar, and stare at it in disbelief and growing fear. I'm four days late. Memories about our sex in the sin-bin come to mind, and I'm not okay.

I rush down the stairs, literally run down the street, and head straight to the pharmacy. A thousand thoughts spiral in my head as I try to find an explanation. I make a list of reasons why it can't be true. We were always careful, except that one time, when I know he pulled out. I don't feel nauseous. My appetite hasn't changed, and I'm eating everything I normally eat. I don't feel tired or sleepy. I'm my usual self, just a bit nervous because of my classes and my new job. That must be it. Nerves.

Back in the dorm, I sigh in relief when I see that our room is empty. Jordan must be at class, which gives me much-needed privacy. I take three tests at once, put them on my bed, and just wait. I pace the room and shove handfuls of M&Ms into my mouth. These candies always help me relax, but they have no power over my nervousness now. I'm a wreck, afraid to even think about an outcome I don't want to see. It will be a total fiasco, a fucking requiem for our future. He's waiting for news from the Thunders, and I can't even imagine telling him I'm pregnant. It would ruin everything.

My phone dings, and I pick it up, opening a message from my dad. He sent me a picture of Smokey lying on my bed. My eyes sting with unwelcome tears as I let him know I'm coming home tomorrow. I can trust him with anything, but I have no idea how he's going to react to me being knocked-up. Just as I see my dad typing a message to me, my alarm starts ringing. I squint at my bed to see the results.

Well...fuck.

I'm pregnant.

Plopping myself down on my bed, I curl into a ball and cry. It's so pathetic, but I need it. To release this tension, to regulate my emotions and reduce my stress. I want to be a little girl again, whose only trouble was her dad not knowing how to braid her hair.

Each new thought I have is more disturbing than the last. He's going to leave as soon as he graduates, and I can't see any happy ending, no matter how much I try to stay positive. It's not working.

ME:

Hey. Can we meet? It's important.

Delete.

ME:

Hey. You're going to be a dad.

Delete.

I'm ready to scratch my eyes out. My eyes are puffy, and my mind is a fucking muddle. I feel like I've lost the ability to think straight, to think in general. As if someone flipped a switch and turned me into the stupidest idiot in the world. Talking to Colton is a must. We're in this together, and I want him to help me make a decision. I don't want him to tell me *what* to do, but I want to hear his take on this news.

The door swings open, and I jump, hurriedly scrambling to collect the tests, pressing them close to my chest. Jordan freezes in the doorway, stupefied. She rakes her gaze over me, twisting her lips as if she's looking at the most disgusting insect. The news about me being Colton's girlfriend made everything even worse than it was. She envies me and hates me altogether.

"Didn't expect you to be here," she hisses, stepping forward and closing the door behind her. "Don't you have class in twenty minutes?"

I look at my phone and curse. I was so deep in my misery, I stopped paying attention to everything else. She's right; I need to leave now to be on time for my next class. I hop off my bed, shove my things in my backpack, and saunter to the door.

"Thanks for the reminder."

Jordan narrows her eyes, finally taking me in. "I think you should look at yourself in the mirror before you go anywhere. Colton doesn't deserve to have his girlfriend embarrass him with how she looks."

I shut the door behind me and head to the bathroom. Washing my face is the only thing I'm going to do. I don't have time for anything else.

The next few hours fly by in a flash. Miraculously, I was able to focus on my classes, not letting my problems catch me in a trap. I even started smiling, talking to one of my classmates when he made a few jokes about one of our professors. It did me a lot of good, and I was ready to kiss him just for helping me to ease my mind. My good cry had a soothing effect, and I'm close to my normal state. My mind has stopped being a puddle, and even now produces more and more ideas about how I should handle my situation.

I'm on my way to my dorm when I pull my phone out of my pocket. It's five p.m., and I'm racking my brain, trying to remember if

Colton has any plans today except practice. Probably not. Otherwise, he would have definitely mentioned it to me.

I want to drop off my stuff at my room, grab a few things, and go to his place. We still have time to discuss what we're going to do.

The second I come closer to my room, I hear the music blasting. Jordan is here, and I sigh, rolling my eyes in exasperation. Next year, I will do anything to change my roommate.

I open the door, amble inside, and go to my closet. I pull a few things from it and shove them into my backpack. Then I edge to my desk and put the books I won't need on it, turn around and walk to the door. Suddenly the music stops, and I whip my head to look at my roommate. Her eyes are on me, and a smug smile plays on her lips. I furrow my brow, not understanding her reaction.

"Leaving already?"

"Like that surprises you?" I say, putting my hand on the doorknob. "I'm barely ever in our room, Jordan. You should be happy to have this place to yourself."

"Oh, I'm very happy. Like super-duper, knocked-up happy."

"Say what?" I wheel around and look at her. The words she chose don't sound like a coincidence.

"You dropped something when you were in such a hurry to leave earlier." *No. Please no.* I haven't checked my tests even once since the moment I dumped them in my backpack.

"Keep your nose out of my business, Jordan. It has nothing to do with you."

"But it has something to do with your boyfriend. He was going to go pro, because he's a very talented hockey player, but you are going to ruin it for him." My cheeks puff out, and I'm ready to fucking strangle her. "I thought he should know."

"You wouldn't—"

"Oh, I did. I couldn't let this opportunity go to waste. He wasn't happy. Dumbfounded, actually. Stunned to the core." She flashes me the fakest smile as I feel my legs give out. "No one likes it when sluts like you try to steal their future."

"Jordan, I swear—"

"You should prepare yourself for life as a single mom. Or get an abortion. Yeah, better get an abortion. Bringing an unwanted child into the world is the stupidest idea ever." With that, she turns her back on me and turns the music up. She's done with this conversation, leaving me seething. I fucking hate this bitch.

I slam the door behind me and stride down the stairs. I wouldn't wish this feeling on anyone—it's honestly a fucking apocalypse. That idiotic bitch had no right to tell Colt about my pregnancy. She had no right to reveal my secrets. I'm so fucking furious I barely see where I'm going, and I tug harder on my backpack. I want to cry, to scream, to punch something, all at the same time—but I also want to see him.

I hear a car horn and freeze. The driver twists a finger around his temple and stares at me. I lift my hands in the air and mouth, *I'm sorry*. He drives away, probably thinking I'm a careless imbecile who wants to die young. I clench my jaw, resuming my walk and banning all thoughts about my roommate and what she's done.

Inside Colt's apartment, I quickly take off my sneakers, hang my leather jacket, and put my backpack on the floor. I go to the living room and plop myself down on the couch, closing my eyes. What a freaking disaster. I can only imagine his reaction when that Barbie told him about my pregnancy, or—even worse—shoved my pregnancy test in his face.

Jordan, I hope you rot in hell for real.

My eyes snap open, and I sit up abruptly. Wait a minute. I scurry back to the hallway, pull my phone out of my backpack, unlock it, and stare at the screen. He knows. He knows and he hasn't called me. He hasn't texted me. He did nothing, not even a single message asking me to come to his place and talk.

I look at the time, calculating in my head when his practice should be over. Usually he's home by seven p.m., and I don't think tonight should be any different. The tiniest voice of doubt prowls inside my head, making it hard for me to breathe fully. I shoo it away, trying my best not to worry yet. There could be an explanation. I have no clue *when* she talked to him—maybe he was on his way to practice already. That's if she talked to him at all. She could be lying, for all I know.

I just want to believe he cares enough about me not to leave me like this.

At seven forty, I'm on the verge of delirium. I pace back and forth between his living room, his kitchen, and his bedroom. My throat is full of pricks and needles, and even my fingers are trembling. The fury I felt has been replaced by fear. Insecurity. I'm slowly dying inside without him.

I take my phone from the couch and dial his number. I press it to my ear and hear a mechanical voice—he sent me straight to voicemail. Did he turn his phone off? Or is his battery dead?

I stare at the screen, and then I call Clay. He's my last hope, because I don't want to accept that Colton would leave me like this. His best friend will know where he is; he'll be able to help me.

"Hey, Clay. How are you?"

"Hey hey, Ava. I'm good, going to watch something with Layla. You?"

"Um, do you know where Colt is? I'm at his place, and I think his phone is off."

There is a pause, and then Clay clears his throat. "Didn't he tell you? He went to San Jose to sign his contract with the Thunders. He was going to stop by your dorm before his flight."

"Oh, I didn't know...I didn't see him today. We probably missed each other. Well then, bye."

"Ava, wait—"

"Bye, Clay." I hang up feeling numb. Everything becomes clear. He probably came to my dorm and met Jordan. He found out I was pregnant, but he didn't call or text me once. He just left me on my own and went to sign the contract. One I didn't even know about.

I count to ten, then I whirl around and go to his bedroom. I have too many things at his place, and I need to get them all. I don't want to leave even a trace of my presence in this suddenly cold apartment. I don't want to cry. I'm not the type to ruin the place either. I'm as calm as fucking Stefan Salvatore with his emotions turned off. I don't want to do anything stupid because I don't care. Just like Jefferson, who couldn't call an ambulance for fear of his future, Colton chose his career over me.

I look like a zombie. I slept for one fucking hour on his couch, and I don't have even an ounce of energy in me to care about it. It's barely eight a.m. when I drag my feet onto campus. My backpack is ready to explode with all my things, and I have another bag pressed to my chest as I head into the library.

"Ava?" Looking over my shoulder, I see Ms. Lewis. "What are you doing here so early?"

"I want to go home after classes," I mumble as she falls into step beside me.

She frowns. Her deep blue eyes wander all over my face. "Are you okay?"

I continue staring at her, as if I'm in some sort of daze. She's the only adult I have here at school. We have become close because of all the books we talk about, because of all the hours I spend studying in the library. I blink and shake my head.

"No. I'm not okay."

Ms. Lewis sighs, grabs my hand in hers, and pulls me down the stairs. She heads straight to her car, opens the door, and only then releases my hand, with one purpose only: to take my things from me and usher me into her car. I slip inside, buckle the seat belt, and wait. I have no idea what she has in mind or what I'm doing here, but I let her.

Starting the engine, she sneaks a glance in my direction. "You're skipping school today. You'll need to check with a classmate about missing assignments."

"Okay." I pull my phone out of my pocket. "Where are we going?"

"I'm taking you home." She smiles at me. "I'll need your address."

I give it to her and quickly text my classmate. Before I hide my phone back in my pocket, I turn it off. I don't want to talk to anyone.

Chapter 49

The Mistake

COLTON

I lock my car and head to the dorm. I have been putting off my talk with Ava for two days, but now I've got to tell her I'm signing a contract with the Thunders. Honestly, I have no idea how she's going to react. I should have told her about the call I got from my agent when she came to see me after practice. Instead, I decided to keep things to myself because I didn't want to steal her spotlight after she told me about her plans for her bookstagram. I wanted it to be all about her. I thought I would have time to tell her later. Like a stupid idiot.

Just as I get to the door, someone pushes it open from the inside. I take a step back and lock eyes with Ava's roommate. Jordan's jaw drops, and she gapes at me in surprise. Then her lips quickly stretch into a leery smile.

"If you're looking for your girlfriend, she already left. Her class started ten minutes ago."

"Dammit." I curse under my breath, wheeling around to go back to my car.

"Colton?" I look at her over my shoulder. "I feel so sorry for you. When someone tries to ruin your future, it must be a hard pill to swallow."

I roll my eyes and resume my walk. This girl is honestly crazy.

"Colt?"

"What do you want?" I snap and whip around.

"You shouldn't have wasted your time on her. She's trouble."

"*You* are a waste of my time. Ava is everything. Get lost."

"She's pregnant."

"What?" I clench my jaw hard, waves of nausea washing over me. I feel like I'm going to puke; my fucking head is spinning. It's mayhem in my chest.

"She ran out in a hurry today, and she didn't notice one of her tests fell on the floor." This girl takes her phone out of her pocket, unlocks it, and then shoves it in my face. I gawk at the picture of the pregnancy test. There are two stripes, and my skin becomes sweaty. It's not good. "I'm very sorry, Colton. I hope you can figure this out. She is putting your whole career at risk."

I take a deep breath and drag my eyes to her face. She's such a snake. Goddamn it, I should have insisted on Ava moving in with me.

I push Jordan's phone back into her hand and take a step forward, hovering over her like a damn wall. I don't have time to deal with this shit, but I want to make myself incredibly clear: "If you tell anyone what you just told me, or if you show this picture to anyone, even your fucking mom, I will ruin you. I will make sure no guy at this school even looks your way, because they will know what a fucking bitch you are. Do you understand me, Jordan?"

She shifts, tucking her hair behind her ears and avoiding looking at me. "I thought you should know."

"That's not what I asked," I growl, taking a step forward. "Do you understand me, Jordan?"

"Yes," she mumbles. Then she turns around and rushes back into her room.

I close my eyes for a second, heave a sigh, and stride back to my car. I better hurry up, because now I need to do a quick detour before I go to the airport. I will deal with all this when I'm back. I don't have the heart to do it now. Showing up to my contract negotiations looking like a trainwreck is not something I can allow to happen.

"Hey," I greet my father, stepping into his office. I called him as soon as I was in my car and asked if I could visit him before my flight. To my surprise, he instantly agreed.

"Hey, Colton." He gestures to the chair in front of his desk. "Have a seat."

I thought I would be nervous, considering what I have to talk to him about, but I'm not anymore. I want answers to my questions, and a little promise from his side. I need to secure my future.

I lower myself into the chair and take a deep breath, focusing on my father's face. I don't want to pretend I don't know about Mom and her affair. And I don't have much time, as I need to be at the airport in two hours.

"Why didn't you ever tell me about Mom and Leo? We had so many arguments. We said hurtful things to one another to make each other suffer. Why did you never mention it?"

"You love your mom. She's everything to you. Avery failed me as a wife, but she never failed you as a mother. What's the point of ruining her image in your eyes?" he says calmly. "I will never understand parents who attempt to turn their children against the other parent. It's the marriage that didn't last. Parenting is forever."

"Unless you're an asshole who abandons their kids for a new wife or husband," I say, and he chuckles.

"True, but that's not the case with Avery and me. She's a great mom to you, and I couldn't ask for a better co-parent. She was always there for you—unlike me—and she's the reason you are who you are. She raised you to be a good man, and I think she handled her job like a real pro."

Ava's image pops into my head, but I banish it from my thoughts for now. I'm acting like a coward, but I can't afford to get distracted. Not right now, when my future is at a turning point. I will go to San Jose, sign the contract, and then I will come back and we'll talk. In that order. Hockey is my life, and I've dreamt about being a pro since the moment I fell in love with the game. It's everything I want, and it will give me independence. I will be able to provide Ava with everything she needs, without asking my father for any favors. I will be able to do it on my own, and that's a very big deal to me.

I exhale, leaning back in the chair. "Did you fuck Helen as revenge? To make Mom pay for her mistake?"

"Yes."

"But why did you let her stay in your life?"

"Getting Helen pregnant wasn't my intention, but it happened. Because of her health issues, she decided to continue her pregnancy without talking to me first. She told me the baby was mine when she was three months along."

"That's not what I asked," I tell him, and he narrows his eyes. *Yes, Dad, I want answers.*

"Your mom never got rid of Leo, even if I asked her to do so. She continued to spend time with him, staying at the gallery late at night. Instead of trying to mend what was broken, she made the crack bigger. I'm not good at dealing with disrespect." I snort hearing that. I have way more in common with my father than I think. "And then there was you and your attempts to fuck my secretary. I had no idea you knew about the pregnancy. With how she was and how much she was flirting with you, I thought she might try to pin it on you. Let you have your way with her, only to tell you she got pregnant. I didn't want that for you, and I played right into her hand."

"Meaning?"

"Helen was flirting with you because she wanted to make me jealous. She let you fuck her because she knew I was keeping an eye on her." He shrugs. "I was afraid Helen would continue to use you, so I made myself believe I wasn't doing anything wrong, just making sure your future was secure."

I'm fucking torn right now. My head hurts. I understand him and don't understand him at the same time. He should have told Mom that if she wanted to save their marriage, then Leo needed to go. He needed to talk to me and Mom to let us know what *his* mistake caused. Everything could have been avoided with an honest conversation.

"Dad, I—"

"I'm sorry for acting like a dick when you found out Helen was pregnant. I despise myself for how I treated you all these years, for how cold I was with Avery. She would have never cheated on me if I was present in our marriage. I was trying to buy her love with expensive gifts, but not even a fucking diamond can fill the void when you're lonely." He looks away for a moment, and then he stares back at me. "I'm a successful businessman. Our family does well financially. But I'm a total failure as a husband and a father. The guilt I felt after Avery's state worsened made me distance myself from Helen's daughter. I just couldn't bring myself to continue helping her."

I'm silent, examining him with an open mind. His reasons to stop helping Helen and Chloe are the same as mine. It makes me realize how many things I still don't know about him. I can hold on to my anger. To my hate. But I don't want to. If I can forgive Mom's mistake, I can try to do the same for my father. I want to try, because if I don't, I will always feel like I missed the opportunity. I'm ready to give him a second chance, but only if he promises me a few things.

"You have another chance to be a good father, you know," I point out. "Chloe doesn't deserve what you put her through because of your mistake."

"Everything I have is yours."

"I know that, but it's not always about money. Like you said, it's about attention. About being there for your child when they need you. That's what Mom does for me. We can't go back in time and change how you acted, but you can change how you act with your daughter. Give your little girl a chance, and you will love her," I say, and he finally smiles.

"Okay. I will try." He eyes me with curiosity.

"If something goes wrong and I don't sign the contract, if I don't find another team, can I work for you after graduation?"

The look on my father's face is stunned. He didn't expect this at all. Neither did I, but things have changed.

"Of course." His brows pinch together. He's probably expecting more from me, but I keep quiet. I'll tell him more after I talk with Ava. Right now, I'm just trying to secure my options. If she's really pregnant and we're going to keep the baby, I will need a job. As simple as that. "I'm sure everything is going to be fine with the Thunders. Your agent sounded incredibly certain about your future with the team when he called me."

"I hope so." Coming here, I expected answers, but I got way more than that. Way more than I even imagined. My mom and dad both made mistakes, and our family was never perfect, but I think this is the first time in years I have both of my parents in my life.

Landing at San Jose International, I literally feel as if I got caught in a hurricane. My agent meets me at the airport and takes me to the hotel he booked for us. Before I go to my room, we talk nonstop about the contract, about things the Thunders might ask of me, about things I want in writing. My head is in such a state I'm barely able to form words by the time he bids me goodbye. We agree to meet tomorrow at eleven a.m. at the reception desk and part ways. Once I'm in my room, I only have time to set my alarm clock before I fall asleep.

Chapter 50

Go Away

AVA

"Ava?" I slowly open my eyes and shift. My neck hurts badly because I fell asleep in my seat. I rub it and turn my head to look at Ms. Lewis. "Is this your house?"

I groan, squaring my shoulders slightly, looking out the window. The corners of my mouth lift, and a very familiar feeling forms in my chest. I'm home. I will be alright. My dad always knows what to say to me, and he will know what to do.

"Well, based on the smile on your face, this *is* your house."

"Yeah, it is." I unbuckle my seat belt and reach for the door handle. "Thank you so much, Ms. Lewis."

"Penelope," she says, and my eyebrows pinch together. "My name is Penelope. You can call me that—when we're not in the library, of course."

"Of course," I laugh, opening the door and climbing out of the car. Penelope helps me collect my stuff from the backseat. "Won't you be in trouble? The library—"

"I called my friend Lena when you fell asleep. Everything is okay," Ms. Lewis says as I take a step back. Suddenly, her eyes go wide as she gawks at something behind me. "Is that your father?"

I look over my shoulder and see Dad strolling in our direction. My whole body warms up with tenderness just from the sight of him. He's my rock, through thick and thin. "Yeah."

"Ava..." she mumbles as her cheeks fire up. Oh my freaking God. This is so adorable, I even forget about my own problems for a moment. Some women in town call him a dilf, and I think my nice librarian is crushing on him hard. And that's just because of his looks. What would happen if she knew what a gem he is? "I didn't—"

"I know how my dad looks, Penelope. I'm not judging." I turn around to face him but lean into her ear. "And he's single."

She sucks in a breath, and I can barely stop myself from laughing. All the shit that has happened to me is worth it just for this situation.

"Hey, kid. I didn't expect you home so early. Don't you have class?" Dad's eyes are on me.

"Something came up, and I decided to skip." I hand him my huge backpack. "I have perfect grades. One day won't change that."

"I have no doubt." He cracks a smile and then shifts his gaze to Penelope. "Thank you for giving my daughter a ride. I'm Dax."

"It's very nice to meet you, D-Dax," she stutters, becoming even more flushed than she already is.

"Dad, this is Ms. Lewis. She works at the library." I decide to take matters into my own hands, noticing as Dad checks her out. "You can call her Penelope. She's incredible."

With that, I head into the house. The only thing I want right now is to go to my room, take Smokey with me, and sleep. I'm drained, and considering the talk I'm about to have with Dad, I need to recharge my batteries.

"So..." Dad trails off, sitting on my bed a few hours later. He let me sleep without trying to wake me up for answers. "What happened? I didn't think you would be home until tomorrow morning."

"What do you think about Penelope? She's cute, isn't she?" I wink at him, and Dad shakes his head with a smile.

"She's cute, yes. What's more, she helped you when she felt you needed it. She wasn't obligated to do that. We exchanged numbers, and I promised to invite her to dinner. As a thank you."

"Definitely as a thank you," I tell him with a meaningful look on my face, and he hits me with my pillow. "Dad."

"Stop making fun of me." He narrows his eyes, trying to look strict. "Start talking. What happened?"

I pull my legs into my chest, wrapping my arms around them and putting my chin on my knees. Then I sigh and lower my face into the blanket that covers them. "I'm pregnant."

"Um, Ava, if you want me to hear you, please stop talking to your legs."

I sigh and look up into my father's face. "I'm pregnant."

His expression doesn't change. He continues to look at me calmly. I want a reaction. Anything. Total silence is the worst. "Did you take a test?"

"Three. They were all positive."

"Did you see a doctor?" I shake my head no and hug myself tighter. "Well, we need to get to the doctor, kid. It's rare, but it could be a false positive."

"Okay." I cried so much yesterday that now it feels as if I don't have even a single tear to shed.

"I'll call Andrea. She might be able to help."

"Dad. She's your ex. I don't want her to look at my lady parts." I probably look like a little bird with its feathers ruffled, but I don't care anymore.

"She's my ex, but she's a great doctor. I don't know anyone better than her in town." He taps on my nose, laughing wholeheartedly. He's so calm and collected, it flows to me too, slipping under my skin and cooling my nerves. "I'll make a call while you get dressed."

Dad stands up from my bed and ambles to the door. Then he turns around and bores his gaze into my face. I grab Smokey as if he's my shield, because I instantly know what my father is going to ask. And I'm not fucking ready to answer. "Have you talked to Colton about it?"

I purse my lips, slide down onto my back, and hide under the blanket. "No."

"Ava," Dad warns, but I stay hidden. *Please, Dad, don't ask me anything about him right now.* "Get dressed."

With that, he closes the door behind him. The only sound I hear is my cat purring, cuddling close to my belly. I dig my fingers into his fur and shut my eyes. Seeing the doctor is the only thing I should focus on.

Layla and I are in my room, watching *Frozen II* together. She's lying on her belly, while I sit with my back pressed to my headboard. My best friend has stayed with me since the moment she walked into my house around ten p.m. on Friday, and it's already lunchtime on Saturday. She refuses to leave, treating me as if I'm a fucking crystal vessel of holy water. I'm just pregnant. Five weeks along, which aligns perfectly with our sex in the penalty box.

"Do you want something to eat?" Layla catches my gaze over her shoulder, and I shake my head. We ate an hour ago, and I'm full. "What about some water?"

"Apple juice," I tell her, and she hops off my bed. "You're the best."

"It's the least I can do to support you." My best friend edges to the door and leaves my room.

I turn the volume up and try to focus on the screen, but it's hard.

All of a sudden, the door opens, and Layla bursts back into my room. "Thompson is here."

"What?" My heartbeat accelerates, and my palms start sweating. I don't want to see him right now, and truthfully I don't understand why my dad let him in. I told him everything once we returned from the doctor, and he said he understood my reaction. So why is Colton in my house?

"Yeah, he's downstairs, talking to your dad."

"I don't care." I lift my shoulder, playing it cool until I hear a knock on my door.

"Can I come in?" His voice sounds quiet, and a million different emotions swim around in me. The biggest one is anger.

Layla rakes her gaze over my face, expecting my decision. I can't hide from him forever. So why not deal with this shit once and for all? I can always cry later.

"Can you please wait downstairs?" I whisper, and she nods, steps close, and hugs me tightly.

"Stay strong, babe." She kisses my cheek, steps back, and opens the door. She strides past him, bumping into his shoulder on her way out and hissing something under her breath.

Thompson saunters into my room and closes the door behind him. I center my attention on the wall, refusing to even look at him. Yet it's impossible. I don't need eyes to feel him. His presence makes my room incredibly small. I feel him move, even if I keep my gaze glued to anything but him.

"Your phone is off. Coming here was the best shot I had."

"A very bad decision. I don't want to talk to you."

"Ava, I'm sorry. I know I let you down—"

"You know nothing, Colton." My stress level is through the roof, and holding myself back is definitely not what I have in mind. I jump to my feet, meeting his gaze and seething. "I thought my life was falling apart when I saw the test results. I spent almost two fucking hours crying on my bed. For two fucking hours, I was pitying my own existence. Then I thought, *Colt and I are in this together. We will figure it out. We will talk, and we will decide what to do.*"

"I just got back from San Jose; I signed the contract—" he blurts, the words rushing out of his mouth.

"I don't fucking care." I shriek, bursting into tears. "When Jordan told me you knew about my pregnancy, I was ready to fucking kill her. It was my secret, and I wanted to tell you myself. I went to your place. I hoped to talk to you so we could figure out our decision together. I was so blinded by my fury, I didn't even realize you knew until I was already in your apartment. My boyfriend knew I was pregnant, and he did nothing. He didn't call me. He didn't text me. I'm eighteen. I'm a freshman with no future, and you left me when I needed you."

"Ava, Thursday was crazy. I went to see my dad before my flight, then I went to the airport. I landed in San Jose around one a.m. on Friday. I talked with my agent for a few hours, and I fell asleep as soon as my head touched the hotel pillow. Yesterday wasn't any different. I tried to call you when I got home, but your phone was off—"

I cut him off. There's only one question burning the tip of my tongue. "When did you know about the contract?"

"On Tuesday morning."

"And you couldn't find a single moment to let me know?" My voice trembles, and my tears are suffocating me. "Not even when I came to tell you about my news?"

"You were so excited about your job, about your bookstagram, and I didn't want to ruin the moment for you. I was going to tell you before, but things were hectic. We haven't spent more than twenty minutes together since—"

"Go away," I mutter, staring him right in the eyes.

"Ava, please—"

"Go the fuck away."

"Babe, please, this isn't us. Let's talk—"

"There is no fucking us, Colton. You left me when I was scared. You disappeared when I needed you. So please, do me a fucking favor and see yourself out."

"I wanted to secure my future, so I could take care of you. Of our baby. I wanted to give you the life you deserve."

"I don't need anything from you, Colton. I will figure everything out on my own." I wipe away my angry, disappointed, sad tears. I'm struggling for breath; my vision blurs, and my heart breaks into a thousand pieces. "There is no need to pretend like you care, like you'll give a damn about me once you graduate and leave the state. You can carry on with your life as if *we* never happened."

He clenches his jaw hard. His deep brown eyes are stormy, like a night cloud ready to downpour.

"G-go away," I stutter. He twirls around, opens the door wide, and takes a step further, glancing at me over his shoulder.

"I don't care what you say, Ava. You're mine. And soon enough, you will be proudly flashing a ring on your finger so the whole fucking world—so every single person on this planet—will know you're Colton Thompson's wife."

The sound of the door slamming is all I'm able to register. I'm too stunned to speak, and I'm too exhausted. I lower myself onto my bed, pull the blanket over my head, and close my eyes. Layla joins me a few minutes later, not saying a word, not asking a question. She just wraps herself around me and holds me close. It's exactly what I need right now.

Chapter 51

The L Word

COLTON

Lying on my back on my bed, I stare at the ceiling. I don't know how long I've been like this, because it feels like eternity. A very fucked-up and lonely eternity. Nothing makes sense without her. I'm the biggest idiot in the world for letting this happen, and I deserve her anger and her hatred. Accepting what I have done to us doesn't make things easier.

The first time I tried calling her was when I got into my car after my plane landed in Michigan. I was so excited to see her and talk about our future. Immediately getting her voicemail felt worse than a cold shower. I tried sending her messages, but they didn't go through. Her phone was turned off.

I called Clay on my way home, and he acted like a friend to both me and Ava. He didn't pick sides, and he let me know what I did wrong. *Sorry, man. When she called me on Thursday, I had no idea you hadn't told her about the Thunders. I bet she was more than unhappy.*

I didn't think things could get any worse until I stepped inside my apartment. There was no trace of her. All her belongings had disappeared, and seeing that made my heart sink lower. The heaviness of not telling her about San Jose was preventing me from breathing freely.

When I knocked on the door of her family home, I felt like a little kid who'd done something bad and was going to have to face his parents. I honestly expected Dax to kick me out, but he let me in. He even invited me to the living room to have a talk. The disappointment I saw in his eyes was the worst. He had faith in me, and I failed him.

I explained what happened and told him I would do anything for his daughter. Dax didn't say much, just let me talk and listened to me. The only thing he said was this: *Ava has trust issues. You made her believe you didn't care about her. Even if it's not like that in reality, you left her when she was in a really vulnerable state. It will be hard to make her listen to you.*

Her telling me to go away broke my heart in two. Her thinking I would abandon her for my career, her tears, and how miserable she looked added heaviness to my chest, and for a moment I thought I would suffocate. I was making sure I had everything to support her, to secure our future together, but she didn't know that. She was sure I got scared and ran away like a coward, and from her point of view, it definitely looked like that.

My alarm goes off, and I slowly stand up from my bed. I can't even imagine what today is going to be like. I honestly just want to see her. I need a chance to explain myself. I know we'll be able to deal with everything, but only if she listens to me. I never plan to leave her. She's way more important to me than she realizes. She's my fucking life, and it's time for her to know that. Keeping my feelings to myself damaged our relationship just as much as my silence about my trip to San Jose. I need to fix it.

It's official. I'm a freaking stalker. I've been following her everywhere, trying to be as discreet as possible. Either I'm good at it, or she just doesn't care, because she hasn't acknowledged my presence even once. Relaxed and smiley. That's how she is today, while I'm a total mess. I remind myself of a bomb, ready to blow up any moment, and it's a fucking mood-killer. Yet I control myself, because she'll never listen to me if I don't.

Stepping out of the building, I look up at the sky and frown even more. It's going to rain, and I'm not a fucking fan. The possibility of Ava getting in my car so we can talk is close to zero, and I definitely don't want her to be caught in the rain.

Rushing down the stairs, I speed up and go after her. She's strolling in the direction of her dorm, swaying her hips and humming something under her breath. Ava is in her element, and my heart swells with happiness just looking at her. It's another reminder of what a strong girl she is. Confident and sassy, independent and always ready to stand up for herself. Since meeting her, I've been a one-woman man, and I'm sure I won't love anyone else.

I line up with Ava, and she doesn't even glance in my direction. I reach over and pull out her AirPod, halting her in her tracks. She turns to me, and her eyes scan my face. My girl is furious, but it makes her even more beautiful to me. Those puffy lips are smacked into a pout, and her gorgeous green eyes are narrowed. She cares enough to be angry with me, and that's the only sign I need.

"Can we talk?"

"No." She tries to snatch her AirPod back, but I hide it in my fist. *You're not getting rid of me so easily, girl.* She rolls her eyes and says, "Whatever."

She twirls around and resumes her walk, as if nothing happened. I clench my jaw, squeezing my fist harder around her earbud. I take off, catching up to her again.

"Ava, we need to talk."

"Why?"

"Because we can't throw away everything so easily. Let me explain myself." This time, I get her undivided attention and also her fury. She stops and faces me, crossing her arms over her chest.

"I'm not the one who threw everything away. You not telling me about the Thunders is the best evidence of where you see me in your future. I don't belong here."

"I went to San Jose to sign my contract. It was about my career, about our future."

"There is no 'our future', Colton. You're leaving as soon as the school year is over. You're going pro, while I—"

"Come with me," I interrupt her, and her jaw drops. Her eyes go round as she gawks at me in bewilderment. "You can transfer to another college. Or just skip a year until our baby is old enough—"

"What makes you think I'm going to do that?"

I take a step closer, taking her chin between my fingers. "Because I know you."

We stare at each other, keeping silent. My heart is going insane in my chest. All because of her. My words linger between us as I wait for her to say something.

"You don't," she finally mutters and takes a step back, letting my hand fall from her face. "I knew you were going to leave, and I was happy for you and your future no matter what, because you're talented and playing hockey is your life. I would have never thrown a fit just because you're moving forward. I would have supported you through and through. That's what people do, Colton, when they care about others. While you? You didn't think about anyone except yourself. You didn't even try to contact me after you knew—"

"That's bullshit," I snap, as lightning crosses the sky. "How do you know anything about how I reacted when Jordan told me about your pregnancy?"

"If you cared, you would have found a way to contact me. On your way to your father's. On your way to the airport. On your way to your hotel." She spits words like venom, a poison that I fully deserve. "Just to make sure I knew you weren't running away, that you weren't leaving me alone in this. I would have been angry with you for not telling me sooner, anyone would have, but I would have known you were going to come back and we would talk. You did nothing."

"Some habits die hard, Ava. I'm used to keeping things to myself. Yes, I put off talking to you till the very last minute, but I wanted you to know. I went to your dorm, hoping to see you during your break—"

"Instead, you saw my roommate, found out about my pregnancy, and carried on with your plans as if nothing changed." She drags her eyes down my form and then back to my face. "Screw you, Thompson."

Ava storms off, and I try to calm my fired-up nerves.

"Everything changed." I bellow, running after her and catching her elbow. I wheel her around and peer down to have a better look at her face. "Everything changed once I knew you might be pregnant. The only thought I had was that I needed to secure my future for *us*."

"There is no *us*, Colton." she says angrily, and the first raindrop falls on her face. "I don't want to have anything in common with someone as selfish as you. I'll figure it out on my own."

"I am selfish," I mumble in disbelief. "The second I heard about your pregnancy, my mind started producing possible solutions. I was going to San Jose to sign the contract, but I still wasn't a hundred percent sure it would happen. Something could have gone wrong, and I would have needed to look for another option, including working for my dad."

Ava's brows pinch together. "Don't tell me you even *thought* about working for your father."

"I not only thought about it, I even asked him, in case something went wrong with hockey. I wanted to be sure I could support you. It's the only thing that matters."

The raindrops become heavier, more consistent. So many emotions change her beautiful face, and I can't look away. Ava is stunning, even when she's angry or confused, sad or happy. She's the most beautiful girl I have ever seen.

"You love hockey," she whispers. The crease between her eyebrows deepens. "And you hate your father..."

"I don't really hate him," I tell her, reaching over to her face and wiping away the raindrops. "My talk with him was refreshing and kind of eye-opening. We're good."

Her eyes are tearful as she chews her bottom lip. I hurt her, and there is nothing I can do to change that. Yet I can do better, and she knows it. In these months I've spent with her, I have become a totally different person. For her and because of her. I'm not afraid to open up, to show my affection and finally confess my feelings. The L word doesn't seem as useless as it did before. The old me would have laughed just thinking about it, but the new me is desperate for her love. It's as if it's the sole reason for my existence.

"I messed up, and I'm incredibly sorry for that. I shouldn't have hidden my news from you. I shouldn't have left you without saying anything. While making sure I'd have the means to financially support you, I almost ruined what we have."

"Almost?" And just like that, I know it's my Ava talking to me. My girl, my only source of happiness.

"Almost," I state, inhaling deeply. "I love you, Ava. I love you more than fucking hockey, and for someone like me, that sounds like the ravings of a lunatic. If anything, I'm obsessed with you, because any time I get to taste you, I crave you even more. You are the only girl I want, the only one I will ever need. And I will do anything for you to give me another chance. Please, Ava."

She lowers her eyes to the ground without saying a word. An empty and glassy stare is definitely not what I expected after telling her I love her. My visit to her hometown comes to mind, and her father's image pops up in my head. Dax told me to be patient with her when I left their house on Saturday. He told me not to give up on her. To give her space and time to figure out what she wants. I only hope she wants the same thing as me. Us. Together. Always.

"Do you have practice today?" Ava asks, fixing her gaze on me.

"Yeah, in an hour. I-I will be free around seven."

"Okay." She takes a step back, and I instantly feel lonely. "See you at your place then."

Ava wheels around and heads to her dorm. I continue to stare at her, squeezing her AirPod in my fist. The rain turns into a downpour, soaking my clothes and hair, but I feel hopeful, even if our talk didn't go as planned.

WHEN I OPEN THE DOOR, I lock eyes with Ava. She stands in my doorway, pressing her backpack to her chest. Her eyes roam over my face and down my body, and I catch the quickest eye roll. Well, I'm not playing fair, wearing only sweatpants. My hair is still wet after a shower.

"Hey." I step aside, letting her in. "I was afraid you changed your mind."

"No, I just had some things I needed to do." She shrugs, ambling inside. "Where can we talk?"

"In the living room." Snatching her backpack, I hold her gaze. "This is too heavy for you."

"Yes, sir," she taunts me, closing the door behind her. "What did you do to Jordan? She told me she's not allowed to talk to me."

"Didn't she tell you months ago being my enemy would be very bad for your reputation?" I ask, and Ava nods slowly. "I proved her right. Rumors spread fast. The whole school will be staying away from her, especially guys. No one wants to have anything to do with someone as nosy as her."

She smiles, her eyes sparkling. "Thanks."

I put her backpack on the floor, and we go into the living room. Once we're both seated on the couch, I turn to face her.

"Ava, I'm really sorry for everything. I shouldn't have put off my talk with you about the Thunders. It was a mistake. But I thought I was doing the right thing, letting you shine—"

She cuts me off. "That's not how relationships work, Colton. At least, not for me. If we're together, we share the good and the bad. If you're sad, I want to know why and help you deal with it. If you're happy, I want to be happy with you, help you celebrate your achievements. We both had exciting news that day, and it would have been absolutely amazing to celebrate it *together*. I understand where you're coming from, but you went about it all wrong."

"I thought you would be upset, because signing the contract means I'll be moving to San Jose. I didn't want to spoil your moment."

"You wouldn't have spoiled anything. I knew it was going to happen. I didn't have any doubt they were going to sign you." She watches me. "You're naturally good at hockey. It's your passion, your driving force, and it's your future. I would have only been happy for you, and it would have forced us to have the talk we had been putting off. We didn't talk about our future, not once, and if you had told me about the Thunders, I would have asked you what it meant for you and me. We could have figured everything out."

"I was so used to keeping things to myself, so when we didn't have time to meet, I thought it wasn't a big deal. I thought I could always tell you on my way to the airport, and that was exactly what I was going to do. But your roommate dropped a bomb on me, turning my mind into jelly. I only knew I needed to make sure you would have everything you need for you and our baby."

"One time I let you fuck me bare, and I got pregnant in a fucking penalty box," she drawls. And then she bursts out giggling. "We conceived our baby in the sin-bin. It will be quite a story for our family."

I move closer, invading her personal space. I drape a hand around her waist and pull her onto my lap. "Quite a story, you said? Does that mean you want a family with me?"

"I do," she says quietly, and I palm her cheek, bending her head down so we sit forehead to forehead. "But, Colt, I'm only eighteen. I don't have a clear vision of my future, unlike you, and it's my first year in college. What if it's just... I'm your first love. What if—"

I press my finger to her mouth, silencing her at once. "There is no what-if. I love you, Ava. I love how strong and confident you are, because it motivates me to be the same way. I love how vulnerable you can be, because now I know sharing my worries and concerns doesn't make me weak. It means I can be myself with you, the real me, flawed and closed off to most people. Just like you can be yourself with me. You let me see you, the real you. And I fucking fell in love with you, babe. With a feisty girl who didn't hesitate to slap a total stranger for his disrespectful words. With a compassionate friend who would do anything for their closest people. With a stunning girl who looks incredible no matter what she's wearing. With a naughty girl who is open to experimenting, who is ready to beg and dominate at the same time. With your beautiful soul, and your constant desire to challenge me, to push my limits. You're the only girl in the world I will ever see. Always."

"I love you too, Colton," she murmurs, wrapping her arms around my shoulders.

"Will you come to San Jose with me? I know it's unexpected, but I will fucking die without you there."

"Dad already sent me info on a few colleges in California. Seems like I can transfer there and continue studying once our baby is older."

"First, I love your dad, for real. Second, you say all that, and my fucking dick springs into action," I breathe, my cock twitching. "I'm screwed."

"And I'm soaked," she comments, and I instantly stand up from the couch, picking her up and hooking her legs behind my back. "What are we going to do?"

"Fuck. Talk. Make love. Talk. And then maybe fuck again."

"I want to know everything about your conversation with your dad," she demands, and I head to my bedroom. "And about the Thunders."

"I'll tell you everything later." I close the door behind us and lower her onto my bed. I drop to my knees, crawl to her, and pull down her panties. Then I raise her skirt higher, spreading her legs wide for me.

"Wait, wait, wait, Colt." She stops me, and I peer at her. "I'm going to tell you something, and I want you to fuck me based on how happy the news makes you."

"Is there anything better than you loving me back? Better than you wanting to have a family with me?"

"Not better, but I think it will make you really happy."

"What is it?" I haul her closer, nestling between her thighs.

"Did you see my backpack?" My fingers skim along her skin and slide lower and lower, to her pussy. "We will need to go back to the dorm tomorrow, for the rest of my stuff."

"Are you moving in with me?"

"Yes." She reaches across my chest and pinches my nipple between her fingers. "Show me how happy you are about it."

"I'm going to make you scream and cream, worshiping every curve and line of your perfect body, just like you deserve." I bend down and hide my face in her pussy. Giving her pleasure is the only thing on my mind.

If someone would have told me I'd meet the love of my life in my last year of college, I would have never believed them. First, I had never been in love. Second, relationships were the last thing I was ever interested in. Hockey was everything to me, and my only goal was to go pro. Funny how different my life became after I met my girl. How much my plans for my future evolved, because now it isn't just about me. It's about my family.

Chapter 52

The Winner Takes It All

COLTON

Ava and I have had time to get used to our new reality. Her moving in with me was the best surprise ever, and it helped me to sort myself out and prepare for the national championship tournament. I am beyond grateful to the Thunders for letting me finish playing my last games of the season with my college team. My contract comes into effect once the championship is over. We won the regional semifinals and rolled on to the regional finals. Making it to the Frozen Four was nerve-racking, but we pulled it off and beat Denver U.

The championship game is all I've been focusing on this past week, barely finding time for anything else. It's my last game with the Panthers, and I'm determined to make it memorable. For me, for the team, and especially for Ava.

Walking out of the locker room, I head back to the ice rink. It's the fucking championship, and our team is winning three to one against Minnesota University. If we win tonight, it will be our fourth title since 1996. It would be iconic to take the championship together, with my best friends Clay and Drake, as it's the last time we'll play together for the Panthers. Bittersweet, and also thrilling. If we ever get to play for the same team again after graduation, I will be the happiest guy in the world. These two dudes are incredibly different, and I'm just glad they want to be friends with a moron like me.

I look around the arena and smile like an idiot when my eyes land on my mom and dad. I have no idea how he was able to convince her to come, but she's here, and she's smiling at me in return. I wink at her and move my gaze further, taking in Dax, who's seated with Benson's family not very far from my parents. He is talking with Ms. Lewis, the librarian, making her grin and blush. Ava is right—those two are cute together, and it would be great if something comes out of it. Everyone deserves a second chance at love.

As soon as I lock eyes with Ava, the whole arena becomes empty and quiet. Such a gorgeous girl I have. I will never stop praising and complimenting her, because that's exactly what she deserves. She plays with one of her braids, grinning at me with the cheeriest look on her face. She's full of mischief, and I can't help but think about her in my bed just this morning. I have a rule: no sex before games, to stay focused and collected. This morning, she made me break it, and I can't say I regret it. My morning was mind-blowing.

"Thompson, are you ready to get back in the game? Or is eye-fucking your girl more important?" I meet Benson's gaze. Nothing has really changed since the day we became best friends. He's huge, and I feel like Tom Thumb near him. He's an amazingly talented right wing. Once he steps onto the ice, he moves effortlessly and fast, as if he's way smaller and lighter than he is. "Earth to Colt, are you even here?"

"I'm just thinking about how big you are. You never thought about becoming a football player?" I nudge him with my elbow, and he laughs heartily.

"I tried, but being on the ice feels different. It's like every muscle in my body comes to life. I feel driven, motivated, and incredibly focused. Once my head is in the game, the world outside the ice rink doesn't exist."

"Same." Clay steps into the conversation as if he's been here the whole time. "Hockey is life, and I refuse to even hear from anyone who thinks differently."

"Amen." The three of us whirl around and gawk at Coach. A smile plays across his lips, but his arms are crossed. "If you're done stating the obvious, how about we win our fourth championship?"

"Definitely." I smirk, putting my helmet on. What could be better than graduating college as a national champion? Only graduating college as a national champion and having Ava in my life, for sure.

The third period is tense, even if we're winning. Our rivals dominate the game, trying to score and pushing us to play defense. Clay is our glue, holding us together and motivating us to do our best with his saves. He's a marvelous goalie, and the Hawks would hit the jackpot if they decide to sign him. I'm proud of him, even though I would have loved to play on the same team with him. Maybe one day.

It's the seventeenth minute of the third period when I see a clear chance for us to score. Not ideal and very tricky, but I want to take the risk. Big chances are never small stakes, and my final year in college is the best evidence of it. If I didn't get over my own ego and follow my desires, Ava would have never been with me. I would have been destined to be lonely, with a horde of meaningless hookups and nothing else. What I have now is a hundred times better.

I meet Benson's gaze, and he shakes his head. He knows what I'm up to, and I have no doubt he's going to help me. Any team should play as a whole, feeling each other out and understanding one another without words. That's what our coach taught us. We are like a family, where every person knows what they need to do so everyone will succeed.

Moving on instinct, I steal the puck from one of Minnesota's player and skate away from him as fast as I can. Being quick is one of my strong suits—not to brag. I pass to Drake, who moves alongside me to our opponent's net. It takes one second, then his stick meets the puck with an immediate slapshot and goes straight into our opponent's net, landing just behind their goalie. *Hell yes.*

I bump into Benson, hugging him tight as other guys join us in celebration. The feeling is marvelous and euphoric, and it helps us to end the game on our terms. The Great Lake Panthers are fucking national champions!

I hear excited chattering, applause, and joyful screams. The entire arena is filled with sound. Yet I'm trying to find Ava with my eyes. I have something I want to ask her, and my heart is ready to jump out of my chest from nervousness. And also fear. A fucking monstrosity spreads its venom all over my skin, and I start sweating. I'm so afraid she's going to freak out, or worse—tell me off just because of *how* I decided to handle it.

The truth is, I want it to be big. Just like my love for her is enormous. I want everyone to know what this girl means to me, even if it means making a fool of myself. She is worthy of only big gestures, not half-assed attempts. Ava deserves the world at her feet, and I intend to give it to her on a silver platter. Or maybe a gold one. Whatever the hell she wants.

Time flies, and my face hurts from the number of smiles I flashed for pictures. Finally sliding away, I see Dad and Dax laughing at something, while Mom is talking to Ms. Lewis. They are waiting for me, and I honestly can't wait to join them, but only after Ava and I talk. I notice her on the team's bench with Layla. I frown, looking more closely, and then I instantly break into a smile. She's wearing my jersey, number eleven. My girl is wearing my jersey, and this simple realization turns me into a lovesick puppy. *Mine, mine, mine*...it's a mantra in my head, getting louder and louder.

I skate over to them, and she stands up. Layla follows her closely, winking at me. She's the best partner in crime I could have asked for. Ava puts her hands on the board and leans forward, arching an eyebrow at me.

"What are you going to do?"

I wind my hands around her waist and haul her to my chest over the board. When I put her on the ice, her eyes go wide. "You're safe with me," I tell her, bending down close to her.

"I'm just a bit surprised. Everything is good." I put my hand on the board, and Layla quickly pushes our secret in my fingers.

"You're wearing my jersey." I ball my fist over the ring as I continue to stare Ava in the eyes.

Ava puts her hands on her hips, smiling from ear to ear. "I'm proud to be Colton Thompson's girlfriend, and I want everyone to know it." She takes a step closer. "Kinda staking my claim on you."

"And I'm staking my claim on you." I drape a hand over her waist and pull her closer. "I know you might be furious for what I'm about to do, but I don't care. You are my most precious treasure, my fucking Stanley Cup, my everything. Even a day without you feels like the loneliest eternity, one I have no desire to go back to ever. I fell in love with you once and for all, and I'm certain you're the best thing that ever happened to me."

"Colt..." she murmurs, her eyes glimmering with happiness. "I love you too."

I take a deep breath and lower myself onto one knee in front of her. Her palm flies to her mouth, covering it as she stumbles back a little. "I'm Colton Thompson. The future center for the California Thunders. A soon-to-be Great Lake University graduate. A fucking stubborn idiot, and a closed off moron. I'm a grump, and I'm not always the best person to be around, but you love me. I don't know what I have done to deserve you, but here we are. You're my life, and I want you forever. Will you be my wife?"

Her lips tremble as she lowers her hand from her face. Ava sweeps her gaze around, noticing people watching us.

"I kinda hate you right now for drawing so much attention to us," she mutters, and I barely hold myself back from bursting with laughter. This is so her, and she's so mine. It's insane how much this girl means to me.

"The winner takes it all, Ava," I state, grinning. "I want to become not only a national champion, but also your fiancé today. So? Will you be my wife?"

"Yes," she murmurs as I take her hand and slowly put the ring on her finger. Layla squeals, and I make a mental note to thank her again. If it weren't for her, I would have freaked out the second I stepped into the jewelry store. She helped me not lose my mind and kept it a secret from everyone, including her brother and her boyfriend. Ava has a real gem of a best friend. "It's so beautiful."

I stand up, and she jumps on me, locking her legs behind my back. I hold her close, coasting my eyes over her face. "So glad you like it."

"How could I not?" Ava asks, glancing around and pouting. "Everyone is watching."

"They all envy me. To have such a stunning woman as you, I'm one lucky idiot."

"Can you imagine what would happen if they knew I'm pregnant?" Her emerald green eyes are full of concern. "They would think that's the only reason you proposed."

"They can all go to hell. I don't care. I would have married you anyway. Pregnant or not."

"So cocky." Ava inches closer to my face, sucking my bottom lip into her mouth and grazing her teeth over it. "And so dominant."

"Just like you love it."

"Absolutely." She kisses my lips and moves away, looking over my shoulder. "I think our parents want to talk to us."

Our parents are a whole different story. I honestly thought the talk with Dax would be the easiest one, and I expected my own father to flip when I told him Ava was pregnant. In reality, both men shook Ava and me to the core. They were in total support of our decision to keep the baby, offering reassurance and help. Dax suggested Ava take a year off, so she can focus on raising our child and then go back to school once the baby is older. My father went further. He bought us a house in San Jose, telling us that we were free to decorate it however we wanted. It was too much, and I told him that. I didn't want him to buy my love with grand gestures. The answer literally made me lose my shit: *It's not about you. It's about my grandchild, and I intend to be the best grandpa in the world, even if the competition is tough.*

I chortle, turn around, and skate over to our parents, not letting Ava go for even a second. "I bet they do."

She sighs, cupping my cheeks with her palms. "I love you, Colt."

"I love you too, Ava," I confess.

This year has brought me way more than I ever could have dreamt of. Family. Happiness. Love. Her kicking me out of her dorm the first time we met is what started us. And even if there were a ton of fuckups, I wouldn't have changed any of it.

Epilogue

AVA

Five years later

I bolt up in bed and snap my eyes open. *What the hell is going on?*

Throwing my blanket off, I swing my legs over the edge of the bed and stand up. God, I hate starting mornings like this. Letting Drake stay at our house for a few days doesn't sound like a great idea anymore. He's not only big, like the fucking Hulk, but he's also incredibly loud. His laughter booms, reaching my ears as I stomp to the bathroom and hop into a quick shower. Then I head to the closet to get dressed.

Walking out of the bedroom, I go downstairs without even checking on Michael. I'm sure he's with his dad and his beloved Uncle Drake. Most of the men in this house these days play on my nerves.

Once I step into the living room, Smokey jumps off the couch and strolls over to me, meowing in greeting. I pick him up, press him to my chest, and follow the noises to the kitchen. Laughter, men's loud voices, and my son's excited chattering make me roll my eyes. Why did they need to wake up so early? It's just nine a.m. on Saturday.

I stop in the doorway. Drake and Michael are sitting at the table with plates full of pancakes in front of them. My son has one pancake in his right hand and another in his left, biting them in turn. Benson holds a cup in his hands, watching him with eyes full of mischief.

"Buddy, you are definitely going to be like your Uncle Drake."

"In your dreams," my hubs comments, wheeling around and gazing at me. "Did we wake you up?"

"You certainly did," I say, fighting the smile that blooms on my lips. Colton in only shorts affects me more than anything, turning my panties into a hot, wet mess. Even five years later. Not to brag, but the title for the sexiest NHL player rightfully belongs to my hubby.

I let Smokey jump on the floor and go to my son. "Good morning, baby."

"Morn-whm-ming," he mumbles as I arch my eyebrow at him, counting in my head how many times I told him not to speak when his mouth is full. Michael finally swallows, noticing me watching him. He turns his head and flashes me a smile. "Morning, Mommy."

I bend down and plant a loud smooch on his forehead. I love this boy to the moon and back, despite all the sleepless nights, struggles, and breakdowns I had when he was a newborn. Books and movies usually paint an idyllic picture of motherhood and parenting, while in reality? I honestly believe our society doesn't realize how hard it is to be a mom. But it's a choice we make, so it's not about complaints. I just think men should be more respectful and more helpful when it comes to their wives, sisters, and mothers.

Colt is here whenever he can be, giving me emotional support or just letting me sleep while putting our son back to bed at night. Our miscommunication in the past gave us an incredible experience, and now we're always there for each other. We talk about everything, the good and the bad. Always.

"Morning, Ava," Drake says, smiling. Even with the very noticeable stubble on his face, a little dimple on his right cheek is visible.

He's twenty-seven, just like Colton. Last season, he got into a fight with a left wing from Toronto, and now his nose is slightly crooked. His hair is short and curly on top. He only got bigger with time, and on the ice Benson is a fucking beast. It's best not to piss him off during a game.

With a smile, he will easily send his opponent crashing into—or flying over—the boards. When he was traded for another player and signed a two-season contract with the California Thunders, it was like a dream come true for Colt. Now he wants Clay to join the team, but for now, he's tied to his contract with the Hawks.

"Morning, Drake. I honestly can't wait for you to move into your house."

"Aw, Mason. You're as nice as always." Drake laughs, taking a sip of his coffee.

"Thompson. She's Thompson," Colt states, correcting him, and Benson chortles harder.

"Sorry, dude. She will always be Mason to me," he mutters once his laughter dies down. "If you think you're getting rid of me once I move, think again. I'm not going anywhere."

"Really?" Michael gazes at Drake, his deep brown eyes full of hope.

"Of course. I love playing with you, kiddo." He reaches over and ruffles my son's brown hair with his huge palm, making him giggle. "Plus, I miss my little niece."

Drake and I lock eyes, and I furrow my brow. Layla is as stubborn as a mule, preferring to struggle alone instead of agreeing to move to San Jose with her brother to be closer to us both. She has financial support, but she definitely needs someone to be there for her. Being a single mom is no fun. Since the moment she broke up with Clay right after his graduation, her life has slowly gone downhill.

"Hopefully we can change your sister's mind."

"She's such a stubborn little sh—" Benson pauses, sneaking a glance at Michael, who has his eyes glued to his face. *Yeah, dude, control your words around our kid.* Colt and I spent a whole week trying to make him stop saying "what the fuck" any time he was annoyed. It was funny the first time he repeated it after me, but when he started saying it ten times a day, it became a problem. No one expects kids at preschool to know swear words. "Shopper," he finishes.

"Really, man? Is that the best you've got?" Colt snorts loudly, grabbing my hand and pulling me to his chest. He wraps me in his arms, and I'm melting already. His warmth envelops me, filling my heart with joy and happiness. The way I love this man is overwhelming and exhilarating. Nothing compares to it.

"It's not easy to find a synonym for 'shit'."

"Drake," Colt and I mumble at the same time, bursting out with laughter. He hides his face in his palms, while Michael looks at all of us in turn.

"What is shit?" he asks once the kitchen goes quiet, and we start cackling like a horde of crazy seagulls again. This day is going to be awesome.

"Michael is fine, Dad. He's having the time of his life, I swear." I sit by the pool; my legs are in the water. My son is running around throwing his toys in the water, while I watch him with a calm demeanor. I found my zen two years ago. I don't think there are a lot of things that can piss me off when it comes to Michael. If he does something bad or rude, he knows there will be consequences. Throwing toys into the pool is definitely not on the list. "Your grandson can't wait for preschool to start again. He misses his friends."

"Does he? Or is it you who can't wait for preschool to start?" Dad laughs.

"Me too," I say, waving at Michael to get his attention. "We're going to have dinner in twenty minutes, so I suggest you go play some more."

"Okey dokey." Michael giggles and runs into the house.

I shake my head and press the phone back to my ear. "Sorry, Dad."

"It's totally fine." Dad chuckles. "Michael told me you're going to visit Isla on Friday."

"Yeah, her mom invited us to a barbeque. Drake is coming too. We're trying to help him get used to a new city, meet new people, show him our favorite places, you know. So far, he likes everything. Except his neighbor," I snort, remembering how exasperated and annoyed Drake was when we got back from his house two days ago. I don't think he will forget Evangelina any time soon. The daughter of Philadelphia's legendary quarterback left a lasting impression on our friend. "He says he hates her."

"Sounds familiar. I remember finding you in the kitchen all those years ago, when you told me about Colton and how much you hate him."

"I still do when he acts like an insufferable jerk." The second these words leave my mouth, someone shoves me in the water. I raise my phone high in the air and turn around, shooting daggers at my husband. A cocky smile plays on his lips as he and Drake stand by the pool with their bags draped over their shoulders. They just came home from practice, and the best idea Colton had was to push me into the water. "Sorry, Dad. My husband just proved why I hate him. Tell Pen I say hi. I can't wait to see you two next week. Love you."

"Love you too, kid. Bye."

Dad ends the call as I swim to the edge of the pool, throw my phone onto the grass, and pull myself out. Drake is still trying to keep a straight face, while Colt grins at me. I bend down, take my phone, and stomp inside, hearing them both break into laughter.

WALKING INTO THE LIVING ROOM, I see Michael and Drake on the couch watching *The Loud House*. Somehow, seeing my childhood friend watching cartoons with my son doesn't surprise me. He's all big and bulky, but Drake is a real teddy bear inside, and it shows when he's around kids. I shake my head and edge to the kitchen. Dinner has been ready for a long time; I just need to reheat everything and set the table. Working from home has its perks, especially when you're self-employed.

What started as a desire to support indie authors has turned into something great and, more importantly, helpful. I hired two girls who I met through the bookstagram community, and they work with me as personal assistants. We're always growing and elevating our business to the next level. Some authors work with us exclusively; some order only certain services. I love reading books and discovering new writers, and I'm beyond happy I was able to turn it into my career.

My smutty stepmother is incredibly proud of me. Without her support, I'm not sure I would have had it in me to continue after

Michael was born. It felt as if I was failing everyone, as I was busy with my son. So she stepped in and helped me to keep going. She still does.

"How is Dax? Penelope?" My husband's voice takes me by surprise, but I masterfully hide it. I'm not angry with him, but I want him to stew a little. And make him all worked up. He deserves it. "Ava?"

I continue cutting tomatoes for a light salad when a hand wraps around my waist from behind, and my back is pressed to a solid chest.

"Dad said he's going to give you a long lecture about how you treat your wife."

"He wouldn't," Colt murmurs, grazing my ear with his teeth. "Dax knows how much I love you."

"Seems to me you love making fun of me just as much," I scoff, enjoying the warmth of his body.

"Definitely not." His big, calloused palm covers mine, and I stop. I put the knife on the cutting board and turn around, looking up into my husband's face. He has a beard now, and it adds a thousand points in his favor. His dark brown eyes are glued to my face, and I see the reflection of my own feelings. Love. Lust. And happiness. I lower my gaze to his chest, and my eyes linger on his wrist. He has tattoos covering both of his arms from his shoulders to his wrists, but there is one that is incredibly special: a tattoo that matches one I have on my lower abdomen. Our secret.

"Hey," I murmur, standing on my tiptoes and kissing his full lips. If it weren't for Drake and Michael, I would have dragged him upstairs and let him have his way with me. I can't wait for Sunday, when it will be just the two of us once Michael goes to sleep.

"Hey, babe," Colt sighs, pressing his forehead to mine. "How was your day?"

"Good. A little less productive than I'd hoped, but overall? Everything is fine," I say, winding my hands around his waist. "Michael was well-behaved. I even took a nap with him for an hour."

"Took a nap?" He arches his eyebrow.

"I started a book, but it bored me to death. It literally lulled me to sleep. I don't know why I'm still trying to give stories with this trope a chance. It's one of the most unrealistic things in the world, and you will never change my mind," I state, seeing him stare at me in amusement. "What?"

"So books with a reverse harem are realistic?" A smile blooms on my lips, and tenderness fills my bones. The number of books we read together is huge—more like the number of chapters and excerpts we role-play. Colton is up for everything except letting another person in our bedroom. It doesn't even matter. Woman or man, the answer will always be no. From both of us.

"It's not my favorite genre, but it has its appeal. It's very entertaining, and educational. Your sex life became a lot richer because of it, so you're not allowed to complain."

"Was I complaining?" He kisses my forehead and takes a step back. "Need some help with dinner?"

"No. I have everything under control. Go check what Drake and Michael are doing." I turn around and toss the tomatoes into the bowl.

My dad's words about our first conversation about Colton reappear, bringing memories back to the surface. I'm not sure I ever hated him, but he definitely annoyed the fuck out of me on more occasions than I could count. All because he had no idea how to express his feelings. The total opposite from how my husband is now. He has a way with words that makes me weak in my knees. The passion we share flares up any time we are alone, always leaving me wanting more.

COLTON

Sitting in my car, I press my phone to my ear. My little sister wants to know if we're coming to her birthday. Chloe is six years old now, and she loves being on the ice. The only difference? She wants to be a professional figure skater. My sister is a very hardworking little gal, and I admire her determination and her talent.

Helen and I had a talk after I told my wife I wanted to be present in my sister's life. There are no hard feelings between us anymore, and we learned how to be civil. Especially since she apologized to Ava for what she said and quit my father's company. They signed an agreement that satisfied both parties. Dad supports his daughter financially and takes her to our family home almost every weekend. He made sure he kept his promise to me. In more ways than I even hoped for.

"We are all planning to come. Don't worry."

"Love you, Colt. Say hi to Ava and Michael."

"Love you too, Chloe. I will. Bye."

"Bye." She ends the call, and I unfasten my seat belt and get out of the car.

The more time I spend with my son, the more I understand Helen's desire to keep the baby all those years back. Considering her health problems, it could have been her only shot at getting pregnant, and she went for it without any hesitation. Her daughter is her life, and she will go all mama bear on anyone who has a problem with her child. It's precious, and I honestly respect her for it. She's just like my mom. And Ava. The love these women have for their children motivates me to be a better father, to be the best role model I can be. There is nothing more precious than a smile from your child.

I lock my car and call my mom. Hopefully she's not in bed yet. The time difference makes my brain hurt sometimes.

"Hey, Colt." My mom's voice fills my ears after the second ring. My insides warm up, and I can't help but grin. She's on medication, and she needs routine. But she's been well for five years, and in all honesty, that's the only thing that matters.

"Hey, Mom. I didn't wake you up, did I?" It's two p.m. in San Jose, but I have no idea what time it is in Biarritz.

"At eleven p.m.? No, I'm still up," she snickers. "Your father has always been a night owl, and that hasn't changed."

I lower my gaze to my feet, shaking my head. If someone had told me my parents would get back together, I would have never believed them. It sounded absolutely unrealistic, but that's exactly what happened. There was a reason Mom didn't leave Dad after her one night with Leo, and that reason was love—love they were able to reignite when Mom returned home from the facility.

They started getting closer because of me. Traveling together to visit my family, to see their grandson. Talking and spending time together like they hadn't done in years. And I think she saw the man she fell in love with all those years ago, the man who made her a priority, who was willing to step away from work and just be with her. Whenever she needed him.

As my wife often says, most of the time, women don't need big gestures, expensive gifts, or declarations of love. They just need their men by their side and present. My dad learned his lesson, and once he noticed the changes in Mom's behavior, he did everything in his power to win her back. And it worked. They look happier than ever, back in love. The smile on her face is the only thing that matters to my father.

"Well, some habits definitely die hard." I laugh heartily. "How do you like France? Is it the same as you remember?"

We talk some more. Mom tells me about their days in France. She and Dad will be back in two weeks and plan to visit us—just in time, as Dax and Penelope will be here too. We never told Mom that Ava's dad was the one who saved her, as it could have triggered bad memories and we were strongly advised against it. But Dad knows, and he barely held his shit together when he realized how much he owes Dax for saving his wife that night. The bond they have is overwhelming.

Seeing Michael running in my direction with a geeky smile on his face, my heart is ready to burst with happiness. He's the most precious little child in the world.

"Okay, Mom. I just got home and need to go change my clothes."

"Sure, Colt. Kiss Ava and Michael for us."

"Definitely, and tell Dad we say hi. Good night, Mom." I hang up, kneeling and catching Michael in my arms. "How have you been, kid?"

"So good." His eyes widen a fraction as I stand up and carry him to the living room. He's super excited about something, and I have no idea what. "Mom is...she's...she's the best."

My brows pinch together, following his gaze with my eyes. My jaw drops at once as I gape at the LEGO town in front of us. There's a train station, a police station, a zoo, and, what's more, a fucking Harry Potter castle. When did she have time to build all this?

I put my son down, and he instantly runs to his toys. I straighten and look at my wife, who's sitting on the couch with a book in her hands. I got myself the sexiest bookworm in the world, honestly.

"What is this?" I ask, coming closer and plopping down beside her.

"LEGOs."

"I know that. I mean, when did you—"

"Here and there. It took me a little over a week." Ava shrugs, and I haul her to my chest, hugging her tightly.

"You're the best mom in the world," I praise her, and she looks up at me, tossing her book on the couch and winding her hands around my waist. "I'm so lucky to have you."

"And I'm so lucky to have you," she murmurs, gently kissing my lips. "You're the best dad in the world."

I rake my gaze over her face, and my skin warms up just from the sight of her. Those emerald green eyes with thick black eyelashes, her little nose, her puffy and so-kissable lips, and my favorite little birthmark on her right cheek. She has her hair cascading over her shoulders, with a little bun on top. I love everything about her, and that only grows with each passing day. I'm the luckiest man in the world to have her as my wife. My twin flame.

We talk about our plans for the day, and Michael hears us. He gapes at me with his mouth half open. "Isn't Uncle Drake coming back?"

"No. He moved into his house, so now he will only be visiting," I tell him, and he sulks, turning away and focusing on his toys again. Smokey carefully steps around the LEGO town without knocking any on the ground.

"I hope he loves his place," Ava sighs, taking her book in her hands again. "Drake is a family guy, and I think he might be lonely."

"He has us," I reassure her, and then I narrow my eyes. "His neighbor looks a lot like you."

"Did you talk to her?" Mischief swims behind her irises, but I'm not quite sure I understand why.

"No, I just saw her walking out of her house. Why?"

"She knows how to stand up for herself, and she won't hesitate to put you in your place if she thinks you deserve it. She flipped him the bird when they were arguing, and called him a moron."

"Basically, she's his type," I say, and my wife laughs. I kiss her forehead and stand up from the couch. "I'm going to go change."

"Okay." She joins me and edges to the kitchen. "I'll heat up some food."

I turn around and head to the hallway, halting in my tracks to look at her over my shoulder. Taunting my wife is still my favorite thing in the world to do. "Ava?"

"Yeah?" She meets my gaze.

"There is no need for dessert." She frowns, but when I say my next piece, she's fuming. "I intend to eat my sweets later...in bed."

"In your dreams." Ava pokes her tongue out at me and stomps into the kitchen. Definitely not in my dreams. Benson's presence made us quieter, but not anymore. Enjoying my time in bed with my wife is exactly what I'm going to do tonight once Michael is asleep.

CLOSING the door to our bedroom, I slowly crawl into bed. It was my turn to put Michael to sleep, and as often happens, I fell asleep myself.

Now it's two a.m., and my wife is in a deep sleep. A blanket is pressed between her thighs as she lies on her right side with her hands under the pillow. She's a real sleeping beauty with her long brown hair spilled over her pillow. I take off my tee and toss it away, getting rid of my briefs as well.

I slide under the blanket, wrapping my body around hers. My hand lands on her hip, and I move it lower, enjoying the softness of her skin. With all my years of playing hockey, I've gained a lot of muscle. She's so small compared to me, and it makes my desire to protect her go through the roof. There is no other girl in the world for me.

"Colt..." Ava's voice is quiet as she looks at me over her shoulder. "I tried to wait for you, but I fell asleep."

"Didn't I tell you about my dessert?" I move my hand between her legs and part them with ease. I press my fingers to her pussy through her tiny shorts, and my cock rises to attention immediately. It hardens as I grind it over her ass while pushing her shorts away and circling my fingers over her clit. Slow and gentle, without rushing anything. I close my eyes, enjoying the friction as my cock throbs. The effect she has on me is absolutely intoxicating. She makes me forget everything. Even hockey, and that's something I never expected to happen.

"You did, and honestly, I was looking forward to your tongue in my pussy. Not just your fingers."

As if she needs to tell me twice. I hop off the bed as she turns onto her back. I grab her legs and pull her to the edge of the bed. Yanking down her shorts, I lick my lips, staring at the little honeypot on her lower abdomen. A matching tattoo to the Winnie-the-Pooh I have inked on my right wrist. I can't fucking live without my honey, and she's perfectly aware of it.

I drop to my knees and slowly lick her clit, and then lower, to her lips. She moans, spreading her legs further and nestling more comfortably. I put my hand on her belly, covering her piercing and holding her in place. I'm hungry for my girl as I swirl my tongue over her swollen clit. I suck it into my mouth hard and then release it slowly, drawing another long moan out of her. She tastes even sweeter than my favorite M&Ms, and it's never enough for me. I could go down on her every fucking day and I wouldn't get bored. It's pure pleasure.

She grabs my hair and tugs, and I lock eyes with her as she props herself on her elbows. "You drive me insane when you do that; it feels so good."

I smile at her, plunging two fingers inside her, and she instantly plops onto her back again. Her fingers dig into my hair. I hold her spread open for me, lapping my tongue over her clit and curling my fingers inside her at just the right spot. She tugs on my hair harder, and I close my eyes. Pain ripples through my body.

"If you continue to act like a brat, I'm going to fuck you like one, babe," I tell her as she rotates her hips, rubbing her pussy over my face.

"Make me come with your tongue, and later do whatever the hell you want," Ava pants, shoving her cunt in my face. "I want you to take control."

Hearing those words, I almost come myself. I glide my hand over her belly and higher, until I have a handful of her breast. Her nipple is a pebbled point, and dear God, I want it in my mouth so badly. I speed up my movements, and she explodes on my tongue, her whole body trembling. The waves of her orgasm make her writhe as her chest rises and falls with her breath.

"So fucking delicious, babe." I stand up, hovering over her. Ava's eyes zero in on my cock, and she grins. "How bad do you want it inside you?"

Well, I definitely should know better. My wife has been compared to a tornado for a reason. She moves away from me, settles on our pillows, and spreads her legs wide. Her fingers fly to her pussy, and I suddenly feel thirsty.

"Tell me how bad you want to be inside me, Colt."

I lunge forward and haul her toward me, sliding inside her at once. She gasps, and I cover her mouth with mine, ravishing her tongue as if my life depends on it. Ava kisses me back, wrapping her legs around my hips as I fuck her. She moans in my mouth, her tongue playing with mine. The feeling of an incredibly strong release builds within me, setting my body on fucking fire and pushing my limits sky-high. I slam into her, going deeper with each stroke. Her pussy is dripping, soaking me in her juices as her breath hitches in her throat.

"I want you to hold your orgasm," I tell her, and her eyes widen. "Hold it."

"It feels too good," she whines breathlessly as my dick fills her completely.

"Hold it, Ava," I command, pinching her nipple through her tee.

"Oh my fucking God." Her brows knit together as her teeth graze her bottom lip.

She grabs the sheets and fists them in her hands. She does as I tell her, trying to stay afloat without letting her orgasm overwhelm her. The sound of our slapping skin becomes louder as I fuck her harder, driving my whole length inside her till I'm balls deep.

I circle my hand around her throat and squeeze. A faint smile crosses her face. She's my fucking brat, and I don't want her to be anyone else. This roughness. This passion. This never-ending desire to challenge each other. It's us. It's how we are, and damn—I don't want it to be any other way. She lifts her hips, inviting me deeper, till I hit her deepest spot with my cock.

"Such a good fucking girl you are, wifey. Such a good fucking girl," I pant, pressing my forehead to hers. "Tell me who your pussy belongs to."

"You." The word spills off her tongue, and her eyes roll back in her head. She's no longer controlling her body, and her pussy clenches around my shaft. Her head bobs back, and she cries out, coming for the second time. I shut my eyes, trying to fight my own release, but it's too good. I grunt and spill my cum inside her as I smash our lips together.

We kiss more, our hands roaming over each other's bodies. Our lust for one another is still strong. Our insatiable desire to become one has only grown stronger, and it's all I want at the moment. My cock is hard again, and I'm ready for another round.

I lean away and roll onto my back, glancing at her. "Your turn."

Ava smiles at me, and then she straddles my legs, taking my dick inside her. She moans, eyes hooded with need. I slap her ass hard, and the change is incredible. My wife frowns, putting both of her hands on my chest. She's not moving, but it only makes me smile.

I slap her ass again, and she flinches. "Fuck me, Ava. Now."

"What happened to me taking control?" she snarls, scraping my chest with her nails. I hiss and just slap her ass again—harder.

"Fuck. Me. Now," I whisper, and my wife smirks. The next thing I know, she takes off her tee and throws it onto the floor. My gaze drops to her chest, and I fucking groan, palming her boobs with both hands. *Mine. So fucking mine.*

Pushing myself from the bed, I sit up straight and wind my hands around her waist. I suck her nipple into my mouth and graze my teeth over it, and Ava moans in pleasure, still digging her fingernails into my back.

"Fucker." When the word leaves her mouth, I'm thrown back in time, to the moment she slapped me for my horrible words.

"But I'm *your* fucker." I cup her ass and push her to start rocking her hips.

Ava holds my gaze. A million different emotions reflect on her face until there is only one: love. She rolls her hips, lowering her mouth to mine. "You're mine, Colton. Only mine."

Our lips collide, and the world around us ceases to exist. Ava is my end and my beginning. She's my weakness and my strength. She's my soulmate, and I'm incredibly grateful to her for giving me a chance. For letting me in and allowing me to love her. For loving me back and being my family. She's my only one, and it will stay like this forever. Always.

Are you curious about Drake Benson's love interest?
Keep reading for a sneak peek of the first meeting between Drake and Evangelina from the second book of the Sinners on the Ice series, BARN BURNER.

BARN BURNER EXCERPT

EVANGELINA

I glance at the clock and smile, seeing my oddly favorite numbers - 12:12. I quickly close my eyes and make a wish for this day to turn out well. It's a habit I've gained throughout the years, allowing myself to believe in a little magic. Even if it's more of an illusion. Magic has nothing to do with what we're capable of.

The second I let the time sink in, I curse. I'm running late. I have a meeting regarding my dessert shop's new menu in a little bit more than an hour, and I still need to take Cooper for a walk. He's been a good boy, waiting for me patiently, but even his patience has its limits. The past forty minutes he was following my every step, looking into my eyes with an absolutely miserable expression on his face. As if I didn't take him for an hour-long walk this morning. This dog is a manipulative asshole...but I still love him.

I quickly collect my hair in two Dutch braids, and twirl around, checking out my outfit. I intend to use this time for a little run, so I'm wearing a black sports bra and black leggings with red sneakers. Coop is sitting near the door, eyeing me with such intensity, you'd have thought I was going to run away. Or have the tendency to run away from him. Both aren't true, but who cares?

"Come on, Coop, let's go." I grab my keys and his leash from the table, and open the front door. He always walks out of the house and waits for me. He's a well-trained dog, and he has never gotten into trouble before. Until fucking now.

Everything happens so fast I'm honestly having a hard time understanding what is going on. Cooper runs off down the stairs, barking and scowling at some guy who is standing dangerously close to my Lamborghini Aventador. No, scratch that, my dog has run at a guy that is as large as a fucking wall.

"What the fuck? Get your fucking dog off me." The guy growls, and his voice snaps me out of my thoughts. Shit. What the hell am I doing? Cooper already has his paws on the dude's chest, and he keeps baring his teeth. I need to get him off.

I rush down the stairs, tripping over two at once and seize Cooper by his collar, dragging him away from the guy. I put the leash on him and take a step back. I press my palm to my rib cage, catching my breath and only now bringing myself to look at this guy's face. His dark brown eyes under his furrowed brows are shooting daggers at me.

"I'm so sor—"

"What the fuck is wrong with you?" he interrupts, making me shut my mouth. "Your dog could have bitten my leg off. Don't you know how to use a fucking leash?"

I'm in the wrong, and I acknowledge that. I want to apologize but this dude doesn't even let me finish.

"Don't you know how to talk to a woman?" I hiss, furrowing my brow. Roaming my gaze over his face, I take in his eyes, his slightly crooked nose and the noticeable stubble on his cheeks. He might be attractive, but in all honesty he's incredibly far from what I consider my type. His build is the biggest turn off. Just fucking no. "My dog is—"

"Your fucking dog attacked me." the guy interrupts me again, clenching his fists.

If I wasn't so pissed, I think I would have been intimidated by him. Just from the shortest glance I know he's into sports. Maybe an athlete. Maybe even a football player just like my dad. And oh my fucking God, I want to run a mile away from him. Athletes are meh, and I literally hate each and every one of them except my father. He's the fucking best.

"I made a mistake letting Coop out of the house without a leash.

But I didn't know you'd decide to check out my car when I took my dog for a walk. He's defending me. Always." I snap, gritting through my teeth. I suddenly hear a door closing and see two girls rushing in our direction from the house next to mine.

Did someone buy it?

"I was just curious about your car. I took a few steps forward to have a better look, and I didn't even touch it. While your dog almost bit my leg off."

I blink and flip him the bird. "A barking dog is not the same as a biting dog, moron. Try to remember that."

"The fuck..." he bellows, and just then a girl appears right in front of him. I focus my attention on her and instantly see that it's Bella.

Eight months ago when I moved to Santa Clara, she worked her magic on the interior design of my house. She's incredibly nice and sweet, and I still like her, despite the fact that her husband is the quarterback for the California Mustangs. Though Xander is kinda cool, he helped me when I was looking for a tattoo artist four months ago.

Okay, maybe not all athletes are so bad, I'm being a hypocrite.

"Hey Eva." Bella steps closer to me and kisses me on the cheek. My brain works at the fastest speed possible, as I put two and two together. Bella's presence here, her walking out of the house next to mine, this jerk lurking near my car. "How are you?"

Her familiar face is like an instant fix for my mood. I smile, feeling my muscles relax little by little. "Hey Bella. I was great until this bull in a china shop showed up. Is he going to be living next door?"

"Yup." A brunette who was silently standing beside the guy takes a step forward and extends her palm to me. "I'm Ava. It's nice to meet you."

"Eva. Evangelina." I quickly shake her hand and then let go, stepping back. Her eyes are glued to my face as she continues staring at me with curiosity."It's really nice to meet you too. Unlike this jerk—"

"I'm not a fucking jerk. Your dog jumped on me, putting its paws on my chest. He was baring his teeth, growling and snapping at me. He didn't look or sound friendly at all. You shouldn't let him off the leash." He bombards me with his accusations, and I pout my lips tighter.

"Again." I pull Cooper to my leg because he is trying to step away from me to Bella. I bet he can smell her dog, Milo, on her. "I didn't expect him to hop up and run at you like he did once he saw you, that's why I wasn't able to hold onto him. He's a well trained dog; he knows how to behave. Unlike you."

The jerk blinks and throws his hands in the air. "Unbelievable."

He turns around and stomps to the BMW X6 parked near Bella's car. He slams the door so hard Ava flinches. Someone definitely has a problem controlling his anger.

I sigh, returning my gaze back to Bella and Ava. "Sorry about that. He just pissed me off to no end, not letting me even apologize to him and only yelling at me." Stepping back, I loosen Cooper's leash a little. "I need to get going or I will be late for my meeting in an hour."

"Sure," Bella murmurs, hugging me briefly. "See you around babes."

"See you around." I tell her and focus my attention on Ava. My eyes travel down her form, her face and all I can say - she's gorgeous. This jerk should be more appreciative of her, instead of acting like the biggest child on this planet. "Bye Ava."

"Bye Eva." She grins at me. My eyes linger on her face for a moment, then I wheel around and quickly stroll away from my house with Cooper. I still have places I need to be, and this whole debacle took way too much of my time. Ugh, I hate it.

BARN BURNER is a fake dating pro hockey romance, the second book of the Sinners on the Ice series. Coming to KU, Kindle and in paperback in 2023.

Acknowledgments

My *little boy*, for being my number one supporter and encourager.

My *husband*, for supporting me in following my dreams.

My dear *Nicole*, for always being there for me, for helping me with my books and believing in me even at times when I'm ready to throw everything away. Becoming friends with you is one of the best things that happened to me since I started writing.

My fabulous girls, *Alwyn*, *E*, *Ina* and *Taniya* for beta-reading this book and helping me make it better. For encouraging me and supporting me, listening to me rant and giving me not only pat on my back but also knocking some sense into me sometimes when my overthinker's side is winning.

My editor *Caroline*, for being incredibly understanding and for perfecting Ava and Colt's story while saving my author's voice.

My friend *Luz*, for creating this amazing cover and giving me tips on how this whole self-publishing world works. You're a rock star!

Being part of booktok and bookstagram community might be overwhelming sometimes, but I'm beyond grateful to *Diana*, *Lily*, *Nicole*, *Norhan*, *Stephanie* and *Tammy*. You are literal gems and I feel so lucky to get to know you.

My *Wattpad* and *Inkitt* readers, for believing in my work and loving my characters just as much as I love them. If someone ever told me in 2019 that one day I'd be a published author, I honestly would have thought they were crazy. Yet your endless support and love is exactly something that helped me to believe in myself as an author. *Thank you.*

In the world full of so many talented authors, I'm immensely grateful to each and every one of you who gave Ava and Colt's story a chance.

You're precious.

About the Author

Anastasija is an indie author and an IT-worker who spends her days creating swoon-worthy and steamy stories that will make your heart race. Her writing is filled with flawed and relatable characters that you'll find yourself rooting for. Whether you're in the mood for angsty drama or steamy romance, her stories take you on a rollercoaster ride of emotions with guaranteed happy endings.

If you're a fan of romance that leaves you breathless and begging for more, Anastasija is the author for you. Connect with her on Instagram and TikTok, where she loves to hear from her readers and share sneak peeks of her books and upcoming projects.

instagram.com/anastasija.white.author

tiktok.com/@author.anastasija.white

amazon.com/stores/Anastasija-White/author/B0BWVDGZS7

pinterest.com/anastasijawhite

Printed in Germany
by Amazon Distribution
GmbH, Leipzig

30241623R00239